GOOD ICE

ɞ • ʗ

Good Ice

A Novel

Forrest Peterson

To: Dave Dorsey

Forrest Peterson

N
S

NORTH STAR PRESS OF ST. CLOUD, INC.

St. Cloud, Minnesota

Front cover photo: Forrest Peterson
Back cover photos: Marilyn Sjotvedt

Copyright © 2007 Forrest Peterson

ISBN-13: 978-0-87839-260-5
ISBN-10: 0-87839-260-2

First Edition: September 2007

This is a work of fiction. Names, characters, places, and
incidents, other than those recorded by historians, biographers, and news
media, are the product of the author's imagination or are used
fictionally. Any resemblance to any events or persons,
living or dead, is purely coincidental.

Printed in the United States

Published by:
North Star Press of St. Cloud, Inc.
P.O. Box 451
St. Cloud, Minnesota 56302

northstarpress.com

GOOD ICE

➶ 1968 ᎒᠀

Mario Ruiz looked over at the stage. In a few hours he would be sitting there singing and playing his guitar. It wasn't much of a stage. A low platform about ten feet wide and six feet deep butted against the back wall of the coffee house in campus town. Painted black, it blended in with the overall interior décor, all black accented with psychedelic designs in bright colors on one of the side walls.

He felt only a little nervous, just enough to spoil any relaxation he might have enjoyed after finals. When the café owner asked him to sing and play, he didn't know why he had agreed. He did not seek it out as did some others. Some read poetry. Others played music or tried to. Some of it sounded quite good, bringing occasional rewards among the more strident, self-conscious, political and self-absorbed endeavors.

He looked at his watch, waiting for Rosalyn to show up. Maybe some of her confidence would rub off. He never could tell for sure if she really was confident or if she just did such a good job of pretending to be. He felt self-conscious sitting there by the window sipping an espresso. He felt people looking at him even though he knew they weren't, and if they happened to, who cared?

Finally he saw her striding along the sidewalk across the street about a half block down. Rosalyn Sommers looked both ways, darted across the street and scampered up the curb on his side. Her bell-bottom jeans swished back and forth along with her long, quick steps. She smiled and waved when she saw Mario sitting at a table by the window. She looked like other university students, long hair, jeans, sweatshirt or T-shirt. Today she wore a pale yellow T-shirt, making her light brown hair appear a little darker than it really was. She often sympathized with the protest and rebellion of her peers. The war, racial discrimination, economic disparity, and general social unrest colored almost every part of their lives the past four years at the university. But it didn't distract Rosalyn Sommers from her goal of getting into medical school.

"Hey, Mario, hope you haven't been waiting too long."

"Hi, Roz."

She sat down across from him, smiling. She reached across and tussled his hair. "You're going to have to trim that a little bit."

"As long as it's off the shoulders," he replied.

"How'd your finals go?"

"Good. It's good to be done. I still got one paper to finish, but that won't take long."

"God, I hope my chemistry final comes out okay. It was a bitch," Rosalyn said, sounding exasperated.

She lit a cigarette. "God, I hate these things. I swore I'd never start."

Mario smiled, remembering how she used to rail against smoking and those who did it. "I'm sure you did fine. I'm sure your four-point-oh is still intact. When will you find out about med school?"

"Soon I hope. I'm not too worried. You know I was accepted here at the U. I'm just waiting to hear from a couple of others."

"Well, good luck."

"Thanks. What about you? When are you leaving?"

"Haven't heard for sure yet. I almost hope it'll be later, maybe the end of summer. At least it won't be so hot there. I don't know. If it's

2

later, I'll have to find some work this summer. Maybe I should go back home to Clareton and work for the Bauers," Mario said with a little laugh. "I could brush up on my farming skills."

"God, I couldn't ever go back there," Rosalyn said, taking a deep drag on the cigarette. "There's nothing to do. They're so narrow minded."

"I know. I don't think I can stand it, either. Maybe I might just work around here. I hope they send me sooner."

"I couldn't believe it when I heard that," Rosalyn said. "A psych major going to teach agriculture in the boonies of South America. So what do you do, have group therapy sessions before hitting the fields?"

Mario smiled but didn't respond.

"Sorry," Rosalyn said. "Bad joke. Really, how'd you get that assignment?"

"I just filled out the application. I wrote down my Spanish language ability. Under 'previous work experience' I told about all the summers working on the Bauer farm. I guess that was enough for them."

"But why the Peace Corps?" Rosalyn asked. "Is that what you really want to do?"

"I don't know what I want to do. I'm not like you. You just know what you want to do. I wish I did. What I really want to do is travel. I thought about just hitting the road, working now and then."

"That seems kind of lonely."

"I suppose. But that way you meet people, too. At least with the Peace Corps, I'll get to travel some. They're sending me to Guatemala. I just haven't heard exactly when."

"If it's not until later, you should go with Aaron to Chicago," Rosalyn said. "But that's not until August."

"What for?"

"I heard he's going as a delegate to the Democratic National Convention. He's been pretty active in politics. He's going as a delegate to support McCarthy."

"Really? How'd you find out about that? I hardly ever see him around these days."

"My mom. She heard it from Aaron's mom. You should at least keep in touch with hometown gossip once in a while," Rosalyn advised.

"I'm not really interested," Mario said.

"Me neither, but sometimes it can be amusing. Although my mom and dad weren't amused when they heard Aaron was going to be a McCarthy delegate," Rosalyn said. "Now if it was the *other* McCarthy, the one back in the fifties, they'd probably be all for it."

Mario laughed with an understanding nod.

(Senator Eugene McCarthy of Minnesota came close to beating President Lyndon B. Johnson on March 12, 1968, in the New Hampshire primary. McCarthy was the conscience and voice of the growing political opposition to the war in Vietnam. His attempt to capture the Democratic presidential nomination rallied student war protesters at the convention in Chicago and led to Johnson's withdrawal from being a candidate.)

"When he heard about it, my dad was really pissed, not that Aaron was going but who he was supporting," Rosalyn said. "He thinks anyone who questions the war is unpatriotic. We never talk about it."

"Probably just as well," Mario said, taking a sip of espresso. "I've never talked about it with my folks, either. I really don't know what they believe. Maybe I should go to Chicago. It might be kind of fun. I'll have to see. That's almost the end of summer. I've got to find out when I'm heading south though."

"Well be sure to let me know," Rosalyn said. "We've got to have a little farewell party. Not like when Jake left. We all just kind of lost track of each other after high school. I got a letter from him last month. Did I tell you that?"

"Really? No you didn't tell me. I got one too."

"It wasn't much. Kind of drippy actually," Rosalyn said. "He never did say a whole lot, but this didn't really sound like him. I think they must censor letters or something. It was nice to hear from him anyway."

"What'd he say?"

"Oh, he just talked about how hot it was, what it was like being over there. He misses our food, going swimming in the lake, stuff like that. Why? What'd he say in the letter you got?"

4

"I got the uncensored version," Mario said. "He even said so in the letter. Their commanding officer has someone go through all their letters and takes out the bad stuff, what's really going on. But some of the guys gave other letters to this newspaper reporter. He sneaks them out and puts them in the mail for them."

"Really? Cool. So what'd he say?"

"He didn't have nice things to say about the CO, that's for sure."

"What's he doing over there anyway? I mean what kind of unit is he in? I don't even know exactly where he is," Rosalyn said. "I guess I haven't paid too much attention the past couple years."

"You know he's in the Marines. He's a gunner on one of those river patrol boats. They drive up and down the Mekong River delta. They get shot at and shoot back. In the letter he told about this one time they were cruising along and started taking small arms fire from one side of the river. The CO sees some people on the other side and orders Jake to open up with the fifty-caliber machine gun. He said you couldn't really see anything because of all the foliage. But he thought he saw some people get hit. He couldn't tell if they were soldiers or civilians."

"I can't even imagine that."

"What?"

"Imagine somebody shooting at you, trying to kill you," Rosalyn said.

"Well you shoot back and try to kill them first. What's so complicated about that?"

"It's not complicated. It's just stupid."

"That's true. I really don't know why we're there in the first place," Mario said. "I mean, fighting Communism and this so-called 'domino theory'—who came up with that anyway?"

"I think they should make the generals and those big-shot politicians get out and do the fighting. You'd never see another war if that happened," Rosalyn said. "Instead they send all these kids like Jake into combat to get killed or maimed. Maybe they should battle on a chess board."

"Then the Russians would win for sure," Mario laughed.

"Yeah, I guess you're right. I just hope Jake gets back okay. What about you?" Rosalyn asked. "Now that you're done with school, you think you might get drafted?"

"Not if I'm going in the Peace Corps. That's what Jim says anyway. He talked to the draft board about it. I don't know. If it wasn't for that and if I got drafted, I'd probably go. I don't know. It's still a duty. Whatever happens happens."

"Sounds to me like you're just resigning to fate," Rosalyn said. "Not even deciding. But I guess not deciding on anything is still a decision. I'd rather make up my mind and decide what to do myself."

"You always did," Mario smiled. "But I *did* decide to join the Peace Corps, and Jake *did* decide to join the Marines."

"I suppose. Maybe I'm being too hard on you guys," Rosalyn admitted. Mario smiled again and said nothing. Rosalyn changed the subject. "So what are you going to sing here? I was surprised to hear about that. I didn't know you kept this up after high school."

"At first I didn't. I didn't play my guitar for a couple years. I don't know. Maybe I got inspired, maybe by Bob Dylan or somebody. I just dug the old guitar out a couple months ago. Man was I rusty. I just hope it goes okay here tonight. I'm kind of nervous."

"Oh, you'll do just fine. I'm sure you can sing better than Bob Dylan," Rosalyn said, shaking her head and pausing to exhale smoke to one side.

"I wish I could write like him," Mario said. "It's not so much the music as the words. Maybe the music is so bad it's good."

"I guess that's what you call going full circle," Rosalyn said. "So, what songs are you going to do?"

"Just some folk songs," Mario said. "There's some Pete Seeger and Woody Guthrie stuff that I did in high school. The Kingston Trio did some good ones. Once when I was going through some of Tom's stuff, I found some poems and things. I made up melodies for a couple of them. I'm going to do one of those, too."

"Really? I'd almost forgotten about him . . . sorry, but that was so long ago."

"That's okay. I'd kind of forgotten about him, too," Mario said.

"What kind of stuff was it? How'd you get it?"

"I don't know. They just found it after the fire. He must have hauled it out of the shack before it burned. Horse had it in a cardboard box, and he gave it to us later. Mom wasn't too excited about it so I just stashed it in a closet."

"Horse!" Rosalyn exclaimed. "I really liked him. That was so cool, him being a cop there in Clareton. He must have really had a lot of courage to stay there as long as he did. That sure drove some of those rednecks wild. All the kids liked him. He really got us off the hook on all that stuff, what happened with Tom. We were just kids. We didn't know any better."

"I saw him not too long ago. Him and Thelma," Mario said. "He's still a cop in St. Paul. They've got three kids, really cute. My family was in town, and they invited us over for dinner. If I'd thought about it I should have invited you, too."

"That's okay. I probably was buried in a chemistry book or something. That's too bad about how all that happened, about Tom," Rosalyn said. "Sometimes I've thought about it. We thought we were doing the right thing. I mean, we were just kids for chris'sake. It's nobody's fault. We shouldn't feel guilty, especially you."

"I don't feel guilty anymore. Back then I did."

Mario hesitated. He almost was going to say more. Ever since he hadn't said anything to anyone except Horse and Grandpa Ricardo, and they knew because they were there at the time, when he saw someone in the alley after Maria and Jim's wedding. It was good that they knew because then he didn't have to carry it alone, and they believed him. Even now he didn't know what to believe for sure. He could still remember the sense of peace in hearing the man's words. He wanted to find it again.

For a moment he thought about telling Rosalyn. He trusted her and she would try to be understanding, but she would not understand.

Like many of the other small town kids who went off to college in the big city, she had separated herself from the religious beliefs handed down by her parents and her church and was searching for something on her own. So far she had found it in science and the study of medicine. The universe was composed of atomic particles, elements that reacted with one another, adapted and evolved over fifteen billion years. The human organism consisted of cells, chemicals, electrical charges, and organs, and when they were not working properly they could be manipulated and repaired as much as possible. Matters of the spirit could be defined in the complex electro-chemical processes in brain cells. The heart was just a muscle that pumped blood.

"The whole family's going to be here tonight," Mario said. "I'm glad they're here, but it makes me kind of nervous, too."

"That's great! I want to see them," Rosalyn exclaimed. "They're so nice. You've been really lucky the way that all turned out. When we were little kids, you seemed kind of lonesome sometimes, just you and your mom."

"It wasn't so bad," Mario said. "Later it was almost harder getting used to having all these other people around. I got along with Jim okay. Then when Emma and Nate came along things really got lively."

"You adore them, and you know it," Rosalyn teased. "You've been such a nice big brother. They adore you."

"Yeah I suppose. It helped to forget about Tom, I mean, not Tom but what happened," Mario said.

"So if you sing one of his poems in a song won't that just dredge things up again?"

"They don't know that. I don't think it will."

"I think that's sweet anyway," Rosalyn smiled again. "In a way you're honoring his memory. It's passing on something he can contribute to the world, not that he didn't contribute a lot anyway. I remember hearing he was quite a war hero before he went on the skids."

"He was. There was some of that stuff in his things, too. I've still got it, some old pictures and his medals."

Mario watched Rosalyn leave for her apartment. She said she'd be back before nine when he was scheduled to sing and play. He thought about asking if she wanted to join his family for dinner at six, but hesitated too long and she was gone. Out on the sidewalk, passing by the window where they had been sitting, she smiled and rapped on the glass. Mario smiled back and waved. His gaze lingered on her lithe figure striding away, her long hair swishing across the back of her pale yellow T-shirt.

If he hadn't finally made the move himself, the butterflies in his stomach would have lifted him out of his chair and onto the small stage. Emma, going on nine, giggled and covered her mouth partly to conceal the fresh gap left by a missing baby tooth. Her six-year-old brother, Nate, looked around awestruck at all the people in the coffee house, their long hair and garish clothes. Mario almost wished his family wasn't even there. He didn't think he would feel this self-conscious. A brief but intense wave of panic left beads of cold sweat on his forehead. Maria noticed and tried to get his attention by acting out several exaggerated, deep breaths, telling him to relax.

He looked at Horse. Horace "Horse" and Thelma Greene walked in just before nine. He was glad to see them. Some of the panic melted away under the warmth of Horse's big, confident smile. He signaled to Mario a "thumbs up."

Back in high school, Mario's repertoire held about twenty songs. He started the set with "Sixteen Tons," the 1947 classic by Merle Travis and recorded by Tennessee Ernie Ford. He thought the chorus would resonate with the audience:

"You load sixteen tons, what do you get?
Another day older and deeper in debt.
Saint Peter don't you call me 'cause I can't go,
I owe my soul to the company store."

The audience applauded politely, sporadically. The most enthusiasm came from the table near the front, especially from Emma and

Nate. Horse nodded his head and in his deep, mellow voice announced, "Amen, brother!"

Mario decided to skip another old classic and move on to some songs he thought the audience would consider more hip. He tried "The House of the Rising Sun," which brought a little more applause, although Maria seemed somewhat disconcerted. He thought he had performed the songs fairly well. The chord changes on the guitar went fairly smooth. He sang Bob Dylan's "Girl from the North Country" and the Beatles' "She Loves You," which generated a few noticeable winces in the crowd. From a solo acoustic guitar it didn't come close to the popular recording.

He felt admonished and embarrassed when he heard someone comment that they thought he was going to do some original stuff. He smiled and said that was next. He sang "Snowy Mornin' in the Spring-time," which he'd written back in April.

He had spent the weekend back in Clareton for Easter. He awak-ened early that Saturday morning to make the three-hour drive by noon. He looked out the window to see an inch of fresh, white snow covering the ground. It sparkled under the rising morning sun, melting it away before noon. It reminded him of the day after Maria and Jim's wedding, Easter Sunday back in April 1959. It had snowed then, too. He laughed when he recalled the reactions of Maria's brothers, Oscar, Juan, and Reynaldo. Living in San Diego his uncles hardly ever saw snow. Like excited children, they ran out outside, scooped up sloppy handfuls of snow and had a snow-ball fight. After a long, cold and snowy winter, the snow brought only dis-may to Mario. It only prolonged the wait for the spring warm-up.

The similar weather nine years later again brought dismay, now intensified by the pressures of college, uncertainty about the future and sometimes loneliness. He sat alone in the coffeehouse Easter Sunday evening and wrote the lyrics in a small spiral bound notebook. Walking back to his apartment, he began to hear the melody.

The audience seemed to like it.

He introduced the next song, one of Tom's poems saying it was written by an old friend, and that he, Mario, had created the melody.

"Put your burden on my shoulder
For I am weak, but I am strong.
Take your hand, put it in my hand
And we shall walk to the end of time.

My father he once told me
That a man must learn to cry.
Turn his head, look at others
And tell them why we all must die.

Then I told him please ask another
There are others stronger than me.
I'm just a child on the great Mandela
It hurts too much when a man is free.

Then he told me don't be frightened
There are many just like you.
Be strong and love my people
And live for all that's right and true."

He concluded his set with "Wayfaring Stranger," which he thought appropriate considering the path Tom's life had taken.

Emma and Nate each took one of Mario's hands as they walked back to the car after leaving the coffeehouse. Jim carried his guitar. The children, excited about staying in the big city and all its new experiences, bombarded their older half brother with questions. They were staying at a newer motel near campus. Saturday morning they would be going to the natural history museum and in the afternoon the graduation ceremony.

Mario soaked up the attention of his family and relished the relaxation he could now afford after the completion of finals and his musical debut. He felt relieved that the discrepancy in his academic records about his name had been cleared up just in time. It had almost looked like he would have to march in the graduation processional without actually receiving his diploma.

When his mother, Maria Ruiz, changed her name years ago to Maria Reese, she did not do the same for her son. When the school secretary who registered him for kindergarten erroneously recorded his name, Mario N. Ruiz as Marion Reese, the new name went with his records all the way through high school. His middle name was Nathan.

Everyone just assumed that Maria had changed her son's name as well. When they called him Mario they assumed it was a nickname. He accepted it when some teachers and others who didn't know him called him Marion, but in his mind he was always Mario.

The university required three signed affidavits and a copy of his birth certificate before they would accept his high school transcript under a different name. The affidavits came from Horace Greene, Clareton High School Principal Albright, and Jim Andersen, his stepfather.

They walked along in the mild spring evening, the last hues of twilight a lingering backdrop to the downtown skyscrapers in the west. Rosalyn accompanied them, walking with Maria and Jim. She was telling them about her next adventure, medical school. She was happy for Mario and his plans to join the Peace Corps, assuring Maria that he would be just fine.

Mario tried to listen to their conversation at the same time Emma and Nate kept up their excited, childish banter. It caught him off guard when Emma asked about that one song.

"Which one?"

"The one about the burden on my shoulder. At first it made me feel kind of sad. But not really. Who was your friend that wrote it?"

"It was just a friend. You wouldn't know him."

Mario tried to change the subject. He started to tell about the natural history museum. It had a dinosaur skeleton almost as tall as a house. The conversation couldn't stop his thoughts from drifting back to ten years ago. During the past four years in college thoughts of Tom hadn't much intruded and when they did he usually managed to deflect them with the many distractions surrounding him, much like he tried to do just now with Emma's questions.

Somehow the question broke through, into his thoughts slightly tarnishing the contentment he had been savoring at the moment. What if he hadn't turned around, went into the alley back in Clareton, back in the fall of 1958? What if he hadn't faced Frank Harley and pounded him? He could have just kept on walking. Where would Tom Nathan be today if none of that ever happened? Where was he now?

ᔈ 1 ᔆ

AT LEAST THERE WEREN'T ANY FLIES. It was too cold this time of year. He looked up and down the alley and then lifted off the lid. Rummaging through the garbage can, sometimes he'd find a half-eaten steak or a piece of chicken. But not today. Sometimes there'd be part of a hamburger. They were so small that most of the time they got eaten, especially after school when the kids barged in to Art's Café.

The place was a magnet, at least for the kids who didn't have sports or play practice right after school. If their daydreams during the last hour of classes drifted to thoughts of food, they were fulfilled with Art's fifteen-cent hamburgers. The small, fresh ground beef patties turned slightly crisp around the edges on the café's big, black grill. For thirty-five cents a kid could get a hamburger, fries, and a soda or milk.

THE MID-AFTERNOON COFFEE crowd of old men all looked up when the door flew open. They paused, one holding a leather cup, ready to roll the dice to see who would pick up the tab. Their quiet afternoon conversation gave way to a boisterous crowd of kids, pushing and shoving, trying to squeeze through the door all at once, red-cheeked faces all talking and laughing.

14

"Better get ready, Art," said one of the men. "Here come the little urchins."

Art smiled. He had already spread a dozen or so patties on the grill and dumped a bunch of potato slices into the deep fryer. More than the business, he enjoyed serving up burgers and fries and watching them disappear. The kids brought in so much energy, laughter, and sometimes rambunctiousness.

Today Mario Ruiz had decided to join the gang heading for the café. He still had fifty cents left from his allowance, and it was already Wednesday. He could manage until Saturday when his funds were replenished. His mom didn't have a lot, but she always made sure he had some spending money, more than some and less than others. He didn't complain. Sometimes he'd earn a little extra doing odd jobs. They didn't have all that much around to spend it on anyway. A hamburger, fries, and chocolate milk at Art's tasted so good after school. That was enough.

All of the round, red vinyl-covered stools were taken, so Mario squeezed in, standing at the end of the counter. Soon Art slid over the little red plastic basket lined with waxed paper and filled with thin golden crispy fries and a hamburger. He opened the carton of chocolate milk. The grayish-brown, rich, sweet fluid went down smooth and cold; it tasted so good. The chatter waned as in their turn each started to eat.

On the front window, water droplets sparkled in the late afternoon sunlight, building and breaking the tensile bond to slide down the glass leaving a clear, straight path. In late November it was cold enough to cause moisture from the warm inside air to condense on the cool glass. Just a thin pane of glass separated the tribal warmth around fire and food from the cold, biting wind swirling through Clareton's streets and alleys.

Mario offered a silent prayer of thanks and then stuffed a clump of fries into his mouth, the salt stinging a bit after the sweet milk. They always said grace before meals at home, and sometimes out in public at restaurants. It made him feel embarrassed and then guilty for feeling embarrassed. If the other kids saw him praying, he was sure they'd laugh and ridicule him. Once in a while at restaurants he'd see people bowing their heads. He admired their courage. Nobody around seemed to notice or care. Perhaps others thought they were showing off some kind of self-righteousness.

"Dear God, thank you for this food, and bless it to my body. Amen," he said to himself, trying to form the words in his mouth like a ventriloquist hoping no one noticed. He ate the little burger in about three bites, pinched his fingers around the remaining crispy slivers of fries, and that was it. Another hamburger basket gone.

Afterwards Mario planned to stop by Jake's place when Jake got back from his paper route. That's if Jake didn't stop by the bowling alley first. Jake earned about five bucks a week from the route. Occasionally he would bowl a line or two. Last year he was even in a league. He wasn't sure about it this year because of the cost, and he had to be there every Saturday morning. In winter that was okay because there wasn't that much else to do, especially if it was really cold.

Mario liked to play basketball when the gym was open. Sometimes it was and sometimes it wasn't. It was never open during the Christmas break from school when he needed it the most. He had thought about joining a basketball league but wasn't sure if he was good enough. Jake wasn't very good at basketball even though he was taller. Mario was better than he was at basketball, but Jake did okay at bowling. Mario had gone to watch his league games the previous year. On Saturday mornings all eight lanes were busy. He marveled at the precision of the new Brunswick automatic pin setters. After Jake's older brother, Larry, lost his pin-setter job, the owner gave Larry a job at the desk. They figured he was old enough by then.

HERE COME THE STRIKE-OUT KINGS," Larry announced once when Jake and Mario entered the bowling alley. "I was referring to girls, not bowling," he laughed.

No matter what time of year, Larry usually wore a white T-shirt with a pack of Luckies rolled up in the left sleeve. He was only seventeen and not supposed to have cigarettes, but nobody did anything. He wore his dark-brown hair in a slicked-back ducktail. He seemed to smirk a lot, at least around the little kids; Mario didn't know if he liked him or not. He wasn't really mean or anything. Mario just didn't feel real comfortable around him. Bowlers had to check the sizes of their rental shoes. Sometimes he would mix two different sizes and slide them across the counter. "Here you go!" It didn't seem to bother Jake much. After they finished their games and brought up the score sheet, which in Jake's case was often in the 160s, his brother would say, "Not too bad, guys," which coming from him was a rare and effusive compliment.

Most of the other kids had left the café before Mario stepped out the door. The shadows cast by the downtown buildings reached the opposite side of the street away from the sun drifting downward in the west. A couple of city workers attaching Christmas decorations to light poles looked cold and tired. An alternating pattern of six-foot-tall candy canes and large wreaths hung from light poles on the side streets. Huge garlands of pine boughs and colored lights stretched across the main street. The Friday after Thanksgiving, people gathered downtown to watch when they turned on the lights, signaling the start of the Christmas holiday season.

Down the street from the café, Mario stopped in the bowling alley, but Jake wasn't there. He went back out, turned the corner and headed for home. Passing by the alley, he saw a bunch of kids halfway down it, by the garbage cans behind the café. He stopped and looked. Something was happening. He started walking down the alley toward them. Some kids were saying stuff to some old man. The man glared and gestured at them. The kids stood around him in a semi-circle, like a pack of predators nipping and taunting, trying to weaken their prey. The old man wore a gray parka—stained, dirty and tattered on the edges. Some stuffing in the lining protruded from a five-inch rip on the upper back. Strands of light-colored hair peeked from the edges of his green stocking cap. Drawing nearer, just behind the other kids, Mario still couldn't tell who it was. It looked like he hadn't taken a bath in a year.

Y OU KIDS GET OUTTA HERE," he growled. "Just leave me alone, okay? Everyone just leave me alone. I'm not hurting anybody."

"You're taking food from the pigs," said one of the kids, Frank Harley. "That's stealing. We should call the cops. Pig food's too good for you anyway!" If anyone would be picking on somebody, it would be Frank Harley.

Twice a week one of the local farmers drove through the alley, collected the waste food and fed it to his pigs.

"Why don't you get a job?" said another kid. "We don't want any bums around town. Why don't you just hop on the train and leave?"

"I've got a right to be here. You kids go home now and leave me alone."

The kids closed the circle around him.

"C'mon, you guys, leave him alone."

Everyone turned, startled, toward the voice, the sound even startling Mario as he heard it come from his own mouth. The adrenaline surging through his entire body, his stomach knotted up. He couldn't believe that he had said anything. The anger that made him speak out quickly yielded to regret.

"What are you doin', Reese?" It was Frank with his customary sneer. "Who asked you? What are you sticking up for him for?"

With the kids' attention turned to Mario, the old man started walking the other way down the alley. Some of the kids noticed, grabbed cans and bottles from the garbage and threw them at the retreating, hunched-over figure. A few thudded off his back. A couple of bottles shattered on the brick pavement. He turned once and cursed back at them.

"Good riddance to bad rubbish," Frank hollered.

Mario turned and walked back towards the street, resisting the urge to run. The rest of the kids started to follow like a pack of hyenas.

"What are you, some kind of bum lover? Just wait 'til we tell everybody Marion is a bum lover," Frank laughed. He pushed Mario in

18

the back. Mario kept walking, a little faster then. If he could make it out of the alley to the street, his chances of escaping without any further confrontation would improve.

Emerging from the alley, he saw a car slowing down on the street, a brand new '59 Cadillac. It stopped, and the driver lowered the electric window on the passenger side. Frank and the other kids stepped out of the alley next to Mario.

"Is that you Frank?"

Earl Harley reached across and opened the passenger door.

"I'm heading home for supper. Hop in."

Normally, getting in the car with a parent in such a circumstance would seriously harm one's reputation. Frank hesitated, but the lure of the shiny new car overcame his initial impulse to stay with the gang. The status conferred by the car exceeded any lost by yielding to a parent's request. Mr. Harley owned the dealership for Cadillacs and Buicks. Every year the Harleys got a new car, usually a Caddy. The other kids gazed in awe and envy at the car, its gleaming chrome and shiny, cream-colored finish. The long, graceful lines sweeping up to the massive, pointed tailfin burned into their memories. And it was a hardtop.

Frank looked around, then walked to the car. He smiled slightly as he climbed in and closed the door with a solid, secure thud. He waved a little salute to the other kids as the Caddy pulled away. Without Frank the group lost its purpose.

"What should we do now?"

"I don't know. What do you want to do?"

"I probably should get home for supper."

"See you guys around."

Freed from the clutches of Frank and the other kids, Mario's tension vanished. He turned slowly and started to walk the six blocks home. Just about down to the horizon, the sun's last reddish-orange light glowed through the dark, bare branches of the tall elms. It had been cloudy all week so it was nice to see the sun again. Losing its warmth and light earlier and earlier every day left a void way too soon for bedtime. A pile of burning leaves in someone's yard off to the northwest sent an invisible smoky aroma drifting along in the cool air. He thought about the old man. "Why did I stick up for him?" he said out loud. His stomach felt a little twinge, and he didn't look forward to school the next day. That was normally the case, but now it would be even worse. Still, he felt as if he had done the right thing. It really made him mad to see those guys picking on that pathetic old man.

AFTER THE CLOUDS CLEARED out toward the end of the week, the temperatures dropped way below freezing. The sheet of ice covering the lake south of town invisibly grew thicker. The lake was their playground year-round. By late fall the kids could usually count on ice skating, the transition from thin to safe ice always an adventure. They tested the limits of nature and their parents' patience by venturing out from shore to see how the ice would hold up. If it was good ice, about two inches was enough, at least for the younger, smaller kids. They had sense enough to stay close to shore until the ice thickened. It was a shallow lake, twelve feet at the deepest.

Friday after school, Jake and Mario headed for the lake to check it out. A few other kids showed up at the city park beach to do the same thing. Freezing over on a cold, calm night, the surface had become a thin sheet of smooth, clear ice appearing dark green over the cold water beneath. Cautiously they took slow, sliding steps out on the ice. It looked almost two inches thick.

"Don't stand so close together," someone said. "You're gonna fall through."

"It's only knee-deep here."

"Yeah, but we don't want to wreck it."

Nobody really wanted to get their feet wet, either. The freezing water gripped a person like a million needles. Walking in wet clothes and squishy, cold shoes, one can't get home soon enough. And if someone was home and found out what happened, the trouble really started.

A few years earlier a kid fell through the ice and drowned or froze to death trying to rescue his dog. The dog had run out onto the thin ice toward an open spot full of geese. The flock erupted from the water in a noisy, flapping cloud, and the dog broke through. The kid crawled out, trying to rescue the yelping, splashing dog. Not too long after, someone saw them and called the fire department. The firemen pushed ladders across the ice toward them. Someone went to get a boat. But it was too late. Now every time kids wanted to get out on the early season ice, they heard the story all over again. Of course, they were convinced that would never happen to them.

A police officer walked down the hill toward the beach.

Out on the ice near shore, the kids stopped and stared, more afraid of the dark-blue uniform than anything else. They were caught.

"Hi there, kids."

"Hi."

"You sure the ice is safe?"

"Yeah, it's okay. We're being careful."

Officer Greene slid one foot out on to the ice, then the other.

"See, it's thick enough," Mario said. "We weren't going out very far or skate or anything. We just wanted to check it out."

About five feet from shore the officer's left foot broke through.

"Damn!"

Submerged ankle-deep, he leaped with his right leg toward shore. Reaching solid ground, water dripped from his trouser leg onto his glistening, soaked left shoe. The kids tried hard to keep from laughing out loud, and the officer's tone became much more stern when a few chuckles escaped.

"Listen, you kids get off here right now! Every year we go through this. You should know better. Remember what happened to Andy Bergquist. We don't want to be fishing anyone out of the water this year. The ice should be a solid *four* inches thick before you can walk on it. Six is even better."

"Yessir, we'll stay off until it's thicker," they promised.

"You'd better, or I can call your parents, too."

That got everyone's attention. If anyone's parents found out about this, they'd be banished from the lake for a month. That would be unbearable. From Thanksgiving to Christmas, they could usually count on clear, solid ice. Later in winter after more snow fell, it was harder to get around through the patches of snow and drifts close to shore, and it was often a lot colder. One more stern look around at the half-dozen kids, and the officer started back up the hill toward the parking lot.

"What does he know?" one kid said. "What does a jungle bunny know about ice?"

Some of the kids laughed. Since becoming a Clareton police officer the previous spring, Horace Greene often elicited such comments, almost never to his face.

"I wish it was summer," Jake said, looking out at the frozen lake.

"Me too, but then we couldn't go skating," Mario said.

"Well, now we can't do neither."

Someone took a last running slide on to the ice.

"C'mon, let's go. You'll ruin it for everyone if the cop sees you again."

It was getting dark, almost suppertime, and everyone started wandering off toward home.

IN SUMMER THE KIDS PRACTICALLY lived at the park. It didn't have much of a beach, less than a hundred feet wide, but two years ago the city had dumped truckloads of sand and started to level it out. They didn't quite finish the job, leaving several mounds on the east half. Somebody said it looked like the beach from the D-Day invasion they saw in a picture in *Life* magazine. The kids were too old to play cowboys and Indians, so they played Army instead. They took turns playing Germans crouching behind the sand piles, firing at the Americans splashing ashore. They took turns because in this case there was a disadvantage to being the good guys.

The Americans always won the battle, but they also were the ones who got wet. That wasn't a problem if you wore your swimsuit, but then charging ashore barefoot in a swimsuit didn't seem real authentic. So they decided that it was necessary to wear shoes even if it meant getting them wet. Almost everyone wore canvas sneakers, and for most of them these were the only shoes they had, except for Sunday church shoes. Sometimes they had to run around in wet shoes for a day or two, which wasn't all that bad except after a while they'd start to stink.

Aaron always got wet shoes because he refused to be a German. Other kids accepted that, even though they didn't quite understand it. Some had seen the picture books on the coffee table at Aaron's house. One had all these photos of the D-Day invasion in June 1944. The other was about the concentration camps. Aaron said his dad insisted that the books always be displayed so they'd never forget what happened. His dad had been in the Army and was wounded in the D-Day invasion. The wound wasn't too serious so he re-joined his unit. They fought in the Battle of the Bulge and eventually went all the way into Germany, helping in the liberation of a concentration camp. Once Jake asked him how many Germans he killed, but he wouldn't say. Aaron said he never talked about it, and we shouldn't ever ask him. Mr. Abrams ran a machine shop and salvage yard on the east side of town and was really nice when kids were looking for things like pushcart axles. He would even drill the cotter pin holes for free.

Some kids always wanted to be Germans when they played invasion. That's what Frank Harley did. He even made a flag with a *"hakenkreuze,"* the hooked cross of the German swastika. He always had the best machine gun, a real-looking toy Tommy gun. Otherwise, kids carried a variety of weapons from toy Winchester rifles to homemade machine guns. That's what Mario used. The kids selected suitable pieces from the scrap pile at the lumber yard for all sorts of projects, including toy guns.

Whenever Frank played, it was never really clear who won the battle. He planted the flag atop one of the sand piles, kept up the pretend machine gun fire, and would never yield to the advancing American soldiers. Lying on the beach with his feet wet and throat getting sore from pretend gunfire and the battle going nowhere, eventually the game just kind of fizzled out as if everyone had run out of ammunition.

Aaron wouldn't play if Frank was there. Mario felt sorry for Aaron because he seemed kind of lonely whenever this happened. Aaron called Frank a Nazi. Aaron was a little different in other ways, too. His whole family was. They didn't attend any church in town, and they didn't make big deal out of Christmas. They gave gifts, but they didn't have a Christmas tree or a manger scene or anything like that. During practice for the Christmas program at school, Aaron would sit in the library.

AARON APPROACHED MARIO after school and said he'd heard about the incident in the alley behind Art's Café. He told Mario he'd done the right thing to stick up for the old guy, and if he ever needed someone to back him up, he'd be glad to. That's one thing about Aaron that kids really liked; he was always fair and honest. He hadn't been at the café that day. He'd heard about it when kids were talking during lunch.

Mario dreaded going to into the lunchroom. Usually he was really hungry. Now his stomach was in a knot, and he hardly had any appetite. When the bell rang at the end of fourth hour and the stampede started to the lunchroom, he just wanted to run the other way, out the door and away and never come back. He felt trapped and almost panicked. "Why didn't I just keep my mouth shut?" he thought to himself. "Why did I even say anything when I saw them picking on the old bum?"

Lunchtime was hard enough anyway with everyone pushing and shoving in line, teasing and trying to talk smart. All the popular kids sat at the same table and acted like they were better than everyone else. Most kids sat in the same groups every day, but a few didn't seem to have any friends, sometimes sitting alone or on the edge of some group. Sometimes Mario noticed these kids and felt sorry for them. If one sat at his table he'd say, "Hi," and that was about it. Then the other kids turned back to their conversation. They never really belonged. If Aaron was there, he'd try to talk with them. He seemed to be really interested in people, and they would tell him about all kinds of stuff. If you wanted to know anything about anybody, you asked Aaron.

HEY, THERE'S THE BUM LOVER. He was trying to stick up for that old guy who was eating garbage behind Art's." Frank said it loud enough to make most heads turn and look.

Mario's ears started to burn even though everyone was looking at Frank and not him.

"Marion over there, he's weird."

"Shut up, Frank," Jake said real loud. "You're real brave, all of you picking on an old man. What did he ever do to you?"

"We should just run him out of town, that's what we should do. He's a no-good bum. He probably steals stuff and everything."

"I think we should run *you* out of town."

"Just go ahead and try."

"Okay, you guys, what's going on over here?" Mr. Anderson walked toward the tables. "What are you kids arguing about?" The boys' gym teacher got paid a little extra to give up a peaceful half-hour in the teachers' lounge to serve as a lunchroom monitor. "What's the big deal?"

"Nothing," Jake replied.

"It must have been something."

"No, really, it's not a big deal. We were just talking about what to do with all the Communists in our country. We've been talking about it in social studies. The Communists are everywhere and trying to take over."

"I find that hard to believe," Mr. Anderson laughed.

"You don't believe there are Communists?"

"No, not that. I find it hard to believe that you were actually listening in class."

The bell rang and kids still remaining in the lunchroom stampeded to bring their trays to the kitchen window. Mario hadn't finished all of his lunch. His stomach still felt all knotted up, and he couldn't eat it all anyway. Only two more class periods remained and then he could escape from school for another day. Jake was going to try get his paper route done early, and they were planning go skating on the frozen lake for the first time that year. Somehow Rosalyn found out and asked if she could go with them. Mario said okay as long as it was okay with Jake. It wouldn't be the same with her along, not bad or anything, just different. They planned to meet at Jake's.

Mario arrived before Jake had completed his paper route. Every day after school he delivered the *Clareton Chronicle* to twenty-eight houses on the west side of town. Saturdays it had to be delivered in the morning. Although it only took about half an hour, if they planned to do something after school it always seemed to use up too much of what little daylight remained, and it made Mario kind of antsy. It didn't seem to bother Jake, though. His parents expected him to work, and it seemed like they always had plenty of money. The Carlsons lived in a newer house by the lake. The light-blue rambler sat at the top of what used to be one of the best sliding hills around. Rosalyn was already there.

"Hi. How long have you been waiting?" Mario asked.

"Oh, not too long. Thanks for letting me go with you guys. When's Jake going to be back?"

"Pretty soon, I hope."

A pair of white figure skates hung around her shoulders, resting on her long, light-brown hair. Her hazel eyes gleamed beneath a white, fuzzy stocking cap pulled down over her ears, and the big wooly ball on top made her seem even taller than she was. Rosalyn was different from most of the other girls. She always seemed calm and didn't talk a whole lot, but when she did she always seemed to say the right thing at the right time. She was probably the smartest kid in the class and was really pretty, and she could have hung around with all the popular girls if she wanted to. Instead, she liked to go skating on the lake and be outdoors. She was always really nice to Mario, and he kind of liked her, too.

"Hi, kids. Are you waiting for Jake?" Mrs. Carlson said from the front door. "He should be home pretty soon. So, what do you have planned?"

"We were going to go skating on the lake," Mario said.

"You think it's safe? I'm not so sure, and it's going to be dark soon. I don't think that's really a good idea."

Disappointment washed over Mario like big wave dousing his anticipation. He looked at Rosalyn, who just kind of shrugged and tried to offer an understanding smile.

"I don't think I'm going to allow Jake to go," Mrs. Carlson said with a tone of sympathy. "I think we'd all better wait until the ice is thicker and you have a little more daylight."

Jake approached on the sidewalk, his empty paper sack hanging from his left shoulder.

"Hi, what's going on?"

"Hi, Jake. I was just telling your friends that it's probably not a good idea to go skating right now. We really don't know if the ice is safe yet, and it's going to be dark soon. Why don't you kids come in and have some brownies. I just made them. I know it's not too long before supper, but we won't tell anyone," Mrs. Carlson said with a sly wink.

ജ 2 ര

MARIA REESE REMAINED IN THE KITCHEN to clean the rest of the meat off the turkey. Thelma stayed to help although there was hardly enough room for one person in the tiny kitchen of the story-and-a-half bungalow. Bowls of leftover mashed potatoes, dressing, sweet potatoes, cranberries, carrots, and dirty dishes covered the small table and what counter space there was. Plates, glasses, and silverware filled the sink. The young women worked well together, like they had practiced the routine for weeks. It was as if they anticipated each other's movements, Maria placing the food in containers and Thelma cleaning off the dishes, pirouetting around the tiny space with only an occasional jostle followed by a giggle and an apology.

They had become close friends over the years working together as elementary teachers, Maria in fourth grade and Thelma second grade. But this was the first time they had spent Thanksgiving together. It was the first time Maria had ever had guests over for Thanksgiving, and the first time Thelma Harris had not been with her family. Even though they were close friends, it was a little bit awkward. Maria could sense that Thelma felt sad about not being with her family. They made small talk as they cleaned up after the big dinner. The turkey had been a twenty-two-pounder so there was quite a bit left. Even though in the past it had been only for her and Mario, Maria always roasted a big turkey because it was the same work as a smaller one and you could eat leftovers for days.

Mario and the men went to the living room to watch the football game. Jim Andersen, a dentist in his mid-thirties, had been spending a lot of time lately at the Reese's. At first Mario didn't know what to think. By now he had grown used to Jim being around. With Horace Greene it was different. He was somehow connected with Thelma. That seemed even more unusual.

Mario had to fiddle with the rabbit ears on the old Philco trying to get a better picture. It was okay—at least you could tell the teams apart. After months of nagging and begging from Mario, Maria finally gave in and bought a used television. She had resisted because, in order to receive any channels you needed a large antennae or to get hooked up to the new cable system in town. You could get one or two channels with an antenna and six with cable, and a much clearer picture, too. But when a new station opened up fifty miles away it came in pretty good without a big antenna. She also thought it was a poor use of time, watching TV. She made sure Mario was always reading a book. He actually looked forward to the new *National Geographic* magazine each month. Mario read each one cover to cover.

But on a cloudy Thanksgiving Day with two football fans in the house, it was a blessing that the one channel, KWCM, carried the network showing the Detroit Lions' game. This year the Green Bay Packers were playing. Jim and Mr. Greene could hardly wait for the kickoff. Mario would have preferred to do something outside after the big dinner, but he also looked forward to the game. It was nice having people around on a holiday, which otherwise sometimes got a little lonely, and they seemed to know a lot about football. They knew all the players and team records and what play they should use on any particular down from the line of scrimmage.

Mario liked to play football. The city recreation department sponsored a football league for the younger kids before they got into junior-high football. Mario had played since the fifth grade on a team sponsored by the Thompson-Harkin Lumber Company. Back then he was a few pounds under the minimum eighty-five pounds, so at weigh-in he filled his pockets with lead slugs the kids had dug from the gravel pit just outside town that the cops used as a pistol range. It didn't fool the rec director. He just chuckled and let Mario play. He knew Mario wouldn't have any problem against bigger kids. Mario would have preferred playing football, even after a big turkey dinner, but as long as everyone was watching the game, he didn't have much choice.

Mr. Greene was rooting for the Lions because he was from near Detroit. Jim was from Minnesota, and there wasn't any pro football team there so he was a Packer fan. Green Bay was the closest pro team, and he also had relatives in Wisconsin. Mario wasn't sure what side he should be on.

Maria asked if anyone was ready for dessert—pumpkin pie. Jim had already gone into the living room and turned on the television. It took a minute or so for the tubes to warm up, and, after Mario adjusted the knobs, a picture finally appeared. The teams were already lined up for the kickoff.

"Maybe we can wait . . . how about during half-time?" Jim suggested.

"Oh, all right," she sighed. "We'll just go put the food away. You boys enjoy the game."

"So, Mario, who you rooting for?" asked Mr. Greene.

"Well, I don't know."

"C'mon, you got to have some favorite. This is a big rivalry."

Mario wondered what difference it would make rooting for one team or the other. They were 500 miles away and didn't even know he existed.

"I guess I haven't really thought about it all that much."

"Well, if you want to be on the winning side, root for the Lions," Mr. Greene laughed.

"Wait a minute there," Jim said. "If you want to feel good about winning after the game, you better back the Pack."

Neither team was having a particularly good season. The Packers had won only one game so far, and the Lions not much better. But that didn't matter on a cold, dreary Thanksgiving Day. Full of turkey, mashed potatoes, dressing, and rich, brown gravy, the men settled in to the couch and easy chair in total contentment. Enthralled by their seemingly vast knowledge about pro football and their good-natured rivalry, Mario settled in too. Except he still wasn't sure who to root for. He admired and respected Mr. Greene. Not every kid could say he was on a friendly, first-name basis with one of the town's police officers, particularly this one. That was just another burden Mario had to bear. Not too many kids knew that Mr. Greene was a friend of the family. At least Mario's friends were impressed and didn't tease him. In fact, they were a little bit awed.

As for Jim, it was a bit more difficult. Mario went reluctantly when his mother took him to the dentist, even though Dr. Jim Andersen did a good job of keeping discomfort to a minimum whenever Mario had a cavity filled. In his early thirties and unmarried, he had been dating Maria for about a year. Mario liked Jim and respected him, but sometimes he felt a little jealous when Jim went out alone with Maria or would give her an affectionate hug or kiss. But they didn't go out alone very often, and Jim tried real hard to pay attention to Mario.

"You let the boy decide who he's going to cheer for," Mr. Greene laughed.

"You're right," Jim agreed. "Mario, it's about time you face up to one of the major decisions in life—which NFL team you're going to be for. If it's going to be between the Lions and the Packers, right now you'd probably be better off being for the Lions. But just remember, things can change down the road, so don't always think you have to go with what appears to be the winner."

"That sounds like a good speech from a loser," Mr. Greene laughed. "So, Mario, what do you think?"

"Well, I guess I don't really know, but maybe I'll root for the Packers. They're not playing at home so maybe it's a little harder playing at the other team's stadium and all the fans are cheering for the home team. Maybe that makes a difference?"

"Well what do you know, we've got us a budding pro football analyst," Mr. Greene chuckled. "That's probably a good choice because the Packers are going to need all the help they can get. Besides, it's probably better if the men in the house are on the same team," he said, winking an eye and then looking at Jim, who smiled and looked a little embarrassed.

The afternoon drifted by in satisfied relaxation, with occasional outbursts of cheers or groans after a big play. With the company, Mario felt content although he looked forward to Friday with no school, ice skates, and a frozen lake beckoning.

HORACE GREENE ENJOYED SPENDING Thanksgiving at the Reeses. He knew it was tough on Thelma, though. He could tell she missed being with her family. When it became clear he was not welcome at the Harris home, Thelma made a very difficult choice. In fact, the conflict drove her even closer to Horace. About the only other person she could talk to about it was Maria. When Maria heard that Thelma and Horace had no place to go for Thanksgiving, she invited them over, knowing that doing so could put her at odds with Thelma's family as well.

During the game Horace commented on how tough it was sometimes for black players to get a fair shake in pro sports. He was proud of Jim Brown of the Cleveland Browns on his way to a record season with well over 1,000 yards rushing. His beloved Detroit Lions, however, disappointed him after taking some steps backward in terms of black players on their roster.

At six feet two, 230 pounds, good-looking and muscular, the twenty-nine-year-old African-American stood out among the descendants of German and Scandinavian immigrants populating Clareton. Horace played football in high school and could have played in college had he been able to attend. Given the opportunity, he even could have had a shot at the NFL and could have made an outstanding linebacker.

He didn't finish high school, at least not right away. In his junior year he started running with a gang—break-ins, booze, hot rods—and dropped out half-way through senior year. He was heading downhill when the high school football coach bumped into him at the gas station. They had a little talk. Horace had been one of the team's most talented players and an outstanding linebacker. Even though it was too late for football, the coach persuaded Horace to get back in school. He had so much potential.

It wasn't easy leaving the gang and going back to school. In 1947 he finally graduated, a year later than normal, and joined the Air Force. After ten years, he'd had enough, received an honorable discharge and bought a bus ticket to back to Detroit, but he never made that far. He'd been on the Clareton police force for about a year now.

"So, how's it going, the job?" Jim asked during a lull in the game.

"Oh, pretty good I guess. Most of the folks are pretty good once they get to know me. But there's a few who'll never accept me. Judge Holmes in particular. He puts me through the wringer every case. All his buddies know if they get a ticket from me it's a free pass. It just ain't fair. I really don't know how much longer I'll stick around."

"That'd be a shame if you had to leave. You've done a really good job here. The kids really like you—most of 'em. They respect you."

"Thanks. But it gets kind of lonesome, too. Most folks are cordial and all, but I don't really have any friends . . . I mean, you're friends . . . but, you know, I kind of stand out around town. Thelma's wonderful, and we really care about each other, but that makes things even worse. If we stay together, we don't really have a future here. And I'm really cut out to live in the big city anyway. If Thelma wants to go along, well I'd be one happy man. I was heading for the city, you know, when Mayor Fairbanks saw me at the bus station."

"How'd that all happen, anyway?" Jim asked.

"What? Thelma or the mayor?"

"I meant the mayor."

"Well, I was just having a quick bite to eat during the bus stop at the hotel. This guy comes up to me and starts talking. At first I thought he was just checking me out, you know, like 'What's this colored person doing in our town?' But he seemed real nice and friendly. Then he sits down and orders a cup of coffee. He asks where I was from and where was I going, so I told him."

"Where were you going?"

"I was heading back to Detroit. I'd done my hitch at that Godforsaken radar base in North Dakota and couldn't get out of there fast enough. I was going to try to become a police officer. If that didn't work, I'd try for prison guard, but I'd probably just end up being a hotel bell-hop. That's what I did in the Air Force you know, military police. Things changed a little after the war for us folks. Anyway, after we'd talked for a while, Mayor Fairbanks offers me this job. I about fell off my chair. No way, I said. No way would this lily-white little hick town's ever going to accept a black police officer.

"But he kept trying to persuade me, and finally I said okay. He was so sincere, and I guess I just felt good that someone was actually interested in me and what I could do. He said it'd be good for the town, too. He said people here needed to start learning about civil rights and equality and all that stuff. I wasn't sure I wanted to be part of the object lesson, but we both agreed if things didn't work out I could be on my way."

"So how did Fairbanks get the police chief to go along?"

"At the hotel coffee shop he asks me if I have a resumé. I said no, so then he tells me to write down everything I've done, like starting from high school and so on. All I could think of was my Air Force experience. He asked about other things, like was I in sports or anything. I put down football, even though I didn't play my senior year, but on the air base we played touch football a lot. I follow college and pro ball and I know the game pretty well.

"Anyway, he took my paper and gave it to his secretary . . . she types it up in a real nice looking resumé and gives it to the police chief. They'd been looking a long time for another officer, and the mayor can be real persuasive when he wants to. The chief goes along and agrees to hire me sight unseen."

"That must've been interesting to meet him the first time."

"You shoulda seen the look on his face," Horace laughed. "At first he looked a little green, then he turns white—I mean *really* white. I look him straight in the eye and hold out my hand. He didn't say a word at first, but he slowly raises his hand, and we shake. Fairbanks has this big smile on his face and says, 'Welcome to Clareton, Horace.' The chief finally gets his tongue untied and says, 'Nice to meet you. I hope—I'm sure you'll do a good job here.'"

"We're glad you decided to stay," Jim said. "Look what you did with the football team this fall as an assistant coach. Their defense was rock solid. And I think it turned a lot of people's minds around . . . especially Thelma's."

"Yeah, well she's really great, too," Horace smiled. "I know it's hard for her family to accept . . . I don't know how all that's going to end up. Around town it's not so bad, at least on the surface. If we stay together, I'm sure we won't be around here too long."

"That's too bad."

"Well, you remember I'm a city boy, and if you ask Thelma she can't wait to get away from here."

"Sometimes I don't blame her," Jim sighed. "We'll probably be stuck here forever."

"You don't have to. What's holding you back?"

"We've never really talked about moving on. I don't know. I guess we like it here. We like the small town life. I know Maria does. We've both got good jobs. Having summers off for Maria is nice, although she still works part of it teaching the migrant kids. That's how she came here in the first place, you know. They were looking for someone—a teacher—who could speak Spanish.

"She lived in California . . . things weren't going too well there, I guess. She saw an ad for this job and here she is. She doesn't care for the winters too much, but she's getting used to it. Sometimes she's been able to get back home for a visit, so that helps. So, what do you think, Mario? How do you like it here?" Jim asked.

Mario was lying on the floor with his chin propped up on his forearms, brown eyes gazing at the television and ears listening intently to the conversation. At first he didn't know what to say. He hadn't much experience relating with grown men, at least at home. Jim smiled patiently and seemed like he was really interested in what Mario had to say.

"It's okay, I guess. I don't mind the winter. We go skating and sliding . . . we play hockey a lot. I don't really remember too much about living in California. I was only about four or five when we moved here, so I guess this is pretty much my hometown. We've been back to California a couple times, but it takes so long to get there it seems like we have to turn right around and head back."

"I can imagine that, especially if you have to take the bus. Wouldn't it be nice to take one of those new jet airliners they've started using?"

"I rode in a jet once. It was an Air Force transport," Horace said. "Man that was something. You could really feel the Gs on take off. When you can cruise at 30,000 feet at about 600 miles per hour, it don't take long to get where you're going."

The conversation dwindled as their attention returned to the game. The Lions won twenty-four to fourteen, but Horace didn't rub it in too much.

Maria hauled out the Monopoly game and finally persuaded the men to play. They needed to kill more time in order to be hungry enough to bring out all the turkey dinner leftovers for another round. Mario gave up any hope of getting outside for some fresh air and burning off some energy. He hoped the other kids weren't down at the rink playing hockey and he was missing out. He'd have to wait until Friday to do something outside when he, Jake, and maybe Rosalyn were planning to go skating around the lake, keeping near the shore as he promised his mom.

ಖ 3 ಝ

MARIO AWOKE EARLIER THAN USUAL for a morning without school. On school days the alarm went off at seven. He relished holidays and weekends when he could sleep in until about nine or so. The Friday after Thanksgiving was like a free day—no school, no weekend chores, no holiday responsibilities—a day he could do whatever he wanted and no one seemed to mind.

There wasn't much going on around town until about 6:00 p.m. when the city turned on the lights of the Christmas decorations. A crowd usually gathered to watch the lighting of the big evergreen on the courthouse lawn, and the stores downtown were busy. If the weather was okay a lot of people drove to Minneapolis, and some even went to the new indoor shopping center in Edina.

Mario scrunched up under the quilt, and for a moment thought about going back to sleep. He peeked at the clock, which showed just before eight, then reached out and pulled back the edge of the shade to see an overcast sky. It looked depressing. Sometimes he just wanted to stay in bed and find refuge in the unconsciousness of sleep. But this morning he remembered the plan to meet at Jake's around nine to go skating. Jake would have been up more than two hours already, so it wasn't all that early for him.

Mario looked back at the clock with the face of Mickey Mouse staring back at him—two big, black ears protruding from the ten and two positions. This souvenir came from their last trip to California three years ago when they went with Grandma Ruiz to Disneyland the first summer it was open in 1955. They could barely afford it—it cost a dollar just to get in—but it was worth it. Some of the rides were thirty-five cents, so they could only go on a few.

Clareton had a lot of things in common with Main Street, U.S.A., at Disneyland. That's where Mario got the clock after begging and pleading. It cost $2.95. They walked around and got some ice cream at the Carnation Ice Cream Parlor. Mario got to do the Main Street Shooting Gallery, and they rode on one of the horse-drawn streetcars. He liked Frontierland the best, especially the Mark Twain Riverboat.

Reminiscing early on a dreary late November morning felt comforting and pleasant, although the memories faded a bit as each year passed. Sometimes now he felt a little embarrassed about the childish clock. Still, he thought it sure would be fun to go back again.

"Mario, are you getting up?" Maria hollered from the bottom of the stairs. "I heard your clock go off . . . why are you getting up so early?"

"Yeah, I'm up. I'm up"

He pulled the quilt back, swung his feet to the floor and sat up looking around the darkened room. He yawned and stretched his arms, arching his back until his head almost touched the wall against the other side of the bed. He walked over to the other window and pulled the shade back. A few snowflakes drifting in a slanting path—showing up against the dark tree trunks—meant it was cold but not too windy.

"Mom, what's the temperature out?"

Already back in bed, she didn't respond, so Mario stepped into his slippers and went downstairs to check the outdoor thermometer showing though the window by the kitchen sink. The arrow pointed just above twenty degrees F. He shivered, went back to the hallway and turned up the thermostat to seventy. The indoor temperature registered sixty-four. Maria had decided it was better to dress warm even inside the house and use lots of blankets. They turned down the thermostat at night to save money on the fuel oil bill.

Since it wasn't a school day, it was cold outside, and they were going to be outside for a long time, it was okay to wear long johns. Mario dug through the bottom drawer of his chest and found the top and bottom pieces. Beneath his blue jeans and sweatshirt they felt like a suit of armor, although soft, warm and flexible. He put on an extra pair of socks. That was necessary anyway because his skates were a size too big. Growing room, his mom said. Dressed for the cold, Mario started sweating a bit as he ate a bowl of Wheaties. He jumped when the phone rang, grabbing the handset before the second ring. He didn't want it to disturb his mom, and even more, was startled that someone was calling early on a holiday morning.

"Hello?"

"Hi, it's me, Rosalyn."

"Oh, hi."

"So, are you and Jake going skating on the lake this morning?"

"Uh, yeah, I guess so."

"Do you mind if I go with?"

"Uh, no, I guess that would be okay. No, we don't mind." Mario hadn't really talked to Jake about it. He didn't want to say no to her, and didn't think Jake would mind.

"Great! I'll meet you . . . at Jake's right?"

"Sure, about nine o'clock I guess.

"Okay, see you then. Thanks."

"Sure. Okay, bye."

"Bye."

Mario hung up the phone and wondered if he'd done the right thing. It was too late now. He rinsed his cereal bowl and went to the front closet for his parka. He pulled his red stocking cap over his ears and stuffed his choppers into the parka pockets. He felt the right pocket to make sure the big spike was still there, the one he carried when he went skating on the lake. He didn't really know for sure if it would be any good if he broke through the ice, but at least it made him feel a little bit more confident. Sometimes he tried to imagine what it would be like, breaking through the ice and plunging into freezing water, trying to grab the spike and using it to pull himself out of the water.

Jake was already skating around on the lake in back of his house when Mario arrived. Mario often felt a little envious of Jake's house being right on the lakeshore. Lying in bed on a mild evening with a breeze floating in the open windows sometimes he could hear gentle waves lapping the shore. Mario had experienced that a couple of times when he stayed overnight at Jake's. When they camped out in his backyard, sometimes that offered a little too much of the sounds of nature. The frogs and crickets often chirped all night long or so it seemed. But in late November the day after Thanksgiving there were no waves, gentle breezes, frogs, or crickets. Just the gray sky with a slight but steady northwest wind blowing across the frozen lake.

Mario made sure to get there before nine before Rosalyn arrived. He wanted to tell Jake before she got there that she was coming along. Jake didn't mind. On the contrary they both felt like brave protectors and could even try showing off a bit. Mario sat on the picnic table, took off his boots one at a time and shoved his feet into his cold hockey skates. He pulled as hard as he could on the laces and tried to hold the initial knot tight while making the bows and tying them. He tried to keep his ankles straight as he walked on the narrow steel blades across the brown grass to the edge of the frozen lake. Pushing off on the first glide of the skating season felt exhilarating. After a few turns around in a large circle, his skating legs were back. Rosalyn walked down the hill in Jake's backyard and waved.

"Hi. Okay if I go with you? I can keep up with you guys."

"Sure," Mario said. "We're just going to skate around a bit."

"Maybe we'll see where that old bum lives," Jake added. "I heard he lives in some shack on the other side of the lake."

Pushing back the white fur-trimmed hood of her powder blue jacket, Rosalyn sat on the picnic table bench and quickly put on her skates. She pulled the hood back up, put on her mittens and tip-toed to the ice on the skate's serrated points to avoid any dulling of the sharp blades.

They pushed off, skating clockwise and keeping close to shore. A cold snap earlier in the week had made the ice thicken to about four inches. It had been calm so the surface froze smooth and clear. The depth of the cracks here and there showed the thickness of the ice.

They skated past the houses along the lakeshore on the east end of town. Mr. Bergquist was down by his dock working on his ice fishing house. When the ice got thicker, he would be dragging it out to the west end of the lake, just off the sunken island along with about a dozen or so other fish houses. The crude little shacks created a little village of ice fishing enthusiasts and those seeking therapy for cabin fever—some a mixture of both.

About six feet square with thin plywood walls they offered shelter from the wind and sun, but not the cold although some used small propane heaters. They sat for hours watching the line dropped through an eight-inch-diameter hole drilled in the ice. In some of the larger fish houses three or four would fish through a hole in each corner, turning occasionally from the poker game going on to check their lines. Some became increasingly mellow, sipping on brandy-laced coffee or schnapps. They appeared earlier than usual this year because of the early November cold snap, and it was good ice.

Mr. Bergquist looked up and waved. "Hi. You kids be careful now. You stay close to shore," he hollered.

"We will," Jake replied.

"That was Andy Bergquist's dad, you know, the kid that fell through the ice and drowned a couple years ago," Rosalyn said after they had passed by. They didn't know Andy real well because he was older, in high school at the time.

"We know," Mario replied. He felt sorry for Mr. Bergquist.

Soon they were past the edge of town, gliding by a patch of cat-tails frozen in the ice along the shallow shoreline. The cattails parted at the inlet to the lake from the mouth of the creek. The slight current created a path of open water a ways out from shore. The skaters did not venture closer, although Mario was tempted to see how close they could get.

"We better not go in there," Jake said. "It's not that deep but I don't want to get my feet wet, either."

"Me neither," added Rosalyn.

The woods started on the south side of the creek and extended about two thirds the way around the south side of the lake. The cattails gave way to a shoreline lined with huge cottonwood trees, box elders, with a few ash and oak trees mixed in. Farther in they could see the shad-owy outline of the fort they had built last summer out of fallen logs and branches. It wasn't weather-tight by any means, but it seemed cozy and secure when they had lit a small campfire casting heat and a warm glow. Along the shore, a few trees undermined by decades of waves had fallen into the lake, some leaving an arch high enough to skate under.

The skaters rounded the southeast shore heading toward the point jutting from the south side. It was about a hundred feet wide, and it didn't go out into the lake too far, but it had some nice, big oak trees surrounded by tall grass and more cattails around the shoreline.

"Look, there's that old shack," Jake said.

"We better not go near there," Rosalyn said. "What if that old guy is there? What if he has a gun or something?"

At the sound of their voices the ears perked up on the dog in front of the shack.

"We better get out of here," Mario urged. The dog barked fero-ciously. The old man emerged from the shack.

"Shush, Ike," he shouted at the German shepherd-cross strain-ing on a fifteen-foot chain toward the intruders.

"You kids get outta here now. If you don't, I'm going to sic the dog on you."

They had already turned and were skating away as fast as they could. Mario looked back, and this time he saw the old man smiling and waving.

"Hey, c'mere, kid," he shouted. "It's okay. The dog's on a chain. He won't hurt you."

"Let's get outta here," Jake said.

"Wait. I think he wants to talk to us," Rosalyn said. "I know, I think he remembers Mario. Let's go back there."

Cautiously, they skated back toward the shack. The dog stopped barking. He sat trembling, poised to spring at any threat. The old man waved and motioned them to come closer.

"Hey, kid . . . you in the red stocking cap. Thanks."

"He remembers you . . . from the alley that time," Rosalyn said.

Mario waved, "Hi. That's okay."

"Say, 'You're welcome,'" Rosalyn whispered.

"You're welcome."

"Not too many people in this town would do something like that," the man said. "That musta took a lot of guts. I appreciate it. C'mere. Who are you kids anyway. It's okay. Ike here won't hurt you. He knows you're friends now."

They skated slowly toward the opening in the cattails toward the shack. The old man tossed back the hood of his parka and smiled. When they got closer, he looked really old, like about fifty, although his hair was colored light sand with a reddish tint. His blue eyes suddenly became brighter and welcoming as they approached.

"You really stuck your neck out doing that, you know," he said looking at Mario. "I really appreciate it. I've been here about a year, and that's the first time anyone paid any attention to me, I mean, in a positive way. Thanks."

"That's okay. It wasn't anything. I don't know . . . it just didn't seem right I guess," Mario said.

"You guess right, boy."

"Well, I guess we better be going. Uh, nice to meet you."

"Sure. Thanks again."

"So, mister, what did you have for Thanksgiving?" Rosalyn asked.

Mario and Jake looked hard at Rosalyn.

"Did you get any turkey or anything?" she asked.

"Turkey? What's that?" he laughed. "Maybe Cold Duck, but no turkey."

"Well, would you like some?"

"What? You got some turkey with you?" he laughed.

"No, but we could get you some."

"Oh, don't worry about me. I don't need any turkey. I hardly remember the last time I had any turkey. I didn't even know it was Thanksgiving time. Right? It's Thanksgiving?"

"It was yesterday. We've got a lot of turkey left over. We can bring you some."

"Okay with me, I guess. You kids are okay."

"We'll be back later," Rosalyn said. "Just tell Ike there to be nice."

"Okay."

The trio waved goodbye and skated off, resuming their circum-navigation of the lake.

"What did you do that for?" Jake pressed Rosalyn.

"I just felt sorry for him. I don't know. We've got all this left over turkey. Mario, you guys always have a big turkey. You must have a ton left over. Can we give some to him?"

"I don't know. I guess it would be okay. I don't think my mom would mind."

"Well let's do it. After we get back to Jake's let's go over to your place and make some turkey sandwiches. We can take them back, and we can bring some scraps for Ike, too. okay?"

"I guess so."

"Okay with me," said Jake.

They continued skating along the south shore of the lake, the northwest wind beginning to bite into their exposed faces. They had warmed up with the vigorous skating, so their torsos allowed some blood flow to their toes, fingers, and exposed areas. But turning directly into the wind as they headed up the west shore triggered a chill that lasted until they reached the leeward northwest shore. Altogether they skated almost four miles by the time they circled the lake back to Jake's place.

"Mom, are you home?" Mario called as they entered the back door.

"I'm in the basement."

"Can we take some turkey sandwiches to this old guy, the one who lives in that shack across the lake?"

"Who? Who is that?"

"You know, he's that one you see around town sometimes. He looks like a bum."

"Oh, that guy. Well, I suppose . . . are you sure it's okay? We really don't know much about him."

"It's okay. We just talked to him, and he was nice. He was that guy in the alley that time that I told you about. Behind Art's Café. He said thanks for sticking up for him."

"Go ahead then . . . just be sure to clean up the kitchen."

Jake and Rosalyn were already digging in the refrigerator for the platter of left-over turkey. Mario began buttering slices of bread. They wrapped three sandwiches in waxed paper and put them in a paper bag along with a smaller bag of turkey scraps for the dog.

It wouldn't be long before lunchtime and the skating had given them an appetite. They made three more sandwiches and each had one with a glass of milk before heading back out the door. Mario led the way, carrying the bag as they skated out on the ice, this time with the feeling of satisfaction that comes from a sense of purpose.

"Hey mister, are you there? We brought you some sandwiches like we said," Jake hollered toward the shack.

The man emerged and commanded Ike to stop barking. He waved and walked down to the shore, warily scrutinizing the young trio. A couple buttons were missing on the red plaid shirt showing from his open parka. His hair looked greasy and stringy, like it hadn't been washed in a long time. Although almost six feet tall, he seemed smaller than he did in the alley that day.

"You really did," he replied. "I really appreciate this. Thanks."

They skated up closer, and Mario handed him the bag. "There's some scraps in there for your dog, too."

"Hey, Ike, you hear that? We're gonna feast on turkey. Thanks, kid. By the way, I'm Tom." He held out his hand to shake. "What's your name?"

"I'm Mario." Mario extended his hand, leaving his mittens on. Tom's hands looked kind of grimy and so did his face, what you could see under his beard stubble. "And that's Jake and Rosalyn."

"Well it's nice to meet you. I can't say that about too many people in this town. You live in town? If I see you there don't worry, I won't act like I know you or anything."

"That's okay," Mario replied. "I don't mind."

"But if you wave at me, I probably won't wave back. In town I kind of pull into my shell, if you know what I mean. I don't want any trouble. Everyone thinks I'm a no good drunken bum. I pick up my check at the veterans' office, rummage around a bit, get a few things at the store . . . otherwise I don't bother anybody."

"Whose shack is this anyway? Do you own it?" Rosalyn asked.

"This is just an old hunting shack. I think the land belongs to a Mrs. Nielsen, or at least it used to. I really don't know who owns it. I guess I don't really want to, either. As long as nobody bothers me here, that's fine with me. Nobody showed up during hunting season."

"How'd you find this place?"

"We used to come up this way to go duck hunting when I was a kid. We never came here, but somehow we knew about it. One time my dad drove back in here to check it out. It was a great hunting spot. Still is, but I don't hunt anymore."

"We've always wanted to hunt over here, but it's a little close to town," Jake said.

"You like to hunt?"

"Yeah, my dad, uncle, brother, and me usually go duck and goose hunting, but not around here. We've got a blind on a big slough a few miles northwest of here. But it's sure tempting when we look across the lake and see the mallards coming on off the point here."

"I suppose I should take up hunting again. Sometimes I could use the food. I don't know if I'd be able to cook it though," Tom laughed. "But I don't have a gun now, so I guess it don't matter."

His initial friendliness vanished. Without saying another word he turned and headed back toward the shack. Ike started to follow, then stopped and cast a hopeful look at the kids, his tail wagging slightly as if he wanted them to stay. After a few seconds with no response, he turned and trotted behind Tom toward the shack. ⇥ 49

"Of course. Just dress warm."

"Don't worry. They'll get plenty warm playing hockey," Jim said. He had been over for supper. "That looks like a lot of fun. If I were younger, I might like to give it a try."

"At least you can skate," Maria said. "You have skates, don't you?"

"Yeah, I've got an old pair somewhere. Probably so rusty they wouldn't even glide."

Maria cleared the table as Jim sipped a cup of coffee.

"That was delicious."

"Thanks," Maria smiled.

"Okay, mom, I'm going now," Mario said after trudging up the basement steps with his skates and hockey stick.

"'Bye. Have fun."

"See you later," said Jim. "Don't score too many goals."

MARIO WALKED BRISKLY ALONG the three blocks to the ice rink. As he neared, he could see some kids already skating around and shooting pucks into the goals. The hockey players used one half of the oblong rink. Jake and Larry had built some goals, frames of two by fours with chicken wire wrapped around the sides and back. They worked pretty well unless one of the bigger kids let loose with a slap shot and the puck would rip right through the chicken wire. When the younger kids played, they had a rule against slaps shots, even lifting the puck.

Even so some of the kids wore some type of shin protection. One kid wore a pair of baseball catcher's shin guards. Sometimes they interfered with skating, but they sure did a good job of protecting against swinging hockey sticks. Sometimes Mario and some of the other kids used magazines. Tonight he had tied a couple of old *National Geographic* magazines to his shins with twine. After a while the twine would slip and the magazines would slide down, so every chance he could, he tried to pull them back up. Mario would never forget the time he caught a slap

4

THE TEMPERATURES HAD DROPPED, COLD enough the past week so the city workers could flood the skating rink at the park. There hadn't been much snow yet, and the ground was frozen enough to freeze the water sprayed on top. It had snowed about four inches earlier in the week, and they cleared the surface of the field, leaving a small ridge of snow around the perimeter of the rink, flecked with bits of grass and leaves.

If you wanted to skate on the lake, that was your business. The city would never plow a rink on the lake even though the lake ice was a lot better. On the outfield of the baseball diamond there was no chance of anyone falling through, plus the rink had the benefit of lights for night skating. A cozy warming house provided a place to put on skates and take an occasional break from the cold, and maybe get a grape soda from the pop machine. Being on solid ground and with a warming house supervisor, when it wasn't below zero the city ice rink was the place to be. At least it was Friday night of the week after Thanksgiving.

"Mom, can I go play hockey at the rink?" Mario asked after supper.

shot in his right shin bone. It left a bruise that didn't go away for three weeks. He could still feel the dent where it hit.

The warming house inside smelled like rotting wood, and after a while like a bag of soggy potato chips. Mario plowed through the noisy *clump clump* of kids walking around the wooden floor on ice skates, talking loud and jostling for spaces on benches along the outside walls. He found an open spot and sat down.

"Hi, Mario."

He looked up to see Rosalyn.

"Hi."

She had already been out skating on the other half of the rink. Girls, mostly, skated on the other side, gliding around in circles and sometimes playing crack the whip.

"So you're gonna play hockey. I wish I could play hockey sometime."

Busy with putting on his skates, Mario didn't respond.

"Well, you have fun." She got up and clomped out the door to the rink.

Mario followed, grabbing his hockey stick from the big barrel by the door.

AFTER SCHOOL HE HAD TAKEN HIS SKATES to the Coast to Coast hardware store downtown to have them sharpened. He was eager to feel how the edges would grab the ice on sharp turns and quick stops.

Jim was over when Mario arrived home from the hardware store, his skates hanging from the laces around his shoulders. Jim had been over a lot lately. At first Mario felt uncomfortable like there was some stranger in the house. He seemed friendly and kind, although it bothered Mario when Jim engaged in some teasing. Mario put up with the usual teasing kids did at school, but he wasn't used to it at home or from an adult. He could sense that his mom seemed happier since she started dating Jim last summer.

Not particularly handsome, Jim wasn't bad looking, either. He kept his dark brown hair in a medium-length crew cut. The lenses in his heavy, black-framed eyeglasses were a little thick, but not as noticeable as those Coke-bottle ones. At the dental office he always wore white shirts with tab collars and a dark tie. It took awhile for Mario to get used to seeing him away from there and dressed less formally, such as the blue jeans and sweatshirt he was wearing now.

"Should be a nice night out on the rink. No wind and not too cold." He looked across the table at Maria. "How would you like to give skating a try?"

"Me? I'd probably fall and break my neck. I've never been on ice skates before."

"I'll help you learn. If you're going to live in this part of the country you might as well try making the best of it."

"C'mon, mom. You should at least try," Mario urged. "It's not that hard. It's a lot of fun."

"Let's do it," Jim said. "Forget the dishes. Let's go to the hardware store and get you some skates. This will be fun."

After more pleading, Maria consented. Mario left for the rink, and Jim and Maria drove downtown to the Coast to Coast hardware store. The holiday lights created a glowing, colorful oasis in the otherwise dark, early December evening. During the holiday shopping season, all the stores stayed open until 9:00 p.m. It looked busy with people shopping and driving around. Jim and Maria had to drive around several blocks before they found a parking space.

"We might as well have walked," Jim said.

F OUNDED IN THE 1870S ALONG A Midwest railroad line, Clareton was named for Clare Knowlton, the youngest daughter of the railroad baron who built the North Central Railroad. Clareton became the county seat and its merchants and other businesses served townsfolk and farms on the surrounding prairie. It had a hospital owned by the county. The grain elevator was the tallest building. With a population of about 4,678 in the 1950 census, it was bigger than most county seats in the region because of the railroad. A state hospital at Dakota Falls over in the next county also employed a good number of Clareton residents. The state hospital housed about 1,000 patients among the psychiatric, drug and alcohol treatment units, many with locked doors.

Jim took Maria's hand as they walked from the parking spot back to the hardware store, passing by Sears and Roebuck, Suzette's Ladies Fashions, and other downtown stores open for holiday shopping. Christmas carols drifted from speakers mounted under awnings at some of the stores. They greeted friends and acquaintances passing by on the sidewalk. These people smiled as they saw the couple approaching hand-in-hand.

Except for food and medicine, the hardware store inventory met almost every other need. Outdoor clothing, gloves, boots, hunting gear, skis, and ice skates took up almost half the floor space. A little bell attached to the front door tinkled as the couple stepped inside.

Mr. Stansberry looked out from the paint aisle. For the past twenty-six years, he had spent almost every waking moment in his hardware store. Even if you didn't know for sure what you needed, his skillful questioning eventually would find the answer for any painting, plumbing, wiring or any other type of repair project. A smile spread below his graying moustache.

"Hi, Jim. Hi, Maria. How are you folks doing? What can I do for you this evening?"

"Hi, George," Jim replied. "We were going to look at some ice skates . . . for Maria here."

"You know where they are in the back. Go try some on. Just holler if you need any help. Remember to leave a little room for heavier socks, but not too much room, either. There's a little box under the bench with some socks if you need them for trying on the skates. I wouldn't say they're real clean, but they're not too bad. Martha actually washes them once in a while."

"We'll be fine," Maria said. "I'm not sure what I'm getting into, though. I've never skated before."

"Oh, don't worry. Jim will be a fine instructor."

Boxes of figure and hockey skates took up one whole shelf in the sporting-goods section. Jim scanned the labels until he found a pair of white figure skates size seven and a half. Maria sat on the bench, took off her right boot and wiggled her foot into the skate. Her socks were heavy enough so she didn't need an extra pair. Jim gazed down as she began to pull the laces tight and tie a bow, noticing the contrast between the shiny white polish on the skates and her smooth, tan, slightly olive skin. He reached down and gently ran his fingers through her long, dark hair tumbling down the sides of her face as she leaned over. She looked up, smiled, and reached up and squeezed his hand.

"So, how do they fit?" asked George as he walked toward them down the aisle. "Sometimes when they're new they need to be sharpened. Should we take a look? If you get them, I'll throw in a free sharpening. Heck, since it's you, I'll sharpen them for free any time you need. How's that?"

It seemed like a lot of money. Maria struggled deciding whether or not it was worth it, and not sure how much she would use them. Eight dollars and ninety-nine cents could buy a lot of groceries, and an elementary school teacher's salary didn't leave a lot for frills.

"Tell you what, if you decide you don't want to keep them, just bring them back at the end of the season. I'll give you a refund. It might not be the full amount but pretty close. There's always somebody looking for used skates. I'm sure you'll take good care of them."

"Sounds to me like a pretty good deal, Maria," Jim said. "C'mon. Once you give it a try you'll be glad you did."

Growing up in southern California, Maria never had the opportunity to learn how to ice skate as a child. Like riding a bike, it's much easier to learn during between five and ten years old. A respect for danger has yet to be fully developed. Fear results primarily from imaginary things and the unknown. And in the event of a mishap, scrapes, bruises, and even bones mend quickly. By adulthood there is enough experience to know that accidents can happen, and more significantly, there's the potential for embarrassment if a tumble should occur while trying to do some childish thing. Maria's sense of adventure, which helped bring a young, single mother to the Midwest far from home in the first place, pushed aside all the negative thoughts and fears long enough to buy the skates. Committed now, she walked out the door with a new purpose, helping pull Jim along by the hand, who just gazed at her as she looked back with her sparkling eyes.

THE HOCKEY GAME STARTED AS IT usually did. An invisible but no less real line marked off about one-third of the oblong rink where the hockey games took place. The first hockey players to arrive began skating around and around, shooting pucks into the goals. Gradually, more arrived, reaching a critical mass sufficient to start a game.

On the surface, choosing sides appeared simple. A few of the natural leaders stepped to the sides. Following an unspoken pecking order, kids began to gravitate to one side or the other, carefully weighing the understood abilities of each as they tried to achieve balance on the two teams. Occasionally, the process would erupt in spoken negotiation if someone didn't follow the order, usually with too many of the better players on one side. Those at the end of the sorting usually knew their place and accepted it. The teams chosen, each gathered in front of one of the goals for a brief strategy session and also to give some time to chase off any non-hockey players who had invaded their territory. Mario and Jake usually managed to be on the same team, and invariably it was the team opposite Frank.

Although unwritten, the rules were fairly well understood. Like flipping a coin, someone tossed the puck in the air and one of the unofficial captains called heads or tails. "Heads" referred to the side of the puck etched with the "X." Checking was prohibited, but that didn't prevent a push or solid hip check from happening now and then. Most of the kids couldn't do a good, hard slap shot, so that wasn't much of a concern, but they were disallowed anyway. Lifting the puck off the ice on a pass was okay, but goal shots had to stay down. They didn't often have a designated goalie, so despite the restrictions a lot of shots went into the cage.

Position playing presented too great of a strategic challenge for a bunch of pre-teens. The teams, one carrying the puck, collided at center ice, each player trying to overwhelm the other with massive force. Every time, Mario and a few others anguished at the sure failure of this strategy, if you could call it that. Their futile cries for someone to hang back and play defense usually went unnoticed. Occasionally, they would become resigned and accept the responsibility. But that also had its advantages.

Observing the melee, often the goalie would see the puck squirt loose. Sometimes he could pick it up and fly around the mass of bodies and sticks toward the opposing goal. Or, as Mario also liked to do, wait for an opposing player to break loose and charge toward him with the puck. He wasn't particularly fast, but he had quick hands and feet. He usually succeeded in stealing the puck with a poke check and would break down one of the sides, thankful for the *National Geographics* tied to his shins protecting them from slashing sticks. Anticipating this, Jake would break open, waiting for the pass from Mario. Immediately after sending the pass, Mario broke for the middle, behind the mass of players, converging on Jake, who was already breaking for the goal. Sometimes he was able to take it in all the way. Other times, if an opposing player had gotten back on defense quickly enough, Jake passed the puck back to Mario, who then usually had clear shot. Frank and some of the others would complain that it wasn't fair to have a planned play like that, but most had a begrudging respect.

Skating up and down just outside the invisible line and watching the game, Rosalyn could clearly see the stupidity and futility of the disorganized, mass confrontation. She cheered loudly whenever Jake and Mario's team scored a goal. Occasionally she had tried to get in a game, which was unheard of, so instead she would hang around the edge and sometimes skate in to the hockey area during the game, only to get severely chastised for the intrusion.

This evening was no different until a loose puck skidded along the ice in her direction. She stopped it with her left skate and then kicked it back toward the game. She skated after it and continued kicking it like a soccer player toward the goal defended by Frank's team. At first the boys watched in momentary bewilderment, then shouted in a chorus for her to leave the puck alone and get the heck out of there. She skated with the puck right up to the goal and kicked it in.

"What'd ya do that for?" Frank shouted. "That doesn't count," he said, looking around at the other players. "Are you cruisin' for a bruisin'?" he glared, skating up to Rosalyn. "Get out of here, now!"

"C'mon, Frank. What's the matter? You afraid of getting beat by a girl?" Jake laughed.

"He just did," Mario added.

"You keep that up and you're going to get a knuckle sandwich," Frank threatened.

"Hey, you kids, what's going on?"

They turned and looked in the direction of the adult voice coming from the sideline. Jim Andersen was holding on to the arm of Mario's mom, who stood somewhat unsteadily on a shiny new pair of white figure skates.

"Oh, hi, Mr. Andersen. We're just playing hockey," someone said. "I guess Rosalyn here just kind of got in the way. It's no big deal."

Mario stared at his mom standing there on ice skates, but didn't say anything, hoping to avoid being noticed and escape the embarrassment resulting from a parent intruding in their world. But he also felt pleasantly happy at the sight of her with Jim. He felt proud of her for being so adventurous, and she looked so glowing and pretty, like she was really enjoying being with Jim.

"Why don't you let her play?" Maria asked.

Nobody said a word. After what seemed an uncomfortably long silence, someone mumbled something about how she might get hurt.

"Well, I guess that's a chance she'd have to take. From what I just saw it looks like she can keep up with you guys."

Although she wore figure skates and not hockey skates, Rosalyn's skating skills were good enough to compete with the boys. She just stood there and watched the encounter, waiting and wondering which way the scales were going to tip in the dilemma facing the boys. Were they going to give in and allow a girl to play, or were they going to challenge the adults? Jim hadn't said a thing, but he didn't have to, his presence and apparent support of Maria being enough to weigh in favor of Rosalyn.

"Aw, let's just let her play," someone said. "C'mon, let's get going. We're wasting time."

Rosalyn quickly detected the emerging consensus, while not really in favor of letting her play, but one of not being overwhelmingly opposed to it. She wheeled around and skated quickly back to the warming house to grab one of the spare hockey sticks.

"So, who's team is she going to be on?" Frank asked with a sneer. "Not mine."

"What makes you think it's your team, Frank ?" Mario shot back.

"If you want her on your team go ahead," Frank replied. "And if she gets hurt, it's your fault."

"As if you'd care. You better not take any cheap shots," Jake warned.

The lull in the game and disruption in the familiar pattern became too much for a couple of the players. They grumbled something about this being ridiculous and that girls shouldn't be playing hockey, and decided to leave early, glaring at Rosalyn as she skated toward them carrying a hockey stick.

"Hey, c'mon, you guys! Where you going? Let's keep playing," Mario hollered.

"That's okay," Jake said. "We still got enough. Let's go. C'mon Rosalyn, you can be on our team."

The game resumed, flowing back and forth across the rink with the sounds of skates cutting and skidding across the ice, the muffled crack of sticks hitting the puck and other sticks, and the occasional urgent shouts of, "Over here. Over here."

In terms of sight and sound, Rosalyn stood out from the others in her light blue jacket and higher pitched voice, but she blended well into the action of the game. Once Frank tried to trip her but was immediately chastised by Mario, Jake, and some of the other kids. Rosalyn called him an asshole, which elicited great laughter from the boys. They weren't used to hearing girls swear. During one scramble for the puck Mario collided with Rosalyn and she almost lost her balance. Normally, such contact would have gone unnoticed, but not this time.

Occasionally Mario looked over toward the other side of the rink to see how his mom was doing. She seemed to be getting the hang of it, skating around holding hands with Jim. A couple times when she almost lost her balance, Jim quickly grasped her arm to avoid a fall. She did fall once. With an embarrassed laugh, she jumped right back to her feet, brushed the ice and snow crystals from her legs and behind and was ready to go again.

"Don't worry about it," Jim said. "If you don't take a tumble once in a while you're not going to learn something new."

ഇ **5** രജ

AS MARIO APPROACHED THE SHACK he expected Ike to start barking. Instead, the young German shepherd lay submissively as far from the shack as the chain would allow, his head on the ground between his front paws and a worried look in his eyes. What was left of his right ear, half gone from frostbite, twitched. His tail lay flat on the ground, sweeping back and forth signaling anticipation held in check by uncertainty.

Suddenly, sounds of yelling and even moans drifted from the shack, triggering in Mario both caution and curiosity. He almost turned around in flight. Then Ike raised his head, alert, waiting to see what would happen next. Seeing the dog boosted Mario's confidence, and he resisted the urge to flee. "Hey mister, Tom, are you okay?" he shouted.

It was a Saturday morning and there was no one was around to play with, so Mario had decided to go for a skate around the lake and had thought about stopping by the old bum's shack. More out of curiosity than anything, but once he looked past the appearance of an old bum, Tom did seem to be a decent man. Meeting him face to face earlier had dispelled the old stereotype that made a grimy drifter an object of derision. Now he was a real person with a name and perhaps even a life.

The paper bag of chocolate chip cookies Mario brought along had dwindled as he skated along, munching on some of them. There were still plenty—more than a dozen at least. That would be enough for a little present even allowing a few for Ike.

"I brought some cookies, chocolate chip. I was just wondering if you wanted any."

Now Ike rose to his feet, his tail slowly beginning to wag. He looked at Mario, then back toward the shack. He shook himself off and began walking toward Mario.

"Hi, Ike. Where's Tom? Is he okay?"

He heard more yelling and some kind if gibberish. It was hard to tell from fifty feet away. He waited, still out on the ice and ready to tear out of there as fast as he could. Then Ike found his voice and let out a whimper and a little yip, like any dog waiting for attention or more likely something to eat. Mario reached in the bag and tossed him two cookies. "At least you can have some." He wanted to move in closer and pet the dog but didn't quite dare even though Ike would have welcomed it.

"This is Mario," he shouted. "You know, one of the kids who brought you some turkey sandwiches after Thanksgiving. I was just out skating around, and I thought I'd bring some cookies."

He waited a full minute for any response although it seemed a lot longer. Ike started barking until a sharp rebuke pierced the thin-walled shack. "Shut up, ya damn dog! They're going to see us! You want to get shot?" Ike retreated and lay down with his head resting on his outstretched front paws.

Mario's confidence and compassion were quickly eroding. He was about to just toss the bag of cookies, minus a couple more, toward the dog and leave when the door of the shack opened a crack.

Tom peered out, then opened the door wider. "Who's there? Whaddya want, kid?"

Now Mario wished he had gone. Tom looked even worse than he did wandering along the alleys downtown. This time he wore a wrinkled blue flannel shirt, again with several buttons missing over a grayish, stained union suit and no pants. His socks had holes in the toes, and his matted hair stuck out in a chaos of spikes. He rubbed his red eyes, blinking in the sunlight of the clear morning and seemed to gradually become coherent.

"What are you doing here? Anybody else with you?"

"No, it's just me," Mario replied, still conscious of his strategy for making a quick escape. "I was just out skating, and I thought I'd bring some cookies. My mom made them this morning."

"Well, son of a gun. I never had fresh cookies for breakfast before," Tom laughed. He hadn't laughed in a long time, at least not consciously outside of one of his many dreams. "Just wait a minute." He stepped back inside the shack and closed the door. In a few minutes he emerged dressed and wearing his parka, stocking cap, and buckle overshoes.

Ike yipped, and his tail wagged vigorously, prancing and jumping at the end of the chain. Tom walked over to pet the dog and scratch behind his ears. "How ya doin', boy? Bet you wondered if I ever was going to get up."

"He usually stays inside nights," Tom said, looking at Mario. "I guess last night or earlier this morning he whined to go out. I must have let him out, but I don't remember. Me and Ike here have been through a lot together, haven't we old boy?" The ninety-five-pound brown-and-black dog rubbed his back along Tom's legs almost knocking him off balance. "You should see him ride the rails. He can jump onto a moving train like a gazelle. He's sure been good company in the hobo jungles. He's about the only one I ever talk to. He don't say much, but he sure is a good listener, aren't ya boy?" Tom said, scruffing the dog's neck and thumping his side. Eyes half closed and panting, the devoted dog soaked up all the attention he could get.

"So, Marion—that's your name, right? Where'd you get a name like that?"

"I don't know." Hearing that name caught him off guard. He heard it used sometimes, in school and from people who didn't know him well. He wanted to try explain it but couldn't find the words.

"Do you like it?"

"I don't know."

"It don't sound like it, but it is a man's name, you know, even if it sounds a little sissy. But that just makes you tough though, right?" Tom laughed.

"I don't know. I'm just used to it I guess. I been teased a couple times maybe, but it's okay."

"Well, don't worry about it. You know John Wayne, don't you? The actor? That's what his real name is, Marion Morrison."

"Yeah, that's what my mom told me."

"The female version is Marian; they just sound similar. Sort of like Francis and Frances."

"Yeah, I know a kid whose real name is Francis. Everyone calls him Frank. I guess there isn't really a good nickname for Marion though."

"You don't always need a nickname. Sometimes they can be worse. Most of the time people get used to a name and don't even think about it. Besides, who we are and what's inside is a lot more important than a name. It's just the movie stars who have to have a classy name. That just shows they're all fake anyway."

"Yeah, I suppose. But my real name's Mario."

"Oh? So, Marion's the nickname then," Tom chucked. "So, what grade are you in?"

"Seventh."

"Let's see, that must make you about twelve or thirteen, right?"

"I'm twelve."

"You like school? What's your favorite class?"

"I don't know."

"You got a girlfriend?"

"I don't know."

"Well, you got to know if you got a girlfriend or not," Tom said with laugh. "I bet some girl's got to like you, such a nice and handsome kid."

"I don't know," Mario replied, starting to feel embarrassed. The thought of Rosalyn flashed in his mind, but he wasn't sure what to think.

"What's your three favorite words?" Tom asked.

"I don't know." Immediately a hot flush swept over Mario's face, embarrassed and angry for being suckered in to Tom's joke.

"Bingo!" Tom laughed. "You win the prize. Here's a dime." Tom retrieved a dime from a pocket and handed it to Mario. Without even realizing it he held out his hand. Embarrassed and not really wanting to, he took the dime. He wasn't used to teasing and didn't know what else to do.

"Hey, it's just a joke," Tom said gently, noticing the downcast look across Mario's face. "You're probably just one of the quieter ones in a crowd, right? That's okay. You know the saying, 'still waters run deep.' But sometimes that just makes life a little tougher . . . getting rolled over by all the loudmouths out there when you know more than they do. Don't worry about it, and for God's sake don't be like them. Just be assertive and stand your ground when you have to, that's what really counts."

Mario looked around at the old shack, with trash strewn around and a pile of empty wine bottles by the door. It didn't add up. Here was a bum, a drunk, dirty and disheveled, yet seeming and talking like a kind, gentle, intelligent person. It must be the booze, or maybe he's sick in the head, or both. Whatever it was, it made Mario feel uneasy.

"Well, I think I got to go. It was nice talking to you, mister, I mean Tom."

"I know you got to go. Thanks for the cookies. Remember what I said before, if you see me around town you don't have to talk to me or anything. I usually go in to town a couple times a week. I scrounge for stuff, pick up a few groceries, and stop at the liquor store. First of the month I stop by the courthouse to pick up my check. The government says I'm disabled so I get a little bit to try live on. It ain't much, but I get by. Like I said before, if I see you or those other kids around I won't let on that we've talked or know each other."

"I don't mind," Mario said, although he didn't really think he would act like he knew Tom. "Well, I got to go. Bye. Bye, Ike."

"So long for now," Tom said and waved.

Mario turned and skated off, around the end of the point heading west. Tom's face returned to its dull, downcast appearance, even when he patted Ike's head on the slow, shuffling return to the shack. The brief encounter with the young boy had pierced the dark cloud over his lonely existence like the first rays of sunlight breaking through after a sudden summer afternoon rain squall. For a moment he had seen the bright blue morning sky, the sun glinting off the frozen lake, and even heard a cardinal calling out in the woods.

WITH WINTER COMING ON, TOM knew he could use more firewood. The job brought some relief and purpose to the morning, which he needed after having been awakened so early. Most days it was almost noon before he emerged from another night that began in a drunken stupor and struggled through a minefield of dreams, or flashbacks and hallucinations suddenly dropping in like mortar shells. In the past, he had enjoyed his morning coffee, but now he couldn't wait to slug down cheap wine if he had any left from the night before.

Jolted from the routine and fueled by chocolate chip cookies, he stepped back outside to hunt for some decent pieces of firewood. *This was just a simple task*, he told himself. *I'm just going out in the woods to gather some wood. There's nothing out there except for birds and squirrels.* Slowly walking warily away from the shack, he kept repeating this to himself, trying to keep in check the sudden pangs of utter terror. It didn't matter what time of day it was or where he was when the nightmares visited, though it was less likely to happen when he was drunk. Terror could explode over him like a starburst shell, and he would find himself flattened to the ground trembling and sobbing.

For years he'd tried to live a normal life. He'd gotten his old job back after the war. He met a wonderful girl. When the demons started digging out of their caves and bunkers, crawling over the horizon of his mind, he even went to a doctor. They tried to talk him through the persistent images and prescribed some medicine. Eventually he just wore out. Day by day, the booze and cheap wine seeped further into his life. He lost his job, his girl, and became a homeless drifter, although for the past year he had been at the shack, the longest he'd stayed anywhere in a decade.

Even though he grew up not far from Clareton, few knew the real identity of the bum living just outside town, if they knew of him at all. Few would have cared anyway. At least nobody bothered him much. Tom wouldn't resort to stealing. Nobody seemed to mind when he rummaged through garbage, except for that one time in the alley behind the café. The first of the month he picked up a meager disability check at the vet's office. The secretary was always nice and tried to be understanding, as if she knew what he and thousands of men like him had gone through during the war.

Tom carried a small hatchet but wished he had a saw. Common sense told him to buy one at the hardware store. He knew it would make wood-gathering a lot easier. It just meant taking some cash that could be used for a couple bottles. Tom could manage that. The hard part would be actually going into the hardware store. The owner was always friendly and even respectful, but he never warmed up to the disheveled stranger like he did to other customers. Whenever Tom had to interact with others in town, he did so with downcast eyes and barely audible mumbling, not from a lack of accomplishment in his younger days, but because of what he had become now.

Watching his master walk away, Ike lay down still attached to his chain. He was used to seeing Tom leave and not return until hours later. This time something was different. His master held some object in his hand. Ike lifted his head and watched Tom intently. The man stopped, turned and looked at the dog.

"Oh, yeah, I suppose I should turn you loose, huh, old buddy?"

More than once a dog had saved his life. Not this particular dog, but Ike certainly could and would protect and defend his master even if it took his own life. Tom had known such self-sacrificing loyalty before, and not just from dogs. He had found Ike as an abandoned pup about three years ago while passing through Nebraska. Maybe the puppy wasn't really abandoned, but it started following him like puppies did, and before long it was too far from home to ever get back on its own.

As he walked along away from the small town, Tom enjoyed the company of the playful pup. It didn't have a collar, so with some modest rationalizing Tom soon claimed the role of protector and master. Miles away as evening approached, the pup started showing some signs of uncertainty, but more likely was just getting hungry and thirsty. When Tom realized this, he became a little disgusted with himself for not thinking about the dog. It had been years since he had been concerned about anyone other than himself.

He found an old rusty can, filled it with water from his Army-style canteen, and the pup lapped it almost dry, scraping his tongue on the rough edges. Tom shared the only food he had, some old donuts, wondering if he had made a mistake. It was hard enough sometimes to get food for himself. A couple donuts and the water seemed to satisfy the pup, and he curled up by Tom's side next to the fire. He decided to call him Ike after the president; "I like Ike," Tom said out loud with a little chuckle, remembering the campaign button he had seen a couple years ago. From then on Tom always took good care of Ike; the grain elevator where they sold dog food was the only store Tom didn't mind entering.

"C'mon Ike, let's go get firewood."

THE FARTHER AWAY HE SKATED from the shack only seemed to intensify the resentment and embarrassment Mario felt. He hadn't done anything wrong, anything to merit being teased like that. He just didn't know how to respond quickly to all those questions. Now he was angry and upset with himself for ever going back there, and he'd even brought cookies. "I'm never going to see that guy again," he muttered.

The breach was complete when impulsively he tore off his right mitten, reached in his parka pocket, grasped the dime and threw it as hard as he could toward the shore. Even before his throwing arm came forward the realization that the dime would have almost bought a hamburger at Art's couldn't stop the impulse, but it did render some regret. It all added up to a surge of energy, and he found himself flying across the ice, away from the shack and back the same way along the eastern shore. Nearing town he saw Jake sitting on the picnic table bench lacing up his skates. He felt like turning around; he was embarrassed about going to the shack and didn't want to have to explain it to Jake. But it was too late. Jake spotted him and waved. Mario skated up to the shoreline by Jake's house.

"You going skating?"

"What's it look like?" Jake replied with his unique blend of amusement and sarcasm toward the obvious. "Where you been?"

"Oh, I just decided to go out. I got up a little early. Nobody was around."

It was always a little lonely when Mario awakened, especially on Saturday mornings. He used to be distracted a bit by cartoons on TV, but the novelty was beginning to wear off. Getting out of the house into the cold, fresh morning air made him feel better. The idea of taking some cookies to the old man's shack even generated some sense of noble purpose. Although now he wanted to hide the fact.

"I thought you'd be home watching cartoons," Jake said.

"I was for a little bit. Then I got bored."

"So where'd you go? All the way around the lake?"

Mario sensed he was getting cornered. At first he was going to say yes, but at the same time he didn't feel right about lying.

"No, I was just skating around."

"But I saw you coming back on the east side. Where'd you go?"

"I just went over there and back, I guess, I don't know, I was just skating around like I said."

"Over where and back?" Jake pressed.

"What's it to you?"

"Jeez, don't have a cow. I was just curious. You going home? Why don't you skate with me a bit? How far did you go already?"

"Well I suppose I could skate for a bit."

"Maybe we should go by that old Tom's shack. He's probably all hung over."

"No, he's not. That's where I was," Mario finally admitted. "Well, he might be hung over, but we talked. I brought him and Ike some cookies. Then I saw them heading out into the woods."

"What did you do that for . . . the cookies?"

"I don't know. My mom just baked them, and it was like we did with the turkey sandwiches. He seemed really happy to get them. It was really weird though when I first got there. Ike didn't even bark, like he was scared of something. I heard this yelling and groaning coming from the shack. It was spooky. I almost took off."

"He was probably having those . . . what do you them, hallucinations or delirious tremblings or whatever they are," Jake said. "Maybe he's just crazy, mental or something."

"Could be. But when he came out and starting talking he was okay, except he started asking me a lot of questions."

"We should go back there."

"What for?"

"I don't know, something to do."

"I don't really want to," Mario said. "You can. Maybe I'll just split for home."

"Oh, c'mon, stick around. We don't have to go there. I was just curious. Let's go check out that spot in the woods on the east side, over where we built those forts. We should camp out there this winter."

"Okay I guess," Mario said.

"I can't stay out too long anyway," Jake said. "I got bowling at eleven. You want to come along?"

"Sure."

They had to walk on their skates a short way from the lake to the fort in the woods. Last summer they had made the lean-to by fitting a long branch in the crooks of two small trees about ten feet apart and piling long branches and brush against it. It only offered the appearance of a roof and wouldn't have kept out much rain, but it still felt secure, sitting underneath with a little fire crackling in front. Somebody had already been there and not too long ago. A lot of the branches were missing. They noticed small furrows freshly scraped through the leaves and dirt heading in the direction of oak savannah jutting out from the south shore where the shack stood.

~ 6 ~

THE NOISY CLUSTER OF BOYS SWAGGERED down the junior high school hall, Frank in the lead as usual. Mario moved in closer to his open locker hoping they would pass by without noticing him. Waiting, he tensed up when they passed behind him. The sudden bump came hard enough to slam his face against the edge of the open locker. Pain shot through his upper lip.

"Oops, sorry, Mario. Didn't mean to do that," Frank laughed.

Mario whipped around to face them. He felt his lip and saw a small streak of blood on his finger. "What did you do that for, you jerk?"

"Hey, it was just an accident," Frank replied with a little smirk. "Somebody bumped into me. I couldn't help it." A few other kids stopped and stood around the two, waiting to see what would happen next.

"You did it on purpose. What did I do to you?" Mario's eyes burned with fury at Frank, who stood about an inch taller and only about a foot away, ominously invading Mario's space. He felt the urge to push him back, but he didn't.

He usually never did, even though he always became incensed whenever Frank or some of the other bullies pushed kids around.

Occasionally he would say something, depending on the situation, but that only turned the unwelcome attention toward himself. Only when the bullies like Frank picked on the really little kids did Mario and some of the other kids stand up to them. It was different when he was the initial target. The other was a gut reaction of anger; this time mixed with fear. He glared at Frank face-to-face for another moment. He could feel Frank's breath and smell the sweet scent of his oily hair cream.

"You better watch it, twerp," Frank muttered quietly through clenched teeth. "Someday you might find those ugly glasses at the back of your ugly head."

As the charged atmosphere around the nucleus of Frank and Mario picked up more observers, the crowd around them grew large enough to attract the attention of Mr. Albright. Every morning before classes started the principal stood in the middle of the intersection of the two main halls. He intervened whenever the usual commotion erupted into pushing and shoving and sometimes harsh words, beyond his fairly tolerant threshold. As soon as he started walking toward the knot of kids in front of Mario's locker, it melted away into the flow of hall traffic. The intended effect quickly accomplished, Mr. Albright stopped and returned to his post. Only Mario remained in front of his locker, feeling angry and humiliated. It was not a great way to start off the morning at school, which was hard enough anyway. Worrying about what the rest of the day might bring, he grabbed his books and headed for first-hour class.

"What happened to your lip?" Rosalyn asked. She was already at her desk and had her social studies book open. Mario swung into his seat feeling angry, embarrassed and not wanting to respond.

"Oh, nothing. I just bumped into something at home. Did you get your homework done?" he replied without looking up, hoping to change the subject.

"What did you bump into?"

"It's no big deal," he said, starting to feel annoyed.

The classroom buzz gradually subsided after the bell rang at 8:15. Mario felt relief now that attention no longer focused on him. He was able to withdraw into his private world where he found peace and sometimes loneliness. The teacher started talking about some little Negro girl down south who tried to go to a school that only white people attended. The school wouldn't let her go there, so the American government said they had to let her attend. The story held Mario's attention for a few moments until his thoughts started to wander as they often did, only more so in the afternoons. Sometimes they were pleasant daydreams, but this morning they hung like a dark cloud, recalling the incident before class. Why do some people have to be like that? Why do they have to pick on others?

"Marion, why do you think Brown vs. the Board of Education was significant?" Mrs. Lane, the seventh grade social studies teacher, always asked questions like that during class. No one ever knew when or whom she was going ask. Some kids liked being asked, but Mrs. Lane always made sure she called some of the others, too. Mario hadn't been listening very closely and felt a tightness in his chest. Everyone looked at him. His slightly swollen lip made him feel even more self-conscious. His could almost feel his mind becoming paralyzed. Then he recalled seeing pictures in *Life* magazine, a somber looking Negro girl in a light dress, surrounded by a crowd of people, many with mean looks on their faces. Slowly, thoughts began to form and emerge into words.

"I don't know . . . I guess it's because we're all supposed to be equal, have equal rights and stuff."

"Yes, but what was the importance of this case? Class, remember from studying our government? The Supreme Court?"

Mario's feelings of self-consciousness eased a bit as she addressed the class and also provided helpful clues to the answer. "The Supreme Court said the school couldn't stop anyone from going there just because they were Negroes?" he replied, more of a question than a statement.

"That's correct," Mrs. Lane said. "In 1954 the U.S. Supreme Court ruled in Brown vs. the Board of Education that a person could not be denied attendance at a public school because of their race or color."

Except for Officer Greene, most kids in Clareton had rarely, or never, seen a Negro in person before. When he was younger back in

California, and on a couple of trips there since then, Mario had seen many other races of people, but didn't think much of it. Maybe the girl did get into the school, but what did she have to put up with to attend there Mario wondered?

A LIGHT SNOW GREETED THE MOB OF STUDENTS escaping when the bell rang at 3:05 ending the school day. Considering how Mario's day started, the rest had gone fairly well. Apparently, someone had told Mr. Albright what had happened between Frank and Mario before classes that morning. Frank kept his distance during the day, although during lunch he occasionally would glare across at Mario several tables away.

Leaving the school building always brought Mario a feeling of relief, escape from the pressures of the junior high jungle. Even though he had a right to worry about what might happen, today was no different. He didn't feel afraid; he almost felt confident in his own abilities to confront any threats or challenges.

"What are you doing after school?" He turned around to see Jake catching up along sidewalk.

"I don't know," Mario said. "I was just going to go home I guess. Maybe watch cartoons."

"I'm going to stop by the bowling alley and roll a few lines. You want to go with?

"I suppose I could, but I'm kind of hungry. I was going to go home and get something to eat."

"I could loan you some money, and you could get something at the bowling alley, or maybe at Art's," Jake said.

Although Mario disliked the burden of receiving such charity, the temptation proved stronger. It wasn't a matter of having to repay the money. It was the slight humiliation of not having enough in the first place. With anyone else he would have refused the offer. With Jake the friendship and trust made it okay.

"I guess I could. I'll pay you back on Friday." The invitation also meant going someplace other than home after school and being around friends. Sometimes it got a little lonely at home until his mom came home.

"You want to go to the café first?" Mario asked.

"I'd just as soon bowl first," Jake replied. "But I guess we could."

The afternoon coffee group of old men had already left, and the café was almost empty. Mario ordered the usual, a single hamburger basket and chocolate milk. Jake said he didn't want to eat too much before bowling, so he just ordered a chocolate malt. Mario was glad that Jake had given him the money before they went in. They paid separately and no one else had to know about the loan.

With wisps of gray hair poking from the edges of his white paper hat, friendly smile and twinkling eyes, Art made all his customers feel they were special. With the kids he often served bits of wisdom along with the food.

"Good to see you. I was beginning to think the whole town was deserted," he laughed. "You kids help keep me going in the afternoons before the supper crowd. The old coffee coots keep things lively, too, but they don't spend much money for all the time they spend here. I should have a cover charge. But it's nice to have the company. And sometimes they bring the Mrs. back here for supper. So what are you guys up to today?"

"Oh, nothing much. Jake here is going bowling," Mario replied.

"So, how was school today? Learn anything?"

"Oh, I suppose we did. You learn anything, Jake?"

"I think you did. Not to stand so close to your locker when Frank's coming down the hall," Jake teased. Mario blushed. Coming from anyone else it would have angered him. By this time he had mostly gotten over the incident.

"What was that all about?" Art asked.

"Oh, nothing. I just got bumped into my locker in the hall this morning."

"Well, those things happen. You'll find as time goes on there are a lot of bumps in the road. You just keep going along and keep focused on what you got to do. And right now I got to get things ready for the sup-per crowd—I hope there's a crowd—and you guys got to go bowling."

Mario and Jake paid their bills, slid off the stools and headed for the door. It opened before they got there.

"Hey, Marion. What happened to your lip?" Frank hollered as he barged in followed by his supporting cast.

"Shut up, Frank." Mario elbowed past and hurried out the door. "And my name's not Marion."

"That's no way to talk to somebody," Frank replied in a loud voice to Mario's back.

"What a fairy," Ronnie said, and they all laughed.

With a questioning look, Art surveyed the small group of boys as they settled onto stools at the lunch counter. Other than the weather or sports, most of the time they ended up talking about cars or TV shows. Even though he was fifty-four and had owned a TV for only two years, Art could hardly remember what it was like before television. It seemed that was all people talked about these days. Some people said it was going to put radio out of business. It had become a great common denominator as millions of people watched "Ed Sullivan" or "I Love Lucy." The ads drove him crazy sometimes. Eventually he resorted to connecting the TV set to an extension cord plugged into an outlet next to the easy chair. When he couldn't take it any longer he simply pulled the plug. Olive said it would ruin the set and it hadn't even been paid for yet. That was anoth-er source of annoyance for Art. People getting suckered into the snare of easy monthly payments.

"So, how was school today?" Art asked, looking back over his shoulder from the malted milk mixer. "I noticed Marion had a little cut on his lip. How'd that happen?"

The others looked toward Frank, waiting for him to respond.

"Beats me. He's kind of clumsy . . . he probably ran into some-thing," Frank replied, looking around at the others with a little smirk on his face. "Where'd he go anyway?"

"Him and Jake went over to the bowling alley. Why?"

"Oh, I don't know. Just curious."

Art distributed the hamburgers, fries, and malts, getting every order right among the six kids. He must have had some system for remembering; even when the café was busiest he almost always got the orders right.

The slurping sound from the bottom of the malt glasses signaled the end of the after-school snack. Now they had to find something else to do. Ronnie leaned toward Frank and said quietly, "You should go find Marion and finish the job. You know, push him around a bit. Show him who's boss."

Although he didn't show it, Frank immediately felt uneasy at the suggestion. "You can take him. You're bigger than he is," Ronnie kept urging. "He thinks he's too good all the time. A good knuckle sandwich would fix that. Why don't you pound him? Serve him right for getting in the way of stuff, like when we were going after that old bum in the alley, or when he told on you to the principal about this morning."

"Now boys, is that really necessary?" Leaning his thick forearms on the lunch counter, Art looked at the boys from lowered eyebrows. "What's that going to accomplish? Fighting don't solve anything. If anything, it makes things worse. If you want to let off some steam or show how tough you are, go out and play football or hockey. When I was a kid on the farm we worked our tails off. We knew what tough was."

At first he had their attention until he got to the last part. Frank, Ronnie and the others looked around at each other and shrugged. "Oh we're just kind of kidding around," Frank said. "See ya later, Art." Laughing and talking, they went out the door.

In the bowling alley at first Frank and his buddies pretended to ignore Mario and Jake. Mario watched as Jake aimed for a strikeout at the end of the first line. Already with three strikes and three spares, he rolled another strike to start the tenth frame.

"Hey, Jake, just play it like you play baseball," Ronnie hollered from over by the pinball machine. "You'll strike out for sure!" And they all laughed.

"Just ignore 'em," Mario advised Jake. "How long are you going to stay? I think I might go home." He would have liked to stay and bowl a couple of lines, but decided to save his money and just watch a bit more. He marveled at the way Jake set the ball down so smoothly and the way it curved into the pocket. He was unaware that the other kids were not merely killing time hanging out at the bowling alley, which was not their custom, but that they were stalking him. Half-way through Jake's second line, Mario decided to go. He said good-bye and walked out the door, pretending to not notice the others standing around the pinball machine. Ronnie was still playing on a nickel after earning two game credits. Just as he was about to press the button to catch the ball and flip it back into play, Frank grabbed his hand. The last ball slowly rolled down past the left flipper and disappeared.

"What'd you do that for?" Ronnie protested.

"We got some business to take care of. Remember?"

"What's this 'we' stuff? Can't you take him by yourself?"

"Course I can. Don't you want to watch?"

Ronnie made a little grimace and let his hands drop from the machine. When he was on a roll with a pinball machine nothing else mattered. He focused so intently that surrounding noise and other distractions didn't matter. Except when someone dared touch him or do anything that would physically disrupt his timing on the flippers. Frank was one of the few who could get by with doing something so outrageous. "C'mon, I'll buy you the next game," Frank said. "You don't want to miss this."

"Miss what?" Jake's brother, Larry, looked over at them from behind the counter, but close enough to overhear some of the talk. "What are you guys up to?"

"Nothing. We were just going, that's all," Frank said.

"Good, get Ronnie out of here. Give the machine a rest."

MARIO WALKED SLOWLY ALONG THE SIDEWALK, head down and shoulders scrunched up against the cold wind. A gust from the alley blew out a dusting of snow. He glanced down the alley with a faint hope that he might see Tom, although he couldn't explain why.

"Hey, Marion. C'mere." Frank shouted from outside the bowling alley about half a block back.

Mario stopped and turned around. "What for?"

"You wanna fight?"

"No, I don't want to fight," Mario said calmly. "I'm just going home."

"C'mon. You think you're so goody goody. Why don't you prove it?"

"What's goody goody about fighting?" Mario said with little laugh.

"Don't get lippy with me, you little punk."

"You're the one who pushed me this morning."

"You're the one who told the principal."

"I did not."

"Well, let's settle this once and for all."

Mario had turned and walked back towards the other boys. He stood facing Frank. "So, go ahead and fight," he challenged. He sensed a slight hesitation as if Frank was taken by surprised how suddenly he had returned.

"You go ahead and fight," Frank said.

"You're the one who wanted to fight. So start," Mario taunted.

"Aw, c'mon Frank, let's go," one of the other kids said.

"I'm going if you're not going to fight." Mario shrugged and started walking back down the sidewalk toward home. Frank and the others followed, stopping when they reached the alley.

"Okay, punk. Let's go. In the alley. C'mon, let's see how tough you are," Frank said loudly.

Mario stopped and looked back. "I told you, I don't want to fight."

"That's because you're chicken. You squeal to the principal, and you hang around that old bum. You must be some kind of a fruit."

Mario walked back toward them and then turned into the alley, stopped and waited. For some reason he did not feel afraid. He felt confident that it would be just Frank and that the others wouldn't interfere. They followed him into the alley. Frank stopped, facing Mario about three feet away.

"So, go ahead, start fighting," Mario said. "I ain't got all day."

Frank just stood there as if he didn't know what to do next. He had been goaded into the challenge, a natural result of his arrogant and pompous leadership among the other boys. He was slightly bigger than Mario, and he actually believed he was as tough as the image he projected.

"You're the one who really wants to fight," he said finally. "You start."

"What? I do not," Mario protested. "If you want to fight, I will. Otherwise I don't care."

"You're just chicken."

"I am not. Go ahead, try hit me. See what happens."

"Hit 'em, Frank," Ronnie said.

Frank just stood there, a blank look on his face.

Finally Mario broke the stalemate. "Okay, if you want to fight, I will."

His right fist lashed out and struck Frank hard just to the left of his nose. Frank stumbled back, recovered, and charged Mario head-on. He tackled Mario around the upper torso, throwing him backward onto the alley pavement. Just as he was about to jump on Mario and pin him down, Mario spun to left, rolled free and jumped back to his feet. Frank swore and charged at him again.

"C'mon, Frank, pound him," Ronnie urged.

Mario made a feint to the right, then side-stepped to the left and came around with his left fist slamming into the side of Frank's head. Although no stronger than Frank, his quickness and agility made a big difference. Frank came at him again. Mario grabbed the front of his bulky coat, leaned back and spun Frank to the pavement. He held him down and began to furiously pound his face, then his gut. Like trying to run in a dream, it felt as if his blows had no strength. The punches to the body felt swallowed up as if hitting a big pillow, the combined effect of Frank's coat and excess body fat.

Also like a dream, the fury seemed to last a lot longer than it really did. Frank's resistance quickly collapsed, and Mario stopped hitting him. "You had enough?" Frank was crying. "You asked for it," Mario said. "If I let you up, you better quit."

He stood up, trying to control his shaking. Frank just lay there crying.

"You got him good," one of the other kids said.

"I thought you were on his side," Mario shouted. "Who wants to be next?" No one spoke. Frank rolled slowly to one side, pulled his knees under him and got to his feet. Mario turned and left for home feeling relieved, yet struggling to hold back his own tears. When he reached the sidewalk he turned and looked back at the others. In the deepening twilight his eyes caught another movement near the other end of the alley. A figure moved out from the shadow of a doorway and slowly walked away. It was hard to tell, but it looked like Tom. Some of the others noticed, too, but paid little attention as they huddled around Frank, who was gingerly dabbing blood from his nose.

"What's going on fellas?" Art stood in the open back door of the café. "What happened? Looks like you didn't take my advice."

"We didn't do nothin'," Ronnie said. "Mario started it."

"Let's forget about who started it. It takes two to fight, so nobody's innocent. C'mon inside."

They entered the back door of the café, and Frank sat at one of the rear tables, facing the back wall, hoping to avoid being noticed by the supper customers starting to trickle in. Art brought him a damp towel wrapped around some ice cubes. Frank wiped away the blood and also some tears, and held the cold compress against his swollen lip on the left side. A bruise darkened the skin below his right eye.

"What are you kids fighting about?" Art asked. "If it's just to show who's the toughest, it don't last long. Somebody tougher always comes along. You got to have a real good reason to resort to fighting. You can keep the towel. It was just an old one, but it was clean. You run along now, and I don't want to see no more fighting. Okay?"

They mumbled their assent and filed out the back door.

"What are you going to tell your parents?" Ronnie asked.

"None of your business. I'll tell 'em anything I want," Frank shot back, the tears giving way to anger.

MARIO DIDN'T SAY MUCH DURING SUPPER. He tried to keep his right hand out of sight, and being right-handed it was difficult to eat with his left, although just then easier than with his right hand, which was red and swollen. Fortunately his mom didn't notice. She did notice that he wasn't eating with his usual appetite either, even though she had made one of his favorite meals, scalloped potatoes and ham. He assured her that he was fine. Busy cleaning up so she could go over to Jim's, she didn't question him further. Mario didn't mind when she was gone occasionally in the evenings; he did his math homework and watched TV. Maria returned after 10:00 p.m., and he was already in bed.

He heard the back door open, comforted that she was home. She hung up her coat and walked softly up the steps. She peeked into his bedroom. Thinking he was asleep, she tiptoed over to the bed, leaned over and kissed him softly on the forehead. Pretending he was asleep, Mario lay still and content, feeling her warm breath and perfumed scent. She backed away, her gaze lingering a few more seconds on his youthful face and fine, dark-brown hair, then stepped out into the hallway.

"Mom?"

"What honey?" She looked back into his bedroom. "I thought you were asleep."

"Mom, can I talk to you?"

"Sure, what is it? Anything wrong?"

Mario's lips started to tremble. "I got into a fight."

"What? Are you okay? What happened?" She walked over and sat on the edge of the bed, placed her hand on his forehead and brushed his hair back, her eyebrows crinkled in concern.

"I'm okay. It was with Frank Harley. He started it. I didn't want to fight but I had to." Tears welled up, and he tried to keep his voice from breaking.

"Did anybody get hurt? Are you hurt?"

"No, I pounded him pretty good. My hand is a little sore, that's all."

"What happened? There must have been a reason."

"I was just walking home. Him and a bunch of other kids stopped me. He said he wanted to fight. I said I didn't want to, but he wouldn't stop. So I punched him and that's how it all started."

"From what I've heard he probably had it coming," Maria said. "We know he's kind of a bully."

But this won't be the end of it, she thought. It's just the beginning. She wondered what she would say when Earl and Louise Harley called, as she knew they would.

"Why did he want to fight you?"

"I don't know. He was picking on me all day. This morning before school he pushed me into my locker and it gave me a fat lip. Somebody told the principal, and he talked to Frank about it. Then I think he followed me after school until this happened."

"Well don't worry about it now. Everything's going to be okay. You say your prayers and go back to sleep. It's always better to wait until morning to clear things up. Just pray and leave your worries with God; he's always watching over us. Okay?"

"Okay. 'Night."

"'Night." She kissed him on the forehead again and left the room.

৯ 7 ৎ

T HE HARLEYS LIVED IN A STATELY, colonial-style house on a cul-de-sac about a block from the school. A large maple tree spread out over the well-manicured front lawn. It wasn't the fanciest house in town—that belonged to the Wrights. They owned the department store. But Mrs. Harley yielded to no one when it came to appearances and furnishings, both interior and exterior, and Earl Harley provided the necessary financial means, although he put up a valiant fight against the three large, wrought-iron lamps strung across the front portico between the four round columns stretching from ground level to the narrow porch roof jutting from the second story. He thought they looked like bulky bird cages. Even if they hadn't been so expensive he still would have complained, but it didn't do any good. It sort of evened things out from when he tore down the old single-car garage and built one that held two cars. Even the Wrights didn't have a two-car garage. That fact was enough for Mrs. Harley to finally assent to the project.

Being a cul-de-sac, Maple Street didn't get much traffic at that end. However occasionally a car would drive in and slowly turn around. Since most everyone in town knew it was a cul-de-sac, the only other reason Mrs.

Harley could think of when she saw these cars was that people were gawking at theirs and the other fine houses at the end of Maple Street. The thought gave her a feeling of smug satisfaction. Someone had to bring some taste and culture to this small town, and set an example to which others could aspire.

Looking out the kitchen window, which faced the street, she saw Frank walking slowly along the sidewalk. It's about time he showed up, she thought. Where had he been since school let out? Often he stopped off at the store after school and rode home with Earl. When Earl came home around 5:30 without Frank, she began to worry. She was relieved to see him, but something didn't seem right the way he walked so slowly and with a downcast face.

"Earl, Frank's coming . . . we can have dinner now," she announced toward the living room. Earl leaned back in his recliner reading the paper, waiting for the 6:00 p.m. news on TV.

Frank entered the side door by the driveway, quickly hung his coat on the wall hook and started up the back stairs. "Frankie, where've you been? I was starting to get worried." Mrs. Harley walked from the kitchen counter toward the back hallway, wiping her hands on her apron. He continued up the stairs without a reply.

"Frankie, I'm talking to you!"

"What?" he shouted back down the stairs in an irritated voice. "I'm just going to the bathroom. I'll be down in a minute."

In the bathroom he looked around for an old washrag or something he could use to clean the blood off his face and then discard so no one would see it. Most of the washrags were newer, some monogrammed with the letter "H." Frank knew better than to use one of those. Consciously or unconsciously his mother somehow seemed able to keep track of such household items. If one were to be missing, she would probably discover its absence, and there would be no peace until the mystery was solved.

He looked through the dirty clothes hamper until he found something he thought he could use to clean his face, a pair of his own underwear. It didn't look too bad. He soaked it in warm water and wrung it out in the sink. He winced as he looked in the mirror above the sink, not from physical pain, but from his own appearance. His upper lip puffed out on the right side, a black-and-blue crescent bordered the outside of his left eye, balanced by another bruise on his right cheekbone. Dried blood rimmed his nostrils, which he tried to clean off with the softest portion of his damp underwear. He dreaded going downstairs to face his parents.

"Frankie, come on now. I made one of your favorites for supper," Mrs. Harley announced loudly up the back stairway. Normally, the aroma of Salisbury steak would have drawn him to the dinner table like young men toward a shiny new '59 Chevy, the most popular car among most kids. Cadillac had nothing like the new Corvettes, and even the '58 Impala was impressive enough to be secretly admired by Caddy and Buick owners. Johnson Motors had the Chevrolet dealership in town. Although the Harleys and the Johnsons were cordial enough, the gap in status between the Chevrolet and Cadillac prevented any deeper relationship, at least as far as the Harleys were concerned.

Frank descended the stairs and quietly slipped behind his mother's back through the kitchen into the dining room. Sitting at his usual spot, he rested his elbows on the table and put his hands up inconspicuously trying to shield his face. He wished his sister had been there to be the focus of attention instead of himself, and perhaps even be there for someone he could talk to about what happened. He wouldn't ever admit it, but it had been lonesome at the start of the school year after she left for college.

If Mrs. Harley hadn't been so concerned about getting the food just right, she might have paid more attention to the fact that Frank was already sitting at the table, which usually wasn't the case. Most of the time Earl had to yell at Frank to come to the table so they could start eating. He would finally arrive, sullen and sometimes ornery. Not this time.

At the table Mrs. Harley finally noticed something seemed different. "Frankie, what's the matter? Is anything wrong?" A warm sense of affirmation from the attention soon dissipated in the dread of what would follow. The persistent inquisition would elicit some kind of satisfactory explanation. He still didn't have one, and he wished she would quit calling him Frankie. His attempt to deflect the attention trying to assure them nothing was the matter quickly failed.

So far Earl had been letting his wife take the lead. He looked more closely at the boy, who was eating slowly, strangely with one hand while the other hovered near his face. Earl noticed something flesh-colored smeared beneath Frank's left eye.

"Son, what's that stuff on your face, by your eye there? Take your hand down so we can look at you," he commanded. Frank slowly lowered his left hand, looked down at his plate and continued eating. Mrs. Harley leaned over for a better look. In the bathroom Frank had smeared on some of his mother's cosmetic cream hoping to mask the bruises. It hadn't worked.

"Oh, my word!" Louise exclaimed. "What happened to you?"

"It's nothing. I'm okay. Just leave me alone!"

The barrage of questions from both flanks became too much. He pushed back from the table, ran to the back door, grabbed his coat and ran out.

"Son, come back here right now!" This time Earl's command had no effect. What little snow there was had been shoveled from most of the sidewalks so Frank could run having to avoid only a few slippery spots. After two blocks he slowed to a walk. He feared getting caught, but he didn't want to keep running, either. He looked back to see the car backing out of the driveway. He felt trapped in the beam of bright headlights, and almost jumped behind a tree like in the game kids played on late summer evenings. They would walk along and whenever a car came along they darted for cover, imagining the headlights to be some deadly, alien ray gun. Earl spotted Frank and pulled up in the Cadillac.

"What in the hell are you doing, boy? You get in here right now!" Earl bellowed. Frank loved riding in the car. Once, out in the country, Earl actually let him drive it.

Frank stopped, turned around and began walking back toward the house. In no way was he going to get in the car alone with his father. In a confrontation, his chances would be better if both his parents were present. Being alone with just one meant that all the energy would be directed at him. Together, eventually they would turn on one another. Frank would become the victim and cease to be the cause of this possible threat to their social status. He jammed his hands into his coat pocket, stared down at the snow-frosted sidewalk, and trudged back toward the house. His thoughts swirled and struggled to seek some kind of explanation.

Earl followed in the car at a walking pace back toward the house, cursing more at the disruption of his dinner and thoughts of the ensuing confrontation. While he didn't like seeing his son get the worst of a schoolyard fight, maybe the boy had learned something. Mrs. Harley, on the other hand, would obsess over the incident until every scrap of evidence, true or false, was uncovered. Nobody got the better of the Harleys.

"Frankie, tell us what happened. Who did this to you?" Mrs. Harley helped him off with his coat and hung it on the wall hook. Earl came in the back door behind Frank, now feeling dismayed and disappointed in his son's behavior and the apparent outcome of his combat. They sat at the kitchen table. Frank fought back tears, generating some sympathy in his parents and softening their initial indignation.

"We should call the police, I really think we should," Mrs. Harley insisted.

"Now just wait a minute," Earl said gently patting his wife on the shoulder. "Let's talk things over. Let's find out what happened first. Frank, tell us what happened?"

"It was some old guy . . . I don't know . . . we were just walking downtown. He must have thought we said something, smarted off to him or something."

"Who was with you?"

"Just me and Ronnie and some of the other guys."

"What did they do? Did anything happen to them?"

"They just took off running. The guy grabbed me, and I couldn't get away."

Mrs. Harley became furious. "This is horrible! Earl, we have to tell the police about this! What if something worse had happened? We've got to find this thug and put him away for good. Who is he anyway?"

"Oh, I've seen this guy around town a couple times," Earl said. "He's kind of a bum . . . doesn't work anywhere that I know of. I think he lives in some shack outside of town. I've heard his name before but I don't remember it. Frank, is that who did this?"

"Maybe. I guess it was." Frank felt some relief now that they had a suspect. He wasn't trying to protect Mario, but he would be ashamed if his parents found out he had been pounded by another kid who was smaller and of a lower status in the community. At the same time, accusing Tom Nathan would get back at Mario, who seemed to have some kind of friendship with the man.

"Don't worry, I'll take care of this," Earl said. "I'll call Harold . . . we'll figure something out. We don't want this to get around, in the paper. But until he's off the street, you be careful, son. Always go in a group, okay? Better yet just call me or your mother and we'll pick you up."

Their dinner had cooled. Mrs. Harley placed the plates in the oven for a few minutes. They finished eating, not saying much. Frank had to force down the last couple of forkfuls. No one had much of an appetite. Earl went to the phone in the front hall and dialed the home number of Chief Stark. Although he still wasn't entirely convinced that his son was telling the whole truth, he went along with his wife's insistence and whatever version of the truth Frank had told them. Had the altercation been with another kid, it would have been settled with a reprimand and perhaps the involvement of the school principal. This was different.

Clareton Police Chief Harold Stark listened to Earl's story and assured him they would get right on it. Although he had never seen any indication of dangerous behavior from Tom Nathan other than his drinking, he did not question the accusation. In fact, he did not question much of anything when it came from Earl and most of the other businessmen in town. He knew that when things went their way, everything would be fine. They all pretty much saw things the same way. The main purposes in life for most citizens were to be law-abiding, hardworking, uncom- plaining, and spending money in town. As far as Tom Nathan was con- cerned, the only shortcoming Harold could think of was the working part. Tom's disability check seemed to provide enough money to buy food, booze, and other basic needs. He didn't have a car, so driving under the influence was not a concern.

Harold worried sometimes when he overlooked such minor infractions among prominent citizens and their sons and daughters. Monday mornings often began with a slight, gnawing concern before he read the weekend report from whichever of his two patrol officers had been on duty. He felt relief when everyone made it home from the club on a Saturday night without any serious accidents.

It didn't take long for the patrol officers to understand how things worked in Clareton. Their shifts consisted mostly of watching for speeders on the U.S. highway that bisected the town, patrolling the downtown at night looking for break-ins, which rarely happened, inter- vening in domestic disputes, and harassing the local teenage hot-rod- ders. The '57 Ford police cruisers still had enough power to keep up with most of the local hot rods. With intelligence gathered from dis- creet visits to the local auto mechanics, they knew all of them pretty well, particularly those with faster cars. But there were always a few who did their own engine work, and Harold was mildly annoyed at not knowing exactly what their cars had under the hood. He didn't mind if they kept their drag races out of town on a deserted county road, although secretly he wished he could go up against Larry Carlson's '55 Chevy. Some time ago Larry had gone to a salvage yard in the Cities and picked up a 283-cubic-inch, fuel-injected engine from a totaled '58 Corvette. Through some mechanical magic, he made it fit under the hood of his '55 Bel Air. Souped up and with dual exhaust, it could burn rubber for a whole block. It tore out the original transmission, so Larry replaced it with a beefed up four-speed.

Harold suspected that once the previous summer that Officer Greene had taken one of the two cruisers up against Larry's car in a drag race, but he couldn't prove it. He resented the way the kids seemed to like and respect Horace. He resented the way he was pressured by the mayor into hiring him in the first place. Earl and the other town big shots advised him to be patient; sooner or later they would manage to get Horace out of town and off to the big city where he belonged, and without stirring up any trouble involving race.

Harold listened intently when Earl called shortly after 7:00 p.m.

"Tom Nathan, is that who you mean?"

"I don't know the guy's name, but that's probably him," Earl said.

"I'd heard about some tussle going on downtown today. It sounded like just a bunch of kids though," Harold replied.

"Other kids were there, sure, but we're pretty certain it was this guy," Earl said. "A lot of us have been worried about him around town anyway. Only a matter of time before something happened. Who knows, it could be him doing some of those break-ins awhile back. We've got to do something about it. You should have done something long ago. Now my son here is all banged up and pretty upset, too. In fact, I'm going to file an assault charge right here and now."

Chief Stark felt somewhat relieved that now he could operate with a formal complaint instead of some off-the-books deal, which were not all that uncommon in Clareton, although he doubted that Tom was the perpetrator. Tom kept to himself, was only slightly known by the merchants at the shops where he bought his basic needs: cheap wine, an occasional bottle of Jim Beam, cigarettes, groceries, and dog food, and also at the library where about once a month he returned a pile of books and walked out with a new batch. Not long after Tom started showing up around town, Harold dropped by the veterans' service and welfare offices to see if they knew anything about the stranger. The secretary at the veterans' office said he had been in the Navy and received a monthly disability check. He had no criminal record, so there was nothing anyone could do but just let him be.

"How about if we just keep an eye on him for a while," Harold ventured.

"What good would that do? You know better than I do the case would get cold and pretty soon everyone would forget about it. What if he did something worse? What if he molested a woman or something? If that ever happened, he wouldn't be the only one to pay," Earl replied.

Harold had received veiled threats before, and some not so veiled. He hated every time it happened, hated himself and felt helpless. He had been Clareton's police chief for twenty-two years. Only three more to go and he could retire. He enjoyed the perks of the job and being part of the informal group of merchants and a few professional-types who ran the town, or at least thought they did. City council meetings were mostly a formality, and the real decisions often were made at the club or out on the golf course. They slipped up when Ralph Fairbanks got elected mayor.

Pharmacist and owner of the Rexall, Ralph was well-known and well-liked around town, and did a real good job of campaigning when he decided to run for mayor. Always cheerful and friendly, he received more trust than any ten people put together. But he didn't belong to the club. He bristled sometimes at city council meetings when the council majority cut corners or handed out sweet deals, but in the weak-mayor system of Clareton's local government he wielded little real power. His greatest influence came from his character, persistence, and integrity. He could be very persuasive when he wanted to be. That's how he managed to get Horace Greene hired. Chief Stark will never forget the recriminations from the boys at the club. Ever since, he had been even more compliant than ever before. All he had to do was hang on for three more years. He had no choice but to go after Tom, and he knew for certain who would get the assignment.

"I guess you're right," Harold conceded. "We'll probably have to wait until he's in town, though. You can't get to his shack unless you hike through the woods, or go over on the ice. I'd just as soon pick him up in town."

"Okay, but you better not wait too long."

"You sure it was him?"

"Who else could it be? Frank said it was him, and I'm sure there were other kids around who saw what happened. Frank usually has friends with him around town. Are you saying Frank was lying?"

"No, no, no. Not at all. I just want to be sure, that's all."

Harold tried to watch television the rest of the evening, which passed slowly in gloomy agitation. His thoughts kept going back to how he was going to explain the assignment to Horace Greene the next day. Horace had proven to be an outstanding cop with great potential. He was tough, honest, direct, yet balanced with great compassion when it was needed. He was effective and well-liked around town, especially by the kids. The initial novelty of a Negro in town, and a cop at that, still hadn't worn off, and perhaps even contributed to his rapport with townsfolk.

Despite that, Harold probably could make a case for poor performance in Horace's conviction rate. The subjects of a fair number of Officer Greene's citations were acquitted in court. Judge Holmes made sure of that, depending on who the defendant happened to be. Members of the club and their offspring often received acquittals, or at worst a reduced charge. This fueled occasional intense arguments between Chief Stark and Officer Greene. A few times Horace prevailed when a violation was so blatant that even the chief couldn't ignore it. This was not going to be one of those times.

ಠ 8 ೞ

T HE SMALL, FOLDED PAPER REFLECTED the streetlights, which had
already been switched on that early winter twilight Tuesday.
Wedged behind the mailbox next to the front door, it caught
Mario's eye arriving home after school. Curious, he pulled it out, unfolded the sheet and held it toward the light. The note, in thick, block letters
from a stubby pencil, read: "Mario, I saw what happened yesterday. You
did the right thing. I'd like to see you again. Come out to the shack today
after school. Tom."

The past two days had been full of mysteries. His fat lip from
Monday had subsided. Now the swollen soreness shifted to his hand. No
one noticed except for Rosalyn, who missed very little. On the way to
first-hour class, she stopped by his locker.

"Hi, Mario. What happened to your hand?"

"Oh, nothing. Why?"

"It looks all swollen."

"Didn't you hear what happened yesterday?" Jake had abeen listening and approached. "Ol' Mario here pounded Frank real good. You
should see him. He looks like a truck ran over his face."

93

"Really? Why'd you do that?" Rosalyn asked.

"He asked for it, he was the one who wanted to fight, not me. Besides, he's been bugging me a lot lately. You know what kind of a bully he is."

"Let me see your hand." She lifted it gently up to her face. She kissed it softly. "There, now it's all better." She patted it lightly and smiled. Her lips touching his hand felt soft and warm, and the scent of her hair as she leaned close sent a shiver through him. He didn't know what to say. He felt embarrassed. He looked around to see if anyone had seen. The memory lingered after he got to class and resurfaced from time to time during the day.

Around school that morning, almost everyone noticed Frank's appearance. By the time classes began, most of the kids had heard about the fight. Frank slouched in his seat, subdued and angry. No one dared say anything. He had managed to avoid Mr. Albright in the hallway before classes started, but Mrs. Lane, always in tune with the lives of her students, noticed. Frank mumbled something about getting knocked down playing hockey last night, and she bought it. Behind her back the kids who knew better made little smirks. They quickly sobered when Frank didn't signal a similar response, which otherwise would have been typical for him.

Throughout the day Mario sensed something different in the way other kids treated him. For some it could have been respect for standing up to Frank. Or it could have been awe for doing such a thing, followed by dread of what might be to come.

Most surprising to Mario, Frank did not seem like himself at all. He had expected Frank to be angry and threatening. He had expected to be called in to Mr. Albright's office to face the consequences whatever they might be. Instead everyone acted as though nothing had happened, especially Frank. Passing in the hall he even nodded slightly to Mario. He seemed to have one of those looks hinting that he knew something more, which added to Mario's worry, like waiting for an attack with no clue where it would come from and in what form.

After school Mario didn't tell anyone about the note, not even Jake. He wondered how he would be able to go out to Tom's shack without anyone finding out. He wondered if he even should go. Would he get back in time to make it to the weekly Boy Scout meeting? How did Tom even know where he lived? What did Tom want? What would they talk about? What would Tom say about the fight? Maybe he might have some insight about what the consequences might be, if any. Still unsure about what to do, he yielded to impulse, grabbed his skates and headed for the park by the lake.

Clouds had moved in, obscuring the late afternoon sun. Mario had no idea, nor did he even think about, how long the visit would take. If it approached suppertime, the sun would have already set behind the clouds. They would actually help as the lights from town reflected off the cloud bottoms, filtering into the surrounding darkness and suffusing the lake with a dim glow. The kids had skated on the lake many times on winter evenings, although they stayed near the shore by town. No one dared venture far out toward the dark, distant shore. It was still light when Mario pushed off on his skates from the park.

The few inches of snow that had fallen so far that winter were not uniformly distributed over the lake. The wind blew the snow around like sand in a desert, leaving large areas of bare ice mottled with low dunes of snow. Mario weaved around the patches of snow, gliding on the clear ice near the east shore of the lake. In the calm air, the only sound came from his skate edges cutting the frozen surface each time he pushed off, back and forth like a swinging pendulum. Looking across toward the point, he could see a small, flickering orange light. Coming closer he could make out a figure sitting by a fire in front of the shack. Tom sat on a stump staring at the flames and scratched Ike behind the ears. The dog's ears perked up. He let out a low growl and then barked.

Mario felt the urge to turn around and retreat back across the lake. *Why did I do this? Why did I even come out here?*

At Ike's bark Tom turned his head and looked toward the lake. Seeing Mario, he smiled and waved. Mario hesitated, then started slowly toward the shack, drawn to the fire more than anything. The orange flames flickered about two feet in the air, casting a glow around the clearing and the shack, replacing the orange glow of the setting sun that was obscured by the dark, gray clouds.

"Hey, Mario! Glad you could make it!" Tom rose from a crouch by the fire and walked toward the shore.

Mario glided up on his skates, still very unsure what he was doing there, although he didn't feel any fear. "Hi. I got your note, so I guess I came out here."

"C'mon up and sit by the fire. Can you walk on your skates?"

Ike yipped like a puppy, jumped and pranced around Mario trying to lick his face and almost knocking him off balance. Mario tried to pet him as best he could, bracing his legs as the big dog leaned into him. He jerked his head back when Ike tried to lick his face, but it was too late and his face got smeared with dog slobber.

"He likes you," Tom laughed.

Sometimes Mario wished he'd had a dog again. He hardly remembered the little cocker spaniel they had when he was younger back in California. After moving to Minnesota they never got around to getting another dog. He walked up to the fire and Tom motioned to a stump to sit on. The older man looked like he'd tried to clean up some. His hair had been brushed although still stringy and greasy-looking. He seemed calm, friendly, and not even drunk.

"Good to see you. How was school today?"

"Okay, I guess."

"I didn't know if you would come out here again. Glad you did. I wasn't sure if I should have left that note. I didn't want to get you into trouble if somebody else had found it like your mom."

"When did you put it there?"

"This afternoon, just before school let out."

"How did you know where I lived?"

"I know it don't sound right, but I kind of followed you home from school one day. It took a couple times because you didn't always go home right away. And I didn't want to be seen too much in that part of town if you know what I mean. People would be suspicious."

"Why'd you do it? Why'd you want me to come out here again?"

"Good question. It's pretty lonesome sometimes, even with Ike here. You know I drink too much. And then I have these crazy times, nightmares and dreams. When you guys brought me those sandwiches, I really appreciated it. You kind of stuck up for me when those other kids were harassing me. Nobody's ever done that around here. Why'd you do that?"

"I don't know. It just didn't seem right I guess."

"Well, thanks for doing that. And then that fight yesterday. What was that all about?"

"I don't know. Frank just stopped me after school and said he wanted to fight. So I did."

"I saw the whole thing. You really took it to him. But be ready if he tries to get you back."

"How'd you see that?"

"I was just making my usual rounds. Just a coincidence I guess."

Mario sat on the stump staring into the fire. Ike sat next to him pressing against Mario's side and savoring the attention of Mario's arm draped over his shoulders and petting him on the side. Tom stoked the fire, adding three more pieces of wood, about the same size as the ones on the lean-to back in the woods. They sat by the fire talking, mostly Tom asking questions.

"So, how long have you lived here?" Tom asked.

"Well, we moved here when I was about four or five. We used to live in California."

"Why'd you move here?"

"My mom got a job as a teacher. She knows Spanish, and I guess they needed someone in the summer to take care of the kids of the migrant workers. They started a summer school or something. Not all the kids . . . a lot of them still had to work in the fields."

"That's nice of them, the school I mean."

"It wasn't the school. I think it was our church."

"What church is that?"

"We go to Immanuel Lutheran."

THE CHURCH STILL SAT ON ITS ORIGINAL 1873 SITE near the west side of downtown, but it wasn't the same building. Growing with the town over the decades, in 1927 the congregation had built a new, red-brick church with tithes from profits of prosperous farmers, merchants, and wages of members who worked on the railroad. In the early 1950s some were moved to apply the Sunday sermons to the rest of the week, and decided to help out the families who came up from the south each summer to work in the fields, mostly Latinos from Texas. The farmers provided housing of sorts, old trailers parked in groves of trees not too close to the main farm house. Running water and plumbing were rare. Most had electricity, which had only been installed in some rural areas around town in the late 1940s.

The Immanuel Lutheran Mission Society, which included a few of the farmers' wives, decided to start a summer program for the migrant workers. The decision wasn't unanimous. A sizeable minority held fast to the notion that missions work only mean overseas locations like in Africa or the Philippines. But Mrs. Bauer's conscience took note whenever she passed by the bean fields, seeing the entire Jimenez family out in the searing heat of midday, large hats shading their unseen faces, hoeing and pulling weeds. The little ones under five hung around the old pickup parked at the edge of the field. The older children, six on up, had to work. The sight reminded her of Jesus' admonition of "suffer the little children to come unto me," and she decided then and there to do something.

She thought of Vacation Bible School until she realized that was out of the question. That would be asking too much of the congregation and other families in town who sent their kids to Immanuel's VBS, which had a reputation of being one of the best. So she thought of a Vacation

Bible School for the migrant kids, only it would have to last more than a week. She didn't give much thought to what Mr. Bauer would say; she knew he would, if not support the idea, at least not oppose it even if they had to pay most of the cost. The Bauers farmed 628 acres, including pasture. An entire section, the farm site and grove took up about twelve acres, more than Mr. Bauer thought was necessary, but his wife wanted a lot of trees to block the frequent prairie winds. He complained once in a while, but since the farm had been her inheritance and not his, it was one of those issues on which she prevailed. A big farm compared to most others; it gave the Bauers significant prominence. It required two hired men, so Mr. Bauer was accustomed to paying employees. In return for allowing Mrs. Bauer to go ahead with the plan to hire a Spanish-speaking summer teacher, the Mission Society failed to appropriate the full financial support. The Bauers had to make up the difference, which she didn't mind, and in fact it added to her feeling of satisfaction and sense of purpose.

In order to reduce the cost, Mrs. Bauer insisted that Maria and her young son stay with them. The big, square, two-story farmhouse had plenty of room. Mrs. Bauer said she would keep an eye on Mario while his mom was off at the church teaching the migrant kids. Maria hadn't even contemplated where they would stay when she took the job. She thought it was a blessing to have room and board and earn a small salary all at the same time. And when they arrived at the farm, she was thrilled at the opportunities it offered Mario.

He helped with chores as much as a five-year old could. Most of the time he just watched when Mr. Bauer milked the cows. He could actually do some good feeding the chickens. Eventually he was able to collect eggs, once he got used to the squawking hens, wings fluttering, futilely beating the air, white feathers shooting all over like the blast from a miniature aerial fireworks rocket.

After a few weeks of fresh air, chores and Mrs. Bauer's cooking, Maria noticed a new exuberance and confidence in her son, a complete turn-around from when they first came to the farm. It was partly her fault.

When she got the job she had overlooked telling the Bauers about the boy. Meeting them for the first time at the bus station, a stony look crept across Mrs. Bauer's face when she discovered that Maria was not alone. Mrs. Bauer had little tolerance for surprises. They strained to be cordial and make initial conversation on the way out to the farm. When they finally arrived at the delicate subject of Maria's marital status, the explanation, while not entirely convincing, was adequate. The little lie had become so familiar to Maria that she no longer felt much guilt. She would do anything to protect her son, who each year was becoming a fine person. With a child's trust, as long as he could remember, Mario believed that his father had been killed in a car crash when he was a baby.

Before too long the Bauers took a liking to Mario, Mrs. Bauer especially because it took her back to the days when her boys were young. They were all grown now, and their daughter, too. She had married the Mulder boy, which didn't go over too well at first with his family. But everything was fine now, and they lived two sections over working the Mulder farm. Two of the Bauer boys moved off the farm to jobs in town. One worked at the elevator in Dakota Falls and the youngest moved to Minneapolis where he worked in a tool-and-die shop. One stayed on the farm.

Maria and Mario became a part of the Bauer family, at least for a while. She was happy to be able to save most of her modest salary. She was happy that Mario seemed to be thriving on farm life. But around the end of July doubts began to emerge. She sensed that the Bauer boy showed more interest in Mario than in her. She confided about this to Thelma. They had become close friends after meeting at church. Thelma offered to let them stay with her and her parents. Maria accepted and with only one week of summer migrant school remaining, they moved to Thelma's, much to the bewilderment and consternation of Mrs. Bauer.

"So THE CHURCH ADVERTISED FOR SOMEBODY who could speak Spanish and be a teacher during the summer. Somehow my mom found out about it, and we moved here," Mario said.

"Well, that's real nice of them. Immanuel Lutheran . . . nice name. Do you know what it means?"

Mario shook his head.

"It means 'God is with us.' It's an ancient Hebrew word. Later they used it about Jesus." Mario didn't know what to say and just looked at the old man sitting there with his greasy hair, grimy face, and worn, stained clothing. "There I go again, saying things that don't fit how I look," Tom said with a laugh. "So, your mom came out here to help out with the migrant kids."

"Yeah, then I guess she got a job as a regular teacher during the school year. That's what she did back in California, but I don't really remember that far back. Do you know Spanish?"

"I used to know a little bit, but it's been so long. I lived in southern California once, too. Say something in Spanish."

"*Algo en Espanol.*"

"Now don't be a wisenheimer," Tom laughed.

"Okay. *Me gusta Ike. Es un perro muy agradable.*" (I like Ike. He's a good dog.)

"I like him, too. So you speak Spanish. That's great!"

"I guess I can speak it pretty good. My mom uses it all the time at home, both English and Spanish. Lots of times whenever she says something she says it in Spanish, too. So I kind of learned it that way."

"Hey, that's great! It's really good to know other languages. You're lucky to have a mom like that. What does she look like?"

Mario hesitated before answering. Tom seemed trustworthy, but it was hard to tell.

"She's about thirty. Dark hair and brown eyes. Pretty I guess."

"That's okay. I was just curious. I didn't mean anything." Tom saw that Mario was uncomfortable. They sat talking for a while, almost hypnotized by the fire. Mario didn't want to let go of Ike, and the dog basked in the company of his new friend.

"He really likes you," Tom said, smiling at the boy and dog sitting across from him gazing into the fire. "You ever had a dog?"

"We used to, when I was little back in California. I don't remember too much about him. I'd sure like to get one again. Mom says it would be just too hard now with us being gone all day."

Tom asked more questions, staring intently at the young boy. Where had they lived in California? Did they have family or relatives back there? How did they like Clareton? Was everything going okay, like did they need anything?

The firelight cast a dim, golden hue on the shack and surrounding trees. Behind them shadows deepened in the fading twilight. The shack looked about half the size of a one-car garage, with a mono-slope, tin-covered roof. In late summer or early fall years ago, the hunters would cover it with brush and small branches to camouflage the metal. Ten-inch-wide, rough-sawn planks set vertically formed the sides, with narrower one-by-threes covering the seams. Each side had a window with a larger one in front by the door, which was made of planks held together by upper and lower cross-pieces, and one diagonal down the length. A stovepipe protruded from the back left corner of the roof. Any paint there might have been had worn off long ago. A pile of firewood sat to the left of the door about ten feet away. A book leaned against the stump where Tom sat.

Tom reached in his shirt pocket and pulled out a pack of Camels. He turned it upside down, tapped the top against his hand and pulled out one that stuck out the farthest. He reached toward the base of the fire for a small branch protruding from the base of the coals, lifted it to the cigarette in his mouth and took a deep drag. The cigarette tip glowed a bright reddish-orange.

"Hey, you want a smoke?"

Mario looked embarrassed and declined.

"Sorry. I should know better. Force of habit mostly. I guess I don't want to be contributing to the delinquency of minors. You ever smoked before?"

Mario felt even more embarrassed and a little guilty. "I tried it once, but I got sick."

Back in fourth grade he and Jake had been leaving the corner store each with a bag of cheese curls and an RC Cola. For some reason Mario never understood, as they were leaving he impulsively reached and grabbed two cigars from a box near the side of the cigarette shelf behind the cash register. The store clerk had turned to help another customer and no one saw. Outside he showed them to Jake, who was deeply impressed. They rode their bikes to the park and quickly consumed their snacks. With a bigger family and each member focused on their own concerns, Jake stood a much better chance of getting matches than if Mario tried and his mom were home. Not that she was particularly snoopy; most of the time she gave Mario a lot of space. They tried Jake's house first.

Back at the park they peeled open the cellophane wrappers. The rich, pungent smell of tobacco at once became tempting yet forbidden. Jake lit up first and took a drag. It wasn't the first time. His parents both smoked and so did older brother Larry. For him the fact that the cigars had been stolen was more exciting than smoking them. Mario took the other one not sure which end to put in his mouth. He struck a match, held it to the end and took a drag. The hot, bitter smoke filled his mouth; he blew it out. "You got to inhale," Jake advised. On the next drag Mario took a big swallow. The acrid smoke poured into his belly; he choked, and his throat felt like it was closing up. A wave of nausea curdled up, and he felt like he was going to puke.

"You dope," Jake laughed, "you're not supposed to swallow it. It's supposed to go into your lungs." Even though Mario didn't feel like trying again with Jake looking on, he had no choice. He took another drag. The smoke hit his windpipe with a hot, stinging sensation, and he let out a loud cough. Besides his stomach, now his throat hurt. "Don't worry, I won't tell anyone," Jake said. "You got to practice more." Mario had tried it once since then, the second time with more apprehension than anticipation.

"Well, it's just as well you didn't smoke," Tom said stuffing the pack back into his shirt pocket.

"You know, it's getting dark," Tom realized. "You probably should head for home. I hope it's not too late already. Sorry I kept you here so long. I guess I'm just a blabbermouth . . . not really. I sometimes forget what my own voice sounds like. I talk to Ike here, but it's not the same as talking to a person. Sorry to put you through this."

Mario had lost track of the time awhile ago, captured by the bond of the crackling fire, loyal dog, and attention from Tom. Only when Tom reminded him did he realize that he was starting to get hungry. Then he felt panic. It was getting late. And dark. And he still had to cross the blackness on the lake and skate back to town. It was already 6:00 p.m., and his mom would be getting worried. He might not even make it to Scouts in time.

"Maybe we can talk again," Tom said. "I go to the library now and then. Maybe you could stop by for a bit. We could have lots to talk about . . . cars, girls, sports, rock 'n' roll . . . what do you think about Elvis? Stuff like that. That okay with you?"

"I don't know. Maybe." Mario wasn't so sure about that idea. "I got to get going. I'm going to be in big trouble."

"Jeez, I'm really sorry." For a moment Tom thought he would never see the boy again. He was angry for losing track of time and putting the boy in jeopardy. He would gladly have defended Mario if he faced punishment. He felt helpless because there would be no opportunity to do so. His heart ached when the young boy stood up to go. He wanted to reach out and embrace him, but still he couldn't be absolutely sure. To say something and then be wrong would be a disaster.

Ike followed Mario on the short walk to the shore, wagging his tail and with a questioning look, seeming to wonder if he would ever see his new friend again. Mario turned to Tom, waved and said good-bye. He reached down and scruffed Ike's thick, furry neck. The sun had set more than an hour ago behind the once gray clouds, now totally dark. The lights from town twinkled along the opposite shore like a miniature Milky Way. For a moment Mario thought about heading straight toward them across the middle of the lake. He knew it probably would have been okay and the ice was thick enough. Then he remembered the stories about the Bergquist boy. A shiver shot down his spine as his imagination created images and feelings of what it would be really like to drown in freezing water, or succumb to hypothermia.

He waved once more and pushed off on his skates counterclockwise close to the shore. Of course, even if he were closer to shore, it still might be too deep and hypothermia still could occur if he broke through the ice. He heard Tom shout, urging him to be careful.

ᔆ 9 ᘔ

MARIA HUNG UP THE PHONE and for the first time started to worry. It was 6:30 and she'd been calling since before six. Mario should have been home an hour or two ago. He was supposed to be at his Boy Scout meeting by 6:30. At first she was not particularly worried, but more annoyed that she had fixed a nice supper, and the longer she had to wait the more annoyed she became. She had already called Jake's and Rosalyn's homes and a few other families that she could think of. She called the bowling alley. Jake had been there Larry said, but he hadn't seen Mario. She called Jim but there was no answer. Some days he worked later doing bookwork or finishing up with a patient. She felt a little hope in calling the only other person in Clareton she really trusted and could confide in.

When Thelma answered, Maria's voice began to tremble as she asked her best friend for advice. They tried to think of who else they could call. They debated calling the police, then decided to drive around town first to check out the ice rink and other likely spots. Maria grabbed her coat to go pick up Thelma when the phone rang. Mrs. Sommers, Rosalyn's mom, called back and said her husband was coming home from work about four. He remembers seeing a kid on the lake skating. He didn't know who it was and didn't think much of it. He argued against calling Maria because he didn't think it was anything and would only get her upset. Maria thanked her for calling.

The searing panic struck before the handset reached the cradle of the black telephone on the little table by the refrigerator. Images of her son in peril, perhaps falling through the ice and struggling for his life were almost too much to bear. She felt helpless. Maria almost never cried, and the few times that she had, she would never let anyone else see. Her throat knotted up, and she squeezed her eyes shut tight trying to hold back tears.

Maria didn't remember driving over to the Harris's. Thelma stood by the window watching and went out as soon as she saw Maria pull up to the curb. The maroon finish on the '48 Plymouth coupe appeared almost black in the early winter evening darkness. Thelma scurried out the door, down the sidewalk and got in. The heater was just starting to give out a weak breath of warm air. Maria tried to not cry as she related the clue from the Sommerses.

"Maria, it's going to be okay." Thelma reached across the seat and put her arm around Maria's shoulder. "Let's not get ahead of ourselves. He's a sensible kid. I know he's going to show up somewhere."

"I don't know what I'd do if anything ever happened to him. I just don't know what I'd do."

"Now don't even think about that." Thelma reached a handkerchief from her purse, handing it to Maria.

"But I've called everyone I could think of. Where do you think he could have gone?"

"He'll be okay. I just know it." Thelma paused. "Maybe we could call the police. We have to start looking," Thelma said, trying to stay calm and reassuring. At the thought of a search party and what they might find, Maria broke down sobbing. "Okay," she finally replied weakly.

"I mean, I think we should call Horace first," Thelma said. "He's on duty tonight. He'll know what to do."

Maria left the car running, and they went back inside. Thelma called Miss Magnuson asking for Horace, Maria intently watching her face to signal contact. Miss Magnuson called up the stairs to Horace announcing the phone call.

Horace Greene lived in a room rented from Miss Magnuson, not much bigger than the hotel room where he'd lived his first three months in Clareton. The hotel had been getting expensive and he started right away looking for a small apartment or even just a room. Every place he went they didn't have anything open. At some places that was true. At some others Horace sensed the little smirk as they lied, or else a cold glare. At a couple places no one would answer the door.

On week nights even when he was on duty she fixed supper for him. She refused when he insisted on paying. She said she would just add a bit to the rent although Horace knew she didn't add much if anything at all. Tonight she had fixed a hamburger hot dish and corn muffins.

"Horace, you have a phone call," Miss Magnuson called up the stairs.

He had been watching TV for a few minutes before returning to duty. He turned it off and came down the stairs. She handed him the phone; he listened intently. Normally, Miss Magnuson would have stepped away, allowing some privacy. She hesitated, watching the concern showing on his face. Sometimes he would get calls from the station about one thing or another. Occasionally there were emergencies and usually she refrained from asking. She watched him listening and asking a few questions. He said good-bye and handed her the phone.

"Anything wrong?"

"That was Thelma Harris. They're looking for Maria Reese's boy, you know, the grade-school teacher's son."

"What happened? Is he okay?"

"He hasn't come home yet. I guess his mom is pretty worried. Somebody said they saw a kid out skating on the lake. I got to go."

Horace grabbed his coat, went out to the '57 Ford squad car and drove over to Thelma's. Although they had been seeing a bit more of each other lately, it wasn't enough. Thelma's parents, while still polite, had cooled their initial welcome when they realized their daughter and the young Negro cop were growing into a relationship that some people in town believed against the laws of God if not man. The Harrises wrestled with their affection for the young man and their hopes and dreams for their daughter's future. Horace no longer felt as comfortable at their house as he once did, so the couple had to find other venues for being together.

Horace wasn't too worried about the boy. He'd show up soon. He probably was still over at a friend's, someone Maria hadn't thought to call. He still might have been hanging around downtown. Trying to reassure Maria about that turned out to be more difficult than he thought. She insisted that they go to the lake. Jim arrived a few minutes after Horace drove up.

Four cars drove away from the Harrises heading toward the park by the lake. Horace led the way, followed by Jim, Maria, and Thelma in her parents' car. They stopped in the parking lot by the beach. Looking up, Horace frowned at where the streetlight should have been shining. He remembered a few days ago on patrol noticing that it was out. He had mentioned it to Carl over at the city maintenance shop, not that it would have made much difference right now. For some reason the bulbs in that particular light never lasted very long. One night he saw a bunch of kids throwing rocks at it. They hadn't seen him. He watched for a few minutes waiting to see if they would hit the target, but not too long and looked around to see if anyone could see him watching them. Seeing the squad car approach, they dropped the rocks but didn't run. Seeing it was Horace they waved and smiled. They denied throwing rocks at the light, claiming they were just having a contest to see who could throw a rock the highest. Horace gave them the speech about how it was costing their parents money each time they broke a light, or how minor acts of vandalism would lead to more serious crime and ruin their lives. Neither argument made any impact and probably inspired more of the same. Playing cat and mouse with the cops ranked near the top among the few real forms of entertainment for a small segment of Clareton teenagers. Of course, they promised never to do it again. With Horace they were a little more sincere than with the other officers.

Following Horace's instructions, the search party fanned out in their cars as near as they could get to the lakeshore, headlights on bright probing the darkness. The sand piles on the left side of the beach cast long shadows out on the lake. Horace and Jim set out on foot on the ice in opposite directions keeping fairly close to shore. The beams from their flashlights wobbled back and forth ahead of them. Maria and Thelma huddled together between the idling cars.

"Be careful," Thelma shouted. "We don't need to be fishing you out of the water."

Maria bit her knuckle and almost started crying again. "Oh, I'm sorry . . . I didn't mean to say that," Thelma apologized. "Don't worry. He'll be okay."

"Where is that shack?" Maria asked, a faint hope rising in her voice. "You know, the one where that bum is supposed to live? What if he's there?"

"Who is that anyway? Why would Mario go there at this time of day and on a school day yet?"

"You remember, Thanksgiving," Maria said. "The kids took some sandwiches out there. I wasn't too worried—there were the three of them you know. I thought it was a nice thing to do. And they went back one other time, too. I don't know. I didn't think it was dangerous or anything. I think I've seen him around town a couple times."

"I think I have, too. I don't know much about him . . . I'm not sure it's a good idea . . . oh, there I go again saying things that don't help," Thelma said. "I'm sorry," she put her arm around Maria's shoulders.

About half way back along the east shore Mario noticed the row of lights at the park. He saw the light bobbing toward him. "Oh man, I'm in trouble now," he said to himself out loud. He almost gave in to the urge to flee. Then he resigned himself to whatever the consequences might be.

Maybe whoever it was, was doing something else. Maybe they weren't looking for him. He knew his mom would understand and forgive him. He could understand that folks might get worried if he was missing for a while, but he didn't think he had done anything wrong. He didn't know who was approaching with the flashlight, and that worried him most.

"Hello, Mario. Anybody out there?" Horace shouted. "Mario. Mario."

"Hello," Mario shouted back, approaching on his skates. Recognizing Horace's voice he felt both reassurance and apprehension. "What's going on?"

Horace shined the light in his face. "That's what we'd like to know. Man, oh, man, are we glad to see you. What you been doing? You scared the daylights out of your mom."

"I'm sorry. I didn't mean to. I was just out skating around. I guess it got late."

Horace switched the walkie-talkie to channel two and called Jim. "You can head back. We found him. He's fine."

Mario glided slowly along, occasionally stopping to wait for Horace to catch up as he slipped and slid on the ice on their way back to the park shoreline. Horace warned about the danger of being on the lake ice until it was really thick. He could have broken through the ice and it would have been all over. Weighed down by water-logged, heavy clothing and skates, he would have floundered in terror before hypothermia set in. Even though the shallow lake was only about four feet deep where they were, it still could have been enough to be fatal. The deep muck covering the lake bottom made footing treacherous.

Horace didn't say anything about how he felt risking his own life in the search. That was just part of being a cop and public servant. Mario got the message without it having to be spoken, but still it wasn't enough to make him admit the real reason he had been out here.

"I can see you were out skating around. The question is, why?"

Horace waited for an answer. In the few seconds of silence that followed, Mario realized he had no choice but to tell the truth.

"I was out at that shack, talking to Tom."

"That's what I thought," Horace replied.

"Do you know him?" Mario asked.

"Yes, I do."

"Was I doing anything wrong? I mean, except being out here in the dark and not telling anyone? We just got talking, and it got late. I never meant to stay there that long. He just kept on talking about all kinds of stuff."

"So, what kinds of things did he ask you?"

"Oh, just stuff, you know, about school, sports, cars, how me and my mom were doing. He talked about a lot of different stuff. He seemed to know a lot of stuff . . . he reads books."

"Well he's not really a bad person as far as I can tell," Horace said. "We've checked him out. He don't seem to cause any trouble. He actually returns books to the library on time," Horace chuckled. "But then he don't have a lot of money so he don't want to be paying any fines."

"What does he live on?" Mario asked. "Sometimes we've seen him digging in garbage cans."

"He gets a disability check. Not much. He was in the war— World War II, not Korea. He got hurt or messed up somehow, maybe it's what they call shell shocked. I don't know too much else. Not long after he showed up around town last summer one of the other officers stopped by the veterans' office. We saw him go there once and decided to make a few inquiries."

"One time when we went out there, he was acting kind of crazy, yelling all kinds of crazy stuff," Mario said. "He must drink a lot. There's bottles lying all over the place."

"That is a problem for sure. You wouldn't believe all the crazy stuff us cops have to deal with because of too much drinking. Drunk driving, why that's just the tip of the iceberg. You can see it when they're weaving all over the road, or worse, getting into accidents. I could tell stories about some people in town you wouldn't believe. At least Tom don't drive, and he don't bother anyone."

"Hallo," Horace shouted as they neared the shoreline. "Look who's here."

Maria and Thelma tried to hurry toward them slipping a bit on the lake ice.

"You had me worried sick. Don't ever do that again!" Maria placed her hands on Mario's shoulders, as much to steady herself on the ice as to hold her son.

"Oh, thanks, Horace," Thelma said. She scooted along the ice toward him and embraced him. Jim arrived from the other direction, thankful that the crisis was over. Heading back to the cars, they scolded Mario for creating such a scare. Thankful for his safe return, no one else asked why he had been out skating on the lake after dark.

A car drove in to the parking lot toward the others lined up on the edge of the beach. Horace recognized Chief Stark's '57 Buick. The chief got out and walked toward the two couples and the boy, preparing to take command of whatever he encountered.

"Horace, what's going on?"

"Hello, sir. We were out looking for Mario Reese here. He was out skating a little too late. His mom got worried. Everything's okay."

"What was he doing out on the ice in the dark and this early in the season? You know the ice isn't safe yet, don't you young man?"

Mario looked down, more embarrassed than anything. "We're careful. We've been out already this year. We check the ice and stay close to shore."

Chief Stark's face took on an irritated look. It was more back talk from a twelve-year old than he cared to tolerate at that moment. He stared at Mario for a moment, then scowled toward Horace.

"Why didn't you call me right away?"

"Thelma called and asked me to come over. We didn't think it was any kind of an emergency. I would have called in right away otherwise."

"That's not the way it sounded on the radio. You were all worried. Someone was missing. You were looking out on the lake. Sounds to me like that could be dangerous."

Horace wondered if the chief would say anything about the spare radio he had let Jim use. He had switched them to a little-used frequency. Even the dispatch center didn't monitor it. A few people in town had scanners. Maybe someone heard the unusual radio traffic and called the chief.

"It was just Jim and me. I thought it would be a good idea if we could communicate after we separated."

"It's not the radio that bothers me. Even the kid out on the ice ain't all that unusual. The question is, what was he doing out there?"

The others looked around at one another, then looked at Mario. He didn't know whether he should run or cry. He wished they would just leave him alone; nothing bad had happened, but he felt guilty anyway. In a shaky voice he told them he had been at the shack and was just talking with Tom.

"You know, don't you, that was the most dangerous thing of all here," Chief Stark said sternly. "He's not just some harmless old bum. Folks have been worried about him doing something for a long time. Now he's a suspect in an assault. We're going to have to pick him up for questioning. You could have been hurt going out there."

"But he's not like that," Mario insisted.

"How do you know that for sure?" Chief Stark scowled at Mario, as if he were angry that the boy had dared retort. "You all listen close now. We've got good evidence that this guy committed an assault. Somebody was hurt. Assault is a felony. We're going to pick him up, and if anyone tips him off or gets in the way they're going to be in big trouble."

He looked straight at Horace. "Now let's all go home . . . we got work to do this week, don't we, Officer Greene?" He turned toward Mario. "As for you, young man, I don't want to hear about you going out on unsafe ice again." He turned and looked at Maria. "And you make sure of that."

No one said much as they headed back to the cars. Horace did not look forward to going to work the next morning. He wondered what the assault charge against Tom could be all about. By this time the car heaters were kicking out warm air. It fogged up Thelma and Jim's glasses when they got into their vehicles. Horace drove away first, leading the caravan from the park. Chief Stark waited until last. Out on the street, he watched to see that the vehicles went in their respective directions. He followed Horace for a few blocks before turning right on Maple Street toward the Harley residence.

✆ 10 ❧

BEFORE 1945 FEW PEOPLE HAD EVER HEARD of the tiny island of Iwo Jima in the South Pacific. Its shape resembling a pork chop, it measured five miles long by three miles wide. Its rugged terrain of rocky ridges and volcanic soil covering eight square miles barely allowed room for three airfields. Strategically located between the Marianas Islands and mainland Japan, during World War II in the Pacific Iwo Jima provided a base for kamikaze attacks against U.S. Navy vessels. By capturing Iwo, U.S. forces would weaken the kamikaze threat and use the airfields in strikes against Japan. Mount Suribachi, with an elevation of 556 feet, took up most of the narrow southern tip. Dug into caves, tunnels and trenches throughout the island, 20,000 Japanese defenders waited.

On February 19, 1945, at 8:59 a.m. the Third, Fourth, and Fifth Marine divisions landed on the southeast shore between Suribachi and Hill 382, the island's second highest point. It took thirty-seven days to defeat the Japanese. Of the 20,000 defending the barren island, only about 1,000 survived. From a total U.S. invasion force of 70,000, 6,821 would be killed, 19,217 wounded, and 2,648 suffer combat fatigue. After the invasion began and by the end of World War II, 2,400 B-29 bombers and their 27,000 crewmen had used the crucial airstrips on Iwo Jima and deadly kamikaze attacks had been greatly curtailed.

W ALKING OUT OF THE RIALTO THEATER on a balmy southern California evening in late March 1944, Tom Nathan knew nothing about Iwo Jima, but he knew what he wanted to do. He placed his arm around his girl's shoulders as they walked along in the twilight. She thought the movie had been okay. To say otherwise would sound unpatriotic. Although she didn't say it, she didn't really care much for John Wayne. So it didn't bother her too much when his character died, and Susan Hayward ended up with the other guy in the innocent love triangle. Still, something about the movie left her feeling a little bit uneasy. She hated the war. Why do men have to fight? Why do they have to go around killing each other? It just didn't make any sense.

The movie infused Tom with excitement. He sensed an answer to the restlessness that had never subsided, even though he was now in his thirties, had a good construction job, and had finally found a girl that he really cared about, not like the others. She was much younger, and he convinced himself that she would wait for him. The following morning, instead of going to the job site right away, he looked up the address of the Navy recruiter office.

When the war started he was already old enough to have passed the stage young men go through in which the prospect of military service promises excitement and adventure. Too young to understand or fear their own mortality, they see military service as a chance to leave a boring hometown and see the world. During wartime the patriotic call to duty trumped everything.

O N THAT INFAMOUS SUNDAY MORNING, DECEMBER 7, 1941, Tom came to around 11:30. Even sleep couldn't numb the throbbing in his head, which gained intensity with each waking second. He swallowed four aspirin, regretting the Saturday night binge; they had become almost routine. He put the coffee on and switched on the radio, anything to try take his mind off the headache, and the loneliness, too. He stood by the table in his small apartment, almost in a stupor listening to the news bulletins from Pearl Harbor.

Tom worked for a construction company with plenty to do building airfields, roads, and military installations. It paid well, and he liked the work. When war came, like many others he felt the patriotic surge following Pearl Harbor and wanted to enlist. His boss convinced him that the company's best 'dozer operator would do a much better job serving his country staying on the job. That lasted for about three years, until seeing John Wayne in *The Fighting Seabees*.

When his girl asked him what he thought about the movie, all he could say was that he thought it was really good. Even if he had tried he wouldn't have been able to express it in words. Like a destiny that he did not fully understand and could not resist, the decision was beginning to take shape, emerging from somewhere in his deepest being. They walked along in silence, arriving at her home before midnight according to her father's wishes. She wasn't even twenty yet, and her father disapproved of her dating an older man, but he accepted it because at least Tom wasn't some horny GI on a three-day pass.

The Naval Construction Battalions—NCBs, or Seabees—needed experienced, heavy-equipment operators. Movies had become a powerful propaganda tool in the war effort. In the weeks following the release of *The Fighting Seabees*, Navy recruiters waited for the seasoned construction workers to arrive at their door. The next morning, Tom Nathan entered the recruiter's office confident in his abilities and experience. He hoped that what lay ahead would somehow transform his life and perhaps bring him peace, a temporary measure of which came from resigning to fate. The decision raised enough courage to call his boss, not because he feared the response, but because he felt badly about letting him down.

Looking down at the vomit and sea water sloshing around his boots, Tom thought wryly about the movie. It didn't show the reality of this part. Grim-faced Marines crammed into an LST bobbing and lurching toward shore. Whether from the anxiety, the tossing vessel, or both, many couldn't hold down their breakfasts. Most of the words spoken during the short trip from one of the more than 450 vessels offshore came from the chaplain. He recited the 23rd Psalm. Many of the soldiers joined in as he followed with the Lord's Prayer, the words muffled by the wind and waves buffeting the LST, and the metallic creaking of light tanks, supply trucks and armored bulldozers straining at the chains trying to hold them still. Tom tried to keep his balance by leaning against the one he would be driving ashore in a few more minutes. He was part of what was to be the largest single operation in the history of the Marine Corps. They couldn't succeed without the support of Naval Construction Battalions.

Driving a large bulldozer off a landing vessel onto a soggy beach would have been challenging enough. Not long after the first wave of invaders landed, Japanese mortar and artillery fire exploded all over the beach. Taking fire along with the Marines, Seabees struggled to lay down steel matting that would enable tanks to join the battle without getting mired in the soft, wet sand. When their trucks became stuck they carried supplies inland on foot under heavy fire. Rounds came in from all directions from mortars and artillery hidden in caves and camouflaged pill boxes. The bombardment left the beach littered with damaged trucks, tanks and bodies. Seabees drove bulldozers furiously, clearing wreckage to make room for more landings.

The mortar shell blast tore a crater in the sand 30 feet from Tom's dozer. The concussion, debris, and shrapnel ripped him from the seat. His body tumbled to the ground on the other side. When consciousness gradually returned, the sounds of explosions, roaring engines, and men shouting seemed far away, replaced by loud ringing in his ears. His head began to ache severely, and a pain in his shoulder spread down his arm. He was lucky. Plates of armor welded around the cab blocked most of the shrapnel. A corpsman crouched beside him and tore away the shirt sleeve. He wiped the blood from the shrapnel flesh wound, cleaned it with antiseptic and bandaged it well. Tom thanked him, took a long swig from his canteen and climbed back on the bulldozer.

The conquest of Iwo Jima was inevitable, but it took longer than expected. The miles of tunnels, caves, and concrete bunkers of the Japanese defenders seemed immune to intense bombing and naval shelling. It took five days to capture the southern third of the island. The original objective was to have control of one half, including the two main airfields, after the first day.

Instead of suicidal banzai charges, Japanese forces waited in their fortifications. The rocky, barren landscape provided little cover for the Marines, who could only engage by frontal assault on foot toward an enemy they rarely even saw above ground. They took heavy mortar, artillery and machine gun fire from all directions. They suffered many casualties, and some days measured their advance only in yards. At times the shooting was so chaotic that friendly fire took its toll. Close air support from carrier-based fighters was almost too close. Although not on the front line, Seabees and other support units took casualties as well. Until silenced one by one, enemy mortars continued to rain deadly explosions with shrapnel tearing through the rear positions. Japanese snipers fired from hidden positions among the rocky ridges, or peeked from camouflaged spider holes in the ground. The 133rd NCB suffered more casualties than the Marine division it supported, forty-two killed and 203 wounded.

By the third day, Tom's Seabee unit had reached the outskirts of Airfield No. 1. He could have gone back to the ship. The shrapnel wound in his right shoulder made it stiff and sore, but he still could drive the bulldozer, and the wound wasn't infected. His commanding officer said he could go back if he wanted to. Tom decided to stay. Sitting atop the heavy equipment at the airfield made Tom and the other drivers prime targets. They learned to keep moving because otherwise the mortars would zero in on their positions. Sniper bullets pinged off the metal shields. As the Marine infantry advanced on the enemy fortifications with satchel charges and flame throwers, the mortar fire on the airfield gradually subsided.

The Seabees worked almost nonstop excavating and repairing the damaged airfield. The sooner it could be secured and made operational, the more B-29 crews would be saved by emergency landings if they had suffered crippling damage on bombing missions over mainland Japan 650 miles to the north. The declining number of mortar explosions brought some relief only to be replaced by utter exhaustion and the occasional lone sniper.

The living conditions alone would have made sleep difficult. Tom had done twelve-hour shifts before, although not under these conditions. Under the hot summer California sun he could at least take a break in the shade of his dozer and guzzle cold water. And when he got back to his apartment he could take a shower, turn up his new window air conditioner, grab a cold beer and settle in front of the TV. As he lay down trying to sleep, like many other soldiers, thinking about home, dreams of a comfortable bed, good foods, and wives or girlfriends brought temporary relief. But it didn't last long, lying there on the hard ground amid empty tins of K rations; still, a glimmer of hope never completely faded.

For some soldiers and Seabees staying in one place too long brought death or injury. After the mortar wound on invasion day, Tom could not escape in sleep even though so exhausted his body felt limp and nauseous. Sometimes the ringing in his ears clanged so loud he wanted to scream; sometimes he did. Sometimes it awakened him further, robbing him of the sleep that was his only escape. Sometimes he envied the soldiers who wouldn't be waking up, the ones he saw by the scores in body bags laid out in neat rows in a large, flat clearing not too far inland.

H ORACE AND TOM SAT IN SILENCE. From the picnic table in the park they could still see the beach in the fading summer twilight. The nighthawks screeched, swooped and soared above the trees. An exceptional sunny day in mid June 1958, its heat soaked into the parking lot and paved street creating an invisible dome of warmth surrounded by cooler evening air.

Most of the kids had already left. A group of boys had been playing Army at the beach. After swatting mosquitoes that emerged at dusk they were ready to leave anyway. The old man's shouts and curses only punctuated their departure, but not until they retaliated with their own epithets. Still, no one dared get too close. While an object of their derision, he nevertheless commanded some respect because of his adult size, and some fear because of his dirty, disturbing appearance. The kids with bikes sat on them ready to tear out of there; those on foot kept farther back toward the street, poised to run. As the arguing and name-calling grew louder, a few porch lights switched on at houses across the street from the park. Maybe someone called the police, or Horace could have been patrolling the area by coincidence. The squad car pulled into the parking lot, sending some of the kids scattering. Some stood their ground, leaving only when ordered to go home. He walked over to where Tom sat on a picnic table.

"What are you doin', man? We told you not to bother anyone," Horace said crossly. "What are you doin' here anyway this time of day? Get in and I'll take you back." Slowly and mutely, Tom rose and walked toward the squad car. Horace wrinkled his nose at the sour mixture of odors from sweat, dirt, and alcohol. "Wait a minute. C'mon back here and sit down." Horace decided it would be better to talk at the picnic table; he had hauled smelly drunks in the squad car before and didn't like the way the odor lingered. Tom came back and sat across the table. He lit a cigarette, said nothing and avoided eye contact with Horace.

"Listen man, we want to help you, but you got to want to help yourself. What're you doin' botherin' these kids anyway? If that kind of stuff gets around town, you're in big trouble."

"I wasn't doin' nothin'."

"What did you do to make them start harassing you? Why were you even around here? Getting this late, you should have been back at your shack."

122

"Why? It's a free country, ain't it? I can go anywhere I want to. Besides, I did my part."

"We're all doin' our part. What makes you think what you did is any different?"

"They shouldn't be doin' that, playing war like that. If they only knew."

"Well they don't know. They're just kids. And you're drunk, too."

"I just told 'em they shouldn't be doin' that. I couldn't help it. I don't want to bother nobody, and I don't want nobody to bother me. I don't hurt anybody."

"Well that may be, but it's what folks think you're doin' is what really matters. Look at you. You look like you're sixty, an old man. You don't have a job, you're filthy and you're drunk half the time. We know you done some good things before. Why don't you try get back on track again?"

Tom looked up at Horace. He couldn't remember the last time anyone showed any concern or care. The secretary at the veterans' office had seemed like she was trying to be nice. She only made small talk when he stopped by each month to pick up his check. If he saw her on the street she looked straight ahead and wouldn't acknowledge him; it would have been too embarrassing if anyone else saw any connection. Horace and the other officers kept an eye on him from a distance; as far as they knew he had no criminal record and had some means of support. When he showed up in town drunk the first couple times they hauled him down to the drunk tank. Once they charged him with a misdemeanor, then dropped the charges because he seemed so pathetic and harmless. Encountering the kids out playing on a summer evening was another matter. Horace wasn't sure what he should do. The radio in the squad car crackled to life with the law enforcement dispatcher asking for his location. Horace walked over and took the mike.

"I'm over at the park by the lake. Every thing's okay. Some kids were playing and things got a little noisy. I sent them home."

"Ten-four. We got some calls from residents about something going on at the park."

"It's all checked out and everything's fine. Over and out."

"Over and out." Horace walked back to the picnic table and sat down.

"You're not going to haul me in again?" Tom asked, smiling slightly.

"You're just no fun anymore," Horace laughed. He outweighed Tom by about fifty pounds. Younger, strong and trained in martial arts, Horace felt completely confident in his ability to handle any physical threat. He paused, "What is it with you anyway?"

"What's what?"

"How'd you turn out like this? Do you really like living like this?"

Tom sat there, his face turning stony, staring with vacant eyes down at some spot on the picnic table. Horace looked at him, patiently waiting for an answer. Tom wanted to say a lot of things, but the words jammed up in his throat and wouldn't come out. He couldn't find the right words anyway to try to explain the blackouts, nightmares, and loneliness of the past ten years.

"What did you do in the military?" Horace asked, trying to find some opening in Tom's wall. Tom said nothing. Horace said, "I was in the Air Force, military police up at Grand Forks. Lord I hated the winters there. It ain't that much farther north, but it's still worse. And then for us folks in a place like that, well we might as well been wearing clown suits or something the way people looked at us around town. Most folks were decent, but there's always a few full of hate and bigotry. I think it's fear, mostly. We ain't no different, just skin color, that's all."

Tom looked up at Horace. "Ever heard of the Seabees?"

Horace smiled to himself, gratified that he found a crack in Tom's wall. "Sure. Naval Construction Battalions. Is that what you did?"

Tom began to tell his story, how he worked on construction before and during the war, how he got into the Seabees and ended up landing on the beach at Iwo Jima driving an armored bulldozer under heavy mortar and artillery fire, how he tried going back to his old construction job after the war, how he and his girlfriend split up. Except for Ike he had never spoken to anyone about these things in more than ten years. Like clearing the beach littered with crippled tanks and trucks, the words unjammed and flowed out; a sense of peace drifted down over his bowed head and hunched shoulders. It battled with the pain rekindled by the vivid memories evoked by hearing his own words, ending in a stalemate like it always did, leaving him more unsettled than before. He cursed himself for the momentary breach in the wall surrounding his inner space, protecting it from external assaults. The words stopped abruptly.

"That's okay, man. It's good to get that stuff out," Horace said softly. He reached across the table and patted Tom on the forearm. "Just be careful to stay away from the kids. I know you don't mean nothin'. They're just kids playing. With all the movies and comic books about the war, I guess you can't blame them for playing like that. They go to the toy store and see those things . . . toy army helmets and guns. I was a little too young for the big war, otherwise I would've probably been there. I'm glad I wasn't because I probably would have been a cook or cleaned latrines or something like that." He laughed, "That's the answer . . . when they play war we should make sure they get the whole picture . . . guard duty, KP, PT, drill sergeants, stuff like that.

"I'm just saying they don't know what it really does to a person," Tom said. "I'm not saying that the war was wrong. We had to do it. We were attacked first. You must remember where you were when you heard about Pearl Harbor; everybody does."

"I was just a kid, and we were getting ready for church. Yeah, I remember."

"The Japs were really stupid to attack us like that. One of their big generals warned them. He said they were waking a sleeping giant. They sure did. I done a lot of reading about it the last few years. Not much else to do I guess."

"We know. The librarian called when you first started hanging out there. As long as you behaved we had to leave you alone. You could try to clean up a bit though."

"I guess so. Sorry. After a while you just kind of lose some of those hygiene habits. That's kind of the way it was on Iwo. It was like one big noisy, hungry, grimy, tired, numbing blur. I don't think I washed decent for three weeks."

"You'll never get over it, will you?"

"Probably not. The only time is when I hit the sauce or when I'm on the road."

"Where are you heading next? You've been here some time now."

"Trying to get rid of me, huh?" Tom said with a little laugh.

"Not me, but a lot of other folks in town ain't as understanding," Horace said. "Why here? Why don't you go to Minneapolis or some other big city? This town's too small, too closed in for your kind. You ought to know that some of the local big shots have been talking to the chief about getting you out of town."

"You ought to know," Tom said.

"What's that supposed to mean?"

"I think there's some in town that would like to see you go, too."

Horace looked at the older, grimy drifter sitting across the table, feeling a little incensed at Tom's bluntness. He had been on the job long enough to start feeling competent and confident. He liked wearing the uniform, carrying a .38 revolver, and driving a '57 Ford police cruiser with a 289 V-8, dual exhaust, and heavy-duty suspension. The problems he'd had trying to make charges stick against certain people in town hadn't yet been too frequent. He still hung on to the belief that that wouldn't last too long. The mayor called him every now and then to see how things were going. His physique and handsomely proportioned face attracted furtive, lingering, blushing glances from many of the women in town.

Miss Magnuson's flat tire last March turned out to be a blessing for both of them. At first she felt a little uneasy when Horace pulled up in the squad car behind her. After he had installed the spare tire, she drove off pleasantly surprised at the friendly, efficient and gallant young police officer. One might even have seen a wistful look on her face. In her mid-sixties, she looked back on more than forty years working as a clerk at the S&L department store and not much else. In the following days she had thought about Horace more than once.

Although still a rookie cop Horace was finding that his growing investigative skills were useful for more than just police work. Miss Magnuson was both startled and pleasantly surprised when he called two days later, asking how she was doing and if she got her tire fixed. He also asked her if she knew anyone who might have a small apartment or room to rent.

"Where are you living now?" she asked.

Horace told about the hotel, how it was getting too expensive, and what he had been up against trying to find a small apartment or room in town. Of course, she knew or had a pretty good guess about much of the story already. When he started the job it didn't take long for the word to spread around town. Some folks didn't believe it until they either saw him, or saw his picture along with a story in the *Chronicle*. The day after the story ran, Chief Stark arrived at the station to find the article taped to the front door, the photo defaced by penciled devil's horns. He took it down and placed it in a new file way back in the lower right hand drawer of his desk. It contained Horace's resume, job application, and several letters—two unsigned.

Before moving into the room at Mrs. Magnuson's Horace usually ate at a café or sometimes at Herm's tavern. It didn't serve much more than hamburgers, hot dogs, and fries. At first the regulars there treated him with cool politeness. Eventually Herm helped break the ice, and once they got to know him better some even became friendly. That never happened at the Lakeside Supper Club. Horace tried going there for a nice dinner once. Although it still made him feel uncomfortable and even lonely, he was used to the stares. Checking his watch it took seventeen minutes before the waitress even stopped by his table. He ordered a scotch on the rocks. When it finally arrived he could tell it had been watered down. The steak, which he had ordered medium-well, came extra rare, again after long wait. He thought about sending it back but decided to eat it anyway. The dark, curly piece of hair on top was about three inches long, and he knew it wasn't his. Still, he smiled at the waitress and left a generous tip.

"I KNOW SOME FOLKS HERE DON'T LIKE SEEING a black person in town, especially in uniform," Horace replied. "I knew that when I started. We just sort of expect it. It makes us have to try even harder. I've been doing a good job here. That's all that matters to me."

"I know you've been doing a good job," Tom said. "I did a good job, too, once. But for some people that don't make any difference. In fact, it pisses 'em off even more. If you're different in any way they just want to put you down. All people seem to care about today is buying things, climbing the social ladder. New cars every year, color TVs, big new houses, nothing's ever good enough. Status is more important than anything."

THE LAST REMNANTS OF THE SUNSET FADED on the northwest horizon, rainbow hues from orange to red to purple blending into the dark blue high in the summer night sky. Stars peeked into view one by one. Swarms of mosquitoes grew in number to match the millions of stars. A car pulled into the parking lot of the park. The radio blared rock 'n roll, probably all the way from WLS in Chicago. Horace wished he could hear the stations from Detroit. He loved listening to the blues, and in the past couple of years an appreciation of rock 'n' roll had started to grow. A hi-fi became one of his first new possessions upon discharge from the Air Force. He bought it in Fargo and had to pay extra for freight on the bus. Every paycheck since his record collection grew by one or two. Miss Magnuson didn't seem to mind as long as he didn't play it too late or too loudly. The accelerator revved the 283 V-8 in the '55 Chevy two-door hardtop to a throaty rumble, then let off, and the engine shut down. The lights switched off and radio became silent.

"Looks like we've got some company," Tom said.

"Yeah, just a couple of kids. I know 'em," Horace replied. "You ever take a girl out to park?"

"Not like they do now. I had some girlfriends, but their parents really kept tabs on things. Sitting on a front porch swing, you can't go too far when you know they're peeking out from behind the curtain."

"Where was that?"

"Just outside San Diego. Ever been to California?"

"No. I'd like to go there sometime, though."

"I'm not from there originally, but I really liked it out there. The weather especially, the ocean . . . I haven't been back in a while."

"So where are you from originally?" Horace asked.

"Not too far from here, actually."

"You got family around here?"

"Some. The folks are gone. I got a brother in Minneapolis and a sister down in Sioux Falls. I've called her a few times over the years. They don't even know I'm here in Clareton."

"You ever want to see them again?"

"A few years back I stopped by my sister's. She's married and got a family. They got four kids. We had a great time. I liked them a lot. But after a few days, her husband wasn't too excited about me bein' around. I got the message and hit the road. Haven't seen 'em since."

Tom looked off into the darkness. He had already talked too much. He felt that emptiness again every time he saw a family with kids or even thought about them. A lonely feeling at the thought that he would never be able to raise kids, like a big piece of him was missing right from the gut all the way up to his throat. If only he hadn't messed things up when he got back from the war. He might still be in California working construction, married to his sweetheart with a house full of kids. The blackouts, nightmares, and fits of panic, the heavy drinking scared everyone. The girlfriend went first, then his boss's sympathy wore thin. The years drifting on the road were hard, the edges dulled by the passage of time but mostly by the booze. Whether he came to Clareton searching for some place to call home, or clinging to some hope that he would find the part of him that was missing, he didn't know for sure. If he found it here, the emptiness might even be greater. It could be within reach, but he would not be able to grasp and hold it as he ached to do.

℘ 11 ℘

TOM WATCHED MARIO DISAPPEAR into the darkness. For a moment he could see the boy's silhouette against the city lights across the lake until Mario veered to the right, staying close to the eastern shore. Ike sat by his side watching too, ears perked, trying to catch the last bit of sound from Mario's skates carving into the ice. His brows twitched up and down above his searching, yellow-brown eyes. Tom was his master and kind most of the time. He always had Ike's devotion, but there was something about the boy that seemed to create in the dog a new bond, a den-mate. He remembered the food the boy brought on earlier visits. He'd anticipated more this time but its absence did not create any lasting disappointment.

Tom talked to Ike a lot; sometimes he did more than talk. There were times when the dog cowered in a corner of the shack or at the end of his chain, times when he had to avoid being kicked, or worse, times when he was thirsty or hungry and Tom would lie on the cot in the shack like he was dead and smelling worse. The sound of Tom's and Mario's voices in conversation around the fire rekindled a sense of brotherhood and stability that Ike had not experienced since he was a puppy. He lay down between them with his head resting on his outstretched front paws, eyes closed and almost lulled to sleep by the mellow sound of human voices talking softly. His head popped up when the boy stood and started walking away.

"What do ya think, Ike? You like Mario?" Tom said after Mario had left. "You'd like a boy to run around with, not some old drunk like me?" Ike looked up at Tom, wagging his tail slowly. Tom gently patted him on the head and scratched behind his ears. "Maybe we'll see him again. Maybe not. Who knows? I need to get something to drink."

Tom walked back to the shack; Ike following behind. Inside Tom rummaged around but didn't find anything more than a bottle of Ripple only about a quarter full. He chugged it down, but that only to primed him for much more.

"Damn, I got to go to town, Ike. Wouldn't ya know."

He reached under the cot, lifted up the loose piece of flooring and pulled out the cigar box holding his cash. He counted $47.28, more than enough to see him through the rest of the month if he stayed with the cheap stuff, although he really wanted a bottle of decent bourbon. Outside he called Ike over to the chain and hooked it to the dog's collar.

"You sit tight boy. I'll be back soon." Tom trudged off toward the path into the woods. It led to the county road along the east side of the lake. It would take him about fifty minutes to reach the edge of town. It would only be about 7:30 when he got there, and the liquor store would still be open.

A short path led from the clearing in front of the shack, through a stand of oaks to a narrow road no more than two tire tracks wide, through a grassy meadow before entering the woods that made up most of the eastern shore of the lake. The track meandered through the woods out to the county road. When he was drunk, Tom usually had no problem finding his way even in the dark. That's how he preferred to navigate the trail—drunk and in the dark. This time, mostly sober, he trembled as he left the open area and headed toward the darkness of the woods. He tried to laugh at himself; only little kids should be afraid of monsters in the dark, not a grown man. But these weren't the monsters of childhood. He saw grotesque shapes out of the corners of his eyes. It was worse when the wind swept through the tree tops. Sometimes he even imagined Japanese soldiers, snipers camouflaged in the trees or popping up from spider holes. A couple times when he heard a branch snap or some other unexpected noise he hit the ground.

Usually he avoided such nighttime excursions, enduring them only in emergencies, such as running out of booze. He cussed himself for not going earlier. He had been distracted from the routine on the day's mission when he left the note at Mario's mailbox. Returning to the shack, he had heated up some beans, washing them down with most of the Ripple. Instead of looking for another bottle, he started a fire in the wood cook stove and set a pot of water on to heat for coffee. He'd wondered if Mario would see the note, and if he did, would he even come? Tom tried to resist the feeling of sad disappointment at the thought that the boy would not do so. He ridiculed himself for even leaving the note and thinking that the boy actually might respond.

The coffee gave Tom energy and even a little ambition. He'd fed Ike and looked around for something to do for the next couple of hours when Mario might show up. There wasn't enough time to go into town for anything at that point. The wood pile was adequate, but he could always use more. "C'mon Ike, let's go get some firewood."

H EADING INTO THE WOODS FOR TOWN LATER, after the boy had left, Tom felt something he hadn't experienced for a long time: a bit of contentment. He was happy for Mario, that he seemed to have a good home, which he didn't really doubt. That he had friends and a good school, and it was a good town where kids could grow up in a loving, stable environment, although not entirely free of life's troubles. Sometimes they were just less out in the open. The thoughts helped distract him from the usual demons lurking in the darkness of the woods and his consciousness. Instead of being threatening and grotesque, this time the barren tree branches, black against the faint glow of the clouds, seemed peaceful, even beautiful as they swayed high in the wind. The snow cover brightened the trail, making it easy to follow.

Out on the road, the snowplow had left a ridge along both shoulders. With little traffic, Tom could walk on the edge of the road, only once having to step off into the snow bank when an oncoming car passed. Tom didn't notice when the car slowed and turned around at the next intersection. It turned back north approaching from behind as Tom resumed walking toward town. He did notice when the car slowed as it neared him. He had nowhere to hide so he braced for something.

Even before the car came to a stop the occupants jumped out the other side, to avoid being seen and at same time be able to quickly retreat back into the car. Snowballs flew toward Tom, most sailing past into the ditch. Tom instinctively hunched over and turned his back toward the assault. One big snowball thudded into the small of his back. The kids laughed and hollered epithets. "Hey, old bum. You'll keep on going out of town if you know what's good for you. Get a job or get out."

Tom tried to ignore them, hoping they soon would leave him alone. He was not afraid; he felt more sad than angry. Sad in his solitude and failed life, sad that these kids had no clue what he had experienced in the past, what he had accomplished, what he had done for his country, what he had become. In his current condition there was no way he could tell them, and if he tried they would not believe him. If only he could warn them.

Shoulders slouched and head down, he continued walking toward town. The kids followed along for about a block still yelling at him. Without the reward of a response, they gave up and the car, a gray '50 Plymouth four-door sedan, accelerated toward town. Tom wished he could become invisible, and he hoped he would not see them later in town. He wished he had more money so he could get a bottle of bourbon and still have enough for some food. He could always rummage through garbage cans, but that meant spending more time in town exposed to its associated risks.

When money ran out, a couple of times he'd hopped a freight heading southeast toward Minneapolis where he sold plasma for ten dollars a pint. That meant leaving Ike alone at the shack for a couple of days, which he didn't like to do. He left the dog on his chain with several pans of water and food hoping that he wouldn't spill it or become entangled in the chain. Somehow the dog knew the difference when Tom left for town for a couple hours and when he was leaving for a longer absence. Each time the dog thought his master was gone for good and was overjoyed when he returned.

"EVENING." THE CLERK IN LAKEVIEW LIQUOR glanced up at the shabby-looking man in the dirty, green parka, then looked away. Just through appearance and behavior he knew a lot about the man who came in about once a week, but he did not know his name.

The man didn't say much. He walked slowly past the liquor bottles sometimes stopping and looking, then continued on to the cheap wine section and made his selection. Setting it on the counter, he dug into his jeans pocket and pulled out a handful of change and some wrinkled bills. In awkward silence he counted out the amount and pushed it across the counter toward the clerk. As he had done scores of times before, the clerk bagged the quart of Ripple knowing it was a waste of a brown paper bag.

The first few times the clerk tried to make the usual small talk. With little response and no indications that the old man had any redeeming value, the clerk soon gave up trying to be friendly; however the habit of remaining cordial was too ingrained. As long as the man could pay, didn't steal and didn't bother other customers, at least he deserved that much.

"Thanks."

"Yep." Tom took the bag under his arm and left. Outside he turned right, walked toward the middle of the block and turned into the alley. He rarely made it back to the shack with an unopened bottle. Sometimes he returned to the liquor store for another before heading for the shack. Sitting on a back doorstep, after a couple long swigs, he contemplated going back for another. He thought he might have enough even for a fifth of cheap whiskey. After the initial assault by the wine the whiskey certainly would finish the job. Just so he waited with the second bottle until he returned to the shack, so he wouldn't fall off the road somewhere. With this plan in mind, he returned to the liquor store then found his way back to the alley.

He sat in the filthy alley, forearms resting on his knees, head down, looking blankly at the broken alley pavement. Remnants of the early snowfall had mixed with grit making a grayish mush. Out on the street several cars passed by. Even though the stores were open until 9:00 p.m. for the holiday season, only a few shoppers and pedestrians walked the downtown streets. The early cold snap helped folks get into the holiday spirit but also kept them home in the dark evenings. In many homes, people sat transfixed in front of the television tuned to "Dragnet," "To Tell the Truth," "Rifleman," or "The Red Skelton Show."

The opposite wall at the other end of the alley lit up, reflecting the beam of car headlights. Tom looked up in apprehension. He didn't want any trouble. He just wanted to be left alone, the stress of human interaction being greater than the yearning for it.

Noticing the red gumball on top of the car, his apprehension increased. He just sat there waiting. A disproportionate number of his contacts with other people involved cops and railroad goons. Some of the cops seemed fair and sometimes even sympathetic. The goons almost never did.

The squad car slowed and stopped beside him. Recognizing the officer's dark face, Tom relaxed a bit. He waited for the gentle scolding from Horace, who couldn't get over his frustration and disappointment about how Tom was spending his time on earth when he had done so much good earlier compared with what he had become now. Horace rolled down the window.

"That you, Tom?"

Tom slowly raised his head, shrugged slightly and raised his left hand at the wrist in a silent hello.

"How much you been drinking?"

Tom held up the bottle so Horace could see it was half full. Horace had received the call about ten minutes earlier. Whenever Tom bought a bottle of whiskey in addition to the wine, the liquor store clerk would sometimes call dispatch. Not for fear of any crime being committed, but the inconvenience of later having to assist a smelly, sometimes puking, old man who didn't make it home and was too drunk to help himself.

"Where's the other one?"

Tom smiled. "You want some?"

"Later. You going to be all right going back? We don't want anyone to see you staggering down the street, do we?"

"I'll be okay."

"So, what was the kid doing out there tonight? You know that really put a scare in everyone."

"How'd you know he was at my place?"

"He told us. He said you left a note telling him to visit."

"I did."

"Why?"

"I don't know. I just wanted to talk. Maybe he would bring some cookies or something."

"Well don't do it again. We were out looking for him in the dark out on the lake. Thank goodness he showed up. You know the ice isn't real thick yet. What if he'd gone through? That would have been it. His mom was beside herself worrying."

Tom looked down at his feet, noticing the two buckles missing from his right overshoe. He had tried using a piece of twine to tighten the fit. It became too much trouble to keep tied so he gave up. He had considered getting another pair, but these didn't have any holes yet and otherwise worked okay.

"Sorry. I didn't even think about that."

"And what's more . . . I shouldn't be telling you this . . . you know that Harley kid? He came home Monday night all beat up. His old man owns the car dealership. You know what he's saying? They're talking like it was you who roughed the kid up. If they decide to go after you, you're pretty well cooked."

"You know I didn't do it. It was Mario, but it was the other kid who wanted to fight. I know because I saw what happened."

"You saw what happened?"

"I was at the other end of the alley. It was just a coincidence."

"Did anyone see you?"

"I don't know. Maybe."

"Oh, great. Now we got witnesses placing you at the scene."

"I don't know if they saw me or not."

"Look. All I'm saying is you better lay low for a while. Stay out of town. You got enough food for a while?"

"I'll be okay."

Now Tom wished he had brought along more money. He would have to stock up on a few more bottles if he couldn't go to town for several days. He thought about asking Horace for another small loan. He still owed him ten dollars. Once, just before the first of the month the owner allowed him credit at the liquor store. Right after getting his check Tom repaid. He wasn't working tonight, and Tom knew the clerk wouldn't accord him that same courtesy. Horace might give him another small loan, but it wouldn't look good for either of them if Tom returned to the store to buy more booze right after the clerk had already called the police. Despite Horace's warning, Tom decided he could try sneak back into town later anyway.

It was almost 9:00 p.m. when Tom started walking back to the shack. Another cold high-pressure system was moving in, pushing the clouds off to the southeast. He didn't notice the stars appearing through the breaks in the clouds. He walked along looking down the road in front, shoulders hunched against the wind that had an extra bite to it after passing over the frozen lake.

He cursed when he saw car headlights heading toward him on the county road. He didn't notice that the car had backed out onto the roadway from the woods about where the trail to the cabin entered. Passing by he saw it was the same gray Plymouth only this time it kept right on going, and he was thankful for that.

When he reached the point where the trail entered the woods, his gratitude turned to alarm. Tire tracks appeared through the snow bank along the road and led into woods. Tom tried to hurry along the trail toward the shack. About halfway into the woods the tire tracks ended. From that point on he saw footprints; he couldn't tell for sure how many sets there were.

People had ventured along the trail into the woods before, but not in winter or in the dark. Sometimes from the shack he could see campfires at the fort some kids had made back in the trees. Once last summer they even camped there overnight. It had caught Ike's attention, and Tom tried to keep him from barking. The next morning he'd heard voices not too far from the shack. When he looked out the door, he'd seen small figures a ways off at the edge of the clearing, scampering back into the woods. Until then he figured no one knew he was even there. He was no longer invisible, and it worried him.

He walked faster, trying to keep his footing. He was far beyond the stage where booze created a feeling of bravado. Damn kids. Why did they have to be like that? He hoped they hadn't made it all the way back to the shack. As far as he knew, no one had ever been out there since he moved in, except for the younger ones who came across the lake on skates bringing him sandwiches, cookies, and even companionship. Maybe they told the older ones, although he knew the trail into the woods was no secret. He knew it was a well-known hangout for high school kids when they got their hands on beer and liquor. Since he had been there, they'd never bothered to continue past the open meadow to the shack.

The tracks kept on going, and so did Tom's concern. He couldn't see anything or hear anything. That worried him most. By now Ike would have heard something, would have been prancing back and forth at the end of his chain yipping and barking. Tom tried to run, as much as a drunk old man could, stumbling a couple times before reaching the trampled space in front of the shack.

Ike lay on his side unresponsive, surrounded by beer bottles, chunks of wood, and rocks, some about the size of baseballs. His smooth black and tan coat looked torn up in spots. A dark stain covered his forehead above his closed eyes. His pink tongue drooped onto the ground from his partially open mouth.

"Ike, Ike," Tom cried. "What did those little bastards do?"

He tried to cradle the dog's head in his arms. "Medic! Medic!" he shouted. "Get a corpsman over here."

His head fell down into the dog's shoulder, sobbing into the furry coat. He looked up, cringing and expecting another salvo of mortars. Everyone else had fled; he was alone. "We got to get back."

He unclipped the chain, then moved around and pushed his arms under Ike's back. He lifted the dog up onto his bent knees, struggled to his feet and began a staggering walk on the trail back toward the road carrying the ninety-five-pound German shepherd. He clenched his teeth expecting a bullet to slam into his back, like being hit hard with a red hot hammer. He just kept going; somehow he kept his feet under him one step at a time. He did not fear the bullets whizzing by; the wind shook the bare branches and rattled the leaves still clinging to them.

Tom carried Ike all the way to the hospital in town. Reaching the emergency room door, he held out a finger and after a few stabs was able to press the doorbell. Soon a light went on and the door opened. The orderly looked bewildered at the unkempt old man carrying a large dog.

"You got to help us," Tom cried. "My son here, he's hurt."

"Mister, that's a dog."

"Please. We were attacked. The Japs are all over. We need a medic. Please, you got to help us."

"Mister, you need a vet. This is a hospital."

"But what about my son?"

"I don't know about your son, but you got a dog." The orderly backed away and started to close the door."

"Please, I don't know what to do. You got to help us."

The orderly paused. "You want me to call the vet? We could call Doc Ahrends. You want me to do that?"

Tom looked down at Ike. The dog felt warm cradled against his chest. He felt the aching in his back and arms, suddenly weak so that he felt his legs were going to collapse. His consciousness suddenly returned, and he found himself in town at the emergency door of the county hospital holding Ike in his arms. He wondered how he got there.

"Sure. Call the vet."

"He lives out in the country. How are you going to get there?"

Tom could hardly manage to stand there holding Ike. How he could walk carrying the dog anymore he didn't know.

"Well, I can call him. Maybe he'll come and get you," the orderly said.

While they waited for the vet to arrive the orderly brought some gauze pads and antiseptic solution and helped Tom clean Ike's wounds. The dog remained unconscious.

Twenty minutes later a Dodge pickup pulled into the emergency room driveway. A man in his early sixties, wearing a dark stocking cap and navy-blue parka got out and walked over to the doorway.

"Hi, Doc. Sorry to bother you like this," the orderly said. "I didn't know what to do. I just couldn't let this guy go. This dog's hurt pretty good."

The vet removed his stocking cap and stuffed it into a pocket. The bright light above the door reflected off his bald head still showing some summer tan and wavy silver hair swept back above his temples. "Glad you called. I get more after-hours calls than your docs do. I'm used to it. So what do we have here?" He looked up and recognized Tom. "Tom, is that you? How'd this happen?"

"It wasn't me that did this," Tom said earnestly. "I came home and there he was all beat up." The word "home" suddenly sounded strange to him; he didn't recall ever using it before in referring to the shack. For a moment his slight hesitation piqued the vet's initial skepticism. "I think it was some kids. I was gone. When I came back I saw a car going away."

"Well let's not worry about that right now. Let's get a look at Ike here."

They laid him gently on an old blanket in the back of the pickup. The vet switched on a large flashlight for a closer look. He felt for a pulse. Slowly regaining consciousness Ike tried to lift his head.

"Looks like a lot of blunt force trauma. He's in rough shape but I think he'll be okay. He might lose that right eye. Could be some broken bones or internal injuries. Only time will tell." He looked at Tom. "He can't go back home like that. I'll take him to the clinic. We'll fix him up and keep him there for a while. We'd take some x-rays, and he'll need some stitches."

"What's that going to cost?" Tom asked.

"Don't worry about it. You can just work it off like you've been doing already."

Tom agreed. He declined the offer for a ride and watched the pickup drive away. Returning to the shack, he hoped no one would see him. He wondered how long it would take and how he would get Ike back.

↭ 12 ↫

EARL HARLEY SET DOWN THE NEWSPAPER, pushed his slightly rotund torso up from the easy chair and walked over to the television. He dialed the channel knob to find the channel with "Dragnet." On the way back to the chair he saw the headlights of a car turning into his driveway. Who could that be, he wondered? In the kitchen Mrs. Harley looked up from the dishpan. "Somebody's here, Earl," she announced. She walked over and switched on the light by the side door. "It looks like Harold." The police chief didn't wait for someone to answer the door, rapping on the window a few times with his knuckles on his way in.

"Hallo. Harold here." He wiped his feet on the entry way rug and hung his coat on a hook behind the door. "Evening, Louise. So what magnificent meal did the Harleys partake of tonight? I could smell it all the way from the street."

"Hello, Harold. It was nothing fancy. Thanks. How are you? Would you like some coffee? I made some apple crisp, too."

"Coffee sounds good right about now. It's a little nippy out there with this early winter. I'll take you up on a piece of that apple crisp, too, please."

Louise cut a big square from the pan of apple crisp, served it on a small plate and poured a cup of coffee. "Earl's in the living room watching TV. What brings you over?"

"You know we're still investigating the incident from Monday. How's Frank doing?"

"He's better now. I just hope it doesn't leave other scars, you know, emotional. I worry about him going to school and what the other kids will say. So far he hasn't said anything about that so that's good. You've got to do something about that man, though. What's happening to our peaceful town?"

"The town's just fine. And when we're done with this case, you won't have anything to worry about. Where is Frank?"

"He went over to his friend Ronnie's. Frank said they got a new pool table, an early Christmas present I guess. I suppose that'll be the next thing, a pool table for the rec room in the basement. Maybe then they'll spend more time here than at the pool hall downtown."

"I wish there were more parents as concerned about their kids as you," Harold said. "Thanks for the treat. I got to go now and bother Earl during his TV show."

"C'mon in, Harold," Earl said loudly. Chief Stark walked into the living room, sat on the sofa and placed his cup on the low coffee table in front of him.

"I couldn't tell if you were here to visit Louise or me," Earl laughed.

"If it was her, I'd make sure you weren't around first," Harold teased back. "I couldn't turn down this apple crisp."

"So, what have you found out so far? How's the case coming along?" Earl turned serious.

"You know that Reese kid, Marion? He was out there again tonight," Harold replied. "That's where I just came from."

"Out where?"

"Out at Tom Nathan's shack, across the lake."

"You were out there? Did you nab him?"

"No, not me. Marion Reese was out there."

"So, what does that have to do with this? Nathan is the one we're concerned about. When are we going to file the assault charge? If we wait too long it's going to lose momentum. What's the holdup?"

"We've been working on it. We spent most of today checking up on Nathan, talking to some of the kids who were there Monday."

"So, what happened today?"

"That's' what I'm here to tell you about. It seems that after school today the Reese kid went out to Nathan's shack. Why, we don't know. I was just sitting down to supper when I heard some radio traffic. I heard Officer Greene talking to somebody else. It sounded like they were searching for someone. They said something about the lake and the park, so I went over there. They had four cars lined up by the beach with their headlights shining out on the ice. Apparently the Reese kid didn't show up for supper so they started looking for him."

"Who was all there?"

"His mom, of course, Maria, her boyfriend Jim Andersen, her friend Thelma Harris, and our favorite officer Horace Greene."

"Andersen, the dentist? He's seeing Maria?"

"What irritates me is that they called Greene first," Harold said. "That must have been Thelma. Maria calls Thelma. Thelma calls Greene. It makes me a little suspicious."

"Why you let the mayor get that through I'll never know," Earl said. "Hiring Greene. I'm not saying I'm against those people, but they should be in their place, and Clareton isn't one of them. And going out with Thelma like that, it just isn't right. Her parents, it's breaking their hearts. We're counting on you to do something. Can't you just fire him?"

"It's not that simple. It might be easy for you, but for us there's a whole long process. Besides, once the bleeding hearts heard about it we'd be all over the papers. Those civil rights people would come to town, and we'd have Little Rock all over again."

Earl sat back, staring at the television. "Yeah, I suppose you're right. We got to do something more though."

"Holmes is doing what he can, but he can only go so far," Harold said. "Greene's still managing to keep his conviction rate at a respectable level. The judge could get in trouble if it became too obvious. The big problem is, a lot of people in town seem to like Greene. It's almost like he's a novelty. Some of those pinkos even brag about our town having a nigger cop."

"Well, don't worry. I've got some other ideas. Maybe we should have a little talk with Thelma. Her dad's been trying to get a loan from the bank so he can expand his construction business. We might have a little leverage there," Earl said with a little smile. "So, tell me, what else did you find out down at the lake?"

"What I told you is about it, but I've got this nagging suspicion there's more," Harold said. "After you've been in this business long enough, you get what some folks call a sixth sense. You've seen enough people in strange situations where you start to get hunches. I don't know. There's something going on here. One thing's for sure, once we pick up this Nathan guy, things will start to shake out."

"So, what do we have on him, I mean, for evidence? Even with Judge Holmes, I don't want to take any chances. This guy's got to go, and that's all there is to it," Earl said, eyes fixed intently on the chief.

Harold Stark started to go over the facts in the case against Tom Nathan. Louise walked over and refilled his coffee cup. He turned down another piece of apple crisp, and she took the coffee pot back to the kitchen. Returning to the living room, she went over to the television and switched it back to "The Lawrence Welk Show." She wanted to hear what Harold had to say, but she also wanted to take advantage of an infrequent opportunity. With Harold there, she figured Earl wouldn't protest, although he might later. They were too busy talking anyway. On some Tuesday evenings, she would go over to a friend's to watch her favorite show while Earl stayed home to watch "Dragnet" and later "Wyatt Earp" and "The Rifleman."

There was a lot Harold wasn't telling the Harleys. The police had checked out Tom's military record at the veterans' service office. One day back in June, Officer Greene approached the chief and told him about talking with Tom in the park. Horace hadn't said anything about him since, but Harold always suspected that wasn't the only encounter, that they had become better acquainted. Horace dearly hoped that Earl would not detect this.

The secretary at the vets' office did not question Chief Stark when he asked to see Tom's military and medical records. Stark leafed through the file, occasionally taking notes on a tablet. It went from one extreme to the other. When the war broke out, Nathan had been working for a construction company as a heavy equipment operator. In the early years they worked twelve-hour shifts and sometimes longer building airfields and military installations. In the spring of 1944 he enlisted and became part of a Naval Construction Battalion unit. On February 19, 1945, he landed on the beach at Iwo Jima right behind the first wave of Marines. After three weeks, two wounds, and suffering from battle fatigue he was taken off the island. Two months later, he was confined to the psychiatric ward at a military hospital in San Diego and later received a medical discharge. He did not attend the ceremony to receive his Purple Hearts and Bronze Star. A hospital orderly brought them later.

Stark asked the secretary for copies of the citations for Tom's military honors.

THE MARINES ON IWO JIMA HARDLY EVER SAW the enemy. Yet they advanced step by step never knowing when a mortar shell would explode with an ear-shattering blast, spraying sand, rock, and shrapnel. Often they bypassed hidden enemy positions, so they always had to check their backs and flanks. The lucky ones had tanks out front. The bulldozers, trucks, and other support units were not far behind. On Day Five of the invasion, one bulldozer with a Seabee at the controls went beyond the threshold of courage for most men.

Marines from the Fourth Division had finally advanced inland far enough to capture Airfield No. 1 about one-third the way up the island.

According to the initial battle plan, they were supposed to have reached that point and beyond by the first day. The cost of the protracted campaign went beyond that borne by the invading soldiers and sailors. Each hour, each day longer took a toll on fighter and bomber pilots needing the barren, ancient volcanic speck in the vast ocean on which land to refuel and repair shrapnel-riddled aircraft. After clearing the beaches to make room for landing more equipment and supplies, Seabees at the controls of heavy equipment moved inland toward the airfield.

Seaman First Class Tom Nathan's skilled handling of heavy trucks, bulldozers, graders, and bucket loaders had become well-known and respected in his unit and beyond. At thirty-five he was ten or more years older than most of his comrades. During training one nineteen-year old said, "Hey, old man, you got a smoke?" Tom smiled and didn't say anything as usual. He reached in his shirt pocket and tossed over the pack of Camels. Somebody else laughed and chided Tom, "You gonna just take that 'old man' crap?" Tom shrugged. "Time marches on and there ain't much you can do about it. Just so the music don't stop too soon. At your age you think it's never gonna stop." They still called him old man, but he didn't mind.

He didn't know where it came from, the impulse that drove him and his bulldozer straight at the cave opening spitting machine gun fire across the north end of the airfield. He tried not to think about it later, but it was hard to forget when all the others wouldn't stop talking about it. The enemy had avoided detection by Marines trying to secure the perimeter. They waited until most of Tom's unit had arrived and began working on the runway. Three days of naval shelling and bombs left many craters to be filled and debris to be cleared. Some of the others laughed at Tom when he welded some steel plates around the cab of his bulldozer.

He ducked instantly at the first rapid *pop-pop-pop* sound of machine gun fire, then looked up toward where it seemed to be coming from. Closer to the edge, another of the bulldozers clanked along, its driver slumped over the controls. Tom turned his machine toward his buddy. With a closer look, he could see the Seabee's neck torn open and blood spilling down. More machine gun bullets pinged off the steel plates and whizzed by his head. This time he saw the gun smoke from what looked like a pile of rocks and dirt about seventy-five yards from the edge of the airstrip. Fifty yards to Tom's left, a squad of Marines patrolling the perimeter hit the ground and fired M-1s and a Browning Automatic Rifle toward the rocks. Tom accelerated the engine and, like an enraged rhino, the bulldozer lumbered roaring toward the enemy gun emplacement. He raised the dozer's huge blade to shield the front and lifted the hinged steel plate with a narrow slit in front of the cab.

In the tool box behind the seat, Tom carried several grenades, a satchel of explosives, and a .45 Colt pistol. Roaring toward the rock pile, Tom reached back for a grenade. Just beyond the pile, he saw the small cave opening spitting bullets. Almost to the opening, he lowered the blade enough to catch a pile of loose rock. Bullets zinged all around and ricocheted off the steel. About fifty feet from the opening, he lobbed a grenade. It missed the opening and bounced back toward the dozer exploding in front of the blade. Tom grabbed the satchel, set the throttle with the machine grinding slowly ahead, and leaped off the right side. The dozer blade caught a lip of solid rock, stopped moving forward but the tracks kept churning. Covered by the smoke and dust from the grenade, he clambered over the rocks and up to the side of the cave opening.

The Marines had fallen in behind the bulldozer, firing on the cave and drawing fire in return. Tom lit the fuse and whipped the satchel charge into the opening. The blast ripped off part of the cave ceiling and blew Tom backwards down the rock rubble. The Marines converged on the smoke and dust-filled gun emplacement, now silent. They found five enemy dead and two wounded. More importantly, they discovered another tunnel leading from the rear of the cave, part of the three miles of tunnels connecting 800 caves and pillboxes. They set off another charge in the tunnel bringing down tons of rock to seal it off. Two Marines found Tom amid the rocks and helped him to his feet, dust-covered, shaking and staring blankly.

Harold wasn't sure how many people in Clareton knew about this part of Tom's past. He and the other officers did and the secretary at the vets' office. Somebody over at the Legion or VFW might though he didn't think it likely. Who knows? It might even strengthen the case. Even if he were a war hero it wouldn't be enough to offset disgust, even fear, about a psycho drunk wandering around town. Some folks just can't tolerate the idea that the object of their attention could be both a saint and a sinner; it had to be one or the other, and it could change in the blink of an eye.

"Has anyone ever tried to help him?" Louise immediately regretted speaking up; it just blurted out.

Earl glared at his wife. "Are you kidding? He assaulted your son."

Her face flushed. "I was just asking." She got up and headed back to the kitchen.

"He's had plenty of help and look what good it did," Earl replied. He looked at Harold and shook his head. "Women. They just don't know when it's too late for that."

Chief Stark smiled slightly. "Well there's a time and place for everything, but I think even Louise would agree that this guy's had plenty of chances. And what he's done now is the beginning of the end for him as far as this town's concerned."

"It better be," Earl said soberly. He lifted the newspaper and started scanning the headlines. "Look at this Harold. Coya Knutson's husband is trying to get her to pay him $3,000 rent for office space at his hotel. Good for him."

"I don't know what those people were thinking in '54," Harold said. "I couldn't believe it when I heard that, when they elected her to Congress. Must be that wind on the northwest prairie up there at Oklee, it addled their brains."

"It's those radicals in the Democrat-Farmer-Labor party," Earl said. "For years she's been trying to get a guaranteed price for farmers – paid for by us taxpayers yet. Can you believe that? What if I could just get a guaranteed price for the cars I sell? Wouldn't that be nice?"

150

"You need a guaranteed price like you need another hole in the head," Harold snorted. "Your margin's probably a lot more than any guaranteed price. You said once that selling cars was the easiest job in the world."

"Well it's just the idea of the thing," Earl replied. "Government setting prices and stuff. Meddling in free enterprise. Sounds like Commie stuff to me."

"Well they finally got rid of her anyway," Harold said. "She's back home where she belongs. When mothers leave home for full-time work, I think it's bad for society. The kids turn into a bunch of juvenile delinquents, I can tell you that."

Chief Stark stood up, catching a crumb of apple crisp falling off his pants leg and dropping into the coffee cup. "I should probably be going. I've got a few more folks to visit yet tonight. If you hear anything about what happened tonight or about Monday give me a call."

"Thanks for stopping by. You going to be at the meeting Thursday?"

"I suppose. But we probably shouldn't be saying much about this to anyone yet."

"I agree," Earl said. "Let's just keep it between us and the judge for now."

"I'm going to pay Horace a visit first, then go over to the Reese place."

"What if Jim's there?"

"That's okay. He was at the lake, too. They have to be warned about Nathan. The boy must be forbidden to ever go out there again. Maybe with Jim there, it'll help get the point across. You know, a kid like that growing up without a man around the house, sometimes they just don't know how to accept authority."

Chief Stark said good-bye and thanked Louise again for the coffee and apple crisp. He backed out of the driveway and drove over to Miss Magnuson's hoping that Horace would be there. Sometimes he stopped home for a break before finishing his shift. On the way Harold passed Immanuel Lutheran Church.

Floodlights lit up the front church yard where kids and adults worked on setting up the annual Nativity scene. Huge shadows of Christians acting out their faith spilled out into the surrounding darkness, jumping up to tall, grotesque images dancing on the church front. On the next two Wednesdays and Saturdays from 6:30 to 8:00 p.m. folks would drive by to look at the live portrayal of the first Christmas. Flashbulbs popped, mostly from cameras of parents whose kids were on duty at the time wearing humble shepherd's coats or dressed up in some curious attire attempting to resemble ancient royalty adorned with crowns of tinfoil wrapped around cardboard. If the weather wasn't too cold and if one of the church families happened to have a healthy infant at the time, they didn't have to use a large doll to depict the baby Jesus. The gender of the young church member so pressed into service didn't matter as long as it didn't fuss and cry too much.

Harold slowed down to see if he could recognize any of the workers. He thought he saw Mario but wasn't sure. If it was, apparently he hadn't been grounded, which the chief certainly would have done had his own kid done something like that. He shook his head. These permissive parents were ruining a whole generation of youth.

On the job he saw it firsthand all the time. Except for some of the farm kids, most seemed to have more money and idle time than they deserved. The smart ones went off to college. Some went to the Twin Cities to find jobs right away after high school. A bunch joined the armed forces, but always there were some who hung around town and continued to express their rebellion in many annoying ways. Perhaps the most annoying was his suspicion of their rapport with Officer Greene. In Clareton, even compared with drinking, hot rodding, and motorcycles, for Stark and many townsfolk that was the most rebellious act perpetrated by some of the town's teenagers, befriending a Negro, and a police officer to boot.

Mrs. Magnuson expressed surprise when she answered the doorbell late in the evening.

"Good evening, ma'am. Is Horace home right now?"

She welcomed the police chief into the front hallway, went to the stairs and announced Horace's visitor. He turned down the volume on the hi-fi and stepped from his room into the upstairs hallway. After nearly eight months in Clareton, this was the first time Chief Stark had encroached on Horace's personal turf. Caution, curiosity and dread all played on the young officer's mind as the chief ascended the stairway.

"Can I get you something, coffee . . . how about some cookies?" Mrs. Magnuson offered.

"No thanks. I just had some," Stark said over his shoulder ascending the stairs. "Hello, Horace. Can I come in?"

Harold Stark entered the large upstairs room and looked around. A small countertop in one corner held a two-burner hotplate. Next to it sat a small refrigerator. Horace turned off the hi-fi and sat on the bed, feeling awkward in the few seconds of silence until Harold spoke.

"Nice record player you got there. Where'd you get it?"

"Fargo. Not much else to do here, I watch TV and listen to records a lot. Is there some kind of problem? Do I have it too loud and folks are complaining? Mrs. Magnuson usually lets me know."

"No, nothing like that." Harold paused. "I want to talk to you about what happened tonight down by the lake."

"I'm sorry I didn't call in first. I should've called John, too. I'm just taking a little break right now."

Chief Stark ignored the apology. "You know, folks in town are talking, talking about you and Thelma. She calls you and you go ahead and try handle this on your own. That doesn't look very good."

Anger seeped into Horace's voice. "Thelma's got nothing to do with this. We're adults, and we can do what we want. When she called, it didn't sound like any emergency."

"Did you know where the boy went?"

"Only afterwards when he told us."

"That man is dangerous you know."

"Tom? Tom Nathan? He maybe drinks too much and acts a little crazy sometimes, but he ain't dangerous. What makes you think that?"

"He's already hurt someone."

"What?"

"He assaulted Frank Harley Monday. We've got a case against him, and you're going to pick him up."

Horace's stomach tightened. "Tom's a good man. He's a war hero for cryin' out loud. He done his part, and now he deserves to be left alone. He ain't hurt anybody."

"Yes he did, and we've got witnesses. Tomorrow or sometime this week you got a job to do. And when I leave here, you better not talk to anyone about this, is that clear?"

Horace sat on the edge of the bed, hands folded in front and stared at the floor.

"Yessir."

℘ 13 ୡ

MARIO FELT EMBARRASSED. The long, fake beard covering most of his face didn't help as a place to hide; it seemed like all eyes were looking at him. He felt too old to be standing there dressed in an orange bathrobe with a long piece of tinfoil draped over his shoulders and a tinfoil crown on his head. Fitted over his stocking cap, it made his head look disproportionately large. Usually it was the sixth graders who made up the nativity scene roster. They didn't have enough this year, so Mario and one other kid, an eighth grader, had to fill in. It wasn't Mario's idea; Maria was on the nativity scene committee this year and had volunteered him.

"Silent Night" played over the loudspeaker in front of the scene. A steady stream of cars passed by slowly, stopping briefly. Every Christmas the Immanuel Lutheran congregation created a nativity scene so elaborate and meticulous in detail that it drew visitors from as far as thirty miles away. The Men's Fellowship spent an entire afternoon erecting the stable and placing the lights. They had rescued a large plastic star from the city garage left over from an older set of decorations. It perched on an eighteen-foot step ladder behind the stable.

The back stable wall measured sixteen feet wide, determined by two sheets of plywood end to end. It allowed plenty of space for the manger, Mary and Joseph, five shepherds, three wise men, and two sheep, a goat, and a Holstein calf loaned by one of the farm families. Four bales of clean wheat straw spread out over the stable floor. The calf was a 4-H project of one of the farm kids playing a shepherd's role, so the animal was accustomed to the youth holding the lead rope attached to its halter. The family assured the Nativity Committee that it would be okay at least as far as docility was concerned. But one evening when the calf defecated right on the set, the city folks were appalled, and it had to go. The sheep and goat remained; they were more manageable and so were their turds.

More so than in some years, the makeup of the cast generated debate between Immanuel Lutheran's Worship Committee and Nativity Committee. A couple of the Worship Committee members opposed allowing a Holstein calf on the set because the species wasn't authentic for depicting Bethlehem 2,000 years ago. However, that was minor compared with the debate about the gender of the infant in the role of baby Jesus. The best the Nativity Committee could do this year was the four-month-old daughter of the Clarks. One Worship Committee member even hinted that it was blasphemy, allowing a female infant to play the role of Jesus. The Nativity Committee prevailed when Maria won the debate, arguing that this was just play acting and not like communion. She firmly believed that Jesus wouldn't be offended, so why should they?

For many families it was a tradition driving to Clareton to view the nativity scene on a Wednesday or Saturday evening of the two weeks preceding Christmas. Many would drive around town looking at decorated houses and stop for pie and coffee at a café. From 6:00 to 8:00 p.m. they could stop in the church fellowship hall for coffee and Christmas cookies if they didn't mind being obligated to leave an offering in the coffee can at the end of the counter of the church kitchen.

As much as Mario had resisted the nativity scene assignment, eventually he warmed to it by the contentment of being a part of the group and the attention of the spectators. He actually thought about the meaning of Christmas. It helped calm the anxiety and loneliness the season often brought. Without school and with many friends gone or busy with their families, and with no cousins, uncles or aunts around it was too quiet at home over the holiday break. Standing there by the manger with the others helped.

Maria often talked about going to California over the holidays but the drive was too long, the weather uncertain, and the money always tight. She was lonesome, too. Sometimes late at night Mario could overhear her crying softly into the phone, talking with her mother in California. It made him feel a little sad until his thoughts wandered off to recall earlier visits there to see her and his cousins. Sometimes when the Mickey Mouse clock approached midnight, Mario didn't think Grandma Ruiz stayed up that late until he remembered that they were two hours earlier. He wondered what it would be like in southern California in December with mild weather and no snow. In photos of the holidays in warm climates Christmas trees, Santa, and decorations looked out of place. How could they get through winter without ice skating, hockey, or sliding down hills on toboggans and sleds?

The spectator traffic past the nativity scene had tapered considerably by 8:00 p.m. Mario hurried into the church fellowship hall for some cookies and hot chocolate. He could eat sugary rosettes all night. He got three before they were all gone and then took four frosted sugar cookies to sustain him on the five-block walk home.

Approaching the bungalow, it was a pleasant surprise to see Thelma's car parked in front. It was nice to have company. Even though he didn't have much to say when she was there, he liked listening to Thelma's cheerful and lively conversation. He noticed another vehicle parked behind Thelma's. He recognized it as a '57 Buick but didn't think anything of it.

"Her real name's Corinne," Thelma said. "But when she was little, she couldn't pronounce it right. It came out as Coya. I think it's a really nice name. Very unique."

"She's very unique," Maria said. "I can't imagine going through what she's done. The good old boys finally got her out, but she won't be forgotten. She'll make a comeback. I wish I lived up there just so I could have voted for her."

The news story in the *Chronicle* about Andy Knutson's demand for $3,000 "rent" for his wife's office space in their Oklee hotel launched the discussion about Minnesota's celebrity congresswoman. Coya Knutson was elected in 1954 and served two terms until her defeat in the November 4th election, caused by a letter during the campaign allegedly written by her husband. He demanded that she come home from Washington, leave her successful political career and go back to being a wife and mother. A slim majority of voters in her district agreed. Apparently, it was no matter that the substance of the marriage had dissipated over the years and their adopted son went with Coya to Washington where he attended a private school. Headlines screaming "Coya, Come Home!" polarized voters in northwest Minnesota's Ninth District.

"It's just criminal what they did," Thelma said.

"I enjoy teaching. She enjoyed teaching," Maria said. "But if she wants to run for Congress and have a career in politics, good for her! She did a really good job, too. I think that's what got to some people the most. She was in there fighting for the ordinary citizens and the farmers, what was best for them and not just for the party fat cats. She stood up to them, and now they got her back."

"That's politics for you."

The doorbell rang, ending the discussion. The women looked at one another, wondering who that could be. Jim or Horace would have entered through the kitchen door, rapping on the window as they came in. Mario would have done the same except for the knock but would have hollered, "Hi, Mom. I'm home!" The front doorbell was a mystery. Maria switched on the outside light and opened the door. She greeted the police chief but didn't invite him in right away, her suspicion equaling if not exceeding his.

"Hello, Maria. May I come in? I'd just like to ask a few more questions if you don't mind."

Chief Stark entered the small living room and sat on one end of the couch opposite Thelma. On TV the "I've Got a Secret" show was just starting.

"That's a good show," he said nodding toward the TV. "Sometimes I can't decide between that and Jerry Lewis."

"How can I help you?" Maria asked, trying to be polite.

"I drove by the nativity scene on the way over. Very nice. You folks did a good job. Was Marion in there by any chance?"

"He was. He should be home any minute now."

"We're very fortunate that nothing bad happened last night out on the lake. I'll never forget the time we had to haul the Bergquist boy out of the water."

"I know it can be dangerous. I've talked to Mario about it, but he's a sensible kid."

"Well, just the same it can happen to anybody. If he's so sensible, though, what was he doing out at that Nathan guy's shack?"

"I don't really know. The kids have been out there a couple of times, I guess. It all started the day after Thanksgiving. Mario and a couple of his friends went out there and brought him some turkey sandwiches. I thought it was kind of nice."

"What's this assault thing you mentioned earlier?" Thelma asked.

"Well, I don't think it's all that serious. We had this complaint and we have to check it out."

"I've heard nothing bad about him . . . Tom . . . except maybe he drinks a bit too much," Thelma said. "I don't believe he'd hurt anyone. He just wants to be left alone. Is that so wrong?"

"You sure seem to know a lot about him," the chief said, lifting his head and looking straight at her. She felt her face become flush and thought it wiser to not respond.

"We just want to talk to him, really. We just want to help him," Stark continued. "You could help us and him by giving us a call the next time you see him. What if something worse happens, and we didn't do anything to prevent it?"

"We'll see what we can do," Maria replied. "Who was assaulted anyway?"

"I really can't say right now. It's under investigation. Like I said, it's not real serious, but somebody filed a complaint, and we have to investigate. You understand."

The kitchen door opened quickly and wide; Mario clumped in, stomping the snow off his boots on the doormat.

"Hi, Mom! I'm home."

"Hi, honey! How'd it go at the nativity scene?"

"Okay I guess. I just hope nobody recognized me."

Mario hung up his parka and went into the living room. He expected to see Thelma. He didn't expect to see the police chief. All the kids in town knew of Chief Stark. He pursued teenage minor traffic violations as though they were heinous crimes. Mario had hardly ever seen him this close before. Tuesday by the lake, it had been dark and everyone wore coats and hats. Here he was sitting about ten feet away right in the living room. The chief's bald head surprised Mario; he had never seen him without a hat. Except for the uniform, Mario didn't even recognize him at first. He looked huge in the small living room and must have been the source of the ominous scent Mario detected, a mixture of tobacco, cologne, and leather.

"Hello, son. We were just talking about your adventure out on the lake yesterday. We're relieved that you made it back okay. But don't do something dangerous like that again, okay?"

"We already talked about that," Maria said. "Chief Stark also wants to know if we can help them find Tom," she said to Mario. "They're doing an investigation, and they need to talk to him about the assault, the one he mentioned earlier."

"Who got beat up?" Mario asked.

"I can't tell you that right now," Stark said. "It happened Monday, though. I guess I can tell you that."

Mario hadn't heard of anyone in town getting beat up Monday other than Frank Harley. His throat tightened; his mouth became dry. Staring at the chief, he felt paralyzed. He had heard of kids going to reform school; he felt a weight of dread that the prospect might be in store for him.

Stark looked at the boy, and instantly knew that Mario knew something more. That could wait; apprehending Tom Nathan came first.

"Well Mrs. Reese—it is Mrs., right?—you've got a fine young man here," Stark said with a smile. "You should be proud of him. Raising a child on your own, that's got to have its trying moments."

"We get along fine, thank you." Maria repressed a flash of anger and ignored the question about her marital status. If he didn't know, he didn't need to; if he did know, he was just rubbing it in. She doubted that he knew. Few in town did and, as far as she knew, for the ones who did know it didn't matter. Over the years of their friendship she had only confided in Thelma, telling her everything. As for Jim, she had only told him what she thought he needed to know.

Although it was only seven years, it seemed so long ago. Sometimes she still felt guilty about changing her name. It just happened and she let it. Toward the end of August 1951 she had to make a decision. Only one week of summer school for the migrant kids remained and she hadn't thought much about returning to California.

ALREADY AT 9:00 A.M. ON THE AUGUST 1951 morning, the warm, muggy air promised another hot, humid dog day of summer. The leaves on the elm trees drooped limp and motionless. The church basement felt cool by comparison. Mrs. Bauer and several other farm wives had driven to migrant camps and fields picking up the small children and dropping them off at Immanuel Lutheran. Maria couldn't imagine how their parents and older siblings could survive the day out in the fields hoeing sugar beets or walking soybean fields, pulling weeds. At least she was happy to provide a refuge for the younger children.

She had heard stories about some migrant workers becoming ill from heat stroke, even dying from it. Some growers did not treat them well. The growers were supposed to provide housing. That was part of the deal. Sometimes that meant an old chicken coop. Since chickens didn't have electricity or running water, neither did the migrant tenants who followed them. Kerosene stoves and lanterns provided cooking and light. They hauled water in buckets from a hydrant in the barn, and outhouses were the standard.

They would rise before the sun, still sore from the hours of hoeing and chopping the day before, boil some coffee and force down tortillas, trying to get enough fuel for the long day ahead. The whole family piled into the pickup, papa and mama in the cab and any number of kids in the box. If the grower was fair and reasonable, the workers could take breaks anytime during the day to spend a few minutes in whatever shade they could find and guzzle tepid water.

Maria knew which growers were not fair, some even cruel, and it made her so angry. She did not feel comfortable talking with Mrs. Bauer about it. She got it out by telling Thelma in detail what life was like for some of the migrant workers. She felt especially sorry for the children just old enough to work in the fields. Most kids their age would be spending a summer day riding bikes, swimming, or playing baseball in the park. When they reached eight or nine years of age, migrant kids were expected to spend twelve hours, six days a week working in the fields alongside older youths and adults. At least they got paid the same. Some families with six or seven kids received substantial checks at the end of the season, but getting there was bitterly hard.

When Maria heard about one grower who docked the pay of workers when they took a water break, even on the extremely hot days, her anger drove her to the police station. When she talked about it with Mrs. Bauer nothing happened. When Mrs. Bauer found out that Maria had talked with the police, she scolded her. It wouldn't do any good anyway because the city police had no jurisdiction in the county. The sheriff said no one was breaking any laws, and no one was forcing the workers to stay on.

Every time Maria saw Chief Stark, it reminded her of their first encounter, of his callous attitude. It became clear to her that the local natives viewed migrant workers as little more than peasants. As long as they did their work and didn't cause trouble in town on Saturday nights, they were tolerated. The chief was quick to apprehend "the Mexicans" if they appeared to have had a little too much to drink, but it was no where near the average amount of the natives at any of the local clubs. In local shops, merchants' eyes followed them intently. The chief really didn't want to arrest them because that was more trouble than it was worth, so he was content to give a harsh verbal warning, salting the words with a few racial epithets. When one of the children told Maria about their family's encounter with Chief Stark, she boiled inside.

When she'd first met him and gave her name, he had not written it down nor asked her how to spell it. Had he known her real name, she didn't know if it would have made any difference. She was more bothered by the little lie about her marital status. When the chief made reference to it as if she had been married, she didn't know for sure if that's what he really believed or if he was mocking her. She wanted to tell him that it was none of his business.

"I'M SURE YOU DO GET ALONG FINE," Chief Stark replied. "But we still need your help getting to the bottom of this alleged assault." He looked at Mario. "If you can help us, we'd be much obliged. You know, really it's everyone's duty as a citizen. We police can't be everywhere all the time. We really rely on folks like you to help us from time to time."

"Why don't you just go out and arrest him?" Maria asked.

Stark's graying moustache twitched with an annoyance, beginning to remember the impertinent questions years ago. It transformed to a condescending exasperation. "It's not quite that simple. We need to have some evidence before we go out and arrest someone. We need to interview witnesses. Besides, where he lives isn't all that easy to get to. When the time is right, we'll see him in town and pick him for questioning."

"What if he doesn't come to town?"

"Well, if he doesn't because somebody warned him, that would make a whole lot more trouble now, wouldn't it?" Stark's eyebrows glowered noticeably looking first at Maria, then at Mario.

"I don't think it was him," Mario blurted out, breaking the tension of the moment. Maria suddenly remembered what he had told her Monday night. But she said nothing, waiting to see how far he would go. Chief Stark's annoyance turned to the boy.

"Well, if you know something you had better tell us. Did you see it happen? We know there were some witnesses. Were you one of them?"

Mario felt like his whole body was on fire inside. Confessing to his mom was one thing. He believed his life would be ruined if he was sent to reform school. With the chief's presence filling the small living room and his mom and Thelma looking on Mario's distraught uncertainty crumbled.

"It was me. I pounded Frank Harley."

Chief Stark smiled, almost friendly and understanding.

"I never said who it was, did I? Then you must have been there, a witness."

"I was there, but it was me, not Tom."

"I know how you feel. It might surprise you but this happens sometimes. People will confess to crimes they didn't commit." He leaned back looking over to Maria. "Who knows why? Maybe to protect someone? Maybe because they feel guilty for some other reason? Sometimes people do strange things."

He looked back at Mario. "So, if you were there, did you see Tom?"

"I don't know. I'm telling the truth about the fight. When somebody came in the alley from the other end, we all peeled out of there. I don't know who it was."

"You know, this is the hard part about being an investigator," Stark said. "You get all kinds of different stories. Young man, you know lying is very serious. In a court they call it perjury. You can be punished for that."

Mario's eyes started to fill up with tears. He couldn't tell which was greater, his anger or fear.

"My son is not a liar, Mr. Stark," Maria's sharp interjection punched through the chief's ominous presence.

They heard a knock on the side door by the kitchen. The door opened. "Anybody here? Hello, it's just me, Jim." He took off his coat and boots and walked through the kitchen to the living room. He looked around, quickly detecting the tension-filled atmosphere.

"Well, hello, Chief Stark. I didn't know you were here. Sorry if I interrupted anything. What's going on?" he asked, looking at the chief.

Chief Stark explained the reason for his presence. More than anything, he had started to become more curious about Maria's past and her present status as far as Jim was concerned. The dentist was well-liked and respected in the community. He had been pursued over the years by a number of young women but none of those relationships resulted in marriage. It angered Stark a bit that Jim's arrival diminished the chief's hold on the others. As he got up to leave, Chief Stark reminded them that they would be talking again soon.

ബ 14 ൽ

M RS. BAUER HAD ARRIVED AT 3:30 P.M. Thursday in late August
1951 right on time as she always did. She parked the '50 Chevy
Suburban by the curb in front of the church to wait for the children's release from summer school for the day. The weather had been
warmer than normal the past week; Mr. Bauer had predicted a thunderstorm by Friday. They could use a little rain, and most of the weeding
had been completed by the migrant workers. The children and their families would be moving on, some back to Texas, others to Nebraska, the
Dakotas or northwestern Minnesota to help with the wheat harvest.

The red-and-white Suburban stood out like a bright carnival ride
among the green background of lawns and leafy elm trees. It gave Mrs.
Bauer a happy reward every day to see the children rushing from the
church toward her parked vehicle. It would last only one more day and
then she would have to find something else to do in the mid-afternoon
although finding something to do never was a problem.

It wouldn't be long before harvest season and its long days and
sometimes nights. Although the men drove the tractors, combines, and
trucks, the women had plenty to do taking over more of the other chores

like feeding the hogs and chickens and milking the cows. They spent more time cooking, too, with more farmhands to feed during harvest. If rain threatened they worked non-stop. Sometimes the women took whole dinners out to the field and the workers ate with hardly stopping.

Awhile ago Mrs. Bauer had asked Maria what she planned to do after summer school ended. The same time she drove to the church each afternoon to pick up the migrant kids, she took Mario back from the farm where he had spent the day. Maria loved to hear him describe his daily adventures. She wished the summer would never end. With so much happening each day and so many things to experience in their new surroundings, thoughts about the impending decision drifted off into the background. She never gave Mrs. Bauer an answer because she didn't have one.

MARIA HAD FOUND A NEW LIFE FREE from the conflicts that had driven her here in the first place. It seemed like she had hardly spoken five words to her father since before Mario was born. A proud, traditional husband and father, Ricardo Ruiz became angry and almost distraught when he learned his only daughter was pregnant and not yet married. He had always warned her about the man she was seeing. He was much older than she. He had a good job, but he sometimes drank too much. While he seemed decent and pleasant most of the time, there were moments of bizarre behavior. Maria never would admit it, but Ricardo had heard stories from others.

No one even knew until she was almost full term. The thought was so remote in Ricardo's mind that even when Ruth told him he didn't believe it. She's just putting on some weight, he said.

"Maria! Maria! Come in here pronto! I must speak to you," Ricardo shouted.

Maria loved her father very much although he had a temper and could be too strict sometimes. She believed he only wanted to protect her, to make sure she got the very best in life. Maria sat in her room, stroked her swollen womb and cried.

"Who did this to you?" Ricardo shouted down the hallway to her room. "I'm going to get that bastard! It's that no-good bum you've been going out with."

Ricardo saw the dream vanish of his beautiful oldest child, his daughter, becoming happily married and presenting him with his first grandchild. He pushed open the door and entered her room. The sight of her sitting on the edge of her bed, hunched over and her bowed head turned away almost moved him to embrace her. His pride and anger held him back.

"I'm sorry, papa. I'm so sorry." Maria covered her face with her hands and turned away ashamed of her tears.

"You're a disgrace to the family! Do you know that? Have you no self-control?"

"Ricardo, please." Ruth pushed past her husband, sat next to her daughter and put her arm around her shoulders. "Try to understand Ricardo. She is your daughter."

"My *daughter* is not a tramp. *This* is a tramp," he shouted. He turned and left the house, slamming the back door.

He hardly acknowledged his grandson when Mario was born. Seeing her husband and daughter this way made Ruth Ruiz very sad. It was almost a relief when Maria and her infant son moved out of the Ruiz house into her own apartment. Ruth paid the rent out of her own earnings, which fueled many arguments with her husband. Things got better, at least financially, when they found a nanny for the baby and Maria got a teaching job. Her mother visited often as did her brothers.

On weekends Maria's brothers played in a mariachi band along with their father. Often Maria would go to see them play, but she and her father remained distant. At first Ruth and the boys became exasperated at their behavior. Eventually they became resigned. When Maria took the job teaching summer school in Minnesota, they thought it would only be temporary. Little Mario was going on five and they enjoyed having the little grandson and nephew around, except for Ricardo. Once when he was four, Mario asked grandma Ruth why grandpa didn't seem as friendly as the others. She started crying, and it made him feel sad. She cried again when Maria and Mario left for Minnesota in the summer of 1951. That was the second time he saw his grandmother cry. He didn't feel quite as sad the second time because they were so busy getting ready for the trip, which he greatly anticipated with excitement and some uncertainty.

Maria's brothers made sure the '41 Chevrolet could handle the 1,500-mile trip. They changed the oil, flushed the coolant and replaced the fan belt. The tires were okay. Oscar worried about the radiator hoses, but the others thought they still were in decent shape. It would be hot crossing the Mojave but not as hot as in August. They worried more about their sister, only twenty-four, and their young nephew traveling across the country alone.

Maria had purchased the car for $275 just before the end of the school year at a used car lot in Escondido. The odometer on the dark blue, two-door sedan registered more than 91,000 miles. Right after the school year ended in early June she went to work packing for the long trip. Mostly clothes because they planned to stay in Minnesota just for the summer migrant school session. Mrs. Bauer assured her that room and board would be provided.

Mario helped pack. He tried to imagine the long trip that lay ahead. He was excited and lonesome at the same time for his friends, uncles, and grandma. She had given him a new pair of blue jeans and tennis shoes—black high-tops with the white rubber soles—the kind he'd always wanted. The smell of the new jeans and shoes followed him into the front passenger seat, lingering until blending in with the dusty odor of the car's gray fabric interior.

They left San Diego just after 5:00 p.m. Saturday. Maria decided it was better to drive through the cool darkness of the desert night instead of the searing daytime heat, hoping that there would be no breakdowns. She mapped a route to just before Flagstaff, Arizona. From there they would leave Route 66 and drive north to see the Grand Canyon, and then northeast toward Colorado because she wanted to drive through the Rockies. After that she wasn't sure if they should go straight across

Nebraska, or head north toward the Black Hills and Mount Rushmore. They had a week to make the trip, so she thought that might give them enough time as long as the car held up. Mario had seen pictures of the four presidents sculpted on the granite mountain in South Dakota. He wanted to see Devil's Tower also, but his mom said they would have to wait and see how far it was and how much time they had.

"Okay, Mr. Navigator, are you ready to go? Can you check the map again?" Maria smiled, reached over and squeezed his hand. "We're off on our adventure." She shifted the car into gear and accelerated away from the curb. Everyone waved, "Adios." Mario looked back and saw his grandma dabbing her eye with a hanky. A thought flashed through his mind that he might never see them again. He rose up in the seat to keep looking back as long as he could still see them. He kept waving but the lump in his throat, which happened all of a sudden, wouldn't go away. He sat back down and stared ahead. Maria noticed a somber look on his face.

"Don't worry, honey. This'll be fun. We'll be back at the end of summer."

He tried to imagine when that would be. He could see the future for about the next week laid out before him in the red line marking their route on the road map across his lap. After that it faded into mist, obscuring any idea of what lie beyond including the end of summer. He had studied the maps and knew where Minnesota was, but little else.

They headed north, reaching Escondido in about half an hour. They planned to stop in San Bernardino for something to eat. Maria hoped that would be before 7:00 p.m.. Then they would head for Barstow out in the Mojave. Mario alternated between studying the road map and looking at the passing scenery. By they time they reached San Bernardino, Mario was getting hungry.

"Can we stop at a drive-in?" He liked drive-ins. It was fun to sit in the car under the canopy. Maria would have preferred a diner where she could get out of the car and sit inside with air conditioning. It was still very hot, but she figured she could wait until the cool night air of the desert. Besides, they could get out of the car and stretch their legs when they stopped for gas before the trip across the desert.

The car hop glided up to the driver's window on roller skates. They all wore white sleeveless blouses, red pedal pushers, and white roller skates. Mario marveled at how they could skate and balance the food trays at the same time. Their tray arrived, and he eagerly awaited his basket full of French fries, the chili dog, and a chocolate malt. Maria had a California burger, fries, cole, slaw and a Coke.

For the first time, Mario thought about the long ride ahead, across the desert and at night. He had never spent the night traveling in a car before. He thought about his room and own bed back at the apartment. He had to go to the bathroom. Maria was anxious to get going.

"Can't you wait a while, honey? We'll be stopping for gas soon. I think their bathrooms might be little cleaner." He couldn't, and she watched while he walked over to the bathroom. It would be a long drive yet to Barstow where she planned to gas up.

She hoped a mechanic would be on duty at one of the service stations in Barstow. She would feel more confident about the night drive across the desert if everything got one last look. She hoped she wouldn't have to change a tire. Her brothers drilled her on the task, making her do so three times. She knew she could do it. They made her take an extra spare tire even though it took up more room. The main problem would be getting at the spares under all the luggage in the trunk. Dusk began to settle in by the time they reached Barstow. If all went well, they would be in Arizona by daybreak.

The old Chevy pulled out of the service station and headed east on Route 66. Maria looked over at her son, smiled and crossed her fingers. He felt secure and excited at the same time. He gazed out the window, every mile a new adventure. The lights of Barstow faded into the distance behind them. Ahead lay a darkening desert sky. Mario leaned forward to look up out the front windshield for stars. As they drove on into the desert night twinkling stars exploded across the night sky. Mario had never seen so many. He could make out the Milky Way and found the

North Star. The only other light came from the Chevy's headlights casting a feeble orange glow on the road ahead. Occasionally pinpoints of bright light appeared far down the road ahead moving closer, getting larger and quickly rushing by in a swoosh of wind and noise, mostly large trucks. Mario fiddled with the radio dial. The farther they went the weaker the KBAR signal became.

"Let's just turn that off for a while," Maria said. "It's so beautiful out here. Let's just enjoy the peace and quiet." The Chevy's six-cylinder cruised smoothly along, harmonizing with the tires spinning over the pavement, their sounds whipped around by the sea of air as the car pushed through at fifty-five miles per hour.

"Mom, how long is it going to take to get there?"

"I told you a whole week and then some. We've got a lot to see along the way. Aren't you excited about seeing the Grand Canyon and the Rockies?"

Mario sat back in his seat. Much of the excitement had burned off and fatigue began to settle in. In the weeks before the trip they had gone to the library to learn about the places they would be seeing. They mapped their route to include the Grand Canyon, then go northeast to the Four Corners. Maria still wasn't sure if they would take the southern route into Colorado crossing the San Juan Mountains or head north to Grand Junction. She worried a bit whether the car would make it over the high passes or if the brakes would hold up on the way down. She didn't mention that to Mario. He could hardly wait to see the sights and places they had read about. But at the moment he wanted to be in his own bed.

Mario crawled into the back seat so he could lie down and stretch all the way out. Maria kept the window open so the cool night air could help keep her awake along with the coffee. Mario lay wrapped in a blanket and dozed, finally falling into a child's serene sleep. It always impressed Maria how young children could sleep so well once they got there. She looked back at him, content that he was sleeping; it gave her all the more resolve to try stay alert and fend off her own fatigue. She poured coffee from the thermos, gingerly balancing the cup on the car seat. The more she drank the more she had to go to the bathroom. It was late when they stopped at the little service station/café in the desert village.

Maria pulled up to the gas pump looking, around not sure if the place was open or closed. A single lamp shed a cone of light from a pole next to the service station section. The gas gauge read one-third. She didn't want to risk going any farther without a fill. Perhaps she could pull off to the side and stay the remainder of the night. It was almost 11:00 p.m. A light shone from a window in back of the restaurant.

"What in tarnation you doing out here this time of night?"

Maria jumped at the sound of a raspy voice. She hadn't seen him walk out from the small living quarters behind the café and approach the car from behind. She whipped around in the seat and saw a man, long white hair askew, a beard, suspenders holding up wrinkled blue jeans over a stained union suit. He walked up to the car and leaned on the door.

"You need gas, we got gas. No hot food, but we got some hot coffee. Don't you know what time it is?"

"I'm sorry."

"Well, don't worry. We'll get what you need and you can be on your way. Aren't you worried about being out here alone at night?"

"I guess I never really thought about it. We're going to Minnesota."

"Minnesota? Where the hell's that?"

"In the Midwest. Up north."

"Well at least it's got to be cooler there than this hell hole in summer."

"It gets hot up there in summer, too. Maybe not quite at hot as here, but it's more humid, so that makes it seem hotter."

"Always somthin, ain't it," he laughed. "Pull over to the pump there so we can get you gassed up. I'll check the oil and water, too. If you need to use the ladies room just go inside the café. Door's open, light's behind the cash register."

The sound of voices and the absence of engine noise stirred Mario from his sleep. He sat up, rubbed his eyes and looked around.

They were at a service station, but it was all dark. The car hood was up, and someone was leaning over the fender doing something to the engine. He realized he was alone in the car.

"Mom!"

An old man pulled back from the open hood and looked back into the car.

"Well, hello there, young man. Didn't see you there at first. Your mom's inside using the bathroom. You need anything? A soda? A candy bar? You probably should use the bathroom, too."

He wiped his hands on an oil-stained rag. He peered into the open driver's side window.

"I'm Mo. What's your name?"

"Mario."

"Hello there, Mario. And how old are you?"

"Almost five."

"Well, you keep an eye on your mom now. You folks got a long road ahead. Should be a lot of fun though. If I was younger, I'd take a long trip again."

"How'd you get named Mo?"

"Oh, that goes so far back I can hardly remember. I guess when I was a little tyke I used to stand up on my high chair and holler, 'Mo, mo,' when I wanted more food or candy or something. That's what my folks said anyway. My real name's Maurice so I guess that fits anyway."

Inside the café, Mo filled Maria's thermos. She paid for the gas. He wouldn't take any money for the coffee. Said it was getting too old and stale. He reached in the cooler and gave her a Milky Way.

"Here. Take this for the young man. You go on now and have a good trip. Sometimes I wish I could leave this place and move on, but I'm too old for that now. Sometimes the missus says we should move. Then we sit out in back in the evening and watch the stars come out. It's so quiet and peaceful. We been here twenty-six years. Maybe you can just send us a postcard."

"We will. How about from Mount Rushmore?"

"That'd be nice. Just send it to Mo's Service here in Fenner. Don't need no more address than that. I'm the postmaster, too."

After the gas stop, Mario tried to sleep again but couldn't. They drove on through the night mostly in silence. Maria wanted him to try go back to sleep although part of her wanted him awake so there'd be someone to talk to and help her fend off fatigue. He finally dozed off, sinking down sideways in the front passenger seat, his head resting on her lap. She stroked his hair and wondered if they were doing the right thing. She felt pulled both ways, by what adventure lay ahead and by lonesome thoughts about her family, friends, and the home she had left. The fatigue became almost unbearable when the pink glow of early dawn crept up on the eastern horizon. She began to question whether or not it was such a smart thing to do, to drive all night.

By mid-morning they made it to Williams, Arizona, the turn-off north to the Grand Canyon. Maria pulled off to a side street in town and napped for an hour; Mario couldn't sleep in the bright morning sun. He passed the time trying to read, looking at the map, and just sitting there. Becoming more and more bored and hungry he finally poked his mom's shoulder.

After lunch at a café, they drove north to see the Grand Canyon. A thunderstorm fired up in the afternoon heat. They watched it from the car parked at an overlook on the south rim. The dark, roiling clouds and rain shrouded the vast canyon that seemed to swallow the lightning bolts. The storm passed to the east reopening the sky to the sunlight; it glowed off the canyon walls streaked with shadows, as if the dark blue storm cloud had stained them. They got out of the car to gaze in awe from the stone fence along the rim.

"Should we get a postcard for Mo from here?" Mario asked.

"Oh, I'm sure they've seen this before. Let's wait awhile. Wait 'til Mount Rushmore. They probably haven't been there."

That evening they stayed in a tourist cabin near the park. For supper, Maria heated a can of chili on the small stove and made bologna sandwiches. They went to bed early; she quickly fell asleep. Mario lay awake, adjusting more slowly to the new surroundings, thinking about the new sights and experiences of the past two long days. He felt lonesome again for the familiar world they had left behind. He awoke to the sound of Maria making coffee. Bright morning sunshine almost filled the cabin not much filtered by the light blue calico curtains over the two windows.

"Good morning, sleepy head," Maria smiled over at her son. "Did you sleep well?"

"Okay I guess." Mario sat up, rubbing his eyes, the loneliness of the previous night replaced by a hungry stomach. He smelled his favorite breakfast. Tortillas were warming up in a frying pan; Maria plopped a column of refried beans down the center of each and rolled them up. She poured a cup of milk and set out a plate with two bean burritos.

"Here you go, sweetie. Let's try to hurry though because we've got another long day of driving ahead."

Mario didn't need encouragement to eat quickly. He had learned the art of consuming large amounts of food quickly from watching his uncles at Ruiz family meals. It was not a matter of scarcity—Ruth Ruiz would never allow that—but more a competition among the boys in survival of the fittest.

They drove away from the cabin a few minutes after 8:00 a.m., the bright morning sun well on its way across the sky approaching the longest day of summer. They crossed the Little Colorado River and passed by the canyons and mountains of northeast Arizona. As they drove, Maria described the geology and native people of the region. Mario had seen pictures. Now he felt the emptiness of such wide-open spaces. Maria tried to explain that it was not empty; up close one could find countless species of flora and fauna, insects and microbes, but not many people. Biology had been her major at the teachers' college.

She hoped that they would have enough time to make the trip and be able to stop and see the sights along the way. The Grand Canyon would be hard to top, although when they stopped at the Four Corners monument Mario had doubled the number of states he had been in to a total of six. He didn't remember much about their visit to Hoover Dam two years before, which took them to Nevada. Now he stood in Arizona, Utah, New Mexico, and Colorado all the same time. He took a picture with the camera aimed down at his feet by the Four Corners marker.

Maria decided to head east toward Durango, across southern Colorado, then head up the east slope of the Rockies toward Denver. She felt a little uneasy about the car holding up on the higher elevations to the north. Halfway between Four Corners and Durango, they took a side trip to see the ancient ruins at Mesa Verde.

"What happened to the Indians?" Mario asked.

"They're still here, at least their descendents are. We'll learn about that when we go on the tour. We'll get to climb up in some places. That should be really interesting."

"But why did they go away?"

"That happened hundreds and hundreds of years ago. We don't really know for sure. Some people think it might have been disease, or maybe a war. Maybe it was a drought so they couldn't grow food."

"Where did they come from?"

"Thousands of years ago people migrated here. We think they came from Asia to Alaska and then spread over North America."

"How did they get across the water?"

"Well, because the ocean was a lot lower then. There were a lot more glaciers holding the water in ice. We think they just walked across the Bering Strait between Russia and Alaska. Who knows? We might even be related. Grandpa Ruiz grew up in Mexico, and some of his ancestors were Indians."

"What about grandma?"

"She came from Iowa."

"Where's that?"

"It's just south of Minnesota, where we're going."

"Will we go through Iowa?"

"Not on the route we're taking. Maybe on the way back we can go that way."

"Why did she come from Iowa?"

"Well, that's where she grew up. She's not part Indian though. Her parents came from Norway—that's in Europe. She left the farm when she was about twenty and went to California. She wanted to be a movie star. But, she met grandpa instead and here we are."

"What about her mom and dad?"

"They died a few years back. You probably wouldn't remember. They were your great-grandparents."

"Am I part Norway?"

"It's Norwegian. Like, you live in America so you're an American. You add an 'N' to the name of where you're from, but not always. I suppose that makes us San Diegoans or San Diegans—that sounds funny—or Californians. Yes, you are part Norwegian, part Mexican and maybe even part Indian if you go way back. It doesn't make any difference though because you're all American."

"What about my dad?"

Maria looked straight ahead at the road. Mario looked at her, waiting for an answer. Back in San Diego with all the family around, the question hadn't really surfaced. He sensed Maria becoming tense. He understood only that the lively conversation was somehow ending, and he felt badly.

"I think I've told you that your dad died a long time ago right after you were born. He was killed in a car accident." Maria repressed the feeling of guilt from actually voicing the lie.

"Was he an American?"

"Of course he was an American. He wasn't a Mexican or Indian."

Maria changed the subject. "Are you getting hungry? We'll find a place to stay in Durango and then get something to eat. How's that?"

RIDING EAST FROM DURANGO, MARIO gazed at the snow-tipped peaks of the San Juan Mountains. He had seen pictures of snow and tried to imagine what it was like. The road over Wolf Creek Pass took them temptingly close. Maria, more concerned about the car, decided to keep on going. Mario tried to protest. They passed by melting drifts of snow right at the edge of the road. He wanted to build a snowman like the one on the Christmas card.

In the afternoons, after driving all day they started looking for roadside cabins or motor hotels. Heading north toward Denver along the east slope of the Rockies, the scenery became a minor disappointment compared to the anticipation of craggy, snow-covered high mountain passes. The flat plains to the east melted off into the horizon. They left Denver for Cheyenne, Wyoming. In the far northwest corner of Nebraska, Maria knew of a prehistoric archeological dig where eons of wind and water erosion had exposed fossils and petrified bones of dinosaurs. Mario had read about dinosaurs and became enthralled at drawings of what they might have looked like.

"Mom, what happened to dinosaurs? How come they're not around anymore?"

"We don't know for sure. That was a long time ago. Some scientists think that some big disaster happened, like a huge meteor crashing into the earth." Right away Maria regretted saying what she did. She knew what the next question would be.

"What if it happens again? Would we all die?"

"Okay, let's try this. Pick a number between, say, one and five million. Just do it."

Mario looked out the window trying to think of a number.

"You have one? Okay, now I'm going to try guess what it is. I'll say it's 256,378. Is that it?"

"No."

"See? We could just keep on doing this and never guess the right number. So you don't have to worry about it."

"But what if you got the right number?"

"Well, then I guess we'd just have to say our prayers and hope for the best."

Mario could tell she was getting a little exasperated, so he let it drop.

"How long is it going to be before we get to Mount Rushmore?"

"I don't know. I'm guessing around five o'clock. Maybe if we find a place to stay we can drive up there in the evening. I guess it's really pretty in the evening."

"Maybe we can get a postcard for Mr. Mo."

"That would be nice. I'm sure he would appreciate that."

After the dry plains of western Nebraska the Black Hills in South Dakota seemed almost more spectacular than the Rockies. Eons ago they were even higher than the Rockies. Millennia of erosion wore them down to 6,000-foot peaks covered with patches of spruce. The malleable granite of a small peak about twenty-three miles southwest of Rapid City, named after a pioneer speculator and developer, had the necessary attributes for the vision of Gutzon Borglum and the promoters of South Dakota. The region was a sacred place for the native Dakota peoples. After Borglum and crew completed the carvings on Mount Rushmore in 1941 it became a destination for millions of American pilgrims. The project began in 1927, an attempt by local visionaries to create something so spectacular it would become a major tourist attraction. Over the years they unveiled the faces of four presidents, Washington in 1934, Jefferson in 1936, Lincoln in 1937, and Theodore Roosevelt in 1939.

Mario gazed at the faces in the mountainside. He tried to imagine how they could have been sculpted. He looked around at all the other people. Some talked with funny accents and a few in different languages. He soon became bored standing there and looking up at the faces. After traveling all that way and having all that anticipation, the short time they spent there somehow didn't measure up. He took some pictures with the Polaroid. He took a picture of Maria with the mountain in the background. A man with another family offered to take a picture of both of them together. It was past suppertime, and Mario remembered he was hungry. They went back into the visitors' center cafeteria and Maria ordered hamburger, fries, and malts.

"Can we get a postcard now for Mr. Mo?"

"Sure. But don't forget grandma and grandpa and your uncles. We should send them one, too."

Mario picked out two postcards from a rack in the souvenir store. Both showed Mount Rushmore. One was just a picture; the other a collage with the faces, a buffalo, and Devil's Tower. He still wanted to go there but Maria had said no; it was too far out of the way.

"Can I write on them? What should I say?"

"Oh, I don't know. Just tell them what you've seen. What you've liked best so far. Things like that."

Mario started with the Mount Rushmore picture card, which he decided would go to Mr. Mo. "Dear Mr. and Mrs. Mo. We saw Mount Rushmore today. It is very nice. We saw the mountains and the Grand Canyon. Thank you for the candy bar. Mario Ruiz."

"That's very nice. They'll like that."

He thought for a moment before starting on the other card. "Dear grandma, grandpa, Oscar, Juan, and Reynaldo, We are having a good time. Riding in the car is very long. I liked the mountains."

"I can't think of anything else to say."

"That's plenty. That's very good. I'll add a note, too." Maria felt proud every time she saw Mario reading and learning how to write. Back home she worked on it with him every day. She felt confident that he would do very well in school.

Leaving Rapid City and the Black Hills felt like leaving a lush, pleasant oasis and heading out into a barren, forbidding desert. The South Dakota heat rivaled the Mojave. At least there was a town about every twenty miles. The signs caught Maria's attention as they did for thousands of other travelers across South Dakota in the summer.

Get a soda
Get a root beer
Turn next corner
Just as near
To Highway 16 and 14
Free Ice Water
Wall Drug

181

They turned off Highway 14 into the little town of Wall. They saw the free ice water sign at the drug store. They did not see any open parking spaces for a whole block either side of Wall Drug.

"My goodness. This must be a popular place."

Maria drove around the block and found a parking place.

"This is really something. I can't believe all these people out here in the middle of nowhere stopping at a drug store of all places."

They found two open stools at the lunch counter. It was too early for lunch so they just ordered malts from the young man behind the counter.

"So where you folks from?"

"California."

"You on vacation? I suppose you've been to the Hills. Or are you heading there?"

"We just came from there. We're going to Minnesota."

"Oh, that's a nice place. We get lots of folks from there in here. Some of those Norwegians are a little stuffy, but they're decent," he laughed. "You going to visit relatives or something?"

"No. I'm going to be teaching. Summer school for migrant worker kids."

"Well that's very nice. Say, on your way back be sure to come this way and stop in. I've got some big plans to really fix this place up. Pretty soon everyone's going to know about Wall Drug. I made these signs." He reached under the counter and held up a sign. "I'm going to give them to tourists to bring home put 'em up. You want one?"

Mario wanted one to add to his growing collection of souvenirs. He remembered the instructions that Bill had given them. The simple white painted plywood had only the name Wall Drug in green letters. Back home you had to add the number of miles from there to Wall, South Dakota, and an arrow pointing in that direction. Mario couldn't make up his mind if he should put it up when they got to Minnesota or wait until they returned to California. The thought made him feel a little homesick again.

ᴤ 15 ᴂ

He jumped at the sound of a voice from behind the evergreen shrubs along the sidewalk.

"Mario. It's me. Tom. It's okay. I just need to talk to you."

Many times walking home after school or especially after dark his imagination got loose whenever he passed by that spot. The shrubs stood so close to the sidewalk that someone could hide in there and grab you in an arm's length. In his thoughts Mario had practiced the drill many times what he would do. A couple of times he even practiced leaping sideways while jerking down with his arm nearest the prickly branches. He tried to make sure no one was looking first.

It wouldn't have worked anyway. When he heard the voice it startled him. Then he just froze, failing to execute the sideways maneuver.

"What are you doing here?"

Tom moved sideways a bit so Mario could see him but remained amid the foliage.

"I just came from the vet. Ike got hurt real bad the other night. I went into town after you left. When I got back he was all beat up with rocks and things."

Mario just stood there staring at him.

"It's okay. I'm not drunk. I'm not going to hurt you. I just want to find out about Ike."

"Is he okay?"

"The vet said he'll recover, but he might be blind in one eye."

"Who did it?" Mario felt bad for Ike.

"I know it was some kids from town here. Maybe you and your friends could help me find out."

"Did anyone see you come to town?"

"Maybe. I don't know. I been to town a lot. Nobody seems to pay much attention most of the time. I just get what I need and go back. Right now I just thought it would be best to stay out of sight, especially near the school and all. Why?"

Mario remembered what Chief Stark said the previous evening. He paused trying to decide what to say.

"The cops are looking for you."

"For me? What for?"

Mario paused again, trying to weigh the consequences. He knew the truth about the fight Monday. He feared what might happen if he were caught squealing to Tom about what the police chief said.

"They think you beat up Frank Harley."

"What? Who's Frank Harley? Where did you hear that?"

It was out now. Mario couldn't hold back even if it meant going to reform school.

"He's a kid in my class. The police chief came over to our house last night. He found out that I'd been out to your shack. I got in trouble because it got late and they were out looking for me."

"I'm sorry. I knew I shouldn't have done that. Leave that note and then blabber on so long. It's all my fault. I didn't even think you'd actually come out there. So what did he say at your house?"

"He said they were looking for you for beating up Frank. I said I did it, and he didn't believe me. I even showed him my sore hand. He kind of laughed and said it probably happened playing hockey or something."

"Did you tell anyone else, about the fight?"

"I told my mom right after it happened. She believed me."

"What did she say when you told the chief that you did it and he didn't believe you?"

"She got real mad. She said I wasn't a liar."

"What did the chief say?"

"I don't think he really said anything back. Jim, that's my mom's boyfriend, he came over just then, and the police chief left."

"Well, Mario, thanks for telling me. Where are you going now? I'd still like to find out from you kids who it was that hurt Ike. You and those other two kids, Jake and Rosalyn."

"I was going home. I was going get some money and meet Jake at the bowling alley."

"Can I meet you kids downtown later? To find out about Ike? Let's say about five in the alley next to the bowling alley. I got to wait for dark, but it shouldn't be too late for you to make it home in time for supper."

Mario agreed although he wasn't sure how he would explain it to Jake. He probably would have to call Rosalyn, too. He couldn't think of who might have hurt Ike. He hoped Jake and Rosalyn wouldn't mind meeting Tom and that they might have some ideas. He couldn't understand why someone would hurt a dog like that. He knew some of the big kids in high school could be mean sometimes. Maybe Jake could see if Larry might know something.

Walking the rest of the way home, Mario started thinking back when they first came to town. He remembered the Bauer farm. Over the years he had been able to visit during the summer. Each passing year he was able to help more and more with chores. This past summer they thought he was finally old enough and big enough to help bale hay.

Not long after school ended for the summer, Mr. Bauer called and asked if Mario could help with baling. He had just mowed the second cutting of alfalfa. It would have to dry a few days and if the rain held off they would be ready to go. He would pay Mario fifty cents an hour. Mario had been trying to hang on to the twenty dollars he had earned so he could buy Christmas presents with his own money. Whenever he was tempted to spend some prematurely, he remembered the hot, itchy and strenuous work.

MARIO AND THE BAUERS' OLDEST BOY had stood on the hay rack behind the baler being pulled by Mr. Bauer on the Farmall tractor. Darwin Bauer grabbed the bales coming off the conveyor from the baler and tossed them to Mario who started stacking them in the back. He braced himself for each one in case it came too hard striking him on his leg. Without gloves, his fingers started to get sore, but with gloves it would have been harder to grab the twine holding the bales together. Years of farm work gave Darwin, now thirty-two, calloused hands and well-muscled back and arms. Mario tried to ignore the pain from the raw skin spreading across the palms of his hands.

They laid down one layer almost to the front of the hay rack, then started another layer from the back. Mr. Bauer said that helped even out the weight. They built successive layers in steps leading up to the start of the top layer.

When Mr. Bauer first called, he advised Maria to make sure Mario wore a long-sleeved shirt and hat. When she relayed this to Mario, he argued about the shirt because of the heat. In summer he always wore white t-shirts. On the hay rack, hot, sweaty, tired and itching from the hay, he began to understand the wisdom of Mr. Bauer's advice. He was ready for the mid-morning break.

They all cheered at the sight of the pickup bouncing toward them across the alfalfa field. Mrs. Bauer drove up and shut off the engine. Mr. Bauer shut down the tractor. Mario sat on the top layer of bales momentarily transfixed by the sudden intense silence. He surveyed the fields dotted with farm groves reaching all around him to the hazy blue horizon, the fields of green wheat and neat rows of tiny corn stalks, the bright sun of a mid-morning in June and the warbling song of a meadowlark.

After three hours of hard work they still had about seven hours to go. He had never felt so tired before. He worried about making it through the rest of the day. He thought about what lay ahead, the hottest part of the day. His friends would be swimming at the lake.

Darwin jumped off the hay rack. He lowered the pickup tailgate and lifted a two-gallon insulated jug and four plastic cups from the cardboard box in back. The ice cold, sweet and sour tangy lemonade sent new energy surging through Mario's sore arms, legs, and especially his back. They each drank several cups. Then it was back to work.

After the break, Mario thought he could make it until dinner at noon. Back in the dining room of the big farmhouse Mrs. Bauer would serve up a smorgasbord of meat, potatoes, vegetables, fresh bread, coffee, milk, more lemonade, and pie. The towering limbs of two huge cottonwoods sheltered the farmhouse from the midday sun, making it about ten degrees cooler inside. The first house built by Mrs. Bauer's grandfather burned down in 1886. They replaced it with a much larger house, two stories with five bedrooms. The cottonwoods had been growing since 1881. It felt good to get out of the sun and sit down.

"Mario, it's so nice to have you visit us again." Mrs. Bauer carried in a bowl of creamy mashed potatoes and set it on the dining room table. "Maybe you don't think so—having to work so hard this time. You're doing a good job I hear."

She went several times between the kitchen and dining room carrying food: ham, fried chicken, mashed potatoes, peas and carrots, big slices of fresh homemade bread. "This'll put some muscle on you. You men be sure to eat up good now." After the morning's work this time Mario accepted being included with the men, not like when Grandma Ruiz said it.

Finally Mrs. Bauer sat down at the table. Mr. Bauer and his son had already started eating; Mario followed their lead. Mrs. Bauer scolded that they hadn't said grace. The men stopped chewing and bowed, waiting for her to start. She did and they followed in unison.

"God is great. God is good. We thank him for our food. By his hand we all are fed. Give us Lord our daily bread. In Jesus' name we pray, amen."

Even after seven summers of daytrips to the Bauer farm, Mario remained impressed at the appetites of the Bauers. They filled and re-filled their plates. Mario tried to keep up. By the time they got to the pie, they were slowing down a bit. Darwin looked up from his plate at Mario.

"So, Marion, how'd you get a name like that?"

"Darwin, what kind of question is that?" Mrs. Bauer shot a scolding glance at her son. "And his real name's Mario."

"I don't know. Just curious."

"And besides, Marion's a nice name. A man's name," Mrs. Bauer said. "You know the movie actor John Wayne? That's his real name, Marion Morrison. He came from Iowa, too."

"That's where my grandma came from," Mario said.

"Oh, really? Grandma Ruiz? I didn't know that. Where in Iowa?" Mrs. Bauer asked.

"I'm not sure. Maybe near Des Moines. That's the capital city. She was from a farm around there."

"How interesting. I always thought she was, you know, Spanish."

"She's Norwegian."

"Really? Well, it's a small world, isn't? So, how did she end up in California?"

"I don't know."

"Oh, I'm sorry. I shouldn't be asking you all these questions. I just remember when you first came here. You were so cute. I remember you and your mom talking in Spanish. You didn't really look Spanish or Mexican, if you know what I mean. I just assumed that you were, at least mostly. Can you still speak Spanish?"

"You should talk, ma, about asking questions," Darwin paused chewing, with a disapproving look at his mother.

"That's okay," Mario said. "Sometimes we speak Spanish at home. I've forgotten a lot, though. Grandma and my uncles, when they call, sometimes they do. My mom says I'm bilingual."

"So, when you're a Reese you speak English, and as a Ruiz you speak Spanish," Darwin laughed.

"Darwin! What a thing to say!" Mrs. Bauer exclaimed.

"Didn't they change their names or something?" Mr. Bauer asked. "I kind of remember something about that."

"I guess so," Mario said, starting to feel uncomfortable.

AT THE TIME MRS. BAUER HAD AGREED with the school secretary that it might be a good idea. After Maria had decided to stay and take the full-time teaching job in Clareton, she went to the school office to enroll Mario in kindergarten. She felt badly that her family would not see their first nephew and grandson off to his first day of school. Her main support in Clareton came from the Bauers and Thelma Harris, the high school senior she had met during the summer teaching the migrant kids. She wondered if her father would ever fully accept his grandson who did not have his father's surname in a union blessed by the church.

THE LINOLEUM FLOOR OF THE MAIN HALL at Clareton's Floyd B. Olson Elementary School had gleamed in the light entering the main door. Maria took Mario's hand. She tried to offer him a reassuring smile as they stepped in from the bright late August morning in 1951 to the darkened building. Light from the main office beamed across the hallway floor at the far end. The pungent, antiseptic scent of detergents and floor wax energized Maria. Mario tried to understand. He wanted to say something, that his life would change and he did not want it to, but he did not have the words. The door closed behind them in the dark hallway, shutting out the sun, the clouds, the sweet scent of cut grass floating in the breeze, the leafy trees, and the melodies of robins and finches.

"Good morning. How can I help you?"

A stout, middle-aged woman in a loose-fitting dark-blue dress looked up from a stack of papers on her desk. Tilting her face downward she looked at them over her rimless glasses that sat halfway down her nose, her graying hair wrapped in a bun. A fine silver chain draped around the back of her neck and hung from the bows of her glasses. She introduced herself as the school secretary. Maria said they needed to register for school, which started next Tuesday right after Labor Day. The secretary appeared somewhat perturbed. *Why do these people come in at the last minute? Can't they plan ahead a little bit?*

"Okay, just a minute while I finish this."

They stood waiting until she set the other papers aside and took out a registration form. Maria's ambivalence began to resurface. This would be a new start. So far she liked the community. She was making friends and acquaintances. The summer on the farm had given Mario new and exciting adventures. Although almost eight years younger than she, Thelma had become a good friend and was very persuasive in convincing her to stay. The apparent chilly reception in the school office opened a small crack in her resolve for a return of unsettling doubt. She brushed it off.

The secretary went through all the questions quickly and efficiently. She didn't bother to ask how names were spelled.

On the first day of school, no one responded when the kindergarten teacher, reading the attendance list to the class, came to "Marion Reese."

"Marion Reese? Are you here?"

The students looked around. The teacher assumed that student was absent, and she continued on down the list.

"Okay, did we get everybody?"

Mario began to realize something wasn't right, but still hadn't made the connection until some of the other students started looking at him. The teacher finally noticed.

"Are you Marion Reese? Why didn't you say anything?"

With everyone looking at him Mario became paralyzed in embarrassment.

"What is your name then?"

"Mario."

"What's your last name?"

"Ruiz."

"How do you spell that? Do you know how to spell that?"

"R-U-I-Z."

"Ruiz? Mario Ruiz? Isn't that a Mexican name? You don't look Mexican. The list here says Marion Reese. I'll have to check this out later. For now I'm going by the list, and you are Marion Reese."

When Maria had said "Mario Nathan Ruiz," the secretary had written down "Mario N. Reese." The N was smaller than the other capital letters and a little too close to the first name. It didn't occur to her to ask for the spelling. When the kindergarten teacher transcribed the information to the class list, it had become Marion Reese. Maria didn't find out until the first parent-teacher conference in October.

After the initial reaction to the assault on their identity subsided, Maria's attitude changed. Her advisers offered different reasons why it might be a good idea to change their names. Mrs. Bauer implied that some people hold some prejudice against someone with a Spanish name. People were accustomed to seeing them around in the summer time as long as they headed south at the end of summer. Thelma said she liked the name "Reese"—it sounded like a good German or English name and besides, names are superficial anyway; people are more than their name. Maria realized that a different name might deflect questions about her marital status. It gave her a sense of new identity. It offered an escape from the unsettling memory of her father's disapproval.

MARIO DIDN'T CARRY HIS BILLFOLD to school like some kids already were doing in junior high. He only carried enough money for lunch. Jake did carry one and right after school let out he went straight to the bowling alley. Mario had to go home first. His mom wasn't home yet. Entering an empty house sometimes left him with a lonesome feeling but not so much this time. It meant that he wouldn't have to hide the encounter with Tom on the way home from school or their meeting plans. He wondered about Ike. He couldn't think of any other ideas about who had hurt the dog and hoped that Jake might have something to say. He wished that he hadn't agreed to the meeting. Then again, he figured Jake and Rosalyn would want to know about Ike, too. And what if someone saw them talking with Tom?

He called Rosalyn and told her what Tom said had happened to Ike. He told her about Chief Stark coming over to his house and accusing Tom of beating Frank. Even though she got really mad, he felt better after telling someone. He told her to not tell anyone or he could get in big trouble. She promised to keep it a secret and agreed to meet at the bowling alley in ten minutes. She sounded all excited and angry at the same time. The mission transformed an otherwise routine school day afternoon into a purposeful adventure.

Mario went up to his room and took two dollars from the billfold in his desk. That left him with $25.67, mostly from baling hay and the rest from his allowance. This time he left a note for his mom: "Mom, I'm at the bowling alley with Jake. I will be home about 6:00 for supper. Me."

They had an hour to kill before the meeting. Mario and Jake bowled three lines. Rosalyn sat on the stool for the scorer's table behind the ball return. Larry noticed they didn't seem to be concentrating on their game; they seemed too hurried. This time when they returned their shoes to the counter the clerk looked at them intently.

"Why are you punks in such a hurry to split?" he said through a cloud of cigarette smoke.

Jake grimaced, waving his hands back and forth to diffuse the sweet, acrid fumes.

"That weed's going to kill you," Rosalyn said crossly. "Why do you have to blow smoke at everybody?"

"It's a free country. Where you guys going in such a hurry?"

"None of your bee's wax," Jake replied.

The door opened with Frank, Ronnie, and some other kids in tow.

Mario, Jake, and Rosalyn looked at each other, hoping that one of them would know how they could get to the meeting without anyone else knowing. The clock on the Hires Root Beer sign behind the counter said 4:56.

The kids in Frank's entourage watched Frank to see how he would react to the three standing by the counter. To everyone's relief he pretended to ignore them. He and Ronnie went over to the pinball machine. Frank took a quarter and flipped to see who would go first. This was their break. Mario, Rosalyn, and Jake headed for the door. It was already dark except for a faint orange glow on the southwest horizon. Light from the streetlamps and Christmas decorations didn't go far into the alley.

Seeing them at the entrance to the alley, Tom leaned out from the shadow along the wall and offered a little wave. Mario looked around to see if anyone would see them enter the alley. It seemed to him that he was the only one who felt scared and nervous; no one said anything.

"Hi, kids. Thanks for coming," Tom smiled.

"How's Ike doing?" Rosalyn asked.

"Oh, he'll be okay. The vet said he might be blind in one eye. He'll have to stay at the vet's for a while."

"That's so mean. I hope they get caught and thrown in jail."

"They won't put anybody in jail for hurting a dog," Jake said.

"He's right," Tom said. "Listen, the reason I came to town was to get a few things. Then I thought I'd try find something out about Ike. Then Mario here tells me the cops are looking for me for beating up that other kid, what's his name, Frank?"

"We could get in big trouble if the cops find out we told Tom that they're looking for him," Mario said to Jake and Rosalyn.

"You did that. We didn't," Rosalyn said sternly.

"Well, if the cops asked you if you'd ever talked to Tom and he knew, they would think you told him, too," Mario said.

"We just have to agree to not say anything. It's no big deal," Jake said. He looked at Tom. "We don't know anything about who did that to Ike. What good would it do for you to know?"

"I guess there's not much I could do about it," Tom said. "It just made me really mad, and I wanted to know who did it. I'm sorry for dragging you kids into this. If the cops are looking for me even if it's for

193

something I didn't do I better lay low for a while. It's going to be tough, though. I've got to get things in town. Maybe they'll just come out and get me."

"Why don't you just leave town?" Rosalyn asked.

"I don't know. I guess it's where I live now. I like this place. Sometimes you get attached to a place."

"Maybe we could bring you stuff," Mario said.

Tom smiled. He reached out and placed his hand Mario's shoulder. "That's noble of you, but probably not a good idea. You'd get in trouble, too."

He could tell the boy seemed uncomfortable and removed his hand. "Thanks again for meeting me. It's good to talk to you kids. I really don't have anyone to talk to. You've been really good to me, bringing sandwiches and all. When you're out skating on the lake if you want to stop by you're welcome, but be careful."

Tom said good-bye, turned and walked slowly toward the other end of the alley keeping in the shadow close to the wall. The three kids turned to leave in the other direction. They froze. Frank, Ronnie, and the others stood at the end of the alley watching. Mario had expected them to stay much longer at the pinball machine. Apparently, this time Ronnie's magic hadn't been working.

This time they didn't say a word. Frank just turned and started walking away down the sidewalk and the others followed.

ॐ 16 ﻋ

NEITHER OF THE TWO GROCERY STORES in Clareton stocked jalapeño peppers. Once Maria asked the manager at the Piggly Wiggly about it. He laughed and said he didn't want to be accused of practicing medicine without a license for cauterizing their hemorrhoids. The vulgar remark embarrassed Maria, and she never asked him again about stocking any Spanish foods. At home she made tortillas from scratch and her own salsa. Her mother sent packages, keeping her pantry supplied with spices, cans of beans, and even fresh peppers.

Maria took a pan out from under the oven broiler. She set a plate with two hot enchiladas topped with melted cheese in front of Mario. She enjoyed watching his eyes light up and focus on one of his favorite foods. He started to eat, but this time she thought he seemed subdued.

"How was school today?"

"Okay."

"What did you do after school?"

"I went bowling with Jake. Rosalyn was there, too."

It made Maria feel good to see her son have friends. He was often quiet, but other kids seemed to like him. He had a sincerity that others felt even though he was not aware of it. Not having any siblings or a father around, she often worried that he would be a loner and get picked on. Sometimes she wished he would be a little more boisterous. But as a teacher she saw enough of that during the day. Even in the younger elementary grades she could see the behavior patterns developing from the different personalities. By the time kids reached junior high the labels and cliques were in control. She tried to identify the wallflowers or awkward ones whom she thought someday would be very successful as adults. She had been in Clareton long enough to have seen some of her predictions materialize, at least in blossoming college endeavors.

Mario seemed to make the transition from sixth to seventh grade okay. He liked going to different classrooms with different teachers. With his own locker, for the first time in his life he experienced having his own personal space away from home on his own, even if it was in a school.

Built in 1919 the high ceilings, undulating wood floors and red brick exterior walls of the Clareton junior-senior high school seemed opulent and majestic compared to the sprawling brick and glass of the modern elementary school, where for the past seven years he dreaded the first Wednesday of the month when the city fire whistle sounded, signaling a practice air raid drill. Teachers dutifully instructed their students to crouch under their desks and hold books over their heads. In their early elementary years, students didn't even notice that the teachers remained at their desks during the drill because teachers were bigger than life. By fifth grade Mario began to question the inconsistency. He felt embarrassed during the drills; nevertheless, whenever the fire whistle shrieked, Mario silently prayed that they were not under nuclear attack by the Russians.

Maria liked Jake and Rosalyn, and the kids in the church youth group expanded the circle of friends even though they socialized because of required membership rather than choice. The youth group organized Friday night parties at various homes. Most parents appreciated the chaperoned events; however, the issue of whether or not they should be allowed to listen to rock and roll music caused some conflict. Some believed Elvis Presley's gyrations to be too sinful. Maria avoided the debate, and Mario didn't seem to care or be too enthralled by the music.

"So, how did you do, bowling?"

"Okay I guess. Jake got a 176."

"Good for him." Maria sat at the table with a plate of refried beans and an enchilada. She kept trying to make conversation, to elicit some explanation why her son seemed subdued, or was it anxious?

"I saw Tom again today," Mario said.

"What? Where? Was he in town? You didn't go out there again did you?"

"I was just walking home from school and he was hiding in the bushes. He said somebody had hurt Ike real bad the other night, and he wanted to find out who it was."

"Who's Ike?"

"That's his dog. Tuesday night after I left he went into town to get some stuff. When he came back, Ike was all beat up. He thinks some kids came out there and threw rocks and stuff."

"That's terrible. Why would anyone do such a thing?"

"I don't know. Then I told him the cops were looking for him for beating up Frank."

"Oh, honey, we know he didn't do it."

"But if the cops think so, then I'm in trouble for squealing to Tom."

"Did anyone see Tom or you talking to him?"

"I don't think by the sidewalk. But he wanted to meet me and Jake and Rosalyn to see if we knew who hurt Ike so we met him behind the bowling alley. Then Frank and the other guys saw us talking to him."

"What did they do?"

"They didn't say anything. They just took off."

Mario fought against tears beginning to overpower him. It was so unfair, it made him so angry. Even though he'd gotten the best of Frank in the fight Monday, it seemed that somehow Frank was still winning. He regretted fighting. He wished he had never met Tom. He wished the whole thing would just go away.

"Let's pray about it," Maria said. She reached across the table and gently placed her hand on his, the sore one. "Dear God, we have a dilemma, and we don't know what to do. Forgive us if we've done anything wrong. Help us do the right thing, and that the truth will come out. Oh, and thank you for this food. In Jesus' name we pray, amen."

"Now we'll just not worry about it anymore and let God take care of it."

"But how are we supposed to know what to do?" Mario pleaded.

"Well, first I'm going to call Jim and Thelma. Jim was going to come over tonight anyway. I think Thelma can make it and maybe Horace, too."

"But he's a cop."

"Well, that would be our next step. We have to tell the police, and he's the only one I trust."

Jim came over sooner than planned when Maria called. Thelma and Horace said they couldn't make it until 7:30. Maria cleared the table. Mario went into the living room and turned on the TV. He protested when she asked him to turn it off so they could talk. She agreed to let him watch until Jim arrived, which he did just before seven. She thought Mario seemed a little irritated but she didn't know why. Jim asked if he could turn on the radio and keep it low. It was almost tip-off time for the Minneapolis Lakers basketball game with Syracuse. Maria said okay. Mario left the TV on hoping she would not object to that, either. The Disneyland show was just starting. Maria looked at both of them, shook her head in mild disapproval and went back into the kitchen to make coffee. She said they could wait to talk until Thelma and Horace arrived. Mario welcomed the break. Thelma and Horace arrived just after 7:30. With five people, the small living room seemed crowded. Even though they were friends Mario still felt self conscious.

"Okay, Mario. Let's start from the beginning, from Monday," Maria said.

"You know, even though I'm not on duty, anything you say is part of the investigation," Horace interjected. "If I was ever caught withholding anything I'd be done for. We've been ordered to arrest Tom. But so far the chief hasn't said anything about actually going to apprehend him."

"This is just terrible," Thelma said.

"We'll back you up on this Horace," Jim added. "That Stark is such a bully anyway. I can't imagine how you've put with working for him."

"If it wasn't for folks like you and the mayor, I wouldn't still be here," Horace said. "I wouldn't have been here at all."

"Oh, don't say that," Thelma said sharply. She reached and squeezed his hand, her small, cream-colored hand barely covering and contrasting with the back of his. "It was meant to be. You know that."

"I hope so. I hope so," Horace replied, looking down at the floor. He looked up at Mario. "Okay, son. Tell us what happened."

They all listened while Mario told about the week's events starting with the incident at school Monday morning when Frank shoved him into the locker. The swelling had receded, but he could still feel a little bump on the inside of his lip. He described what happened after school Monday, the fight with Frank. He told about the note and going out to Tom's shack on Tuesday, then about what happened today.

Maria said they had nothing to hide except for Mario getting the best of Frank in the fight on Monday, which most people would consider a schoolyard scrap and not a serious assault. The former was considered a pounding. You pounded someone not so much to hurt them but to show domination. Frank had been goaded into an attempt to pound Mario. He always put on a bold front and probably wasn't even aware of his insecurity and self-doubt, which greatly increased the odds of him losing the fight even before it started. But he found another way to save face and seek revenge.

A beating was different. It could be spurred by anger, fear, hatred or revenge. As for Mario, it might have crossed the line because he tried to hurt Frank, but Frank had it coming. Mario had gained a few pounds of muscle working on the farm over summer and took it to Frank more than he realized. Remorse swelled in the aftermath, and he felt guilty and terrible when he had told his mom that evening after it happened. But all the adults still seemed to consider it minor thing, children's play. After confessing, he felt much better.

"So, how do you think Tom became a suspect?" Horace asked Mario.

"I don't know. I think he might have been in the alley. I don't remember seeing him all that much. Kids said they saw someone, and we all ran."

"So, it was you who beat up Frank Monday. Tom wasn't even near you, except for Tuesday and today, is that right?"

"Right."

"But you say that today Frank and some of his friends saw you and Jake and Rosalyn talking to Tom."

"We couldn't help it. Tom was the one who wanted to talk to us. We didn't know anything about what the police chief was talking about last night, when he said they were looking for Tom. And we felt bad about what happened to Ike. We just wanted to help," Mario pleaded.

"You know, I think Tom's basically a good man but he can get crazy sometimes, but did you ever think that it was him who hurt Ike?" Horace asked. "That's not all that uncommon, people beating on their dogs."

"The way Tom described it, Ike got hurt pretty bad, not like somebody kicking their dog once in a while," Mario said. "He said Ike is at the vet clinic and will be there for a while."

Horace thanked Mario for his cooperation. He rose from the couch. He drew the early shift Friday and wanted to get to bed at a decent time. He wanted to interview Frank again but dreaded seeking permission from the chief and the Harleys. He believed Mario was telling the truth. He feared that up against Frank's version of what happened it wouldn't matter. Except for meeting Thelma, like many times before he wished that he had stayed on the bus last spring. It was only supposed to be fifteen minutes, just enough time to use the bathroom and grab a cup of coffee and a doughnut.

Thelma and Jim stayed awhile longer watching TV and listening to the game. Maria popped corn. They talked about other things, the weather, the high school basketball team, getting ready for Christmas. Thelma said Horace was planning to go to Detroit to visit his family. She would miss him but knew that it also would avoid any awkward tension if he were to spend Christmas in Clareton with her family, but she did not want him to be alone at Christmas, either. The company and conversation helped Mario relax a bit. At nine he decided to do some homework. He had forgotten all about the math assignment; they were starting to learn about algebra. Each time he found the value of X in a simple equation it gave him a small sense of accomplishment and certainty. After completing the assignment's ten problems he felt better and ready for bed. Just one more school day before the weekend.

They had been planning to go with Jim, Horace, and Thelma to Minneapolis to do some Christmas shopping. Now, because of the investigation, Chief Stark said Horace couldn't leave town. It disappointed Thelma greatly but they decided to go anyway without him. At least she could buy his presents without secrecy. Mario fell asleep thinking about the trip.

LIKE MANY SCHOOL DAY MORNINGS, Mario awakened with a knot in his stomach only this time there was a reason. That it was Friday didn't help much. Surprisingly, Frank hadn't been much of a bother all week. Several times he'd even smiled at Mario, but it hadn't been a friendly smile, more of a smirk.

Sitting in class provided refuge from the jostling and banter in the hallways, bathrooms, and lunchroom. Every Friday Mrs. Lane in social studies spent the first half of the class period talking about current events of the week. 1958 was the state's centennial year, so each week she included something about Minnesota history. She'd clip articles from the *Minneapolis Journal* and sometimes the *Clareton Chronicle*. This Friday she talked about a story from Alabama where the U.S. government

201

and the state were arguing about the voting record of Negroes. The state wouldn't release them because it would show racial discrimination.

Mrs. Lane left some time to ask the class if anyone would like to mention any other current events. Someone said the state traffic death toll stood at 654 compared to 635 in all of 1957. Someone else told about a nineteen-year-old kid from Duluth who got killed playing Russian roulette. Mrs. Lane could tell that some students didn't know what that was, and she hoped to just let it slide. When one kid asked about it, she had to explain, trying to ignore snickers rippling through the classroom. Jake raised his hand and told about the atomic-powered aircraft. An Associated Press story in the *Chronicle* said the project was not going well. Listening to the discussion, Mario's thoughts escaped Clareton for a while. The bell rang and, almost in unison, the students grabbed their books and hurried to their lockers before going to the lunchroom.

"HEY WETBACK, HOW YOU DOING? How do you like the cold weather?"

Mario spun toward the voice behind him. He saw Frank looking at him with a little laugh. All week Frank had ignored him almost completely.

"What are you talking about?"

"You. So you're part Mexican. Say something in Spanish, like 'adios amigos,' only we're not amigos," Frank laughed.

"Just bug off, will ya? I'm sorry what happened Monday. But I didn't start it. Just leave me alone."

"You mean when that bum assaulted me? We'll take care of him. But I just don't like Mexicans in our town. They should stay in the fields where they belong."

"I'm not Mexican."

"That's not what I hear. You came from California, and your mom's Mexican."

"Where'd you hear that? She's not Mexican."

"It's for me to know and for you to find out," Frank laughed.

Mario couldn't think of anything to say. He closed his locker door and headed for the lunchroom, hoping to find refuge at the table where he, Jake, Aaron, and several other friends sat.

Frank followed him down the hall.

"I'm sure you've heard the cops are looking for that bum friend of yours. When they catch him he's done for."

"He didn't do anything, you liar," Mario replied back over his shoulder.

"You calling me a liar? You're the liar, trying to pretend not being a Mexican. And you're trying to help that bum, too. We saw you yesterday in the alley. You and Jake and Rosalyn. What were you talking about?"

"You should know. It was probably you and those other guys who beat up his dog."

"I don't know anything about no dog. Who cares about some old bum's dog?"

"Somebody beat up his dog real bad, and he was asking us about it, that's all."

"What else did you tell him? Did you tell him the cops are looking for him?"

Mario didn't know what to say. He hesitated before denying that he had said anything about that to Tom.

"You did, didn't ya. You squealed," Frank said. "Now he's going to get away, and it's all your fault."

"Why are you lying about this?" Mario asked. "We all know what happened. Why are you blaming him?"

"I'm not but some other people are. We don't want bums around here anyway. Or Mexicans either."

"He's not a bum, and I'm not a Mexican, and you're a lying jerk," Mario said.

Frank let it go and sat down to lunch at his table. Mario sat at his table. They avoided contact the remainder of the day. Most Fridays Mario felt relaxed walking home from school; today he felt like he would explode.

SOMETHING ABOUT THE HARLEYS' ACCOUNT of what happened to their son Monday caused Chief Stark to let the investigation cool awhile. He wanted to believe them. Five kids testified that they had seen Tom Nathan strike Frank Harley in an alley downtown. Then the Reese kid said he did it. The boys at the club were pressuring him to arrest Nathan and boot him out of town. The scales tipped when the wife of one of the club members told him she happened to see someone who fit the description of Nathan in town Thursday. He said she saw a man talking to three kids and placed his hand on the shoulder of one of them, and she thought it was a girl. It added to the weight of evidence that the drifter drunk was bothering, even molesting, children in town. Stark decided to go ahead and turn up the heat.

೫ 17 ೫

H ORACE DIDN'T GO STRAIGHT HOME after leaving the Reese's
Thursday. His strength and stature, his direct, decisive manner
tempered with an adequate amount of empathy made him a good
cop. It could ruffle feathers, more so among those whose fear and insecurity became manifest in prejudice. It strained the working relationship
between him and the chief. However, this time the circumstances of the
case gave Horace the courage to go directly to Chief Stark's home.

Mrs. Stark answered the door. Horace felt a brief moment of relief
when she said Harold wasn't home. He almost lost his resolve and
returned home. But he knew where Stark was, downtown where every
Thursday evening the Clareton Order of the Knights gathered for a short
business meeting followed by poker, pool, cigars, and whiskey. He
decided to go to the club.

As far as the current members knew, it was the first time in the
club's history dating back to its founding in 1884 that an African-American
had ever crossed its threshold. Horace stood before the oversized wooden
door of the two-story brick building in downtown Clareton. He held back his
apprehension and pressed the buzzer. He didn't recognize the man who

answered the door, but the man recognized Horace. He politely told Horace they were in a meeting and no visitors were allowed. Horace said he had urgent business with the police chief. The man excused himself and closed the door. A minute later he returned and invited Horace in.

Smoke hung in the air drifting in and out among the islands of light above the card tables in the high-ceilinged room. A hush replaced the sounds of voices and laughter. Entering the main room Horace nodded around to club members; he knew almost all of them and some too well. He spotted Stark's table and walked over, trying to ignore two dozen pairs of eyes that followed his every step. Stark looked up in mild annoyance at Horace's intrusion. He laid his cards down and stared at Horace for a few long seconds before responding. He was holding a full house and sensed that he would not be able to reap its rewards.

"What are you doing here?" Stark asked with more irritation than curiosity.

"Good evening, sir," Horace said. "I'm really sorry to bother you like this. But I'd like to talk to you about the investigation."

"Can't this wait 'til morning?"

"That's up to you, sir. But I was hoping we could try clear some things up now."

Stark looked at his table mates. They shrugged with facial gestures and open palms indicating they would yield to the police chief's decision even if they really didn't concur. That unsettled Stark the most. Since Horace was hired, they had been fairly easy on Stark, mostly because the young officer brought more talent than the town deserved and most of the citizens liked him. Now, with Horace standing in front of them at the club, perhaps things had gone too far. Stark had to do something. He excused himself from the card game. Horace followed him to a smaller room off the main meeting room, all eyes following them in silence.

It was actually the second time an African-American had entered the clubroom. Several of the older members who knew the club's history knew about Jeremiah Colton, a black Civil War veteran and charter member of the Knights. He led the fund-raising effort and took the first ceremonial step across the threshold of the club's new building in 1888. A surveyor known for his accuracy and integrity, he became well-known and accepted in the dynamic, growing prairie community. After he died in 1902 his family left town. His legacy remained only in his name in the club's files; his role in the building had been forgotten.

"Now what's this all about?" Stark asked when they were alone.

"I just interviewed the Reese kid again. I think he's telling the truth. I know Tom Nathan, and I know he wouldn't do the things he's accused of."

"*You* think? *You* know? What's the evidence?" Stark said gruffly. "You came here to tell me *this*? I think you should go home and sleep on it. We can talk in the morning."

Horace hadn't thought the chief would actually listen to him and briefly regretted making the intrusion. He knew better than to hope so but he did anyway because he had been looking forward to Friday and the weekend with the shopping trip to Minneapolis they had planned. Still, he persisted.

"I think Frank Harley made up that story about getting beaten by Tom," Horace said. "And I think somebody put him up to it. I can see real easy where he would get his pals to back him up on the story. They think it's real funny. Frank saves face by accusing Tom when Mario really did it. And he gets back at Mario because Mario and some of his friends had befriended Tom. But what I'd like to know is how Frank got the idea in the first place."

Stark's initial irritation softened. He smiled a bit and placed his hand on the young officer's shoulder. "Horace, you're a good cop, but you're young and you've still got a lot to learn. You just can't get personally involved in a case, and you can't speculate. It's tough in a small town when you know everybody, believe me I know. Now I think we have to stick to the facts and the witnesses we have. Some of us think this is an opportunity to make this a better town, and that's what really counts, you know. People just don't like seeing an old drunk around town. Why does he have to live here?

He'd be better off in the big city. As police officers, it's our job to protect and to serve, and if folks don't think they're being protected and served well, then we better do something about it."

"So it's not the law that counts but what folks think?" Horace said.

"Like I said, you've got a lot to learn."

"You don't believe Frank's story, either."

"I'll believe the facts and the truthful testimony of witnesses."

"I'd go along with that if it was truthful."

"You better be careful with that kind of talk, young man."

"I'm sorry. I just don't believe Frank's telling the truth."

After the chief's reprimand, Horace stopped himself from saying what he thought next, that it wasn't Frank who was making up the story and where it might be coming from. He got up to leave, thanking the chief for talking and apologizing again for the intrusion. He tried to fend off feelings of defeat and self-consciousness that followed him, along with twenty-four pairs of eyes, back through the clubroom and out the door. Stark appeared in the doorway of the side room and motioned to Earl Harley.

"So, what's this all about?" Earl asked after entering the room and closing the door. "Was he talking about the investigation? How's it going? When are you going to get this Nathan guy?"

"Horace says that Reese kid, you know, the school teacher's boy, claims that he was the one who assaulted your son," Stark said. "He's convinced Marion, or Mario—that's his name—is telling the truth."

"So, you're telling me that it's my boy's word against his?"

"That's pretty much it."

"But it's not just Frank's word," Earl said. "Three or four of his friends said the same thing. This Reese kid, maybe he's just talking big. What witnesses does he have?"

"It was just him on Monday."

"Well, I've got something to tell you," Earl said. "Tonight at dinner Frank said he and some friends saw Nathan in town today after school. They saw him behind the bowling alley downtown talking to this Marion and a couple of other kids. What do you think about that?"

Stark tried not to look surprised.

"If you would have been on the job, you would have picked him up by now," Earl continued. "I'll bet they told him you were out to get him."

"Listen, I know you want to get this over with," Stark said. "But we've got to make sure. If he gets into court with a lawyer we might not have enough evidence to make it stick."

"What makes you think he'd get a lawyer?"

"He looks and lives like a bum, but he's got some money. And he's got a brother in Minneapolis and a sister in Sioux Falls. You never know, they might decide to back him up."

"It sounds like you're backing out of this, Harold. This is our town. This guy is nothing but a drunken bum, an eyesore, a blight on the community. Let's get rid of him and fast. Now's our chance, don't you see?"

"I know. I know. We could make a case. But a lot of the evidence is circumstantial. If he's got a lawyer Holmes might cave. And what if there's a jury? Right now I'd say it's fifty-fifty that he gets off. Then what? We look like fools, and he's still here."

"Okay. I guess you know the system better than I do. But we've got other options," Earl said, smiling slightly.

"What would that be?"

"Well, everyone knows he's kind of crazy sometimes, not to mention the booze. Did you ever think about sending him to the looney bin?"

"Earl, I think that's going a little too far. That's a long process, too. Besides, if we did he'd be a ward of the state and we'd be picking up the tab for the rest of his life."

"But it's not all that much. They can work on the farm there. And from what I hear, they usually don't live to a ripe old age anyway."

Earl continued pressing the argument. After years of selling cars it came natural. Without even thinking, he could detect a person's needs, desires, vulnerabilities and emotions no matter how well hidden or unknown even to them. He liked to say that selling cars was the easiest job in the world. Eventually his persistence led Stark to accept the logic of his scheme although without great enthusiasm. He agreed it might be a solution with somewhat better odds. Holmes certainly would sign the commitment order if they could get Doc Croft to go along with it.

They emerged from the side room. Although Judge Holmes sat at one of the card tables they decided to wait until Friday to bring him in on the plan. Earl returned to billiards and Harold to his seat at the card table. During their absence Earl's billiard partner had taken over Harold's poker hand and won the pot. The other players chided Harold that he should share it with his substitute but he declined. The other member who took his seat owned the Ford dealership in town. Harold figured the guy had already made enough money off him from the two 1957 Ford police cruisers the city bought last year.

About 9:45 Harold excused himself again from the poker table. They had played long enough. At 10:00 p.m. most of the members would either go home or move to the TV lounge to watch the late news. He knew that's what Doc Croft would be doing, so he wanted to call him before the news started. He apologized for calling so late before telling Croft he would stop by the clinic about nine Friday morning. He didn't elaborate on why, saying only that he was investigating a case and needed some information. Stark already had all the information on Tom Nathan he could get his hands on: military records, relatives, some employment history, comments from local merchants where Nathan bought supplies. He even called the former police chief, a law enforcement profession acquaintance, in Nathan's hometown in southern Minnesota. He was having a hard time convincing himself that Nathan was nothing more than a drunk and perhaps still suffering from the vestiges of World War II battle fatigue. More than anything Nathan was a danger to himself.

STARK ARRIVED AT THE CLINIC FRIDAY MORNING just after nine. He figured he would probably have to wait anyway. Dr. Louis Croft had been practicing in

Clareton for more than thirty years. For two generations of Clareton area residents, a sizeable number entered the world cradled in his hands. Stark didn't know if Croft knew Tom Nathan or had treated him for anything. Earl had objected to bringing Croft in, favoring another physician instead. Harold didn't back down, insisting that if they were going to try the commitment route he wanted to see Croft.

Years ago as a young police officer, Stark would have marched down the hall of the clinic looking for the doctor. Now he sat patiently in the office, calmly flipping through an old *Time* magazine. He welcomed a few moments of peace and quiet when no one made demands on his time and he didn't have to answer the phone. He looked forward to talking with Croft, anticipating wise advice. It wasn't the first time felt squeezed between what the good old boys in town wanted and what he thought was right or could reasonably justify.

Lean and fit with a silver crew cut, Louis Croft looked more like a Marine colonel than doctor. At sixty-three, he could have retired several years ago. No one would have blamed him, but most everyone would have missed him. He had been slowing down a bit in recent years to make more time for golf, fishing and occasional trips with his wife to visit their children and their families. Between the clinic and hospital he still put in fifty-hour weeks and couldn't think of doing anything else. At 9:20 he entered his office with quick, fluid steps, a warm smile, and a firm handshake.

After exchanging pleasantries and talking about the weather, Stark delved into the investigation and their proposed solution. Croft listened attentively, interjecting a few questions for clarification and jotting down some notes.

"So, Harold, tell me, what's the real purpose here, to get this guy out of town, to close a case or to help him?" Croft asked.

"Depends on who you're talking to."

"I'm talking to you. What do you think needs to be done?"

"I'd like to see him leave town. I'd like to help him, I guess. He's a war hero for crying out loud. A drunk one most of the time but still a decorated veteran. And I'd like to get Earl Harley off my back."

Resting his chin on his folded hands, Croft looked at Stark for a moment. Stark waited, returning the gaze in hopeful confidence of hearing a wise response.

"I don't know if this would get him out of town, but I know how we can help him and maybe appease Earl at the same time. I don't see any evidence that Nathan is mentally ill. That's not a diagnosis, you understand. Just from what you've told me I don't see it. Battle fatigue is real. The trauma of combat can have some lasting effects. And alcoholism—that's now considered a disease. It can be treated."

"And how do you do that? Either they just have to get up the gumption to quit or else you throw them in jail or someplace where they can't get it."

"There is another way. There's a program over at the state hospital where they've had some success treating alcoholics. Now it certainly could be this guy has other problems—they usually do. But the program can help with those issues, too."

"It sounds like it might be worth a try. It would probably appease Earl just to know that this guy's going to the state hospital. If Nathan goes through the treatment and decides to come back, I'll just have to deal with that then I guess."

"You'd be doing the right thing to try help him. I'd be glad to help. I'd talk with him if you want."

"Thanks. The job right now is bringing him in. Somehow we'd have to let him know he has two choices, face an assault charge or agree to the alcohol treatment program. I don't expect that'll be real easy. He seems to want just to be left alone and not have much to do with anybody. We might have to apprehend him forcibly."

"You're the cop; I'm the doctor," Croft smiled. "Like I said, it's the right thing to try help him. I know the doctor at the state facility who runs the program, Bradley Nelson. He's young but very able. Talk to him. I'm sure he can help."

Stark thanked Croft for the information and left the clinic. He drove back to the station thinking about the next step. Coming directly from home he had driven his Buick to the clinic. The weather forecast called for snow in the afternoon followed by strong winds and colder temperatures. He wasn't worried about the weather. He could make it to Dakota Falls and back in plenty of time.

Although it was only thirty miles, he decided to drive the Buick instead of one of the squad cars. He enjoyed cruising along the highway in the big car. It had a two-way radio, and he would be reimbursed for the mileage. He stopped at the office first to tell the secretary and call Dr. Nelson at the state hospital. Nelson was busy so Stark decided to chance leaving a message and departed.

In 1891 the state bought a farm just outside Dakota Falls as a site for another insane asylum. Some residents opposed the proposal; others supported it as noble and humanitarian. When it grew and brought more jobs to the area overt opposition to the "funny farm" subsided. An expansion in the 1930s brought a series of new, ornate buildings. By the 1950s, the brick-and-stucco wards housed nearly 1,000 mentally ill patients, alcoholics, drug addicts, and an assortment of other misfits.

Faced with a growing caseload and limited staff a young doctor and a psychologist on the staff listened to their instincts and compassion. They turned away from the conventional belief that drunks were hopeless dregs of society. Dr. Nelson began treating alcoholics with a program based on Alcoholics Anonymous. They brought in counselors, ministers, and people from the community to form a support network for the patients. It was unheard of, treating drunks as ill people and treating them with respect.

Viewed from the highway several miles off, the red-tiled roofs of the "red roof college" stood out among the dark, barren trees and snow-covered landscape. Looking out his office window Nelson saw the '57 Buick pull into the parking lot of the main building just before eleven. He had found a few minutes to fill out some reports and didn't pay much attention, except for noticing the police uniform on the man getting out of the car. He watched the man approach the building. He recognized Clareton police chief Harold Stark. It didn't look good.

213

He remembered Stark from a case two years ago, a psychopath who killed a whole farm family with a shotgun over a hunting dispute. Nelson couldn't decide which he detested most, Stark's arrogance or the insecurity that it attempted to hide. But he understood society's need for those willing and able to use necessary force no matter what the underlying psychological drives.

Stark introduced himself at the reception desk, apologizing for the short notice. The receptionist said she had left a note on Dr. Nelson's desk but wasn't sure whether or not he had seen it. She went into his office. Stark followed.

"Dr. Nelson, Chief Stark is here to see you. From Clareton."

Stark looked into the empty office. The secretary turned toward Harold, mystified.

"He was just in here. He just walked in five minutes ago. I didn't see him leave."

Harold looked around. He thought he felt a slight draft or a temperature difference between the office and the hall. He walked over to the desk and felt the warm coffee mug. He went over to the window. It had not been closed all the way and was unlocked. He peered out the window to the ground below and saw footprints in the snow.

"Looks like someone just made an exit and didn't use the door," Harold said wryly.

"You mean he jumped out the window? Why on earth would he do that?"

"Beats me. You know him better than I do. If you see him, tell him that I really need to see him. We're trying to help this guy in Clareton, an alcoholic drifter type. It's not real serious, but Doc Croft there in Clareton suggested we check with you folks."

"I certainly will," the secretary said. "I still can't imagine why he did such a thing, jumped out the window. But sometimes he can be kind of silly if you know what I mean. He does crazy things sometimes, jokes and pranks. Around here sometimes you have to just to keep your own sanity. He'll show up sooner or later. It's up to you if you want to wait. Or I could make a formal appointment and make sure he's there."

Stark decided to wait. Soon it would be lunch time, and he could get a bite to eat in the hospital coffee shop. He asked to use the phone to check in with the station at Clareton. Horace answered. Stark expected to hear the secretary. He forgot for a moment that he had told Horace he couldn't take Friday and the weekend off. He told Horace where he was and what he was doing, at least trying to do. He didn't mention the doctor's apparent avoidance.

Horace said the vet called the station asking if they knew anything about Tom's dog. While such things didn't usually require police involvement, the beating in this case was particularly nasty. The vet, Doc Ahrends, wanted the police to know about it. He said Ike was recovering but should probably remain at the kennel for a while. If a dog is property, then there was a fair amount of property damage that could be costly to the owner.

"What happened to the dog? I didn't know he had a dog," Stark said.

"It's a German shepherd named Ike. The night we were out looking for Mario, apparently later Tom went into town. When he returned to the shack he found Ike all beat up. He carried him back to town, to the hospital. They called Doc Ahrends."

"To the hospital? Who did it? Maybe he did it for all we know. You know how some people treat their dogs. He was probably drunk and started kicking the dog. Or he went berserk like a lunatic."

"According to Doc Ahrends this wasn't your average dog-kicking," Horace said. "Ike was severely beaten with sticks and rocks and who-knows-what."

"Whatever happened it has nothing to do with our case," Stark said. "Let's not get sidetracked here. You wait until I get back. We're going to bring Tom here and I want you to pick him up. Understand?"

"Yessir. He said Tom stopped by the vet clinic yesterday to check on Ike. Then he went into town, at least that's where Doc Ahrends thought he was going."

"I know."

Horace wondered if the chief knew that he also knew. He wondered how the chief knew, but it wasn't hard to figure out. If Frank Harley saw Tom in town Thursday, it wouldn't take long for word to get back to the chief. Although he knew it wasn't right, he held back from telling Stark about his meeting Thursday night with Maria, Mario, Jim, and Thelma. He hoped no one had seen him over there. If the chief ever did find out, it wouldn't be good.

Horace almost started feeling sorry for himself. He imagined Thelma, Jim, Maria, and Mario getting ready to leave on the shopping trip to Minneapolis. He wished someone who cared would be around to help him though this. He hung up the phone and looked dourly out at the leaden winter sky and biting northwest wind whipping up stinging snowflakes.

౩౦ 18 ౭౩

THE GOONS HAD DRAGGED HIS LIMP BODY from the rail yard to the edge of the highway. They let go, and Tom's arms flopped askew, one landing across his chest and the other stretched out above his head like a Nazi "Seig Heil" salute except the hand was clenched instead of fingers stretched out open.

Most of the blows had been to the body although at first the clubs landed on his head to render him unconscious and leaving several bleeding welts. When he crumpled to the ground, they went to work on his torso with their heavy boots.

Seeing light, feeling warmth and hearing soft muffled voices Tom felt the black nothingness recede behind him. He heard a woman's voice calling his name. Slowly his eyes regained focus to see a young woman standing next to him. Her white uniform shone in the bright light in a white room. She looked pretty with red lipstick and a crisp, white nurse's cap.

"Tom, can you hear me? How are you feeling?" She placed her hand gently on his shoulder.

"Where am I? What happened?" He tried to raise his head. The slight effort sent pain burning across his chest. His head throbbed.

"You lie still now. You're in the hospital. In Billings."

Tom lay back looking around the hospital room. He looked down at his feet and the bed. A cold sweat broke out on his forehead. Panic pressured him to flee, but he couldn't move; like a strait-jacket the pain wouldn't let him.

"You're going to be fine. The x-rays show you have four broken ribs and a fractured vertebra. But don't worry. It should heal okay. You have a pretty good concussion. Do you know what happened?"

"I was just riding the rails. It was a couple of railroad goons."

"Or some other drifters."

"It was goons. The bums would only do what's necessary to steal your stuff."

"Well, don't worry. We'll take care of you, for a while anyway. Your personal belongings are in that bag over there. We see you're a veteran, in the Seabees. Where were you stationed?"

Tom relaxed and lay back in the clean, soft hospital bed in Billings, Montana, 1954. So far it wasn't like the last hospital he was in.

"I was on Iwo."

"Really? To come through what you've been through, then and now, it looks like somebody's looking out for you."

"I can't imagine why."

"Oh, come on now. Everybody counts for something. That's why we do what we do here in the hospital. Do you have any family?"

"I did. A brother, sister, some nieces and nephews. Don't see any of them. I'm pretty much on my own."

The nurse picked up on the reluctance in Tom's responses and didn't pry any further.

"You rest now. If you need anything just press the button there."

"What kind of hospital is this?"

"What do you mean? It's just a regular hospital, a county hospital. If you can you'll probably have to pay something. But if you can't we'll take care of it."

"I can pay. I want to."

The last time Tom had been in a hospital things had been a lot different. He didn't pay and he didn't want to be there. They kept him locked in a room that was more like a cell. A bare mattress on the floor, toilet but no sink, a small high window covered on the inside by heavy-gauge mesh. At meals they slipped a tray through a notch in the bottom of the door. Except for weekends they let him out into the day room for half an hour accompanied by two male aides. One tried to be friendly. Both carried key rings, which they extended from their belts whenever they had to open a door, all of which were locked.

Those who knew of his service gave him a little better treatment compared with many of the other patients at the psychiatric hospital in Stockton, California. Yet he remained a prisoner, a ward of the state after the incident at the highway construction site where he worked after the war. No one could explain why he went on a rampage with the bulldozer that October in 1947 crushing a construction company pickup against the side of a bridge abutment. The court committed him to the hospital. His legacy continued only in the lunch-break tales among the construction workers about the crazy guy who crushed the foreman's truck. It was something many of them wanted to do, or at least they joked about it.

He didn't remember much about the two years and seven months in the hospital except for the odor. No matter how well they tried to clean the ward, the smell of human waste, sweat, and cigarettes permeated the walls, ceilings, and floors, overpowering the lye soap. It filtered through the wispy fog of sedatives and shock treatments they used to keep him subdued. Even the bare light bulbs in the ceilings were caged. Then one morning they cleaned him up, dressed him in clean work clothes, handed him a bag with his belongings along with $200 and sent him out the door.

The alcohol took over where the sedatives left off, and he hit the road, always moving, trying to keep one step ahead of the lost hopes and dreams that followed, haunting him in his nightmares and sometimes when he was sober. He vowed never to let himself become trapped like that again. He had been on the road four years before the attack in Billings.

219

Sometimes he found work, construction jobs mostly. After saving a little money, he moved on. He never really fit in among the other workers who talked about their families, baseball, fishing and hunting. They tried to be friendly but put little effort into trying to bond with the silent stranger into their group. In the early summer mornings it didn't take long for them to see that he had been hitting the bottle the previous night. Given menial jobs and having to watch others operate the heavy equipment only half as well as he could added to his resentment and alienation. In most cases he left the job before he was fired.

He carried some clothes, food, some books, and paper in an olive green, canvas duffle bag, the kind found in an Army surplus store. That's where he bought most of his supplies: a mess kit, sleeping bag, small pup tent, K rations for times when he was out in the middle of nowhere and needed food.

He wandered among the small towns and cities of the plains and mountain states. In the larger cities, he sometimes joined in the camaraderie of the hobo jungles. They found shelter in clumps of trees and brush near the rail yards. After days and weeks alone with no one to talk to except himself and his notebooks, he welcomed the companionship around the fire at least for a day or two. None of them ever stayed too long. Occasionally they all had to scatter when the railroad goons swept through beating a few just to make the point and destroying the small, crude shelters some of the hobos had built.

Back out on his own, Tom struck back the only way he could, writing in his notebooks or writing another letter to her. At first he mailed them to her old address. He had no way of knowing if she ever got them or even cared enough to read them. As the years passed he wrote fewer letters. He no longer mailed them, instead watching them slowly curl at the edges, turn brown and burst into bright orange flame in the campfire.

The days and nights passed like a slow-moving train. The months and years slipped by until he lost all hope that he would ever see her again. And what he had become no one else would ever want. Evenings under the starlit sky, he sat staring into the fire chain-smoking Camels and pulling on a bottle of cheap wine until it dulled the painful, sharp edges of his thoughts. Sometimes he talked out loud just to hear the sound of a voice resonate in his chest. Sometimes, when an interesting thought or insight flashed in his mind he picked up his notebook and wrote comments about life, politics, love, and sometimes poetry.

> It ain't easy to be a loser
> It's hard to be poor
> I've felt this way
> Many times before
> Anyone can make money
> Have a nice car
> Own a fancy house
> Not knowing who they are
> I've only been here just a little while
> I've seen a lot and more
> And most of what I've seen
> Makes me want to be poor

During his time at the hospital in California, his sister would call twice a month. After he left and hit the road, she had no way of contacting him. At first he didn't care. For years his shame kept him from calling her until the morning of his fortieth birthday. He had realized that his life was half spent, and he wanted to talk with her again. He knew she would try to understand. She'd insist that he come to Sioux Falls. She would help him find a place to stay and get a job. It lasted just over six months until he arrived at the job site late one morning for the third time obviously hung over. They paid him for the hours that week and told him to not come back.

Back at the rooming house, he took what he could carry and left the rest, a small refrigerator, a radio, a toaster and a coffee pot. He gave the landlady his sister's phone number and asked the landlady to call and see if she wanted them. He went to the bus station and bought a ticket for San Diego.

He tried to find her without her knowing it. He called the school where she worked. The secretary who took his call said she had resigned several years ago but didn't know where she was. He went to the restaurant where they used to hang out. The waitress remembered Tom but remained aloof; the man she saw now appeared to be a weary, repulsive shell of the good-looking but unpredictable man she remembered. But she was sympathetic and believed in his sincerity; she told him that she had heard something of the whereabouts of his former girlfriend. He left San Diego heading east, this time hitching rides, walking, or jumping a slow-moving empty box car. A faint hope remained after all.

TOM REMAINED HOSPITALIZED IN BILLINGS for two weeks, mostly because of the fractured vertebra. The nurse asked about his sister. She had found Nancy's name, address and phone number written on a playing card, the Ace of Hearts. She thought it might be a girlfriend. Tom said she was his sister in Sioux Falls. He finally agreed to let the hospital call. Nancy invited him back to Sioux Falls. She scolded him for not keeping in touch over the past few years. Suddenly he felt lonesome and missed her. He wanted to accept but the reluctance he thought he heard in the tone of her voice made him hold back. The embarrassment and strain on her family he caused the last time hadn't gone away. He left the hospital and went to a rooming house in Billings for several more weeks and then hit the road again.

He would have liked to go to Yellowstone. He remembered seeing pictures of the geysers, caldrons, and hot springs. He thought about trying to hitch a ride but decided against it. Families and tourists probably wouldn't stop to give a ride to an old bum. It was already September and with kids back in school the tourist traffic had subsided anyway.

He left Billings, walking along the highway southeast toward Sheridan, Wyoming. Whenever he heard a vehicle approach from behind he turned and held out his thumb. Hitching rides with truck drivers, he made it to Cheyenne. Riding in a truck offered more comfort for his back and ribs than a boxcar. He could take the required conversation for a while. Then the lies in his story would start to challenge the reality of his life. The truckers didn't know nor did they need to. Any conversation and companionship helped pass the hours on the narrow highway stretching out to the horizon where the blue sky turned hazy and blended into the earth, sometimes blocked by a distant mountain range.

He found a clump of cottonwoods along the Crow River outside Cheyenne and camped there for a week. The soreness had subsided by then, and he hopped an empty box car heading east into Nebraska. Where the tracks came close to Highway 30, he watched the cars and trucks. Once in a while a driver would see him sitting in the boxcar's open door and wave. He waved back and even smiled a bit.

The small towns strung out along the rail line about ten miles apart. Five miles off he could see the grain elevators and water towers. Even though the train didn't stop, Tom moved away from the door to avoid being seen while passing through the towns. Sometimes he would like to have seen other people, but the risk wasn't worth it. When the train stopped in the rail yard at North Platte, he hoped he could exit unnoticed. He relaxed a bit after leaving the tracks towards town to get some food and a bottle. At first he was annoyed when a dog followed him.

"Go on, get out of here."

Mostly German shepherd, he figured the puppy wasn't more than three or four months old.

"What are you doing out here by yourself? Where do you live? Go home now."

It was the first time he had spoken out loud to anyone other than himself since the last time he hitched a ride in a truck. It felt good. Though reprimands, his words seemed to encourage the dog even more. Tom turned and continued walking toward the downtown. The puppy followed, gradually closing the distance with its nose close to the ground trying to pick up the scent. Tom walked along, ignoring the dog until he felt its wet nose touch his hand and pink tongue lick his fingers. He stopped, turned and looked at the pup. It stood still, looking up at him with bright yellow-brown eyes, wide mouth, and alert ears. When Tom smiled and reached down to pet the pup, it moved closer and leaned into his leg, tail wagging fiercely. Tom scratched through the soft puppy fur on its neck. He didn't find a collar.

"Well, little fella. You better go home. I'm leaving town, so if you keep following me that's your business."

By the time Tom left the other side of town along Highway 30, the puppy was completely lost. It had no choice but to keep following the kind, soft-spoken man. Tom was beginning to enjoy the company more and more. His thoughts progressed toward accepting the belief that the pup probably didn't have a very good home anyway and he would be doing it a favor by leading it away and becoming its new master.

THE PHONE RANG AGAIN. HORACE SIGHED and picked up the receiver. That's what made police work interesting and stressful at the same time even in a small town. Mornings could be busy with calls from citizens or shop keepers who discovered vandalism or a break-in, though these were less likely in the cold winter months. He preferred break-in calls to the late-night domestic squabbles or pulling over drunks. His heart ached for the kids cowering and sobbing in homes where comfort and security became uncertain amid the shouting, cursing, crying, and sometimes physical abuse. His belief that he was doing some good in trying to help them still provided sufficient buffer between the external conflict and his inner peace. Faced with having to bring Tom in, the inner barrier didn't seem to be working.

"Hello. This is Dr. Nelson . . . at the state hospital in Dakota Falls. Is Chief Stark there by any chance?"

"Not yet. This is Officer Greene. Is there anything I can help you with?"

"He stopped by this morning, but we just missed each other. Perhaps you could tell me what he wanted?"

"He did call me just a while ago. We're looking into some treatment for an individual here in Clareton. He's a suspect in an assault, but instead of filing charges we're going to see if he could get some help there at Dakota Falls."

"What kind of an assault? Who is this person?"

"He's about fifty or close to it. Name's Tom Nathan. A drifter type, drinks a lot. He lives in an old shack outside of town. I'm pretty sure he's innocent in this assault case, but I guess the powers that be here in Clareton think otherwise. You didn't hear me say that."

"Don't worry. We're just here to help. If he's an alcoholic we can help him."

"Well, there's probably more than that, too," Horace said. "Sometimes he acts crazy, like he's hallucinating or something. He was in the war, and I think he might have been shell-shocked or something. I don't think he's dangerous, but folks in town who have seen him like that think so."

"It can be very complex. You're right, he's most likely not dangerous other than to himself. It sounds like we could help him here. We've had real good success for quite a few years now treating inebriates. We treat alcoholism as a disease and not some kind of character flaw. It's amazing the difference it makes, treating them with respect instead of condemnation. It's certainly not easy. Each day is a new battle, but with the support we give them, the majority get back on the wagon and stay there."

"I'm glad you called, Dr. Nelson. I sure feel better now. I've been ordered to bring Tom in. I just hope that somehow I can convince him it's for his own good. I hope he cooperates and goes along peacefully."

"Would it help if I or someone from our staff comes along?"

"Probably not, but thanks for the offer. Seeing a stranger might scare him off, especially if he knows they're from an institution. He knows me. I can talk to him. The question is will he listen?"

"Okay. Sounds like you know the situation. Good luck and call if you have any questions or anything. And please extend my apologies to Chief Stark. When he returns tell him that I called. He's welcome to call me anytime or I can call back, too."

Horace thanked Dr. Nelson for calling. He felt much better. He actually looked forward to Stark's return now that they had a solution that could please everyone. He hoped that Harold wouldn't become angry that Dr. Nelson talked with him first.

What if Tom resisted? If he didn't go voluntarily they would have to get a court order. With Judge Holmes that'd be no problem. But it would mean that Tom would have to come in with force, and Horace would be the one to have to do it. He thought about the kids, Mario, Jake, and Rosalyn, how they had befriended Tom. He probably should have mentioned that to Dr. Nelson. The kids, maybe they could help. He wanted to call Thelma, but she was in school so he'd have to wait.

Chief Stark returned to Clareton in a bad mood, which in itself wasn't unusual. It usually happened when he couldn't control everything to his liking or when one of the good old boys in town needled him about something or other. In either case he took it out on anyone he could. Sometimes Horace considered going out on patrol before Stark returned just so he could avoid any harassment. This time he decided to wait; if he didn't tell Stark right away about the call from Dr. Nelson it would only make things worse. He sat at his desk reading the paper.

Although he knew it by memory he liked looking at the television schedule. The Friday evening line-up promised an escape from the day's troubles. Several evenings a week, he and Thelma went to Maria's to watch TV. He felt safe and comfortable at the Reese's as long as everyone agreed on which program to watch. Everyone liked "Rin Tin Tin" at 6:30. At seven the consensus no longer prevailed. Horace and Jim liked "Ellery Queen," but Mario preferred "Disneyland." Sometimes this strained Maria's diplomacy skills. Some evenings Mario went to Jake's where they had two TVs, one in the living room and one in the rec room, eliminating much of this conflict. Then the burden of choice fell on Mario because he enjoyed watching TV at home with Maria, Jim, Thelma, and Horace and also at the Carlsons.

Horace looked at the clock. The time passed like trying to see a distant cloud move across the sky. It was after two when he looked out the window and saw Stark's Buick pull up along the curb. It was still snowing lightly. Horace wondered how the roads would be Saturday when the others would be driving down to Minneapolis. He wished he would be going with them, although he knew they would be safe with Jim driving. And without him they wouldn't have to endure the stares when they entered the department stores. He hoped Tom would understand what they were trying to do. He heard the key in the back door. Chief Stark entered, stamped the snow off his shoes and hung his jacket on the wall hook. He went straight for his office and motioned to Horace to follow. It didn't help much that this time Horace knew the reason for the chief's bad mood.

"I drove all the way to Dakota Falls, and this guy doesn't even show up," Stark muttered. "I think he even tried to skip out. When I got in his office he wasn't there. I looked out the window and saw fresh tracks in the snow. Can you believe that? He must have just jumped out the window."

"So what did you find out?" Horace asked.

Stark glowered at his young, dark-skinned officer. "Nothing. If I didn't see Nelson, what could I find out? I waited awhile, even had lunch in the coffee shop there. It gave me the creeps, all those drunks and psychos around. Nelson just disappeared, so I finally left."

"He called here not too long ago. He apologized for missing you and said he would like to help in any way he can."

"What a crock! He could have helped by staying put in his office. What else did he say?"

"He thinks they can help Tom. Apparently they've had some success treating drunks. They can help with the mental stuff, too. He offered to send staff to help bring Tom in."

"That won't be necessary," Stark cut in. "That's your job. The way you talk about him, it sounds like you know him pretty well."

Horace's skin flushed in guilt and embarrassment; Stark didn't pick up on it except for the sudden increase in the blinks of his eyes. Horace didn't say anything. Stark looked back at him in silence, both

227

knowingly using the "no response" tactic hoping the other would succumb to the tense silence and blurt out something that either revealed more information or weakened their position. That standoff lasted only a few seconds and ended in a draw, which always irritated Stark. He retreated to his position of authority and spoke first.

"This is what we're going to do. You're going to pick up Nathan. If he doesn't go voluntarily, we'll get Holmes to sign a commitment order. You make sure he understands that going to Dakota Falls will be the best thing to do. If he doesn't we'll make sure he goes to prison for ten years after we escalate the assault charge into something more, if you know what I mean. By Monday I want him either in jail here or on the way to Dakota Falls. Is that clear?"

"Yessir."

"If he resists I'll get somebody to help you. But I hope we can do this quietly. Right now that's up to you."

๕ 19 ๛

ALMOST THREE INCHES OF SNOW HAD accumulated by suppertime and another four or five inches had been forecast through Saturday. Friday after school Mario shoveled the sidewalk anyway. He had to do something to burn off the tension from the school day. He tried to erase the words and images of Frank's taunts.

The shovel scraped the concrete sidewalk, pushing fresh, fluffy snowflakes into a heap. He scooped only far enough to fill the shovel but keeping the snow from falling off the back and onto the sidewalk. The scoops of snow piled up a long, low mound paralleling the sidewalk. Most of the time shoveling snow or mowing grass created an immediate sense of accomplishment. He could see the fruit of his labor and it felt good. While it still snowed, he looked back along the sidewalk where he had shoveled to see a soft, white coating. It didn't bother him because he was just glad that school was over for another week. It was Friday, visitors were coming over in the evening to watch TV, and they were going to Minneapolis Saturday. It was a lot to look forward to.

By the time he finished shoveling the driveway, the power plant workers had switched on the streetlights. Millions of large, fluffy snowflakes emerged, sparkling from the darkness above into the halo of light spreading from the large incandescent bulb under the round metal shade of the street-light at the corner. Mario stopped shoveling to look. The blanket of snow swallowed sounds, leaving the early winter evening quiet and peaceful. Maria leaned out the kitchen door to say supper was ready; she thanked Mario for shoveling and admired the good job he'd done. He could almost taste the grilled cheese sandwich and tomato soup that awaited.

Starting his eighth winter in Minnesota, he hardly remembered the tropical winters in southern California of his early childhood. He didn't like the early darkness and the bitterly cold days when the temperatures dropped to twenty and thirty degrees below zero. But he liked the snow and the ice-covered lake. He couldn't imagine how people in warm climates could get excited about Christmas without snow. Sometimes it didn't snow very much by Christmas, and it was a great disappointment for most people. That had been especially true for Mario two years ago. His main Christmas present was a six-foot toboggan, but there wasn't enough snow to use it until early January.

One doesn't really appreciate the warmth and light of a cozy home until one steps inside from a cold, snowy winter day. The buttery aroma of a grilled-cheese sandwich turning crispy brown in the frying pan greeted Mario; he hurried to remove his overshoes, mittens, and parka. Tomato soup simmered in a small kettle on the stove. Maria added a dash of cinnamon, and with oyster crackers floating on top, it tasted much better than the stuff they served at school.

She was talking on the phone. She pointed to the stove and made a swirling motion with her hand. Mario stirred the soup and lifted the sandwich with the spatula to check the underside. It was just about right. Maria hung up the phone. Horace was coming over unexpectedly. She opened another can of soup. Mario filled his bowl first so he wouldn't have to wait until the kettle reheated.

Maria wished Thelma could come over, too. Thelma had stayed home for dinner with her parents tonight, hoping to drain off some of the tension arising from the amount of time she had been spending with

Horace. She still hadn't told them about the shopping trip they planned to take to Minneapolis Saturday. Her parents' concern about the weather would be bad enough. Knowing that Jim, Maria, and Mario would be going along might help although for some time they had been acting as though Thelma's friends were traitors helping lead her astray.

"Horace can't go with us," Maria said with a rare sad expression. "He has to work this weekend. That Stark makes me so mad. I hope Thelma still goes. I'm going to have to call and tell her. And then her parents. You'd think they'd quit treating her like a child for goodness sakes!" She looked at Mario, sitting at the kitchen table contentedly eating his soup and sandwich. "We've got to stick together so this whole thing doesn't get spoiled."

"Why's he coming over?" Mario asked.

"He wants to talk about this Tom guy and their investigation. They're going to try get him to the hospital, to get some help. He was wondering if you and Jake and maybe Rosalyn might be able to help."

"Are we still going to Minneapolis?"

"Yes, we are. Don't worry about that. It's just for the day anyway."

"At least I won't have to ride fruit."

"What's that?"

"You know, sit in the middle. If he goes him and Jim will be sitting in front and I'll be sitting in back between you and Thelma," Mario complained. He would prefer to sit on the outside of the backseat next to the window; eliminating any awkwardness from having Horace along was even better. Even though Horace had been a guest in their home numerous evenings watching TV, Mario still couldn't relax in the presence of the police officer's engaging personality and his appearance.

"Oh, we're not so bad," Maria laughed. "Besides, that Packard of Jim's is big enough to hold a whole Scout troop."

"How are we supposed to help get Tom?"

"I don't know. Let's hear what Horace has to say."

Stark agreed to let Horace off early Friday to make up for having to work the weekend. Originally, Horace was scheduled to work late

Friday so he could take the weekend off. His instructions were to be on patrol around 10:00 p.m. near the main highway. Fans would be returning from the high school basketball team's away game. Stark considered the effort a failure if the officers didn't snag at least one teenage driver for speeding or drunk driving, or at least a repair ticket for a burned-out taillight. Those happened more than the law of averages would predict because of deliberate pranks. Now and then just for fun or perhaps retribution, someone would sneak into the parking lot and disconnect the wire to a taillight. If noticed by the officers and if the driver happened to be a teenager, it was almost certain they would be stopped. Horace knew this because he saw someone do it one evening in the Clareton high school parking lot during a choir concert. Staked out in his own car in the far corner of the parking lot he couldn't recognize them for sure in the darkness. One used a slim jim to unlock the car door. The other crawled in the back seat, pulled open the back rest, crawled into the trunk and disconnected a taillight wire from the inside. It took about two or three minutes. They ran to the street behind the school parking lot toward a waiting car and driver, who also served as a lookout. Horace thought he recognized the car.

On this particular Friday night any young motorists committing minor traffic violations would be getting a free pass.

Horace knew he was taking a chance going to the Reese's. When he left his place he didn't go directly over. Whether from guilt or his knowledge of Stark, the thought occurred to him that he might be under surveillance himself. He drove downtown to the drug store and bought some Christmas cards. It made him feel a bit lonesome for his parents and siblings back in Detroit. The stores stayed open until 9:00 p.m. and were busy with holiday shoppers. Horace figured if he parked downtown and left his car there for a while, it would not be noticed. He would walk the six blocks to the Reese's although not directly. The darkness made him feel less conspicuous; leaving tracks in the fresh snow on the sidewalk annoyed him.

Sitting at the Reese's kitchen table, he talked while eating a grilled cheese sandwich. He felt a little guilty because he could have grabbed a burger downtown; it was much more enjoyable sitting at the kitchen table of one of the few friends he had in town.

"Thanks for inviting me over. Sorry to have to trouble you with this again. Don't let it worry you on your shopping trip."

"We wish you could go."

"Me too. But that's the way it is. With this snow, I hope the roads are okay. The plows do a pretty good job keeping the main highway open."

"I'm sure we'll be fine. Jim's a good driver. We're taking his car. So what happened today?" Maria asked.

Horace described the events of the day without elaborating on the details of the tension working with Stark. He didn't have to. It lingered in all of them from the confrontations with the police chief by the lake Tuesday evening and again Wednesday right in their living room.

"So, Mario, what do you think about all this?" Horace asked.

"I don't know. It still makes me mad that they think he beat up Frank. But I guess I'd rather see him go to a hospital instead of jail. I guess he drinks a lot. When he acted crazy I wasn't really scared of him."

"Well I'm going out there tomorrow to talk to him," Horace said. "I just hope it goes okay. At least I won't have to worry about his dog. I mean, he's a nice dog and everything. It's too bad what happened. Maybe that's how I can approach him . . . saying something about Ike. I wish we did have some clues about that."

"It was a terrible thing for somebody to do," Maria said. "We wish you luck tomorrow. We'll be praying for you." She patted him on the back. Horace looked up, smiled and reached up and patted the back of her hand. Sitting at the kitchen table and eating soup and sandwiches together, watching his mom and Horace touch one another, for the first time Mario saw him as a real person, not a cop in a uniform, but a friend who could be trusted.

THELMA CALLED HORACE A FEW MINUTES before eight, just before they left for Minneapolis. She apologized for waking him up. He had planned to be up by then anyway. He lay awake for a long time Friday night thinking about today. He finally fell asleep around 2:00 a.m. and must have shut off the alarm without even realizing it. It had been set for seven.

A light snowfall continued adding to the four inches that had fallen overnight. The thermometer read ten below zero. Winters here were a little less cold and windy than Grand Forks but still plenty cold enough to freeze lake ice to a foot thick and more, although he still thought it foolish to walk out on it. And people who drove their vehicles out on the frozen lake were crazy. With the snow already on the ground and the threat of the wind picking up later to blow it around, he had decided to hike to the shack through the woods.

Horace waited at the station until noon. He tried to keep busy reading the paper and looking through files of old cases that accumulated and lingered, pushed aside by urgent matters of the moment. On Saturdays the *Chronicle* came out in the morning. He read the entire sports page with area high school basketball results from the night before. The Clareton Comets upset the Dakota Falls Flyers sixty-eight to sixty-six. At 11:30 he unwrapped his bologna and cheese sandwich and poured coffee from the thermos.

The snow had stopped, but the increasing northwest wind whipped it into a soft, white veil obscuring distant trees blending their dark shapes into the gray winter sky. The plow had already cleared the county road east of the lake. Horace left the squad car at the roadside and stepped out into the woods. Closer to the shack, he smelled the sweet, smoky scent of a wood fire. He wondered if it came from embers smoldering from the night before or from a newly started fire. Knowing Tom, it still could be the former, but he hoped Tom was already up. He approached close enough to shout but not too close.

"Hello, Tom . . . Hello. Anybody home?"

An almost transparent wisp of smoke floated up from the stovepipe until a gust of wind blew it away. Horace rapped on the door. He started to reach for the .38 revolver at his side, then lowered his hand and tried the door handle. He rapped one more time. Slowly he pushed

234

open the door and peered inside. A rumpled Army surplus sleeping bag and wool blanket covered a cot in the corner by the barrel stove. A small table and one chair stood in front of the stove. A metal platform on top of the stove held a kettle still steaming with warm water. Stacks of newspapers, magazines, and books lined the wall opposite the door. To the right of the door, food sat on a counter—a loaf of bread, some sausage, potato chips, a few bottles of cheap wine, a carton of cigarettes. At the other end of the shack from the stove, it felt cold enough to make mechanical refrigeration unnecessary. A pail half full of lake water sat on the floor by the stove. Looking at the books and magazines, Horace knew why Tom seemed to know so much. Too bad it didn't do anything for his hygiene; he wondered when the last time was Tom took a bath. The wood smoke mingled with the odor of stale food, cigarettes, dirt, and grime.

Horace stepped back outside and took a deep breath from the fresh, cold air. He noticed the tracks in the snow leading away from the shack and became a little disgusted with himself for not noticing earlier. He walked back through the woods to the squad car on the road. He tried to guess where Tom might have gone. He remembered Ike and drove toward Doc Ahrends' vet clinic.

Driving into the farmyard, Horace could see lights on but no sign of the vet's pickup. He went into the former dairy barn that served as the clinic and kennel. An oil stove heated the former milk house converted to an office and exam room. White-painted concrete block walls shone under the sharp glare of fluorescent lights. A gray parka hung on one of the coat hooks next to the door. The smell reminded him of wet cardboard mixed with the scent of cleaners and medicines. He thought he heard sounds coming from the main barn where the kennels and stalls were located. He opened the door leading into the barn.

"Hello! Anybody home?"

He saw Tom stand up by the kennel.

"Tom, is that you?"

Tom walked over and greeted the officer. He looked calm but tired. The barn was kept just warm enough to keep the water in pails from freezing when nested in a pile of straw. To Horace it felt colder inside than outside; he shivered a little just to look at Tom standing there in his flannel shirtsleeves.

"Where's doc?" Horace asked. "Are you here to see Ike? How's he doing?"

"Doc's out on a call. Ike's doing okay. He's pretty sore."

"That's too bad, what they did. I wish we could do something. So, you're here all by yourself?"

"Not sure if his wife's home. She could be in town shopping. I'm kind of taking care of the place, the clinic here, until he gets back."

Tom explained that he'd been helping around the clinic since last summer. He cleaned stalls and kennels, fed and watered animals being cared for. Doc Ahrends' practice focused mainly on farm livestock; he had been looking for someone to help out and watch the place when he was away at farms. He paid Tom a small wage and offered him a place to stay. Tom turned down the room offer even though living in the shack meant a two-mile walk one way. He appreciated that Doc didn't mind if Ike came along to work.

Tom led Horace back to the stall where Ike lay sprawled out on his side. His tail wagged weakly; he lifted his head off the straw slightly trying to greet the new visitor. His black and brown hair looked matted around his head and one shoulder where it had been shaved around the stitches. One of his long legs stuck out straight wrapped in a splint. Horace looked at the dog and shook his head.

Tom knelt next to Ike and gently scratched behind his ears. "You know, dogs and horses are the only people you can really trust."

Horace smiled. "That's what all the kids call me, Horse."

"I know."

"I don't mind. In fact I kind of like it. I've been called a lot worse, that's for sure."

"So, are you here about Ike or what?"

"Actually I wanted to talk to you," Horace said.

"Me? What about?"

"You know the talk that's been going around town, about the Harley kid getting beat up."

"You know I didn't do it."

"I know, but the problem is others think you did, or want to think you did."

"Are you here to arrest me then?"

"No, but there is something we've got to talk about. Maybe it can turn out for the better for everyone in the long run. Let's go back to the office and talk about it."

Back in the office Tom poured a cup of coffee, offered it to Horace and poured one for himself. Horace did his best to explain his conversation Friday with Dr. Nelson. He told Tom that he had two choices, face an assault charge or get in the treatment program at the hospital. Tom sat there sipping his coffee, stoic and silent.

"I'll have to think about it."

"Well, you better think fast. There's not much to think about. Look at your life. Drunk half the time, living like a bum. If you shape up you've got a lot of good years left. I know what you've done. You could get a job on one of those interstate highway projects. Maybe even meet someone. It's not too late. You never know."

Tom looked out the window in silence. Through the white clouds of blowing snow, he saw the headlights of the vet's pickup turning into the driveway. Doc Ahrends stepped inside the office looking surprised and slightly mystified at the police officer's presence. He hung up his coat and extended his hand, warmly greeting Horace. Horace began by asking him how Ike was doing; Tom excused himself and went back into the barn.

HORACE COULDN'T SEE A THING THROUGH the snow blowing across the field. He returned to the barn, which he and the vet had already searched. Tom had vanished. Horace had explained to Doc Ahrends why he was there. They decided Horace would go to the shack; Doc Ahrends would drive back to town and look around. They figured Tom would have to find some shelter because the dropping temperature and strong northwest wind pushed the wind chill past twenty degrees below zero.

Doc Ahrends saw him first, leaving the feed elevator. Because of his travels in the countryside, the vet served as a useful contact for the sheriff's department with his two-way radio patched into dispatch. He called the dispatcher, asking her to call Horace on his walkie that Tom was heading west from the elevator toward the lake near the inlet of Miller Creek. Doc Ahrends turned off his headlights and slowly followed in his pickup from a distance. He lost sight of Tom trudging through the snow into the cattails.

In Tom's shack, Horace felt a little warmer out of the wind and cold. He sat in the chair flipping through a magazine, angry about Tom's stubborn resistance. The dispatcher's voice crackled, relaying the message from Doc Ahrends. Horace decided to wait in the shack, but the more he thought about it, he decided to venture outside to look for Tom. He wanted to follow the trail through the woods back to the road. His gut told him to head out on the ice across the lake. His sense of duty backed up his intuition, overcoming the anxiety he felt about going out on the ice even though folks told him four inches was plenty enough to support a person. He zipped up his coat all the way, pulled down and secured the ear flaps on his warm hat and left the shack. He pointed his flashlight's bright beam into the blowing snow. He turned it off because it didn't help and would only reveal his position.

Between the intermittent wind gusts, he could see the dark line of the opposite shore and outline of buildings in town. He walked toward the northeast shore about where Doc Ahrends had lost sight of Tom, occasionally slipping and cussing where the wind had exposed bare ice. About half way across, he saw a figure moving in his direction. They closed to about forty yards, then Tom turned and started trying to run back the way he had come. Had they been on dry ground, Horace would have overtaken him in less than fifty yards. Running and slipping on the ice, he gained slowly. He worried if Doc Ahrends were to encounter Tom back on the shore before he got there, and if Tom were to became violent.

The exertion of trying to run on the ice felt like someone switched on a heater inside his jacket. He closed within twenty yards of Tom, shouting for him to stop. He thought they were far enough out on the solid ice from the inlet of Miller Creek. This early in the season the current kept it ice-free near the mouth. Where the ice sheet began it appeared solid, but the current narrowed the thickness to an inch, enough to hold up snow but not much else.

"Tom! No! Get away from the edge." Horace stopped well out on the thicker ice, watching in anguish as the thinner ice gave way, dumping Tom into the dark, freezing water. Horace called for help on the walkie-talkie. Tom flailed his arms in the water and tried to pull himself up on the ice. The frigid water soaking into his heavy parka and clothing soon would drag him under even before the hypothermia set in. He did not cry out for help, but Horace could see terror in his eyes and his gasping breath.

Horace took off his jacket and cautiously approached. He lay down on the ice and crawled closer, hoping to get near enough to throw Tom the other end of the jacket. He was just about to throw when he heard a scraping noise. He looked to his left. Through the swirling snow, he saw a man pushing what looked like a small boat. About ten yards away from the open water, the man climbed into the boat. Using a long pole tipped with a metal point he continued pushing the boat across the ice. The boat carried a twelve-foot wooden ladder with a rope tied to one end. Drawing close enough, he slid the ladder toward Tom still clinging to the edge of the ice. Now Horace could see the panic in Tom's eyes, the searing pain from the icy water gripping his entire body. Tom reached out hooking his numb hands over the second rung of the ladder. At the boat, Horace helped Mr. Bergquist pull on the rope. Slipping on the ice, they tried to keep traction, slowly pulling Tom onto more solid ice. Horace helped him into the boat, and Mr. Bergquist covered him with blankets. Together they pushed the boat toward shore.

"Somebody sure is looking out for you," Horace said shaking his head and handing Tom a cup of hot coffee. Tom sat on a chair by the furnace in Bergquist's basement still soaked and shuddering under the olive-green wool Army surplus blanket around his shoulders.

"We better get you some dry clothes," Mr. Bergquist said. He came down the stairs a few minutes later carrying a pair of old jeans, socks and a sweatshirt. "Here, you can have these. Just keep them. The wife's been trying to throw them out anyway." Tom slowly reached for them and nodded. Mr. Bergquist brought in a red-and-black plaid wool jacket and an aviator style winter cap with pull down ear flaps. "There, now you'll look like a lumberjack, like Paul Bunyan," he chuckled.

"Well, sir, you sure came to the right place at the right time." Horace said. "How did you get all that gear out so fast?"

Mr. Bergquist looked away, off to some distant place only he could see. Tom thought he could see tears filling up the corners of his eyes.

"If only I'd had this stuff three years ago." Mr. Bergquist choked a little as he spoke. Finally he said, "My son fell through about the same place. It was late fall. The ice was hardly more than an inch thick, and his dog ran out after some geese in the open water by the creek. Andy tried to save him. Ever since in winter I've had this duck boat and gear by the shore. He would've been nineteen now."

Tom stared at Mr. Bergquist, hurting for his loss, guilty about his own rescue, comforted in the warmth, uncertain about what to do next.

"Damn ice." He spoke for the first time. "Sorry to put you through all this. Thanks for what you did."

"You're welcome. I'm glad I was there," Mr. Bergquist said. "You're a Minnesotan. Ice shouldn't be any mystery. Actually, there are many variations of ice. I've read about it a lot. It's not all the same.

Tom laughed. "Minnesota nice? It sounded like you said, 'Minnesota nice.'"

Horace gave Tom a curious look, then laughed. "There ain't no such thing, 'Minnesota nice.' Minnesotan ice maybe, but not Minnesota nice. You sure got a subtle way with words."

Mr. Bergquist looked at both of them blankly. Ever since they lost Andy he did not take lake ice lightly, nor could he see any humor in the situation.

"You ought to know about the currents, especially by the inlet," he scolded. "You have to know what you're doing on the ice. And you too, officer. You should know better."

Horace shrugged. "I suppose. I was just doing my job. Thanks for being there. You ought to get some medal or something." He looked at the shivering man sitting by the furnace, hair matted here and askew there.

"Tom, we got some business to take care of," Horace said. "What in heaven's name are you still doing around here anyway? Shouldn't you be farther south this time of year? It's only December. Wait 'til January or February if you want to see some real cold weather."

Tom looked up, then looked away. He still wore the wet clothes. Outside in the wind and bitter cold they would freeze in a minute. He would have to change into the borrowed clothing. This time he would not be able to escape the younger, stronger and faster police officer, unless he blacked out only to find out later what he had done. He liked Horace and hoped it wouldn't happen.

"I come from around here. I know what to expect."

"We have to talk about what we're going to do," Horace asserted. "Like I said, you've got two choices. This Dr. Nelson, he sounded real decent. This could be a big turnaround in your life. Change is tough, but once it happens you're much better off. Now you come with me. You can stay in the jail tonight—heck—it's a warm bed and meals. Tomorrow we'll take a ride to Dakota Falls."

"Okay. But I'd rather stay at my place tonight. I need to get a few things. I'll meet you tomorrow at Doc Ahrends' place."

"And what if you go back, get drunk and change your mind?"

"I won't change my mind." Tom looked up at the officer. "Could you do me a favor?"

"What's that?"

"Could you see if Maria Reese and her son are there, too?"

Horace tried to conceal his surprise. He decided against telling Tom that he was going to ask them along in the first place. He would wait and see where this goes.

"I suppose I could ask them. They're supposed to be driving back from Minneapolis tonight. It probably would have to be after church. May I ask why?"

"Just ask them, okay?"

Horace agreed and didn't press the issue. He knew that Tom had talked with the kids from time to time. He had hoped just the kids' presence might help persuade him to come in peacefully. Tom changed into the dry clothes and accepted a bowl of chicken noodle soup, thanking Mrs. Bergquist and saying he was sorry to hear about their son. The wind was letting up, but the temperature kept dropping. Horace gave Tom a ride in the patrol car to the vet's to see how Ike was doing, then dropped him off at the trail leading through the woods to the shack.

"You better get a fire going quick," Horace advised. "And good luck." He took off his glove and held out his hand.

Tom did the same, and they shook hands.

"Thanks," Tom said. "See you tomorrow. One o'clock sound okay?"

"See you then."

Tom got out and Horace watched until he couldn't see him anymore through the dark gray almost black tree trunks. He drove back into town feeling more hopeful that everything would work out. He looked forward to hearing about the shopping trip after the others returned. He wondered what Maria would say when he told her that Tom asked if they could be there.

ഉ 20 ര

DURING SUNDAY SCHOOL THE KID WHO STOOD in for Mario at the outdoor nativity scene Saturday evening wanted payback. No matter how much he'd stomped his feet, they still grew numb out in the bitter cold even though they closed down the scene early because of it, and he'd expressed his displeasure. Mario told him that's why he had been chosen as one of the wise men in the first place; he was smart enough to avoid the duty when it was so cold. The other kids laughed.

Some had never been to Minneapolis and wanted to hear about his trip. He told about shopping at Dayton's and Donaldson's. They'd eaten hamburgers and sandwiches at the big F.W. Woolworth lunch counter. For supper they stopped at the Forum Cafeteria. The tall buildings, crowds of people, holiday lights and decorations of the big city left them in a relaxed, festive mood on the three-hour drive through the dark winter night back to Clareton. For Mario the mood began to dissipate when thoughts crept in about going back to school Monday and the nagging, unfinished business about the fight and who was to blame.

The regular Sunday school teacher had stayed home nursing a cold. Unprepared for the regular lesson, the substitute teacher spent the class time talking about the St. Lucia story. After the last worship service parishioners and visitors gathered in the fellowship hall where young girls dressed in white gowns and wearing tiaras with candles walked gracefully among the tables serving coffee and Scandinavian pastries. Maria told Mario that would have to hold them for a while; they wouldn't have time for a regular Sunday dinner before one o'clock. Mario filled his plate with rosettes. Maria suggested that lefse would be more substantial fare. He liked lefse, too, slathered with butter, sprinkled with sugar and rolled up. He ignored the disapproving stare from the lady looking at him trying to balance the pastries he'd piled high on his plate.

OFFICER GREENE ARRIVED AT THE REESE house at 12:45. Mario hung up the phone feeling lonesome and little anxious. Jake said he couldn't go along because they had company for Sunday dinner. That meant, even if they didn't have to go to the meeting with Tom, Mario probably wouldn't be able to watch the football game at Jake's place anyway. Putting on her coat, Maria told Mario to do the same.

"Do we really have to go?" Mario pleaded.

"We said we would. Now I'm not so sure why. I suppose because it's Horace. If he thinks we can help—you can help—then we'll try. Horace said Tom asked if you could be there. He must trust you or something."

"I don't know what to say. What am I supposed to do?"

"You don't have to say or do anything. Horace is in charge. We'll let him handle it."

DOC AHRENDS LOOKED OUT THE KITCHEN window and saw the '53 Pontiac pull to a stop outside the clinic. He had expected to see a Clareton police car. At the last minute, Horace had decided to use his own car just in case the squad car might spark something that upset the plan. He hoped the chief wouldn't find out, and if Stark did, that he would be able to explain. Horace opposed Maria's request that Jim and Thelma accompany them. He said too many people might scare Tom off.

Tom stood behind a cottonwood tree in the grove watching them exit the car and walk toward the barn. He saw Doc Ahrends leave the house and follow, jamming his arms into his jacket as he always did to save a few seconds of time. Tom looked around and down the driveway. The temperature had just crept a few degrees above zero, but the wind had subsided and the low-hanging sun shone bright in the clear, deep-blue sky, making it seem warmer.

The trees in the grove surrounded him like a cordon of strong, silent guardians. He saw the only people in Clareton he trusted: Horace, Doc Ahrends, and Mario. He squinted hard trying to make out the features of Maria. The longer he waited, the more he felt his courage fade. He turned away and started walking back through the grove trying to keep the trees between himself and the barn. From the kitchen window, Mrs. Ahrends saw a dark figure moving in grove, head cast downward, hands jammed in parka pockets. She picked up the phone and started dialing. Still looking out the window, she saw the figure stop; she stopped dialing. It turned around and began walking slowly back toward the barn.

Four old, wooden high-backed chairs served as the clinic waiting area next to the desk. Maria opened her purse, took out her compact, stood by a window and peered into the little mirror inside checking her makeup. She dabbed powder on her forehead and nose; she thought they looked a little moist. Mario sat quietly looking around the office and exam table all together in one room. He tried to read the labels on the bottles and boxes on the shelf. A stack of fifty-pound bags of therapeutic dog food leaned against one wall. Horace stood by the window making casual conversation with Doc Ahrends. Both familiar with working weekends or nights, they commiserated about missing the Chicago Bears-Detroit Lions football game. Again Horace thanked Doc Ahrends for helping out. Mario asked how Ike was doing and if they could see him. Doc Ahrends agreed and led Mario back to the stall in the barn. Horace and Maria remained waiting in the office.

"Here he comes," Horace said.

Hands jammed in his pockets, a green stocking cap pulled down over his ears, Tom crossed the farmyard toward the barn, head downward, looking about ten feet ahead as he walked. He pushed open the milk house-clinic door and stepped in.

"Hello, Tom. How're you doing? You thaw out yet from yesterday?"

Tom looked up at Horace with dull, deadpan eyes. Horace silently cussed himself for alluding to the incident on the lake. The meeting wasn't getting off to a good start. Then a slight smile turned up the corner of Tom's mouth.

"I needed a bath anyway."

Horace relaxed and smiled.

Tom turned away momentarily in a fit of coughing.

"Tom, this here's Maria Reese. Mario's mother. Mario and the doc are out in the barn visiting Ike."

Tom looked down at the floor, then slowly turned his head toward Maria. His gaze slowly lifted and locked in on her face. Maria looked back frozen in silent astonishment. Horace watched them, suddenly sensing that this was something different than an awkward meeting of strangers. He wanted to say something, but he had learned the value of patience. He held his hand close, waiting to see what the others would do, waiting for the right time. Most of the time people revealed the truth when led and not forced in that direction.

"Maria, this is Tom Nathan."

"Hello," Maria said. Years ago his face, well-tanned in the California sun set off iridescent, blue eyes like the deep, clear water of Lake Tahoe. His clean, close-cropped blond hair had become darker and thinner; his eyes looked weary and faded. Beneath his short beard, Maria could still see the familiar lines of his square jaw. Was it really him? The age difference then was part of the attraction. Now he was past his prime and she saw what time could do.

"Hello," Tom replied quietly. Maria recognized the voice.

"Tom's agreed to go to Dakota Falls," Horace said.

"I hear they have some real good programs there," Maria said looking at Horace. "It's too bad about what happened, about accusing him of assault."

She looked at Tom.

"Mario told them what really happened," she said firmly. "They just ignored him. It was like they had already made up their minds. It made me so mad."

Tom watched her speak, slowly nodding in understanding assent. After all the years of searching and running, it now seemed so unreal standing there in an old milk house attached to a Minnesota barn on the doorstep of another bitter cold winter. So many times he had tried to write the words. So many times he imagined speaking them. He could not let go of the vision. With Horace there, he could not try speak them, which was almost a relief. The words were so inadequate anyway. Just to see her made his heart swell and begin to ache. Now he knew for sure.

"Mario's a good kid," Tom said quietly, gazing at Maria. "He stuck up for me when he didn't have to. For a kid to do something like that, it's really something. We had some good talks. He's smart, got some good friends. Must be doing good in school. Tough kid, too, whipping that Harley kid like that. You've done a good job."

"Thanks," Maria replied blushing faintly.

"Your last name. Reese. You're married, or were?"

"I'm not married. We changed our name not long after we moved to town. It's a long story," Maria said with a slightly embarrassed smile.

"You two talk like you know each other," Horace broke in. "Is there something going on here I don't know about?"

"Not anymore," Tom looked at Horace, a wisp of sadness in his eyes.

The door from the barn opened. Doc Ahrends and Mario entered breaking off the tense encounter, which the vet vaguely sensed in the three standing there looking toward them as if they'd just heard shocking news. He spoke first.

"Hi, Tom. Ike's coming along well. We should keep him a few more days though. That okay with you?"

"Looks like it might be longer than that," Tom said wryly. He looked at Horace. "They don't take dogs where I'm going, do they? I mean real dogs, the four-legged kind." He tried to laugh at his own joke but no one else did even if they understood.

"He can stay here as long as necessary," the vet said. "He's used to the place. We get along well. He's a good dog."

"Thanks," Tom said. He looked around at the others. "You folks sure been good to me. It means a lot. I know I can be a handful sometimes. I wish I could explain it. I don't want to be like that. I'd change if I could. Maybe this'll do it."

Tom zipped up his parka, getting ready to leave. He walked over to Doc Ahrends and shook his hand. The vet smiled back warmly, thanking Tom for helping out at the clinic. Tom faced Mario and held out his hand. Mario offered his and their hands clasped, this time without gloves or mittens. Tom lingered, holding Mario's smaller hand in his rough, chapped hand with the dirty and cracked fingernails. Almost serenely he looked down at the boy.

"Thanks, Mario. For being a friend. Maybe you can come and visit me. Maybe you can help Doc here take care of Ike."

Mario said he'd like to do that. Doc Ahrends nodded. Tom walked over to Maria and looked in her eyes. Long ago he would have picked her up and embraced her. He offered his hand. She hesitated and slowly raised her hand, and they gently clasped.

"Thanks for being here," Tom said quietly. "You've done well. Good luck."

He turned toward Horace and nodded. They walked out and got into Horace's car, Tom just staring ahead with no outward hint of the sweet, painful memories flashing through his mind and the thought of them having to be all he would have the rest of his life. He suddenly realized he would miss Mario. Maybe they would visit. He stopped his thoughts on the brink of starting to feel sorry for himself. While he had not chosen the path his life had taken entirely of his own conscious will, by now he accepted it.

RIDING BACK TO TOWN, MARIO LOOKED across the snow-covered fields glistening white beneath the December sun, already starting its way down toward the southwestern horizon. In just a couple hours it would become a glowing, orange disk in the early winter dusk. Although he knew the explanation from science class, he still marveled that it looked so large just before it set compared with the much smaller appearance high in the sky. He looked at Maria, who seemed much more quiet than usual. She sat at the wheel looking straight ahead. It wasn't like her on a sunny Sunday afternoon. It made him feel a little melancholy and he didn't know the reason. He hadn't wanted to go to the meeting with Tom, but it went better than he expected. It had been a stressful week. Maybe things would settle down now. He thought about calling Jake to see if he could still go over to watch the rest of the football game. He shivered at the thought of how they played football in December even if it wasn't quite as cold in Chicago. This game he would cheer for Detroit because of Horace. Maria welcomed the space when Mario called Jake. It was okay to go over to the Carlson's because their dinner guests had left. Maria watched him hurry out the door; she reached for the phone. Thelma's father answered. He handed Thelma the phone, and she answered sounding upset. It distracted Maria from her own crisis, for a moment.

"Thelma, what's the matter. Is everything okay?"

"I can't talk now. No, it's not okay," she whispered.

"Can you come over? I need to talk about something, too."

"I don't know. I don't know where to go. Every time I go someplace, they think I'm seeing you-know-who. Even at your place."

"How about church? We could say we're going to help clean up after the St. Lucia lunch."

Earlier Thelma casually mentioned that Horace was on duty today. That's when it started all over again, the arguing with her parents about the man she was beginning to love. Now it worked to her advantage. Her parents did not become suspicious when she told them she was going to church to help clean up. Any other day they could have met downtown at a café or the drugstore soda fountain. On Sunday everything was closed except the churches. They would meet at the back door and find an empty Sunday school room. Just in case, they decided to drive separately. On the way over, Thelma's anger again brought thoughts of moving out. She was twenty-four, and it was about time.

An elementary school teacher's salary wasn't much, but enough for her to live on her own. Every time she talked about it, her father argued against it, and she backed down. He believed that marriage was the only way a young woman could leave home. Thelma wanted that, too, but as the years passed, the opportunities dwindled. Clareton offered few in the first place. To put Horace in that category was so remote that no one even considered it, not even Thelma until today. The argument with her father tore a small opening in the shroud of convention that protected but also limited her mind.

Mrs. Hanson looked startled when she saw the two young women sitting in the darkened room. They sat in folding chairs in the small room in the church basement, the only light coming from the fading afternoon sun filtering through a small window high on the wall. She told them the women had finished cleaning up and were getting ready to leave. Maria said they were just talking and would turn out all the lights when they left. Mrs. Hanson smiled and returned to the kitchen. Thelma told her story first. Her face looked steadfast even with smudged makeup around her eyes.

"I'm going to do it," Thelma's voice quivered. "I'm going to go with Horace. He's been asking me ever since school started this fall. He can't take it here anymore. Neither can I. We love each other. We really do."

"I know," Maria said quietly. "I know it's not going to be easy. I'll do anything I can to help you. I'll really miss you."

"I'll miss you, too. But you've got Jim. And with Mario getting older and into high school you've got a lot here."

"More than you know. More than I knew up until today," Maria said in an even, serious voice.

"What do you mean?"

Maria's hands went to her face to cover the tears, but not the spasms that the sobs sent through her body and out her shoulders. She wiped her eyes and began telling about the meeting, about Tom, about their past. Thelma listened, stunned.

"Are you sure?"

"I'm sure."

"Does anyone else know?"

"Horace. He was the only one in the office when we met. He took Tom to the hospital. I'm sure Tom told him everything."

"What about Mario and Jim? You have to tell them."

"I know. But I'm so scared. I think Mario will be okay. I just hope Jim understands."

"How do you feel about him, about Tom?"

"I don't know." Maria started crying again. "After all these years I had almost forgotten about him. Every now and then when I'd see Mario talking or acting a certain way it would remind me of him. Then I would remember the bad times. I just couldn't live like that. And my family— papa especially—would have nothing to do with him. Finally I just tried to run away from it all."

"How did he find you here?"

"I don't know. I knew he came from some place here in the Midwest. Back then it didn't really matter. Once when we were back visiting my family I heard from a waitress at a drive-in we used to go to that he had been around looking for me. Maybe he found something out. And here I thought I was getting away from it all coming out here," Maria said with a little laugh as though disgusted with herself.

"There are some things we can't just run away from all the time," Thelma said. "What if it's part of God's plan? Did you ever think about that? You'll just have to trust in God that everything will work out. We both will."

Although it was difficult to believe with deep conviction, just hearing the words Maria felt some relief. She smiled and squeezed Thelma's hand.

"I hope so," Maria said. "You know, I'm not sure Tom even knew about Mario at first. By the time Mario was born, he was already going over the edge. We had broken up long before that, but he still hung around. Papa acted like he would have killed him if he could."

"I never was really convinced about Mario's father being killed in a car accident," Thelma said. "When we first met, I figured your past was your business. I wasn't going to pry if you wanted to keep that to yourself."

"I'm sorry. I know I haven't been totally honest. I had to say something. When Mario was little it was easy. Back in California he had all his uncles around. When we came out here and he entered school, I had to say something, both for his sake and for the school board. Nobody questioned it."

"Well, I think it's going to work out," Thelma said trying to sound confident. "Tom's going to get helped at the hospital. I think Mario would like to visit him, and I think Jim will be supportive."

"I hope you're right."

"I hope it's going okay with Horace taking Tom to the hospital," Thelma said.

"I hope so, too."

HORACE WORRIED ABOUT TOM'S REACTION if he stopped at the police station to switch his vehicle for a squad car for the ride to Dakota Falls. He explained that since this was official business, he had no choice. Seeming to be resigned and docile, Tom shrugged in assent. Horace decided to take a chance and let him ride in the front seat. He prayed that Chief Stark would not see them or find out. Horace figured right now he most likely would be watching the football game.

At the station Tom waited in the front lobby while Horace went back to call the hospital; they would be waiting for him at the admissions building. In the squad car, Horace asked Tom if he minded if they listened to the football game on the radio. Leaving town and out on the highway, Tom sat quietly, gazing at the snow-covered fields and groves of trees shielding farmsteads from the cold northwest winds. Horace tried to follow the game, but his thoughts tried to frame questions he wanted to ask Tom but that would not disturb the present calm.

"That Mario, he's a good kid," Horace said looking at Tom and trying to detect some reaction.

Tom smiled. "Him and a couple other kids brought me turkey sandwiches on Thanksgiving. Can't remember the last time I had turkey."

"Good thing we didn't eat it all," Horace chuckled. "I can really pack it away. Jim, too. You know him?"

"Not really."

"He's Maria's fiancé. He's a dentist."

"I could use a dentist."

"They'll take care of all that at the hospital. I think it's good you're going there. So, how'd you know Maria?"

"We met out in California. She was just a kid. I was working on highway construction in San Diego. I don't know what she saw in me, being older and all. We had some good times. Then I got this wild hair up my ass and joined the Seabees. She was waiting for me when I got back, but it wasn't the same. Her old man never did see much in me. To him I was just another horny gringo chasing his beautiful daughter. Maybe that was part of her wanting to be with me. She was trying to get back at him. I don't know. I'll never figure 'em out, broads."

"You can say that again," Horace nodded, smiling. "And you're right about that, she is beautiful." He paused, contemplating the next question. "So, about Mario. Maria's said his daddy was killed in a car crash long time ago. You know anything about that?"

"I found out for sure today. And as far as I know, I ain't been killed in a car crash. Been in a couple but not killed."

"There is a resemblance. So, now that you have a son . . . that going to make any difference?"

"I'm going with you to the hospital ain't I?"

"Yep, that you're doing."

Tom clammed up and the remainder of the trip Horace counted off the miles in his mind, listening to the game. They turned off the highway into the campus of the Dakota Falls state hospital. Even in winter it was beautiful. Large lawns with ancient, gnarled oak trees—it rivaled some country clubs. Horace stopped by the curb in front of the admissions building. Two large men emerged. They wore white uniforms. Tom looked out the squad car window, and Horace could see his body turn rigid, his hand grasping the door handle and knuckles turning white.

In the backseat of the squad car, behind the heavy wire screen separating front and back and without interior door handles, a passenger would be unable to get out unassisted. Sitting in front, Tom suddenly opened the door, sprang out and started running down the street. Horace jumped out in chase. "Tom, Tom," he shouted. "Stop! Don't do this!"

In less than two blocks Horace closed in, still shouting. In a full run, Horace suddenly dove forward and tackled Tom to the snow-covered pavement. At first Tom struggled and fought back furiously. Horace grabbed his arms from behind and held him to the ground. The hospital workers finally caught up, winded, heaving in gasping breaths.

"Tom, we're not going to hurt you. They're going to help. C'mon now and cooperate," Horace pleaded. "This ain't easy for me either. Don't make it hard on everyone now."

Tom's struggles subsided. A sudden wave of exhaustion swept over his body; his face felt hot and cold at the same time. He felt weak as if someone had pulled the plug on his energy. Without any warning a hospital worker produced a syringe and thrust the needle into Tom's thigh right through his jeans, quickly injected the sedative and pulled it out. Tom's whole body stiffened in reaction to the needle. He raised his head, trying to look back at the assailant. He cursed and started struggling again to escape.

"What the hell'd you do that for?" Horace complained to the hospital worker. "He was going to cooperate. You don't need to dope him up. I got him under control."

"You'll stick around then to keep him in line?" the hospital worker replied sarcastically. "We do what we gotta do. He's become violent once, he'll do it again."

Tom's struggling surged in one final effort to defy the sedative seeping into his body. Horace held tight. A small, white panel truck drove up. Two hospital workers unloaded a wheeled stretcher from the back. The first one looked close at Tom's face, lifted his eyelids and nodded to the other two. They told Horace to move aside and lifted Tom's limp torso into a sitting position. They shoved Tom's arms into the sleeves of a white, canvas jacket. Straps hung from the ends of the long sleeves, which were sewn shut. Other straps held the overlapping flaps of the front tightly secured. The sleeve straps held Tom's arms wrapped tightly around in front. They lifted him onto the gurney and buckled heavy straps around his body from ankles to shoulders.

"Jeez, you guys," Horace complained. "Take it easy. We were doing fine until you showed up. He isn't going to hurt anybody."

"That's what they all say," one of the hospital workers said, breathing heavily. "We know what we're doing. You got him here; your job's done except for signing some papers."

Tom's head rolled to the side looking toward them, through them. Horace felt a pang of regret. He couldn't tell if Tom was looking at him or if he was looking at anything at all.

"I don't know what they told you, but he didn't do it. They accused him of an assault. They said he could either face that charge or come here. He came here by his own choice. He deserves to be treated better than this," Horace said angrily.

They loaded the gurney into the truck and closed the door.

"He'll be fine. We just have to get him settled down first," the hospital worker said, offering a little smile. "Thanks for doing the legwork. You're fast. You must have been some kind of track star. How'd you ever get to be a cop there in Clareton anyway? We don't see too many of you folks around here. I mean, it don't bother me but, well, you know what I mean."

Horace hesitated, trying to find a response. No one ever talked about it, at least to his face. He had grown used to the stares from strangers out in public; still it bothered him from time to time. Back in Clareton citizens had become accustomed to seeing him around town, and his new-found friends and acquaintances made it bearable. They offered sympathy and support at times such as when he arrived at the station early one morning and found a white pillowcase draped over the back of his chair. It was tilted so that one corner pointed up in the air and with two eyeholes cut out. He ripped it off and threw it in the garbage can out back. He never said anything until weeks later and then only to Thelma.

The truck turned around back toward the admissions building; Horace followed on foot. In the hospital admissions office, all the papers sat ready for his signature. Judge Holmes had already signed them and, according to the date, three days earlier. Horace signed them and then took a chance on calling Chief Stark now rather than wait until returning to the station. The football game was over anyway. Stark didn't say much; he didn't even say good job or offer thanks. His tone of voice revealed irritation and enunciation suggested whiskey. Horace drove off the hospital campus feeling unsettled and melancholy, the mood matched by the early-setting December sun and darkening sky, barren trees the color of coal, and the Detroit Lions had lost to the Chicago Bears twenty-one to sixteen.

∽ 21 ∾

ONDAY MORNINGS, ESPECIALLY in the middle of December, came with all the anticipation of a visit to the dentist, at least before the Reeses switched to Jim Andersen two years ago. Their former dentist, in his seventies, had started slowing along with his worn-out drill and believed Novocain was for sissies. Dr. Andersen showed empathy, used more up-to-date equipment, and Novocain. Their visits to the dentist became more frequent, and after a while that's all they had become, visits.

Mario rolled out of bed and looked at the Mickey Mouse alarm clock, again thinking about California; it still would be warm in San Diego but it wouldn't seem like Christmas. Friday and the start of the two-week Christmas break seemed so far off.

He didn't know what to think about what his mother had told him Sunday evening. He understood that his family differed from most other kids' families, but they all understood that whatever circumstances comprised a kid's home life it was all part of the normal community fabric.

Only once in a while did a particular kid's family structure or status become an issue. Once kids found out that Mario lived alone with his

mother and didn't have a father around, they accepted it. This new revelation most certainly would become an issue unless no one found out.
Maria said that at least for now they would keep it to themselves. The
whole town didn't have to know. That was fine with Mario.

Only a few times in recent years had he wondered about the other
half of his parentage, more out of curiosity than anything. A child's trust
helped him to believe his mother's explanation that his father had died
in a car crash long ago. Simple rationalization kept the trust intact; it
could have happened, maybe she actually thought it *had* happened.

In any case there was no place for a father, no empty part of his
life that he was aware of. Now he would have to try to find a place. He
tried to understand where Tom would fit in. He seemed kind, friendly
and totally attentive during their previous encounters. Now he was a
drunk locked up in a mental hospital. Mario felt nothing except concern
about what might await him at school and the weight of the burden of this
new information that he now carried. Sometimes when he would see his
friends with their fathers, he sensed that he was missing out on something but it never really bothered him. In the cases of some fathers that
was a good thing.

It helped having Jim, Thelma, and Horace over Sunday evening
to talk things over. They relaxed for a while watching "The Ed Sullivan
Show." They promised to do what they could to help and to keep the matter private. Thelma admitted she couldn't remember exactly what she
told her parents. Horace described what happened taking Tom to the
hospital and that he had to call Chief Stark, but that he didn't say anything more than they already knew about Tom's identity. He couldn't
promise though what would happen Monday when the chief would want
a full account. Concealing such information would have serious consequences. He dreaded Monday more than Mario.

Chief Stark would have already been at the station three hours
Monday morning when Horace arrived at 9:00 a.m. Stark always started
his work day at six going through reports and other paper work a couple
of hours before the rest of his world. Not finding a report from Horace,

even though it would have been reasonable to let him wait until Monday morning to write it and which Horace intended to do, gave Stark another opportunity to browbeat the young officer. He called Horace into his office. Without even a "Good morning," Stark began his interrogation.

"I didn't see your report. Why didn't you do it Sunday?"

Horace settled into the heavy, wooden chair in front of Stark's desk.

"It was getting late. I was going to do it this morning. I called you yesterday."

"So, how'd it go? Did he cooperate?"

"For the most part, yes. He sort of got cold feet when we got to the hospital. We had to restrain him a bit when he tried to run."

"Would've helped if you'd put him in the back of the squad car," Stark said, revealing his ominous 'gotcha' expression—a little smile curling up on one side, head tilted slightly forward and unblinking eyes leveled at the victim—that Horace had seen before. How did Stark know? Horace shifted in his seat trying to decide how to respond.

"I know him. He's not a criminal. He was cooperating."

"He's a suspect in an assault. He's a drunk, and there's evidence of mental instability. It was a serious breach of rules to not keep him under control at all times. What if he became physical when you were driving on the highway? What could have made you decide to give him special treatment?"

Horace began to feel flushed and angry at the chief's badgering. It seemed no matter what he did or that he did something very well the chief would zero in on the tiniest flaw as if he relished picking away at the young officer, who in the eyes of a goodly number of people prominent in the community, stood as evidence of the chief's inner weakness and ineffectiveness.

"I just got back from Dakota Falls," Stark continued. "Talked to Dr. Nelson. This time I caught him before he could sneak away. Looks like Nathan will be there a while. By the way, I saw you with him outside the station Sunday, in your own car."

Stark leveled an accusing look at Horace; the chief picked up a manila envelope from his desk and pulled out the contents. Horace returned a steady gaze and remained silent.

"This is some of the stuff they found on him," Stark said. "They hang on to the money and other valuables. These are just some papers and stuff they found in his pockets."

He picked up and unfolded a newspaper clipping, partially torn and frayed at the edges.

"Now why do you think he had this?" He held it up so Horace could see.

The farm page of the *Minneapolis Journal* featured a story about migrant workers. The reporter and photographer had traveled to small farm towns in western Minnesota. One of several sidebar stories told of a young teacher who came to Minnesota to teach summer school for migrant workers' kids. If it hadn't been for the picture, Tom never would have noticed. Horace leaned in for a closer look, and Stark handed it to him. Horace read the headline: Clareton church hires Californian to teach summer school for migrant children. Maria's smiling face looked out from the photo. Another photo showed her reading to a group of children.

"So, tell me Horace. What's the connection here?"

Horace scanned down the article, unconsciously biting on his lip. He prayed that what he was about to say would not bring harm to Maria and Mario. He told the chief about Sunday afternoon's revelation. Stark leaned back in his chair listening and showing a slight, satisfied smile. He could hardly wait to see Earl Harley. His next call would be to Mayor Fairbanks. Withholding information and violating apprehension and custody procedures were more than enough to force dismissal and not have to worry about political repercussions.

EARLY MORNING SHOUTS AND LOUD VOICES burrowed through Tom's unconscious stupor. He lifted his head from the bare mattress on the terrazzo floor. Light shone through a heavy screen over the window of the door faintly illuminating the room's interior. He felt nauseated and sore all over, punctuated by a dull ache on his right thigh. Once he had vowed never again to become trapped like this. He lay back looking around at the bare walls of the small, empty room except for a sink and toilet. When he tried to sit up his head felt as though spinning like a top. Another wave of nausea surged through him, and he flopped back down on the mattress.

Soon a face appeared behind the window screen. The bare bulb covered by a wire cage in the ceiling burst into bright light, searing through Tom's eyes, which he instantly winced tightly shut. Then panic began to well up in a clenching grip around his throat. He quietly cursed himself. His eyes began to fill with moisture, almost a new sensation or one he couldn't recall ever before experiencing. The door opened in time to stop him from beginning for the thousandth time to think about the way things could have been. A slight, young man entered, flanked by two larger men. His face looked friendly, even sincere, still young enough to hold ideals. The young man smiled, walked over and crouched down by the mattress, and extended his open hand.

"Good morning, Tom. I'm Dr. Nelson. Bradley Nelson. How are you feeling?"

Tom pulled his right elbow under himself, raised up his shoulders and reached across with his left hand. He hesitated putting his grimy, rough hands in the soft, clean hand of the doctor; he laid his fingers lightly on the doctor's open palm. He let his hand drop and looked down; he couldn't return the eye contact.

"We're going to help you. That's what we do here. We're glad you decided to come."

"I didn't exactly decide to. How long am I going to be here?"

"That's partly up to you. We'd like to find some things out first. After that we'll have a better idea. We know some things already. You're addicted to alcohol, you know that I'm sure. Even if you don't admit it you know it. Anything else you can tell me right now?"

Tom lay back on the mattress, staring at the ceiling. A fly flew in a crazy pattern around the ceiling light. He kept watching it, forgetting for a moment where he was and what he was, almost going into a hypnotic trance. Patiently, Dr. Nelson waited. One of the aides asked if he still needed help. Dr. Nelson said they could go.

"Do you have any family around?"

Tom mentioned his sister in Sioux Falls and brother in Minneapolis. He asked that they not be contacted.

"We won't right now, but eventually we'll have to. That's the rules. I'm sure they'll want to know how you're doing. Is there anybody else?"

"No, that's it." He thought about Maria and Mario, but said nothing.

Dr. Nelson patted him on the shoulder and said he'd feel better after getting some breakfast. They would talk again later.

Tom watched him leave, closing the door behind him; he heard the metallic click of the deadbolt lock. He knew about the state hospital at Dakota Falls. After his experience of two-and-a-half years at Stockton, he would not be here had it not been for Sunday. He closed his eyes to see the picture fresh in his mind of Maria standing just a few feet from him at the vet clinic so close he could smell her perfume. He replayed in his mind the conversations with Mario. He began to feel pride about the young boy's life and promise even though he had contributed nothing to it until now other than the seed, and if you could call those conversations a contribution. He would try to get better. He dared hope that Mario would visit.

CHIEF STARK ARRIVED AT THE HOTEL COFFEE SHOP more than half an hour past the usual 9:00 a.m. coffee time. Some of the men already were getting up to return to their offices and shops. Earl Harley and a few others remained. They set their own hours and could stay all day if they had wanted to. Earl was telling about the trip to Florida they planned to take right after Christmas. They would fly into Miami on one of those new Boeing 707s. They would borrow a car from an auto dealer acquaintance and drive down to the Keys leaving ample time for golf.

Chief Stark sat down at the large, round table toward the back, the same table they had used for as long as he had been in Clareton. Everyone in town knew who sat there at 9:00 a.m. every weekday morning, so it always was available when they arrived in ones and twos. Only occasionally did a waitress have to advise someone else who unknowingly sat there that it was reserved. The men said their greetings, and Harold reached for the coffee pot.

"So, Harold, how'd things go this weekend?" Earl leaned in speaking more quietly than usual. "I thought you were going to call me last night. Then you don't show here at nine. I was beginning to wonder."

"Everything's fine," Stark replied, slightly irritated. "I went to Dakota Falls this morning. Talked to Nelson. Nathan'll be there a while."

"Better be more than a while. If they let him go, it better not be back here."

Stark leaned back as the waitress brought the small plate with a single piece of wheat toast. While most of the others had pie or a sweet roll with their coffee, he always ordered toast in his ongoing battle to keep his waistline in check. He looked at the toast and called the waitress back. He suddenly felt a desire for a piece of banana cream pie and yielded to it. He would savor it as he would do the same in reporting to Earl and the other boys. No ordinary kind, this pie with its fresh, made-from-scratch filling and flaky crust had earned a reputation even beyond Clareton. The waitress took back the toast and returned with a slice of banana cream pie. She winked at Stark and said they wouldn't charge him for the toast. He picked up a fork and carved off the point of the piece of pie, thinking of the words to begin his piece of news and how it would surpass whatever Earl had been talking about.

"Part of him's still here," Stark said with a slightly mischievous smile.

"What's that supposed to mean?"

Chief Stark reached into his shirt pocket, pulled out the newspaper clipping and handed it to Earl Harley. "Get a load of this." Earl carefully unfolded it and looked it over.

Stark reached out and tapped the yellowing newsprint. "That was in Nathan's pocket. Notice anyone familiar?"

Earl tipped back his head to scan the clipping through his bifocals. Stark began to recount what Horace had told him back at the police station just a few minutes ago. Earl listened while he read, slowly shaking his head.

"It figures. I always wondered about her. How long has she been in town now, five, ten years? I always said it would be just the beginning. I don't mind if they come here and work the fields in summer. Just so they don't stick around. You know that, Harold. We see 'em around town in summer and who knows what they're up to. Makes more work for you don't it?"

"Not really. They pretty much keep to themselves. I think they're too tired to cause any trouble."

"So, what are you going to do?" Earl asked with that accusatory tone that Stark privately detested. He already knew what he was going to do and he didn't need Earl to tell him.

"Horace is gone."

Earl leaned back, looking at Stark with a raised eyebrow that said 'tell me more.' "I meant about Nathan and Maria Reese."

"What's there to do about that? Nathan's gone and that's it."

"What if he gets out, comes back and they get back together?"

"That's their business. I doubt that'll happen anyway. I'm talking about Horace."

Chief Stark described how he saw the young police officer and the felony suspect arrive at the police station Sunday afternoon, in the officer's private vehicle. They transferred to a squad car with Nathan sitting in front as if they were two friends going for a Sunday afternoon ride. Stark took pleasure in telling how he had a few of the other boys helping with the stakeout to watch Horace and alert the chief, and that he did so without including Earl Harley.

"We now have cause to get rid of Horace," Stark said with deliberate arrogance. "To transport a felony suspect without proper restraint procedures—that's a serious breach of tactical policy. What's more, he's been withholding information germane to the investigation. He's gone, and there's nothing Fairbanks and those pinko do-gooders on the council can do about it."

"Two for the price of one, huh?" Earl chuckled.

"You could say that."

"Maybe this'll help us get three."

"What do you mean? Fairbanks?"

"We spent a lot of money this fall. Maybe it won't be wasted after all," Earl Harley said, smiling and nodding knowingly.

Their candidate in the 1958 mayoral race, Henry Bloom, lost to Ralph Fairbanks by fifty-four votes, which, after a recount, increased to sixty-seven. The chief election judge, Mrs. Wiley, still hadn't recovered from the embarrassment. It had been the first recount ever in the eight elections for which she had been responsible.

The re-election of Ralph Fairbanks greatly disappointed Earl Harley, who had led the campaign for Bloom. They had spent the most ever on a Clareton mayoral race mostly due to the full-page ads in the *Clareton Chronicle*. The ads compared the qualifications of the two candidates, noting with prominence that back in the 1920s Ralph Fairbanks, as a college student, had attended a Socialist meeting. It was true, but Fairbanks did not have any idea how they knew. The ad said his opponent was a patriotic American who would stand strong against the insidious Communist threat.

Fairbanks had complained, saying that he only had attended out of curiosity and that it had been so long ago. He asked *Clareton Chronicle* publisher August Ditmarson to pull the ad or at least change it, but Ditmarson refused. If the information was true, there was nothing he could do about it. And as long as Earl Harley said it was true, that was good enough for him. With the campaign ads, plus the usual grocery store and car dealer full-page ads, the weeks leading up to the November 4 election set a new revenue record at the *Chronicle* for October. Ditmarson was very happy with that.

"It's too bad we have to wait four more years," Chief Stark said.

"Maybe. Maybe not," Earl Harley said, staring into his empty coffee cup.

RETURNING TO CLASS MONDAY MORNING it seemed to Maria that she had been gone two weeks instead of two days. The long trip to Minneapolis on Saturday followed by the events Sunday made the time seem to almost stand still. Some weekends just flew by, but not this one. The longest part came at the end when she lay in bed late Sunday night crying until sleep moved in, if not evicting at least superseding the memories and thoughts that left her drained and worn out.

Thoughts ricocheted inside her mind from happy memories of a brief love to regret that her life had not taken a different path, to devotion to her son, to loneliness for her family, to the young school children and the job she loved, and wondering what could have been had Tom survived the war with more than just his body intact. She had tried to pick up where they left off. He tried to remember where that was, but somehow became so lost that he couldn't find his way.

Whenever she asked him about what it was like in the Seabees or what he did on Iwo Jima, he had become irritated. He wouldn't talk about it at all, so she quit asking. He was often moody. He startled easily followed by angry outbursts at whatever noise or movement triggered his jumpiness. But she didn't give up and tried to reach out to him in other ways. She ignored her conscience and traditional upbringing to invite physical intimacy. She didn't tell Tom about the pregnancy and never saw him after Mario was born. Many times over the years, she would look at her son and wonder. What was Tom doing now? Had he gotten any better? Was he even still alive? What would he think if he knew that he had a son who looked so much like him except for darker hair?

Jim was so different. With more planning than passion, they both pursued a vision of happiness. He hadn't actually come right out and asked her to marry him; they had talked about everything else and had been approaching a mutual understanding. Shortly after Thanksgiving she thought he had almost reached the point of asking, just before everything happened. Several times he chatted to her about what it would be like to have children. She tried to explain that a child was a blessing and a burden, both wonderful. Under different circumstances she would have liked to have more, but as the years slipped by that thought faded. Now she thought she was too old. Jim politely disagreed.

She enjoyed Jim's company and was beginning to care about him. Not particularly handsome, he stood five feet, nine and one-half inches. Financially secure, and she believed also emotionally, he offered the stability needed for well-functioning family. He always seemed optimistic and enjoyed a good joke, and he was kind. When she cried, it was for losing Tom, the love that no longer existed, and the fear that what he had become would re-enter her life and might somehow destroy any hope of a happy future with Jim. She also cried about what all that had happened would mean for Mario. Finally, sleep brought relief.

Getting into the routine Monday morning, Maria felt much better except for the memory of the nighttime anguish and the tiredness that it left in its wake. The coffee smelled wonderful, and the radio weather report predicted a warm-up. It had been bitterly cold the last week, much below normal. She and Mario ate breakfast without much conversation, which wasn't all that unusual. Most mornings Maria did most of the talking. This morning Mario sensed she was being more quiet than usual although he didn't think about it or say anything.

Sunday afternoon at the Carlsons, Mario told Jake about the meeting with Tom at the vet's and that he went to the state hospital. Jake laughed and said he wasn't surprised; the guy did seem like a nut case. Mario wanted to tell more, but he couldn't bring himself to do it. They dropped the subject and tuned into "Bonanza" until Mario had to leave for nativity-scene duty at the church. He thanked the Carlsons for the bowl of chili. It had tasted good because he had been very hungry, but it was no match for his mother's chili. When he told the Carlsons about adding chocolate and cinnamon to neutralize the acid in the tomatoes they were skeptical, and he felt embarrassed for even mentioning it.

IN THE SCHOOL LUNCHROOM MONDAY, Rosalyn sat at their table, which she occasionally did in total disregard of the gender segregation among seventh graders. This time she did so with a purpose: to find out more about what happened Sunday. Her father had returned that evening from his job at the state hospital with another story to tell. This he often did although with discretion so as to maintain some degree of confidentiality.

But it was late, nearly midnight and everyone already was in bed, although Mrs. Sommers remained awake. Her husband couldn't resist telling her about Clareton's own Officer Greene chasing a man and tackling him to the ground. As usual when he worked the late shift before retiring to bed, he checked in on his sleeping daughter. He gently tucked the blankets around her shoulders and smoothed her hair. Sometimes he would lean over to leave a soft kiss on her forehead. Many evenings Rosalyn tried to stay awake and only pretending to be sleeping, waiting for those welcome but unspoken gestures of fatherly affection. Sometimes straining to hear her parents' late-night conversation, she had learned things her parents never would have discussed in front of the children. Her father stood in the open bathroom doorway wiping his face with a towel as he told his wife about the excitement at work, just loud enough for his voice to carry into their bedroom and also Roslayn's.

"YOU GUYS, DO YOU KNOW WHAT HAPPENED YESTERDAY?" Rosalyn sat on the end of the lunchroom table and leaned toward the boys. Some looked at her with disdain even though they knew she would ignore any rebuffs and forge ahead with whatever she had in mind to do. Almost every Monday kids brought accounts of activities and events from the weekend. Mario told about their trip to Minneapolis on Saturday. Rosalyn's intrusion saved him from revealing anything about what happened Sunday.

This might be something interesting, so they listened although with varying degrees of skepticism.

"They've got that bum at the funny farm. My dad came home from work last night and said he tried to run away. The cop had to run after and catch him."

"You mean Horse?" Jake asked.

"Yeah, him. And you know what they do there? They're going to cut part of his brains out. That's what they do to the crazy people. It turns them into zombies."

"Oh, please, not while we're eating lunch," one of the kids complained.

"They do not. How do you know?" another kid said.

"Yes they do," Rosalyn insisted. "I know because my dad works there. They do it so they don't go wild and hurt people."

"Tom wouldn't hurt anybody," Mario said. "They won't do that." He swallowed the other words that something in him wanted to get out. He believed that if those words did get out, the reaction, while he was unsure exactly what it would be, would most certainly be swift and intense, and most likely followed by ridicule.

"Well they just might," Rosalyn said sounding defensive.

"So, what if they did?" Jake said, tacitly declaring the subject to no longer of interest. It was just a bum who incidentally became part of a temporary diversion. Curiosity started it and sympathy may have sustained it for a time, but these became insufficient up against the outward circumstances of this man's life. It wasn't worth their trouble, and, had their attention continued, it certainly would have threatened their status among the other kids.

Occasionally Mario still heard taunts about being a "bum lover." As far as he and Jake were concerned, it was time for that to end. All last week Frank Harley had been particularly obnoxious, which seemed peculiar because he had been the one to get pounded. Yet he continued to taunt them, mostly Mario, but also his friends by association, about their connection to the old bum living in the shack outside town. It

269

annoyed them how some people in a conflict always managed to turn things around in their favor. It just wasn't fair.

Frank almost acted proud of the greenish-yellow bruise below his left eye and still slightly swollen lip. Many kids believed his story about how it had happened; he relished the sympathetic attention from some of the girls. It made him out to be almost a hero. When kids heard the other version, many didn't believe Marion Reese would or could do such a thing. Mario wouldn't talk about it except to say that Frank was a liar, so the collective seventh grade opinion on the matter remained divided.

EARL HARLEY ARRIVED HOME MONDAY after work in a good mood. It had been a good day. He had sold two cars, a Cadillac and a Buick. He was glad to see Frank already home. The boy had been spending too much time at the bowling alley playing pool and pinball. He should be learning how to make money before wasting so much time spending it. Earl mixed a martini before they sat down to dinner. He sat in the large easy chair reading the paper, scanning down the story under the main headline, "West to Stand Firm on Berlin."

"Got to stand up to those Commies," he said to no one in particular. Frank sat in front of the TV, trying to adjust the color. "Big mistake letting them take half of Germany," Earl muttered. He scanned further down the page pausing to read at least the first few paragraphs from several of the stories that drew his attention. "House Committee to Decide on Coya Probe of Her Charge of Malicious Conspiracy." He wagged his head in silent disdain. What a waste of taxpayer money. If she'd stayed home where she belonged in the first place, none of this would have happened. Even if her husband had been duped into writing that letter, he had done the right thing.

The martini went down smoothly. Mrs. Harley called from the kitchen that dinner would be ready in about fifteen minutes. Earl ordered his son to fix him another martini, one job that never drew a protest from Frank. At the liquor cabinet in the dining room and out of his parents' view Frank took a shot himself while mixing the drink, undetectable compared to the amount the Harleys consumed. Mrs. Harley typically took her two drinks, and sometimes three, while preparing dinner before her husband arrived home. By the time they sat down to dinner, the conversation sometimes became loud and occasionally belligerent.

This time Earl Harley had something interesting to talk about. He told everything he'd heard from Chief Stark about Sunday's events. He had already told them right as he arrived home that the bum had been apprehended. It took the martinis to elicit the rest, not because he was holding it back deliberately, but he had almost forgotten; he still didn't comprehend there could be anything favorable about an old drunken bum.

"This Reese kid, what's he like?" Earl asked his son.

Frank gave him a questioning look, continuing to chew a mouthful of Salisbury steak. Why in the world would his father ask something like that?

"I don't know. He's just a kid at school," Frank said.

"His mother's a teacher, but I don't know anything about her husband," Louise Harley added. "I don't know if she even had one. They came here from California a few years ago."

"I know that," Earl said with some irritation. "I was asking about her son. But you're right, she doesn't have a husband, but her son still has to have a father, right?"

Louise Harley remained silent, confronted with that familiar air of sarcasm coming from her husband. On this occasion she sensed something else, an attitude of smugness, as if he knew something that they didn't. She wanted another drink.

"The kid, what's his name, Marion? What's he like?" Earl pressed his son. "Does he get into trouble? I don't want you hanging around with kids like that. Who'd name their kid Marion anyway?"

Frank looked up from his plate, a slight sneer in his expression. "Are you kidding? I'd never hang around with him. He's nothing but a little punk. He thinks he's such a goody goody."

271

"John Wayne's real name is Marion," Louise interjected, inflecting a little defiance, although not too much. When Frank was born they argued about his name. Francis had been her paternal grandfather's name, so Louise won out. Earl relented but never used it; he even wrote down "Frank" when he brought the birth announcement to the paper, for which Louise never really forgave him. Her husband shot her an annoyed expression, then returned his attention to Frank.

"He's got no right to be conceited," Earl said. "Guess who his daddy is." He paused, looking from Frank to Louise and back to Frank. "Anybody?"

"I don't know. So what?" Frank finally replied.

Mrs. Harley's thoughts raced, trying to collect the bits of gossip accumulated over the years. She hadn't heard anything about Maria Reese fooling around. The young teacher hadn't been a topic of discussion at Louise's bridge club since Maria first arrived in Clareton. In any case, it would have to be before she and her son arrived in Clareton. For a moment, Louise was stumped until bits of evidence began to form a thought, encouraged by her husband's knowing look and slightly nodding head.

"What are you saying, Earl?"

"I'm saying that this bum we picked up is the kid's daddy. Can you believe that?" Earl Harley chuckled.

"I guess it figures," Frank said. "One time downtown, we saw this guy trying to steal stuff. We hollered at him to stop, and Marion comes along and yells at us for yelling at the bum."

"You shouldn't be downtown in those places in the first place," his mother said.

"Oh, ma," Frank said rolling his eyes.

"That's okay Louise. These kids have to get some street smarts, too," Earl said. "Whoever or whatever this guy is, he won't be a problem anymore. It's probably a good thing for this Marion kid. Having a drunken bum like that for a father can't be too good for a kid."

Frank left the dinner table, saying he was going over to the ice rink to play hockey. By now the early December cold snap had hung on so long, folks had become resigned to it. At first it kept people indoors evenings to the dismay of merchants counting on crowds of holiday shoppers. In the homes with kids who had televisions, arguments broke out over whether or not they should stay indoors and watch TV or play outside despite the cold. As long as they dressed warmly and kept moving, the cold wasn't so bad, and playing hockey did the job except for occasional cold toes. Skating was slower because in the bitter cold the friction of skate blades didn't quite melt a sufficient, microscopic layer of water necessary for a fast glide. Even the puck moved like it was sliding on sand instead of ice. But after nearly two weeks of high temperatures in the single digits and below-zero lows, everyone looked forward to the forecast of a warm-up, almost with more anticipation than they did Christmas.

Frank left the house with his skates and hockey stick. He set them down behind the garage and headed instead to the bowling alley to meet Ronnie and some of the other guys. It was still too cold for hockey and he didn't care to see Marion at the rink if he happened to be there. He would rather wait until Tuesday at school to divulge what he knew. That way he would have more authority with other kids around, and it would be more embarrassing for Marion.

At the ice rink, Mario felt relieved when Frank didn't show up. They had a couple good games, which for a while provided some escape from the thoughts and worries of the past two days. Only four more school days remained until the two-week break, and the weather was going to warm up.

❧ 22 ❧

MARIO STARED AT THE SHEET OF PAPER on his science classroom desk. Worry began to simmer deep in his bowels. Mr. Hanson, the seventh-grade science teacher, had just distributed the test papers. Mario made it through the first page of multiple-choice questions without too many guesses. He regretted not studying more. Had Maria known about the test, she would have made him stay home Monday night and study instead of playing hockey. On the other hand, if she did know perhaps she would have relented, realizing her role in the weekend's events, which didn't leave much time for studying. Maybe her son needed some escape even if it meant not being well-prepared for a test.

The second page of the test showed a sketch of a typical cell, surrounded by blank lines connected to various parts of the cell. Normally Mario liked science, particularly biology, but this time his mind went blank. The nucleus was obvious as was the cell membrane. The exact spelling of the other parts remained hidden somewhere deep among his own brain cells, the neurons failing to transmit the memory into his consciousness. If only he had studied, tracing the paths one more time. He began to feel sweaty.

Mr. Hanson, who saw in every bright student a future physician or research scientist, made his tests more challenging than perhaps appropriate for seventh graders. He could have included a list of the cell parts on the page for reference, but he didn't.

When Mr. Hanson collected Mario's test, two lines remained blank. He felt like a failure. He couldn't stop being distracted by thoughts about what Rosalyn said Monday. The bell rang just as Mr. Hanson finished collecting the tests. Leaving the classroom, Rosalyn asked Mario how he had done, which only made him feel worse. It was the first time he could remember ever turning in an incomplete test paper. She said she did pretty good. She always said she wanted to be a doctor when she grew up. They blended into the avalanche of kids in the hallway heading for lockers and their next class.

At lunch Mario would have devoured the hamburger gravy over mashed potatoes, even the green beans. Today he forced it down, past the tightness in his throat, mostly from his disappointment and even shame about the test. He tried to ignore the obvious looks directed toward him from the table where Frank and his friends sat. Not just looks, but also laughter.

"What's the matter with those guys?" Jake said, sopping up hamburger gravy with a piece of white bread. He leaned over his tray to take a quick bite before it dripped. Frank continued to look at them, shaking his head and pretending to laugh.

"Who knows?" Mario said. "Who cares?"

Seeing that he had their attention, Frank spoke out over the lunchroom clatter of utensils and chatter of kids.

"Hey, Marion, how's your old man?" Frank grinned, bobbing his head and looking over at Mario, then around at his tablemates.

"What the heck is he talking about?" Jake asked.

Mario froze. He stared down at his plate. His hands became damp and clammy, and his face burned. He wanted to get up and leave but he couldn't move. Anger welled up. He hated Frank.

Jake looked at Mario. They had been friends since kindergarten. Only in later years did it occur to Jake that Mario didn't have a father around. It didn't really make any difference. They accepted things the way they were. A few years ago he'd asked Mario where his dad was. Mario said he was killed in a car crash a long time ago. Nothing more was said, nor did it need to be. Now Jake's curiosity required some type of answer even though the question had been raised by Frank, whose credibility could be questioned.

"What's he talking about?" Jake repeated.

"I don't know," Mario said. "Are you done eating? Let's get out of here."

"Hey, Marion, that's your old man at the funny farm. No wonder you're such a spaz," Frank said loudly.

Looking down at his tray, Mario got up from the table and walked quickly over to the window that received the dirty dishes, not even looking back to see if Jake followed. He did, passing by Frank's table, asking him what was he talking about and what his problem was.

"That bum you guys know, that's Marion's old man." Frank laughed again, looking around the table at the other kids for a concurring response.

"What're you talking about? How do you know?" Jake challenged.

"That's what my dad said," Frank said, chewing on a piece of bread. "They picked him up Sunday and took him to the funny farm. Otherwise he was going to jail. The cops found out who he was and that he was Marion's old man."

"You're such a liar," Jake scoffed. "You lied about the bum beating you up. You lie about everything."

"Swear to God I'm not lying. You can ask the cops. Ask Marion."

"I will." Jake walked away. He didn't see Mario at his locker; he would find him in shop class. Passing him in the hallway, Rosalyn asked Jake what was the matter with Mario. She said he looked kind of upset and didn't even respond when she talked to him. Jake tried to shrug it off. "Frank was saying stuff in the lunchroom. Mario got mad. No big deal." For Rosalyn the explanation wasn't even close to being good enough. She persisted, asking exactly what Frank had said.

"Frank was saying something about that bum, Tom, being Mario's dad," Jake said. "He's such a liar."

"What? Well, what if he is?" Rosalyn challenged. "It's possible. And what if they're going to operate on him like I said? Maybe that's why Mario's so upset."

She had not been aware of a physical resemblance until this moment when her intuition told her something if not yet on a conscious level. During their encounters with Tom, parkas and stocking hats left only faces visible. Along with mannerisms, the way they walked and talked, it was enough to create an unconscious hint of some connection between Mario and Tom, something more hidden behind the outward appearance of a drunken bum in dirty clothes. It only added to the initial adventure of going out skating on the lake with the boys in the first place.

"I didn't think he was mad," Jake said. "He just got up and left the lunchroom. I don't know."

"You boys are so stupid," Rosalyn scolded. "You just don't see anything. I'm going to ask Mario."

"Go ahead. See if I care."

Rosalyn spun in disgust and walked off for home economics class.

AT CHRISTMAS, THE PARENTS OF BOYS in the seventh-grade shop class would be receiving an identical gifts, identical at least in the planning. The quality of the finished plastic letter openers varied considerably. Most had completed cutting the piece of clear plastic to the proper shape, narrowing it to a point at one end. Some kids also rounded the handle as they were supposed to do. Some didn't care. For them shop class offered a wonderful environment for goofing off. The teacher, Mr. Wick, didn't seem to care either as long as the class appeared to be focused on their work. Once he had to intervene when two kids pretended to be having a sword fight with their letter openers. Mr. Wick scolded them, saying someone could get an eye poked out if they weren't careful. If they play-fought again, he threatened to confiscate their letter openers and send them to the principal's office.

Instead of desks and chairs, shop had six thick, wooden work tables each surrounded by four tall wooden stools. These took up most of the shop classroom space. A vise grip was attached to each end of the work tables. An array of power tools lined the back wall, available only to senior-high classes except for the small jig saws, which the seventh-grade boys used to rough-cut their letter openers. Under the rote super-vision of Mr. Wick, they could use the torch to heat the handle of their letter opener if they wanted to, then carefully twisting it 180 degrees. This provided a better grip and some measure of aesthetic quality.

Since last Friday, Aaron Abrams had been polishing his letter opener to unblemished perfection, mostly out of boredom. Already with several years of experience with the tools in his father's machine shop, he could have operated the power tools in back almost blindfolded, even better than most of the farm kids. He sat across the work table from Mario and Jake, occasionally offering suggestions about their projects but in a way that seemed constructive and not demeaning. The whole Abrams family was like that, friendly, helpful, competent, yet they often kept to themselves. At Abe's Machine Shop and Salvage outside town, Mr. Abrams provided excellent service, quality workmanship and fair prices, with a sense of mastery and dignity that could have been directly trans-planted from the Old World. He excelled at repairing and refurbishing old shotguns, pistols, and hunting rifles, which greatly enhanced the fam-ily's reputation.

"Mario, I heard about your dad," Aaron said quietly, still looking down and polishing his letter opener. "I'm sure everything will work out okay."

Jake looked over at Mario, waiting for his response before asking the question himself. Mario got off his stool abruptly and went over to the buffer to polish the edges of his letter opener, which he had just sanded. Jake watched him go and then looked at Aaron.

"What's his problem? What do you mean about his dad?"

"Didn't you hear Frank at lunch? He asked Mario about his old man."

"You mean Tom, the bum? You know Frank. That's a piece of crap."

"No, it's not. It's really true."

"How do you know?"

"My mom heard about it," Aaron said. "She was at the state hospital Sunday and found out. She goes there Sundays to do stuff for the patients . . . you know, volunteer stuff."

Jake looked over at Mario still at the buffer, really a power grinder, but with a soft pad afixed to it for polishing.

"I guess, if you say so," Jake conceded. "So, he wasn't killed in a car crash after all. I guess Mario should've made two letter openers," he laughed. The other kid at the table laughed, but not Aaron.

"You guys talked to him a couple of times. So, what was he like?" Aaron asked.

"He seemed okay, I guess. We brought him food a couple times. That was mostly Rosalyn's idea. Mario talked to him the most. He went out there last week when they had to look for him out on the lake. Then we saw him in town last Thursday. That's when we told him the cops were looking for him for beating up Frank. I can't believe that. They believed Frank when he said Tom did it. I think he just said that so he wouldn't have to admit that Mario pounded him."

"That's really not fair," Aaron said.

Mario returned to the work table and exchanged glances with Jake. Neither knew what to say or even felt like saying anything. Mr. Wick walked by, making the rounds among the work tables, gravitating toward sounds of what he considered excess conversation. He admired Aaron's work and looked around the table momentarily before moving on to the next.

"What Rosalyn said . . . that's true you know," Aaron continued after Mr. Wick had moved on. "They do something to the front part of their brains. It's like the Nazis used to do in the concentration camps. They did experiments on prisoners."

"Oh, shut up, Aaron. How do you know?" Jake challenged. "This is a hospital, not a concentration camp."

"I know, but they still do stuff. Rosalyn's right. I bet they're going to do an operation and turn him into a zombie. He shouldn't even be there in the first place. He didn't do anything. It's all because of Frank."

"Is Tom really your dad?" Jake asked looking over at Mario.

"That's what my mom said," Mario said quietly.

"We should do something," Aaron said. "We should try to get him out of there."

"What? Are you nuts?" Jake was incredulous. "How would you do that? What for?"

"I'll think about it. What are you guys doing after school today?"

Mario said he had to study for the math test before supper because he had to go to Scouts in the evening. After what happened last Tuesday, missing Scouts and causing the search out on the lake, this time he had to be there. Jake said he was going to play hockey after delivering his paper route. Aaron shrugged and said he was going to think of something anyway. What had happened was just too unfair to sit back and not try to do anything.

Rosalyn could hardly wait for Home Economics class to end. They had been baking Christmas cookies, and the teacher made some of the students stay a few minutes over while they waited for them to come out of the oven. Rosalyn rushed out, hoping to intercept Mario coming from shop class or find him at his locker. She didn't see him until English class. She walked in a few minutes tardy and handed Miss Quale a note of explanation from the Home Economics teacher.

The entire class watched her take her seat; Rosalyn ignored them, staring at Mario instead, trying to see something in his eyes, trying to read his mind. He offered a fleeting glance, then looked down at his English grammar textbook. While Miss Quale lectured about sentence structure, their minds wandered, looking for the words they would need after class, questions for Rosalyn and explanations for Mario. He knew there was no way to avoid her after class even though he knew her questions would be out of compassion and not ridicule. When the bell rang, she waited at the door, closing in when he approached.

"Mario, is it true what they said?" At least she looked around to see if anyone could overhear, and she tried to hold back with a loud whisper. "Is Tom really your dad?"

"That's what my mom said. They found out when they picked him up on Sunday."

"What are you going to do?"

"What do you mean? What am I supposed to do?"

"I don't know. Are you going to see him again? What's it like to know he's your dad?"

"I don't know. I don't feel any different. Maybe we'll visit him there."

"I'm sorry about what I said, about operating on his brain. I mean, they do that sometimes, but not always."

"That's okay. That's what Aaron said, too. You won't believe this. He said we should go and break him out of there. Even if somebody did, what good would that do?"

"Well if they did operate on him and you went to visit, it wouldn't be the same talking to him as before."

Mario stopped at his locker and said he had to go right home and study. Rosalyn said good-bye and that she hoped things would work out. She said she was going home to study, too, although it wouldn't necessarily be for one of their classes. Often she would peruse an old medical encyclopedia at home that her parents purchased used when they realized her ambition of someday becoming a surgeon. She also planned to call Aaron.

"HI HONEY. HOW WAS SCHOOL TODAY?" Maria called from somewhere in the small house when Mario entered the back door. He gave a bland, noncomittal response. He fixed a snack, peanut butter and jelly on two slices of

toast and a large glass of milk, taking it into the living room to watch cartoons. Maria started to fix supper, reminding Mario to leave some room for
hamburger hotdish. As he settled down to review math problems, the aroma
of spices and hamburger browning in the frying pan drifted into the living
room. He left the television on. He expected her to suggest that he turn it
off, but she didn't. He could do math problems with the TV on, and it helped
distract him from other bothersome thoughts.

The hotdish tasted good. Maria agreed to eat in the living room
on TV trays where they could watch TV instead of conversing, which she
usually tried to do. Mario was her child, but also her friend and com-
panion. Until Jim, it had been just the two of them. She still hadn't figured out what the sudden appearance of Tom might mean. Any feeling
for him had been destroyed and buried long ago. As the memories resurfaced, she began to feel confused and somewhat sad. Seeing Tom
Sunday, dirty, disheveled, and downcast, she'd felt only pity. She still
hadn't fully recovered from the shock.

"Mom, why didn't you and Tom get married?" Mario asked quietly, the question buffered by the noisy cartoon voices and shrieks coming from the TV.

Maria closed her eyes, took a deep breath, wishing none of this
had ever happened, that the past couple of days could be erased. Life
seemed to be going well. Now this. How could she explain to Mario how
it all started, how he started, without hurting his feelings? She remembered one of her friends back in California. In 1944 three months after
they were married, her husband, a Navy pilot, left for duty in the Pacific
theater. A month later his Corsair, riddled with shrapnel, crashed into
the ocean. Two days later, the woman received the news from her doctor
that she was pregnant. Eventually she remarried. Her first child would
know his biological father only by pictures and letters.

It was kind of like that with Tom. The man she knew before he
went to Iwo Jima never returned. The man who returned appeared the
same except for the hollow look in his eyes. She might have tried to stay
with him, but she was young and her father, who disliked and distrusted

him in the first place, became even more forceful in keeping them apart. She tried to convince him and herself that Tom would get better, that the outbursts, the unpredictable and sometimes bizarre behavior and the drinking eventually would subside. After seeing Tom Sunday for the first time in more than ten years, she realized for certain that they hadn't.

"When you kids play war or Army or whatever you call it, it's fun and it's all pretend. But in real life, the glory is only a small part of the story. In real war, a lot of soldiers and pilots never come back. Even if they do come back, sometimes they're not the same as before. They have wounds and injuries to bear the rest of their lives. It was kind of like that with Tom. He was in the battle on Iwo Jima. He wasn't the same when he returned. But the wounds in his mind were far greater than the wounds on his body. Eventually they put him in a hospital, a mental hospital out in California. He stayed there a couple of years, and then they let him go. Maybe if all this hadn't happened, things would have been different. Every night I prayed that I did the right thing. When we moved here and things seemed to be going well, I started to think it was the right thing, but I always felt guilty about not having a father around for you."

"How come you didn't tell me before?" Mario asked.

Maria's composure cracked. She dropped her fork and covered her face with her hands. Immediately Mario felt guilty and sorry. She recovered and looked up. Seeing his distress, she tried to explain, not knowing if it would do any good.

"When you were little, it didn't seem necessary. Once when you were about five, you asked about it. It caught me off guard, and it just came out about an accident happening. Right away I felt bad about it, but I didn't know what else to do. If I had tried to explain, you probably wouldn't have understood. Then I told myself that I would explain it when you were older. I just kept putting it off. I'm so sorry. Please forgive me."

Mario felt sorry for her, too. "That's okay."

"Thank you," Maria said. She leaned over on the couch, put her arm around his shoulders and gave him a little sideways hug. For a moment she felt the relief of a burden being lifted.

"Rosalyn said that at the state hospital they're going to operate on Tom's brain," Mario said matter-of-factly. "Can we still visit him?"

"Sure, you can visit him. Where did she get an idea like that?"

"She reads a lot about that stuff. Doctor and hospital stuff. She said she wants to be a doctor when she grows up."

"Well, I'm sure that he'll be well taken care of. They'll do what they have to do."

"But Rosalyn said if they operate like that, it turns people into zombies."

"I think she's exaggerating a bit."

"Could we still visit him if that happens?"

"I don't think that'll happen, but even if it does you can still visit him."

They finished eating, and Maria took the plates to the kitchen sink. Soon Mario would have to leave for Boy Scouts but he had enough time to watch the first part of the 6:00 p.m. news. The newscaster, wearing a crew cut, heavy dark-rimmed glasses, light sport coat and striped tie, sat behind a plain countertop holding a sheaf of papers. He read straight-faced in an almost monotone voice, which sometimes even flickered with color, at least compared with the black-and-white image on the tube. The first story reported that Coya Knutson's husband now claimed that he had been "taken" by the political intrigue and that had he known what really was going on he wouldn't have signed the "Coya come home" letter. Maria heard the story from the kitchen and came into watch. She remained to see the next story about the state government allocating nearly nine million dollars for the mental hospitals, two million of which was earmarked for Dakota Falls. Mario watched, too, as he put on his parka, getting ready to leave for Scouts. He smiled and said, "'Bye." Maria smiled, went over and gave him a little hug. "'Bye. Love you. Be home at eight."

MRS. ABRAMS ANSWERED WHEN ROSALYN CALLED, saying Aaron was at the shop helping his dad. She would ask him to call back when he came home

284

for supper. She asked if she could take a message. When Rosalyn said, "No thanks," Mrs. Abrams continued to talk, asking how she and her family were doing, how school was, what she planned to do over the holiday break. Rosalyn said school was going well. She launched into a detailed account of the seventh-grade social studies class project about the state's centennial year, 1958. Mrs. Abrams listened for a few minutes, then said she had to go and fix supper but that the project sounded very interesting.

Aaron returned home just after five-thirty. His mother told him about Rosalyn's call. She followed him to the phone as if she were going to show someone how to use it for the first time. It was the first time she could remember a girl had called the Abrams' home asking for her son. Aaron questioned her attentiveness, and she returned to the kitchen where she turned down the radio a bit.

"Aaron, I've got to talk to you about Mario and his dad," Rosalyn said with the tone of determination and excitement that she usually reserved for very important matters, which for her were not in the same category as topics of the other girls who talked like that all the time about some movie star, music, clothing, makeup, or boys. "I think that's so exciting about Tom being his dad. It's a miracle. Did you ever talk to him? We did a couple of times. We skated out to his shack and brought him turkey sandwiches on Thanksgiving. That's too bad about his dog. Mario told me about that. Someone went out there when he was gone and threw stuff at his dog—rocks and things. He had to go to the vet. He's still there. His name is Ike. I think he's a German shepherd or something. Do you know what they do at the mental hospital, where they took Tom? I think that's so rotten, blaming Tom for beating up Frank. He's such a liar. It makes me sick. Sometimes they operate on their brains – they cut the nerves or take out the front part. It makes them like zombies. I've read about it before. So what do you think we should do?"

"Aaron, are you still on the phone?" Mrs. Abrams called from the kitchen. "I don't hear you talking. I need to make a call soon."

"I'm still on the phone," Aaron said, turning his head away from the receiver. "Sorry. That was my mom. I can't stay on the phone long. I told Mario in shop class we should get him out of there. It's not fair what they did. Tom didn't do anything wrong. They're being mean just because he's a bum. I think they're afraid of him."

"Why would they be afraid of him?"

"Just because he's different. But that's no reason to be mean to him like that."

"I think so, too. But what can we do?"

"In shop when I said that to Mario, I was kind of kidding. I told my dad—about Tom and what happened—not about getting him out of there. My dad thought it was really wrong, and somebody should do something. Talk to the mayor or police or somebody."

"We should go with Mario to visit him and then leave the door open or something so he can get out," Rosalyn said.

"How would you do that?"

"I don't know. Maybe we could take him for a ride or something and then he would escape."

"They'd never let us do that. We'd have to sneak him out or something. We could really get in trouble. But maybe we could do it so we wouldn't get caught. I'll try think of a plan, and you do too. We can talk about it tomorrow."

Rosalyn agreed. They would talk about their plans tomorrow and tell Mario.

❧ 23 ❧

D R. BRADLEY NELSON COULDN'T BELIEVE what he was reading. His colleague on the medical staff at Dakota Falls State Hospital, Dr. James Walters, had conducted the initial assessment and diagnosis of the new admission from Clareton, a forty-eight-year-old male, single, no permanent address or immediate family. Decorated World War II veteran, a Seabee who served on Iwo Jima. Likely suffered psychological trauma in combat. Obviously alcoholic. Physical health reasonable considering circumstances.

"Patient appears to be suffering from acute psychosis," the report continued. "Hallucinatory. Propensity for violence. Resists medications. Little confidence will take medications consistently. For the safety of staff and community, recommend frontal lobotomy."

Walters' report followed with two pages of detailed support for the procedure. His arguments could be convincing.

Chronically under-staffed and under-funded, the state hospital system struggled to manage the workload of dealing with the detritus of society coming in the door almost every day. The hospital needed stern and certain measures to maintain control. Nelson was too soft. His methodology required too much work marshalling the support system necessary to try to rehabilitate patients. It seemed like Nelson spent all his time on the phone rounding up pastors, priests, counselors, social workers, and anyone who would volunteer to surround the patient with support. Walters resented Nelson's success; he held stubbornly to the swift and effective procedure, at which he had become very adept. But it had been two years since he had performed one, since just before Dr. Nelson joined the staff as medical director. Walters resented him for that, too, a young, innovative, and annoyingly enthusiastic intruder on his turf who banned lobotomies.

"Jim, you can't be serious," Dr. Nelson said, looking up from the report.

Dr. Walters sat in front of Nelson's desk, sullenly resenting being called into Nelson's office.

"We just don't do this anymore," Nelson continued. "You know that. In a third of these cases they actually get worse after lobotomy."

"But in a third they get better," Walters replied. "And if there's no change, there's no harm done. Two out three isn't bad odds, especially when you consider the amount of time and cost."

"It's barbaric. I just won't allow it. And what do you mean by better? Better for whom?"

Dr. Walters sat impassively, glaring at his superior who was twenty years his junior, remembering the day Walters learned that he would not get the director position he had assumed would be his. His graying hair swept back in a modest pompadour showed meticulous grooming, unlike the bushy eyebrows furrowed above his glowering eyes. Now he was just counting the days toward retirement. The thought of defying Nelson played on his mind. He knew he probably could do it anyway and there wasn't much Nelson would be able to do about it except chastise him and put a report in his file. Walters had been around a long time and knew how the system worked. Any dispute would become bogged down in seemingly endless reports, counter-reports, meetings, and phone calls between Dakota Falls and St. Paul. With no sign of resolution in sight eventually Nelson would give up.

Walters' tenure was almost unimpeachable, vulnerable only to the most outrageous behavior such as some hideous, highly-publicized crime, or more likely some indiscretion that publicly embarrassed the political power structure at the department headquarters and governor's office. He had seen careers ruined by the latter.

On the other hand, he couldn't be sure how Nelson would respond. If he did perform the procedure despite Nelson's prohibition and Nelson went public gaining support from the social workers and liberals, it could backfire. As Nelson continued to lecture him about the ineffectiveness, even immorality, of the procedure comparing it to such mistaken treatments as blood-letting, Dr. James Walters' thoughts wandered back to the days when lobotomies were common, when he had even gained some notoriety for the speed and skill with which he performed them.

One of the early practitioners used a small ice pick. Since then the instrument had been refined and made of stainless steel, but still basically it was the same. Like an ice pick, the tip curved to a sharp point. Placed on the forehead just above the eyes, a quick, sharp rap from a mallet drove the point through the relatively thin bone of the skull, penetrating the brain's frontal lobes. The tip would be swished back and forth like a windshield wiper, severing nerve connections. Sometimes doctors performed the procedure under local anesthetic so they could converse with the patient, immediately detecting changes in speech and behavior. The patient recovered quickly, often with a splitting headache, but were never the same again. Dr. Walters had performed the procedure twenty-seven times in his early years at Dakota Falls.

"I still think it's a mistake, not allowing this anymore," he argued. "Maybe they overdid it years ago, but that doesn't mean it no longer has a place anymore. Have you seen today's report on Tom Nathan? Oh, he was calm when you saw him yesterday morning. You know as well as I do what can happen. He was just waiting for a chance to make a break."

After lunch, two aides unlocked the door to Tom's eight-by-ten room. They led him down the hall to the day room where other patients were playing cards or checkers, watching TV, and smoking, always smoking. A few sat off to the side in their own world, sometimes rocking back and forth, sometimes letting out a burst of laughter or stream of profanity. Steam knocked through a thick, heavy radiator squatting on the floor between two large windows—both covered with heavy, mesh grating—filtered what little afternoon daylight late December allowed.

Even though Tom's lungs were long accustomed to acrid, toxin-laden cigarette smoke, the heavy, odorous atmosphere of the hospital ward day room felt suffocating compared to the fresh, outdoor air of the countryside. With the aides' attention turned elsewhere, he had bolted for the front door. On the way, he grabbed a free-standing ashtray and tried to batter the doorknob in a futile effort to break the lock. The aides rushed up, trying to grab his arms and wrestle him to the ground. Another came to help, holding up a syringe and shouting at Tom to stop or they would put him under again.

"You can't keep me here," Tom shouted, trying to turn his head toward his captors as he lay pressed face down on the floor. "I'll go face the assault charge. I don't care. Just get me out of here."

"I'm afraid it doesn't work that way," one of the aides laughed. "You've been committed by the court. It's for your own good, for everyone's good."

Tom stopped struggling. Betrayal suddenly weighed on his back greater than the knee of the largest of the three aides pressing into it. What court order? Who did this? He cursed himself for believing them. He'd trusted Horace. Mario was just a boy and too young to be involved in any scheme. It must have been Maria.

Tom felt his body go limp, suddenly drained of strength. He stopped fighting, and they led him back to his room. He pleaded for a smoke. An aide said that, when he behaved, he could sit in the day room and smoke; for now at least for a while he was going back into his room, where smoking was prohibited. The last time he lit up was in the car with Horace.

Lying on the mattress in his room, Tom tried to console himself by thinking about his son, what a fine boy he was. Tears spilled from the edges of his eyes, moistening the hair on his temples. Why did it have to be this way? Why didn't he make things work years ago? He was trapped, caged like those mangy-looking lions pacing behind the bars at the zoo. He would go crazy if he had to stay locked in these buildings the rest of his life. Even if he could see Mario again, it might be more painful and awkward than anything. He craved a drink and a cigarette even more.

DR. NELSON LEAFED THROUGH THE FILES SITTING on his desk, found the one for Tom Nathan, and began to read. "The first thing we have to do is work to build trust," he finally said.

"Psychotics, schizophrenics are not capable of trust, you should know that," Dr. Walters replied with a tone of sarcasm.

"He's not schizophrenic. He's suffered psychological trauma, but he's not psychotic. We will treat him with medication, counseling and emotional support."

Dr. Walters' contempt for Nelson's soft approach grew every time they confronted each other on a case. He saw the younger colleague's integrity and sincerity only as weakness. He even thought that he could do the procedure without Nelson's knowledge and conceal it after. With the overwhelming caseload it might be possible unless Nelson took a personal interest and followed Tom Nathan's progress. Walters stood up abruptly and left Nelson's office, saying only that he had to get back to work and without clearly concurring with Nelson's assessment and recommendation. "I thought we were working," Nelson muttered to himself as Walters disappeared out the door.

MARIA FINALLY SUCCUMBED TO THELMA'S insistence that they call the hospital to see how Tom was doing. She had resisted because she didn't know where it might lead, and she did not want him back in her life. It brought back the feelings of bitter loneliness that clouded those early days after Mario's birth, and the tense anxiety of trying to conceal from

291

her family her condition leading up to it. Slender, wearing loose-fitting dresses, she'd succeeded almost until the time arrived. The love and support from her mother and brothers sustained her, but never quite compensated for the wall that enclosed her father's love, which, despite his wife's urgings and his own conscience, he couldn't prevent from turning into anger and sorrow.

At first Maria blamed herself. As the years passed and Mario grew, she gradually began to blame Tom. Where was he when Mario took his first step, when he said his first words, when he started his first day at school? She did a good job of resisting those kinds of thoughts, but still they always hovered, ready to strike whenever she dropped her guard, or sometimes let them. At times Thelma became her conscience, and this was one of those times.

"You really should call. It's the Christian thing to do," Thelma said evenly, calmly. "Just to see how he's doing. You don't have to talk to him. I know Jim would understand. He would want you to call, too."

THE HOSPITAL SWITCHBOARD NEVER CLOSED. The evening operator transferred the call to Ward Nine. The hospital aide on duty said Tom Nathan was doing fine, but she couldn't talk to him right then. If Maria wanted more information, she would have to call back in the morning and ask for Dr. Nelson. Thelma stopped Maria from hanging up the phone, urging her to ask if it were possible to talk to Tom. The aide asked if she was family. Maria didn't know what to say. She stammered something about him being the father of her son. It wasn't good enough for the aide; he had seen almost every manifestation of domestic dysfunction, which had worn down his sympathy years ago and now chipped away at empathy. The bizarre behaviors of his work world provided an endless supply of fuel for the cynical attitude, that people on the outside just didn't understand what they had to go through each day to keep these people out of sight.

Maria left for school a bit earlier than usual in the morning. Normally she would have dropped Mario off at the junior-senior high on her way to the elementary school. He was getting into his parka when the phone rang.

"Hello. Is this Mario? This is Tom."

He sounded normal, even a bit cheerful. He asked how everyone was doing. Mario said fine and that he was just heading out the door for school.

"Sorry to hold you up," Tom said. "I should have known better. But do you have just a minute? Can I ask you a couple of things?"

He asked how Ike was doing at the vet's. Mario said he didn't know but would ask his mom to call and find out. Tom said he was okay but was a little concerned about what might happen to him at the hospital. He had changed his mind and didn't want to stay there anymore, but they wouldn't let him go. Did Mario know anything about some papers they signed that said they could keep him there even if he didn't want to? It just wasn't fair, everything that happened. He didn't blame Mario for what they said about the fight. When he went to meet them at Doc Ahrends on Sunday, he had gone of his own free will. He thought that maybe he could straighten out and live a better life. He hoped it would be okay if they could at least do things together like going fishing or bicycle riding. He could hardly remember when he last rode a bike and wanted to try it again. What kind of bike did Mario have?

"I've got a Schwinn. I got it for my birthday last summer," Mario said. "We could go bike riding. That'd be fun."

"I'd like to do that," Tom said. "I can't stay on the phone here much longer, though. They let you call for only so many minutes. Maybe you can help me. I've got to get out of here. I know about some of the things they do here, and I don't want that to happen, do you?"

"One of the kids at school said something about some kind of brain surgery," Mario said.

"That's what I'm talking about. I can't let that happen. I've got to get out of here somehow. I'll have to think of something. But don't you worry. I've been in tough spots before, and I've always figured something out. You better get on to school now. Have a good day. I'll try to call again soon. I'd like to talk to your mom, too."

Mario said good-bye and hung up the phone. He felt a little sad and helpless having no idea what he could do to help Tom. He realized it was the first time he had talked with him knowing who he was, and it hadn't even been acknowledged, at least not in words. He stood by the phone in the silent house. He looked out the living room picture window, a still life of houses across the street, dark tree trunks and snow-covered yards. A small pile of wrapped Christmas presents lay on the floor beneath the window waiting for the Christmas tree, which still remained in the lot next to the hardware store along with scores of other balsam firs and spruces leaning against a framework of two-by-fours. They had planned to get their tree and set it up last Sunday until the meeting with Tom intervened. Now it was Wednesday morning, just a week before Christmas Eve, and they still hadn't set up their tree. It never really felt like Christmas until the tree was up. They would have to get one this Saturday for sure. Mario grabbed his books and left quickly for school hoping he wouldn't be late.

After that day only two more remained before the Christmas break when he could relax away from school for two whole weeks. Even though he wasn't thrilled about being there, it still felt good to step into the warm school building after walking in the cold, just a few degrees above zero. He didn't see Frank, and no one else bothered him on the way to his locker, which surprised him a little bit because his self-consciousness had convinced him that everyone knew about Tom and that was all they were talking about. No one seemed to remember or care until he arrived at social studies just before the bell. Rosalyn and Aaron stood on either side of the classroom door looking directly at him as he approached.

"Hey Mario, we've got to tell you about our plan," Aaron said. Rosalyn nodded. "We planned it last night. We'll tell you about it at lunch."

She sounded so confident, it sometimes irritated him. He still didn't comprehend that kids could even conceive of doing something on their own in that distant, mysterious world of adults. He had no choice but to consent to hearing about it. Aaron said that's what happened to the Jews in World War II. They didn't do anything wrong but were arrested and thrown in concentration camps. At first they didn't even know what was going on. When they found out about the atrocities and gas chambers, some tried to fight back. That's what they had to do with Tom. He didn't beat up Frank Harley, and now he was in the mental hospital, and they were going to turn him into a zombie.

"He called this morning," Mario said. "He said he wanted to get out of there. He said something about the brain surgery. I don't know. I don't know what we can do."

"See! See! That's what I mean," Aaron whispered urgently, backing his way into the classroom ahead of Mario and Rosalyn. "You've got to hear about our plan."

They tried to find some privacy at lunch. Their surreptitious behavior could have been a neon sign attracting the attention of all the other kids as if they were passing by the marquee of the Clareton Theater on Saturday night. It seemed like everyone was staring at Mario, Rosalyn, Aaron and Jake when they tried to sit at a different table. And why Rosalyn was sitting with them? This time it was as if there were no question she was part of the group.

While Mario was at Boy Scouts Tuesday and Jake was playing hockey, Rosalyn had called Aaron. They had a plan except for one big problem: they needed help from some big kids, high school kids who had a car. They wondered if Larry would do it.

"I'm not going to ask him. Are you kidding? He'd tell us to go jump in the lake," Jake insisted. "He got in trouble last summer with the cops for drag racing. They said if he got in trouble again they'd take away his license. He'd go nuts if he couldn't drive his car."

"C'mon," Rosalyn pleaded. "All we need is a ride to Dakota Falls. We'll just pretend we're going to visit Tom. He can't get in trouble for that."

"We couldn't just go do that," Mario said. "My mom wouldn't let me go."

"We don't have to say *that*. We'll say we're going to the basketball game or a movie. It'll be Friday night," Aaron said.

"That's lying," Mario replied.

"Sometimes you have to if the reason is good enough," Rosalyn said. "Just think what'll happen to Tom if we don't. You ever think of that? C'mon Jake, just ask him."

"We need to hear about this plan of yours," Jake said.

"You can. Let's meet right after school," Aaron said. "Where should we meet? Can we go to your place?"

Jake agreed. Mario said he had to be home by five so he would have time to eat supper and get ready for the nativity scene. The remainder of his school day withered under the worrisome thoughts that kept intruding on classroom work. Why did all this have to happen? How could Rosalyn and Aaron even think of doing what they said? What if they got caught? Would they get arrested and be sent to reform school? Just because they said Tom was his father, it didn't feel any different. The thoughts amplified his self-consciousness. It felt like all the other kids were looking at him and thinking about the same things even though no one said anything, not even Frank.

Larry Carlson always tried to park his '55 Chevy Bel Air right in front of the bowling alley so he could see it through the front door from his post behind the counter. He'd started saving up for a car at age fourteen. He bought the Bel Air last spring with his savings and mostly a loan from his father, the payments for which inspired him to work sometimes up to thirty hours per week. The bowling alley job didn't pay much, but it would have to do until he got a better job. His ambition focused on being a mechanic at the Chevy dealership. Mr. Henderson had been encouraging but said they didn't have any openings and that he would have to graduate from high school first anyway. Larry had learned a lot already working on the car this past summer at Thorson's Auto Repair. Leonard Thorson responded to the young man's enthusiasm for cars and his apparent work ethic by allowing him to work on his car there evenings in return for doing odd jobs and even some small repair work. Larry's skill working on engines and drive trains grew immensely with only a few minor mistakes. He didn't much care for body work, though.

He had big plans for the Chevy, a four-door hardtop, two-tone white-over-aqua finish, and 265-cubic-inch V-8 engine. He'd found it at the Chevy dealer in St. Cloud, a trade-in from a man who owned a movie theater, or so the salesman said. The odometer read 36,278 miles, many of which registered on Highway 10 between St. Cloud and Minneapolis, and one long road trip to Las Vegas, the salesman said. The movie theater owner almost traded it in when the '57s came out. He was glad he waited for the '58s, according to the salesman. He traded it in for a 1958 Impala with a 283-cubic-inch engine and air conditioning, which he vowed never to be without again after the trip to Las Vegas. The salesman said he could have afforded a Buick, but he liked the Chevys better. The body showed no rust, and the tires were almost new. Getting in for a test drive, the first thing Larry did was turn on the radio. He paid cash, $525 from his savings with the $1,000 loan from his father, Hank Carlson, who made him promise that he would graduate from high school on time and get a job immediately unless he got drafted or enlisted in the Army.

Larry had done about all he could afford to fulfill his vision for the car. Working Sunday evenings at Thorson's Auto Repair, he had installed a dual-exhaust system, four-barrel carburetor, and baby moon hubcaps. He was saving up for a four-speed, floor-shift transmission. It turned out to be a necessity later anyway after he had installed the fuel-injected 283 engine. Leonard Thorson shook his head, musing that it would be cheaper in the long run to trade it in for a car already with all those things. Why these kids had to soup up their cars, he couldn't understand. But underneath the ducktail hair, tight blue jeans, white T-shirts with a pack of cigarettes rolled up in the sleeve, he thought Larry was a good kid.

Larry looked out the front door of the bowling alley at the Chevy parked in front, its gleaming black finish reflecting colored light from the Christmas decorations on the streetlight post, thinking about taking it to the car wash after work to clean off all the road salt and snow under the wheel wells. Just before school started he had it painted black, the whole thing. The guys at the body shop just shook their heads in bewilderment. They asked him why he would want to do a thing like that. He just said he thought it would look really cool, so they didn't question him anymore about it, and he had the cash to pay for it.

Larry got out of school an hour early every day because he had a job, so he was already at the bowling alley door when it opened. Jake entered first, looking around, followed by Rosalyn and Mario and some other kid Larry didn't recognize right away. Aaron Abrams usually didn't hang out at the bowling alley. They approached Larry, whose condescending amusement this time came with a little curiosity.

"Hey, what are you punks doin'?" Larry pulled a cigarette from the pack of Luckies lying on the counter, tamped one end on his watch and lit up with a flourish, ending by waving the match up and down in front of the younger kids and flicking it into an ashtray. He took a deep drag and blew a cloud of smoke toward their faces.

"Larry, we got to talk to you," Jake said. Rosalyn grimaced, waving away the smoke in front of her face.

"So, go ahead and talk."

"You know that bum, that guy that's supposed to be Mario's dad? You know what they're going to do to him?"

"They're going to cut part of his brains out. They're going to turn him into a zombie," Rosalyn interjected. "We've got to get him out of there."

"So what do want me to do about it?" Larry said. "I think you got a screw loose, that's what I think."

"We need a ride to Dakota Falls," Aaron said.

"What for?"

"We're going to get him out of there," Rosalyn said.

"What? You think you're going to rescue him? I think you guys are psychos, just like him," Larry laughed.

"He's not a psycho," Mario said. "He shouldn't even be in there. They think he beat up Frank so they made him go there."

Larry looked at Mario, trying to figure out his little brother's friend. Usually he didn't pay much attention when Mario was at the Carlson house. Sometimes he wondered why Mario didn't seem to say much. Larry thought it made him seem kind of sneaky. However, after hearing about the fight last week, he had to grant Mario some respect for pounding Frank Harley like that, even though they were just a couple of little kids, not like a big rumble or anything.

"Who thinks the bum beat up Frank?" Larry asked.

"The cops do," Rosalyn said. "They said they'd put him in jail unless he went to the state hospital. That's what Mario's mom said. They tricked him, and now they're going to turn him into a zombie. He didn't do anything wrong."

"So, what are you going to do about it?"

"We're going to help him escape," Aaron talked for the first time. "He's totally innocent. If we don't do anything, that would be worse."

"You punks are way out in left field." Larry surveyed them, shaking his head and taking another drag on the Lucky.

"Please, Larry. You got to help us," Rosalyn said, leaning into the counter, the words hissing out through clenched teeth. "All we need is some way to get there. You got to give us a ride. That's all you've got to do. You won't get in any trouble. Promise."

"So, if you get there, how're you going to help him escape?" Larry said, his skepticism beginning to erode under a faint but budding intrigue.

"Don't worry, they've got it figured out," Jake said. "All we need is a ride on Friday. We can say we're going to a movie there or something."

Larry looked at his younger brother. Their five-year age difference kept sibling rivalry in check for the most part. After he got his '55

Chevy, sometimes he took pleasure in giving the younger kids a ride. He liked showing off the car with a bunch of enthralled kids on summer evening rides to the A&W. It didn't seem to bother LeeAnn. Larry's girl-friend seemed to like the little kids, and eventually he noticed that her warm and receptive mood when they were around sometimes lingered when they were alone together later.

"So, all of you are going? There won't be enough room," Larry said.

"I'm not going. I'm just helping with other stuff . . . planning and stuff," Aaron said.

"Well, I don't know what we're doing Friday night. I'll see what LeeAnn wants to do. I think you guys are nuts, but, hey, it could be fun," Larry shrugged with a slight smile that read mischief. He aimed a stern look at Jake. "You better make a good story for mom and dad. We're tak-ing you guys along to a movie in Dakota Falls, right?"

"Okay, don't worry," Jake said.

"Thanks," Rosalyn said with a big smile, reaching across and patting Larry's forearm on the counter. Mario nodded and said thanks.

"I'll let you know tomorrow," Larry said. "I'll see what LeeAnn says. Nobody say anything to anybody. Got that?"

"We won't say anything," Jake said. They hurried out the door and headed for the Carlsons.

ಔ 24 ಞ

TOM NATHAN PUSHED THE FOOD TRAY through the opening in the bottom of the door. He had eaten everything. He never much cared for fish if you could call barely warmed, breaded fish sticks fish. Two days without a smoke left him feeling frayed and fidgety. He began eating everything on his food trays and would have eaten anything. Leroy said he could have a smoke Saturday if he behaved. Tom cursed himself again as he had done numerous times since Sunday. He lay back on the mattress staring at the bare light bulb making his eyes ache and trying not to go crazy. He heard the tray scrape along the floor. Leroy set it on the food cart and looked into Tom's room through the grated door window.

About half of the patients on Ward Nine remained locked in their rooms in the evenings. Some could come and go as they pleased to the day room until 10:00 p.m. They smoked, drank coffee, and watched the TV housed in a box behind a clear plastic shield. The hospital auxiliary had donated the first one, which survived only a week when one patient charged it during "The Jerry Lewis Show" putting his fist through the front of the picture tube, resulting in twenty-eight stitches. Before they would donate a replacement, the auxiliary insisted on the protective box. At ten it was lights out, and everyone went to their rooms. The night staff person walked down the halls on both floors, checking on the patients and making sure their doors were locked.

Tom picked at his teeth, still angry about the news from the dental exam Thursday. At first they tried to convince him that he would be much better off if they gave him dentures. Some of the cavities did hurt a bit. Some had been filled at his last dental treatment almost ten years ago at the hospital in Stockton. He'd had nice teeth once, straight and even, giving him a pleasant, friendly smile looking even whiter against his smooth tan skin years ago back in California. He had tried to remember to brush his teeth. Most nights he slumped into unconsciousness from the effects of alcohol, until now.

Since coming to the hospital Sunday, he'd brushed his teeth six or seven times day as if that would make up for the years of neglect, as if it would somehow purge the rot eating through the enamel like leprosy. The helpless anger, which pervaded almost every waking moment of the past week, surged again when he recalled their response to his plea for keeping his teeth, that they probably would pull them anyway. He did not fear pain, but he couldn't stop thinking about some dentist holding pliers, twisting and yanking out all his teeth. He scoured his mind for some ideas to prevent that from happening. He ran his tongue through the gap once occupied by the left bicuspid, before it had been knocked out by the truncheon wielded by one of the railroad goons four years ago in Billings. And it hadn't even had a cavity.

Leroy Liipcek regularly worked the second shift, Monday through Friday on Ward Nine at the Dakota Falls State Hospital. Now at age thirty-eight, the habit of sleeping late had become deeply ingrained. With no family or children forcing him to start the day earlier, any change was highly doubtful. There weren't many jobs where one could spend most of the evening smoking, watching TV and getting paid for it. While he smoked and watched, he also drank Nehi orange sodas and ate potato chips, slowly adding the pounds that made his skin stretch like a balloon over the turgid layer of fat.

With each new patient on the ward, he had to establish the norm for what TV shows they would watch. Some had never watched much TV, making it easier in those cases, such as the new patient in room eleven. Friday evenings Leroy had always insisted on watching "Ellery Queen" from seven to eight. At eight he let them switch over to the "Phil Silvers Show," which he didn't care for much. Shortly after 8:00 p.m. he went to the desk in the ward office, closing the door behind him. He pulled open the lower left drawer of the desk, reached way in back and pulled out a magazine, more to look at the pictures than read the text. At first he wasn't sure, then he heard it again. It sounded like a female voice outside, shouting or yelling. He got up and looked out the window. He could see a figure on the sidewalk in front of Ward Nine not too far from the streetlight. He returned the magazine to its hiding place, put on his coat and went out to investigate.

"Hey there, you okay?" he asked when close enough to be heard without shouting, which would have put additional strain on his breathing anyway. She was sitting up now and holding her right ankle pulled up across her left leg. He couldn't see her face in the shadow of the streetlight, but he noticed her skirt pulled more than half way up her thigh. Her unbuttoned car coat revealed a tight-fitting sweater. She looked young and very pretty; her ponytail swayed when she looked up at him.

"I slipped and twisted my ankle," LeeAnn said, trying to make her voice sound hurtful. "You should do a better job clearing this sidewalk." The weather had warmed up during the week, although it still dipped below freezing. Periods of afternoon sunshine had warmed the sidewalk enough to melt some of the snow piled along the edge into small pools scattered in low spots, which refroze after sunset. It would have been simple to avoid the ice patches even in the darkness illuminated only by occasional lamp posts. LeeAnn tried to make sure no one was watching when she carefully sat down near a patch of ice. Then she opened her coat and hitched up her skirt.

Leroy didn't know what to do. He knelt down and reached for her ankle.

"Don't touch me!" LeeAnn shouted.

His hand snapped back. "I'm just trying to help."

"It hurts too much," LeeAnn whimpered.

"What do you want me to do?"

"Just wait for a minute. When it quits hurting so much you can help me get up."

"Do you want me to get a stretcher or something? Where are you going? What are you doing here anyway? It's after eight o'clock."

"I was visiting someone. I was just going back to my car."

"Nobody's supposed to be out here on the hospital grounds after curfew."

"I know that. It was an emergency. I got permission from the director."

His skepticism subdued by the perfumed scent and pleasant appearance of the young girl, and also the firmness of her voice that in other circumstances would have been exposed as an almost convincing attempt at acting, Leroy waited patiently crouched next to her, looking at her, trying to not acknowledge that she seemed to be avoiding looking at him.

JAKE'S HAND SHOOK AS HE TRIED TO FIT THE KEY into the door on the back side of Ward Nine. They lost critical seconds when a car approached right after they left Larry's car, which was parked on the street just west of the building allowing visual contact with both front and back. Seeing the head-lights coming down the block, they jumped behind a tree. The trunk, only a foot in diameter, provided just enough cover for one person standing side-ways. Jake did so right next to the tree. Mario stood next to Jake but farther away; they turned in unison keeping in the tree's shadow as the car passed by. Jake kept repeating under his breath, "Damn damn damn."

Mario still didn't believe they were actually doing what they were doing. His stomach churned; he almost felt like he wanted to cry. Once they started, the adrenaline had taken over, temporarily evicting the guilt he felt for telling his mom they were going with Larry and LeeAnn to a movie in Dakota Falls.

Rosalyn sat in the backseat of Larry's '55 Chevy trying to watch the boys as long as she could. At first she felt helpless, then angry when she saw the other car approach. *Those idiots in the car, they better keep on going. They better not mess things up,* she breathed against the rear window, wiping away the moist fog condensing on it. She wanted to go with them but relented when Aaron convinced her that only Mario and Jake should go in. And besides, it would be better for Larry if Rosalyn stayed in the car in case some hospital official stopped to check it. Rosalyn had her story: She thought her dad was working that night and they were going to visit him; they had stopped to figure out the direction to his building.

Jake couldn't wait to begin the operation. He wore a dark-blue denim jacket, olive green GI fatigue cap, and wanted to smudge his face with charcoal, but Aaron said that would look too suspicious.

The car passed by, continued for two blocks, turned left and disappeared behind a building. Jake took off running down the sidewalk toward the back door of Ward Nine. Mario's legs felt weak and shaky as he tried to keep up, carrying the duffle bag with two pillows and a blanket inside. He almost hoped the key wouldn't work. They would have to retreat, go home and forget about it.

Jake tried without success to turn the key in the lock. He tried not to force it, carefully wiggling it backward and forward, up and down in the keyhole. The seconds dragged on, and Mario felt like he was going to explode. Finally the key turned all the way, and the lock snapped open. Mario stayed out on the sidewalk far enough back so he could still see Larry's car. He watched and waited, the seconds seeming like minutes. Then he saw the brake lights blink three times, the signal that the hospital worker had left the building to help LeeAnn. He whispered loudly to Jake, "All clear to go in."

"It worked!" Jake whispered, looking over his shoulder at Mario. "The key worked! Way to go, Aaron! Let's go. We got just a couple minutes."

Jake removed the key and slowly opened the heavy wooden door, trying to be quiet as possible, like when they played Army and he was a Special Forces soldier infiltrating enemy lines. He stopped halfway when one of the hinges squeaked, sending a shiver along his arm and down his back. He stopped opening, and they slid through the half-open door into a back hall with a stairway leading up to the main floor. They could hear a TV. Compared to the fresh, crisp winter air outside the suffocating indoor air smelled of cigarette smoke, body odor, and cleaning fluid. They crept up the stairway, solid limestone slabs. At the top, Jake crouched and peered into the main hallway. The office door stood open. The only voices they heard came from the TV in the day room through a door to the right. Jake looked back at Mario and motioned with his head to advance.

They had studied the floor plan almost to the point of total memory. Rosalyn had visited her father at work enough times to easily recall the layout: The main floor of the long, rectangular building stood a half story above ground level with an identical second floor above. The small ward office stood just to the left of the front entry and next to that the doorway to the day room. A long hallway extended in the other direction, to the left as they entered from the back of the building.

Jake stepped into the hallway, first toward the front door to see if the hospital worker was still being detained. He saw Leroy crouching on the sidewalk next to LeeAnn, who was sitting holding her ankle.

Quickly and quietly the boys tiptoed down the hall to room eleven, right where it was supposed to be according to Rosalyn's drawing of the building floor plan. Mario stood on his toes to look through the window. He knocked on the door, not too loudly, but the sound churned up the butterflies in his stomach even more. Jake cupped the key in his hands and exhaled a breath like he was rolling dice. This time he tried to work the key in the lock more gently than the first time under the greater force of tension. He prayed Rosalyn was right, that Aaron had made a copy of a master key, that it would work in all of the doors.

EVERY NOW AND THEN, AARON WOULD ASK HIS PARENTS if he could work on projects in the machine shop, so it was not unusual when he asked permission Thursday evening. Lately, they had allowed him to be there alone, although Mrs. Abrams still worried and insisted that he not use the welder. Aaron promised and said he would be careful. Rosalyn told her parents she was going to the skating rink. Aaron was already in the shop when she arrived shortly before seven.

"Did you bring it?" He was excited and determined, as much for the challenge of their plan as for the risk he would be taking in using the welder.

"I got it. I hope it works." She looked around the machine shop. The white-painted concrete walls helped reflect light from the long, cylindrical fluorescent bulbs hanging from the ceiling. Although appearing reasonably neat and clean, the place smelled grimy like grease and oil. "Wow, I didn't know you had all these machines. My parents think I'm at the rink. What did you tell your parents?" she asked, lifting her ice skates from her shoulders, their laces tied together and draped around the back of her neck. Aaron shrugged. It was no big deal, working in the shop in the evenings.

Rosalyn carefully reached into the right skate and withdrew a Calumet Baking Powder tin. Aaron watched closely as she turned the cover off and pulled out the form wrapped in several pieces of facial tissue.

"Good job. This'll work fine," he said, gently taking the thick bar of clay, about five inches long. He held it up to look closely at the impression of the skeleton-type key made into one side. Rosalyn smiled and shivered. Her father suspected nothing yesterday when she apparently became curious about all the keys on the key ring attached to a leather lanyard he wore on his belt when he went to work. At home it hung on the key rack by the kitchen door. He had worked the day shift at Dakota Falls State Hospital, arriving home right after she did from school. Just before supper she lifted the key ring off the rack and began to inspect them.

"Roz, what are you doing with daddy's keys?" Mrs. Sommers asked. "Supper's just about ready. Can you go get daddy?"

"I was just looking at them."

She carried the key ring with her into the living room where her dad was reading the *Chronicle* and occasionally glancing at the TV. "Daddy, supper's ready. Daddy, what are all these keys for anyway?" She held up the key ring. Mr. Sommers put down the paper and looked affectionately at his daughter. Her curious, childlike demeanor drew his attention and made him much more responsive than that generated at other times recently when adolescent outbursts and sullen moments seemed to predominate. This seemed a welcome respite from the other moods that had been occurring more often. He realized the days of his daughter's sweet and charming childhood were ending. He smiled, explaining that most of the keys were from work.

"Why are there so many? Why can't you have one key that fits everything?"

"Honey, there are just a lot of different locks," he said. "Different doors, medicine cabinets, things like that. There is one that's a master key for the main doors of the buildings. Everyone has one of those."

Rosalyn asked which one that was. He lifted up the master key. Casually she reached for it, said thanks and turned to take the key ring back to the kitchen, holding it by the master key. She passed through the kitchen, unnoticed by her mother still busy with supper, and quietly slipped down the basement stairs. At the workbench she firmly pressed the master key into the block of clay she had ready, wrapped the clay in tissue and inserted it into the baking powder tin. Returning the key ring to the holder in the kitchen, the whole procedure had taken all of about two minutes.

Aaron rummaged through the scrap barrel, a thirty-gallon steel drum containing a jumble of aluminum, steel, and iron odds and ends. He found a short length of steel rod and held it above the key impression in the block of clay; too thin. He tossed it back and pulled out three more. As long as it was reasonably close, the diameter of the shaft wasn't that critical. He found one that looked close and set it on a counter. He leaned over the barrel looking for a small scrap of sheet metal.

"Are you sure you pressed the key all the way in," he asked looking over his shoulder at Rosalyn. "I have to know how thick it should be."

Rosalyn said she thought so. He reached back into the barrel carefully to avoid any sharp, jagged edges of metal. He took out a small, flat piece of steel from a job over at the grain elevator. Cleaning up after the job it easily could have been tossed in a garbage can, but at on-site jobs, his dad always picked up every scrap and took it back to the shop. It measured three millimeters thick, just about right.

"Can you really do this? Are you sure it's going to work?" Rosalyn asked.

"I can do it. I can't guarantee it'll work," Aaron replied, a slight tone of irritation in his voice. Rosalyn flinched back half a step and said nothing.

He cut the steel rod to a five-inch length; the shaft and handle would be the easy part compared with the key's notched pattern. He used the power metal saw to rough-cut the pattern from the steel sheet. Clamping the small piece in a vise grip, he trimmed a bit more off using the grinder. It was barely large enough to hold in the table vise, so he could refine the pattern with a steel file. Holding it carefully with a needle nose pliers, he tried to lay it into the pattern in the clay block.

"Darn it, it's too small," Aaron shook his head, exasperated. "I should have checked it better when I was making it."

"That's okay. It didn't take too long. Can't you make another one?" Rosalyn said trying to sound optimistic and hopeful. "There's still time."

Aaron sighed and repeated the process. This time the notches fit snugly into the clay pattern. The pieces were too small to weld so he braised it to the shaft and also a small, flat piece about the size of a quarter to the other end for a handle. He clamped the homemade key in the table vise and filed down the rough edges.

"There, how's that for a masterpiece?" Aaron said looking at Rosalyn and smiling. She grinned and patted him on the back. They laid the key into the clay mold and, except for the handle, it appeared to fit.

"Wow, that's amazing how you did that! Good job!" Rosalyn said. She put the key and clay block into the Calumet Baking Powder tin. It was her job to see that Jake and Mario got the key on Friday.

JAKE TURNED THE KEY IN THE KEYHOLE of the door to room eleven. It wouldn't turn. He jiggled it back and forth. Nothing.

"Who's out there? What's going on?" Tom's voice whispered from inside.

"It's me. Mario and Jake," Mario whispered loudly. "We were going to get you out of here, but the key won't work."

Tom got up and looked out the door window. "What the hell are you kids doing? How'd you get in here? Where's Leroy?"

"He's outside, helping LeeAnn. We don't have much time," Mario said. Jake fought off panic still trying to work the key. "It's no good, it's not going to work," he said.

"What do you need a key for?" they heard Tom say through the door. "Look up. There's a little knob. They just use the deadbolt from the outside. They don't use the key lock."

Mario turned the knob and felt the bolt slide back. They stepped back as Tom pulled the door open.

"What in the hell you kids think you're doing?" Tom said smiling, almost laughing. "How'd you get in here?"

"Aaron made a key. C'mon, we gotta go," Jake urged. "We're going to get you out of here!"

Mario carried the duffle bag into the room. He pulled back the blanket on Tom's bed and emptied the contents of the duffle back—two pillows, a pale yellow towel and another blanket. He laid the pillows end to end, rolled the towel into a ball and rested it on Tom's pillow. He pulled Tom's blanket over the pillows and tried to make it look like a human form.

"That's good enough, Mario. Let's go," Jake whispered urgently.

He looked down the hallway. It looked clear. Quickly they headed for the back stairway. Reaching the central hallway, Jake peeked around the corner toward the front door, then went closer to look out the window. LeeAnn still sat on the sidewalk holding her ankle. Leroy stood over her, looking like he was getting ready to go back to the building. Tom, Jake, and Mario went down the back stairway. Another patient stood in the doorway of the day room, nervously smoking a cigarette. He started laughing and hopping back and forth from foot to foot. "I wanna go too. I wanna go too," he said through clenched lips holding a cigarette and clapping his hands vigorously. "Here comes Leroy. Here comes Leroy. You better hurry. You better hurry," he said excitedly. They ignored him and scurried toward the back door.

"You kids are something else," Tom kept repeating, shaking his head on their way down the back steps and out the door. "I've been praying for a miracle to get out of this place." He stopped suddenly in a coughing fit, doubled over and hung onto the railing. Jake and Mario stood down by the door waiting. "Hurry," Jake said. "C'mon, Tom. Let's go," Mario whispered. "Are you okay?"

Tom nodded, holding onto his chest with his left hand and used his right to steady himself down the rest of the stairway.

Outside Jake looked up and down the street for traffic. He saw the brake lights on Larry's car blink continuously and rapidly, the signal that LeeAnn's diversion had ended and Leroy was heading back to the building.

Leroy walked slowly and with great effort up the stairway, entered the front door and looked back out the window at the young girl, who was walking away apparently fully recovered from her twisted ankle.

He watched, puzzled, as she faded into the darkness farther away from the streetlight.

He removed his coat and turned back toward the office. Arvid stood in the doorway of the day room excitedly stepping up and down with his feet like climbing some imaginary stairway, clapping his hands, laughing and giggling through his lips pressed together holding a cigarette.

"Tom's gone. Tom's gone. Tom's gone," Arvid giggled, puffs of smoke escaping into the hallway.

"Go back and sit down, Arvid, or I'll take away your smokes," Leroy said gruffly.

Arvid had felt the draft of cold air entering the back hallway. Just coming in from outside where the temperature had dropped to fifteen above zero Leroy hadn't noticed. Foot prints left by dirt and snow blended into the mottled pattern of the terrazzo floor.

Leroy felt irritated that the incident had ended so quickly. He had never been so near an attractive teenage girl before except perhaps in a movie line or checkout at the grocery store, much less try to touch one. He entered the office and hung up his coat. Arvid followed, standing in the doorway still giggling and stepping up and down. "Tom's gone, Leroy. Tom's gone, Leroy."

"Arvid, shut up and go sit down," Leroy ordered. He looked at his watch, not yet eight-thirty. Normally he waited until about ten to make the rounds, checking to make sure all the patients were in their rooms. He took Arvid by the elbow and escorted him back into the day room, looking down the main hallway on the way. Everything looked quiet except for the TV blaring in the day room and a radio coming from somewhere on the second floor. He sat down to watch TV and one of the other patients in the room wanted to play cribbage so he did.

"Here they come," Rosalyn said excitedly. She opened the back door and got out, waiting to usher Mario, Jake, and Tom into the backseat. She waited for LeeAnn to get in the front, skooch over next to Larry, then climbed in herself. Larry shifted the '55 Chevy into first gear and slowly drove off, looking carefully for other traffic because he did not turn on the headlights. Rosalyn turned, looking toward the backseat.

"We did it! We did it!" she said excitedly. "Hi, Tom. We're going to get you out of here. Where do you want us to take you?"

"Hold on a second," Larry said. "The deal was just to give you guys a ride back to Clareton, or we can let Tom here off in Dakota Falls. That's as far as we go."

Tom erupted in another coughing fit, waving his hand back and forth trying to speak. He shivered visibly, his shoulders hunched, making the overly large blue-cotton shirt he wore look even baggier. In the rush leaving his room and the building he had not taken a warm jacket, but his was locked in a storage closet anyway. Mario sat in the middle scrunching his legs and shoulders together trying to not touch Tom or Jake, noticing for the first time that Tom was not wearing a jacket, but he didn't say anything.

Tom finally stopped coughing enough so he could speak. "Just let me off by the trail to the shack at Clareton. I'll just get some of my stuff and high-tail it out of here. You kids are something else. You saved my life. I don't know how to thank you."

"We ain't out of here yet," Larry said sardonically. He wheeled the Chevy out on to the main highway and turned in the direction of Clareton. Tom asked Larry if he had a smoke. LeeAnn took a Lucky from the pack sitting on the dash, handed it to Tom and reached back with the lighter. He leaned forward to reach the flame with the cigarette tip and took a deep drag. Mario watched quietly, looking at Tom's face illuminated in the bright orange glow. Rosalyn shook her head slowly with a look of disgust. "Those things'll kill you," she said to no one in particular.

In Dakota Falls, thirty miles closer to Fargo, LeeAnn had fiddled with the radio dial and picked up KRRV, hoping to hear a better selection of rock 'n' roll. The signal began to fade the farther they traveled back toward Clareton. Larry wasn't paying attention to the music, anxiously studying each oncoming vehicle as it passed by but trying to avoid looking directly into the headlights.

Now that the break-out had actually occurred he was regretting the adventure. If the cops stopped them with Tom in the car, it could be big trouble. Larry agreed to the plan partly because he didn't believe these kids would actually pull it off. He thought once they actually arrived at Dakota Falls, they would chicken out or that their plan to get Tom out of the building wouldn't work. He thought it would be just a joyride, something to do for a while on a Friday night in December after which he and LeeAnn would go to the late show. In the trunk he had a six-pack of Schlitz malt liquor and a pint of peppermint schnapps in an insulated cooler more to keep it from freezing than anything else. Now he had a car full of little kids, an old psycho, and LeeAnn wasn't paying him much attention. After her role in the encounter with Leroy, all she wanted to do was go home and take a bath.

"Tom, are you okay? You don't look so good," Rosalyn said. He looked damp and pale. His breathing sounded like wheezing. Even though Larry's car smelled of tobacco, they could almost taste the sweat and cigarette smoke permeating Tom's clothing.

"I'll be fine," Tom said, trying to suppress the coughing as he spoke. "You kids didn't have to do this, but I really appreciate it. I sure hope you don't get in trouble."

"As long as nobody saw us at the hospital we're okay," Jake said.

"The story is that we were going back to Clareton from the movie, and we picked up this hitchhiker," Mario said. Rosalyn nodded, smiling. That was her idea. Despite signs warning, "DO NOT PICK UP HITCHHIKERS," along the highway near the Dakota Falls State Hospital there was no law prohibiting it, and in the dark it was hard to see the signs anyway.

Moments of awkward silence as they drove along through the dark winter night made Mario feel even more self-conscious that he was sitting next to his father; he didn't know what to say. Tom just sat there, head hanging, quietly wheezing, eyes fixed on some imaginary spot on the seatback in front of him. LeeAnn rocked her head back and forth to the beat of a Buddy Holly song on the radio, softly mouthing the words, and everybody strained to listen.

Larry relaxed a bit as they approached the Clareton city limit. In a few minutes, it would be all over as far as he was concerned. He turned left on to the county road before getting into town and soon he'd be letting Tom out.

"Shit," he blurted. A Clareton police squad car passed by in the opposite direction. Larry looked in the rear-view mirror and saw the brake lights. The squad car made a U-turn.

❧ 25 ☙

MARIA RETURNED FROM THE KITCHEN with a fresh bowl of popcorn. Already nine o'clock, they had just finished watching "Ellery Queen." It was the first time she had allowed Mario to go out of town with a group of kids and no adults along. She had been quiet all evening and noticeably fidgety.

"They'll be home soon," Thelma said. "Don't worry so much. I'm sure they had a good time and everything will be fine."

Jim agreed. "That Larry Carlson . . . he's a good kid," Jim said. "I know he looks like one of those rock 'n' rollers, but inside he's decent and responsible. He'll make sure they get home all right. And the roads are okay."

Maria sat down on the couch next to him and forced a smile. They were spending a quiet evening at home watching TV. Horace had had to work so Thelma had joined them. During the TV shows Maria sat looking almost absent-minded, munching on popcorn and sipping a Coke. She would find her thoughts drifting back to the past and the brief, passionate moments with the handsome construction worker, how it all fell apart, and the years of loneliness that followed. Her devotion to her son kept her going but she often had to suppress obsessive thoughts that something bad might happen to him. She didn't know what she would do if anything did happen to Mario although the prospect of a better future with Jim brought some comfort as long as Tom kept his distance.

"You know, Mario's getting old enough now to strike out on his own a little bit," Jim said gently. "We can help, but kids also have to learn things for themselves. He's got a good head on his shoulders . . . look where he got it from."

Thelma nodded and smiled. "I'm sure he'll be okay. They'll be home before ten. Just you wait and see."

"You're right. I know I shouldn't worry so much. And it's a group of kids—Jake and Rosalyn and Larry's girlfriend. I guess if the Sommerses allowed Rosalyn to go along, I shouldn't worry," Maria said trying to reassure herself.

HORACE RECOGNIZED LARRY'S CAR RIGHT AWAY. Because of the bright, oncoming headlights piercing the darkness, he didn't get a good look inside the car other than to see that it held five or six people. He knew they would be returning from Dakota Falls about now, but he wondered why they were heading back out of Clareton on the county road. His indecision about following them ended when he looked in the rear view mirror of the squad car and saw only one taillight glowing red on the '55 Chevy.

In a past similar circumstance, Larry punched the accelerator and disappeared into the night. On a hot summer night with five beers in his belly, he yielded to panic instead of to the cop. Lucky for him it had been Horace who decided to not pursue. He would approach Larry later and chew him out but good.

When he saw the red flashing gumball gaining on him, this time Larry slowed to a stop. He had done no wrong, he said to himself, but his mouth felt dry and sticky anyway. He hadn't been drinking, yet. He wasn't speeding, and the passenger was just a hitchhiker they'd picked up.

"Damn," Jake muttered, looking out the back window at the flashing red light. "All this work for nothing."

Tom hung his head, and everyone else in the car sat still, almost petrified and not saying a thing. Larry looked into the side mirror and watched the officer get out of the squad car.

"Whew," he said quietly. "It's Horse!" He rolled down the window and a blast of cold, fresh air rushed through the car's stuffy interior. The officer approached the car, the beam from his flashlight bouncing along the roadway.

"Evening, Larry. You mind if I asked where you kids are going?"

"How ya doin', Horse. I mean Horace, Officer Greene. Sure, I don't mind. We was just driving around, we just got back from Dakota Falls. Went to a movie. We took the little kids here."

"Yeah, I heard about that. Nice of you. What movie did you see?"

Larry looked at LeeAnn, caught off guard without an immediate response.

"It was *The Defiant Ones*," Rosalyn replied quickly. "It was really good."

"So, what's up, Horace?" Larry asked.

The officer leaned back and sideways so he could peer into the car without getting too close to the open driver's window, the motion mostly out of habit and not any particular concern about this particular traffic stop.

"I heard that movie is pretty good. Wish I could've seen it," Horace said. "Did you know your right taillight's out?"

"What? For real?" Larry exclaimed. He looked at LeeAnn. "They were all working when we left." She nodded.

"That can happen sometimes even without any help," Horace said with a wry smile. "There's something else, too. Dakota Falls sent out an APB about a runaway from the state hospital. A male patient, late forties, about six feet tall with light hair."

Larry felt the hair under his ducktail prickle on the back of his neck. He gripped the steering wheel and stared straight ahead. From the second they saw the police car turn around, he knew they were caught cold.

"They said he's high risk, dangerous," Horace said, with what Larry thought sounded like a little chuckle. "Anyway, if you say you haven't seen him that's good enough for me. I'll just have to believe you. Course, you all have to say that so we're all of the same understanding." He leaned over again to look at each person in the car, except for deliberately ignoring Tom sitting in back on the driver's side.

"We haven't seen him," Rosalyn finally said, looking around curiously at the others and shrugging her shoulders.

"Good," Horace said. "But if you did see him, say, give him a ride or something, what would you do?"

Larry turned and looked at Mario and Jake in the back, then at LeeAnn and Rosalyn. LeeAnn poked him in the side with her elbow, whispering something about picking up a hitchhiker. Larry looked at her and then back toward Horace.

"If there was a hitchhiker, we might give him a ride someplace," Larry said. "That's all."

"Like maybe give him a ride home or something like that," Horace said.

"Right."

"If you had picked up a hitchhiker, do you think anyone would have seen you?" Horace asked. Larry said he didn't think so. It was dark out. Then Horace asked Larry if he'd been drinking, and he said no.

"Good," Horace said. He looked at his watch. He rested his hand on the car top where the door met the roof and ran it slowly along the smooth, shiny finish, briefly scanning his eyes over the roof and down the back. Ever since Larry had had it re-painted all black last August, the car turned heads around town for both its looks and throaty muffler.

"Why'd you do that anyway?" Horace asked. "Why'd you paint this all black?"

"I don't know. Just felt like it I guess. You like it?"

"I think it looks great," Horace grinned. Then he turned serious. "You get these kids home soon now, okay? And you better remember what we all said, that we didn't see anything about the runaway."

319

Larry nodded. He felt relieved and relaxed back into the car seat. The others relaxed, too, except for Tom who sat motionless the entire time still gazing at the imaginary spot on the seatback in front of him.

Horace reminded Larry to get the taillight fixed right away and walked back to the squad car. Larry rolled up the window. He took out a Lucky and lit up, shaking slightly as he did so.

"Can you believe that?" Larry said, exhaling a cloud of smoke. "Why is Horse covering for this guy?"

"It's because he didn't do it. He didn't beat up Frank Harley," Rosalyn said. "Frank lied about it, and the cops made Tom go to the state hospital for it. It's just terrible."

Mario looked at Tom and saw a little smile curling up.

"It looks like you're home free," Mario said.

Tom looked at him and smiled. "For now anyway." He reached across with his left hand and patted Mario on the shoulder. "You kids saved my life. I won't ever forget that. I don't know how you did it. Must have took a lot of gumption."

Larry drove about a half mile down the county road stopping where the trail led into the woods and Tom's shack. The temperature had already dropped almost to zero on the way down to the fifteen below forecast by morning. Mario offered Tom his parka, but it was way too small. Tom hesitated, then asked instead if by any chance it might be possible to get something to drink. Because of the kids Larry didn't want to say anything about the malt liquor and peppermint schnapps in the trunk. Jake knew about it anyway and cajoled his older brother into offering it to Tom. Reluctantly and with some embarrassment because of Mario and Rosalyn, Larry got out, took the schnapps from the trunk and handed it to Tom. He smiled again and reached out to shake Larry's hand. Then he reached back into the car and held out his hand for Mario. Mario took off his right mitten and shook hands with Tom.

"Thanks again," Tom said. He wondered if he should address Mario as his son, but he could tell the boy felt awkward, as he did himself, so he didn't.

"Bye," Mario said. "Good luck."

"Maybe we'll see you again sometime," Tom said. "Say hello to your mom for me. I hope things work out for her and Jim, and you, too. You're a good kid." He reached in and gave Mario's hair a tussle. He asked Larry if he could have a couple of smokes; Larry gave him the pack of Luckies about half full. Tom said thanks, smiled and waved, then turned and headed into the woods toward the shack. They watched him fade into the wall of darkness among the trees.

For the first time since leaving the hospital, the bitter cold sent a shiver through Tom's lean body. He took a swig of the schnapps, the minty, sweet, cheap liqueur warm and comforting on the way down. Two inches of new snow on Thursday had left a fluffy, white frosting on tree branches and transformed the footprints on the trail through the woods into smooth, concave indentations. Tom trudged along, shivering on the outside but warmed in his belly each time he stopped for another swig. He didn't have much time to return to the shack, get the belongings that he could carry and make it back to the train station in time for the 11:15 to Minneapolis. That was his only option now, to get out of Clareton and disappear into the skid-row section of downtown Minneapolis. He couldn't risk getting caught again.

He couldn't take Ike on the train even if he had healed from his injuries. Although he'd miss Ike, Tom was glad that Mario promised to ask his mother if they could take him. Mario felt confident that she would agree if he promised to take good care of him and take him for walks. Doc Ahrends said he'd be willing to keep Ike, too. Tom's anger resurfaced again about what they did to Ike. So trusting, loyal, and completely innocent, there was no explanation for the attack other than human cruelty lurking beneath the imperfect constraints of laws and moral values, much less care and compassion for other living things.

Other than losing Ike, the time spent here had been worth it; for the first time he could remember he had accomplished something more than drifting from town to town and working odd jobs when he needed money. Even though he didn't know it at first, he had found what he was looking for in Clareton. Sometimes during the past months he fantasized that he would be able to stay, that by some miracle they could all be together again. He hoped that in the future he would be able to see Mario again, see him graduate from high school, go to college, meet a nice girl, have a family—live a happy, productive, normal life. He tried to push aside the thought that he might never see him again.

After seeing the story in the *Minneapolis Journal* when he arrived in Clareton almost a year ago, he did so with some anticipation, but no great expectations. Although alone there at the shack as he always was except for the few times the kids had visited, when he had confirmed that Maria and Mario were here, he would sit by the fire at night comforted by knowing they were right across the lake, and at the same time anguished because while they were within reach, they never would be in his grasp. He took more swigs on the bottle of schnapps, waiting for the desired effect that would dull the painful thoughts and eventually make them go away, at least for a while.

On the ride back from Dakota Falls, he questioned Mario about everything that happened; he had no choice but to believe Mario when he said he knew nothing about any legal commitment to the state hospital. When Tom came in from the cold last Sunday and agreed to enter treatment, he did so trusting them—Maria, Mario, Horace, Doc Ahrends. At first he blamed them, believing that they were the ones who betrayed him. He cursed himself for trusting anyone, something he once vowed never to do again.

He was not angry with Mario about the fight with Frank Harley a week ago Monday. He did not blame Mario when the Harleys and police accused him instead. The boy tried to convince the police about what really happened. In fact he felt proud about the boy's courage in standing his ground, his honesty, and his physical toughness. What angered him were the same things that always did, the injustice, intolerance, selfishness, and discrimination that infiltrated and tainted the community and people in it, especially among those who had more power than the rest.

Emerging from the woods into the clearing he could barely see the dark shape of the shack against a background of snow-covered shrubs and trees. It wasn't the same returning to it this time. No welcome from Ike leaping and yipping at the end of his chain. Fresh snow covered the ground in front making it appear as if it had been uninhabited for a long time. He walked up and opened the door. He heard some small critter scurry for cover; he hoped it was a mouse and not a rat.

It seemed colder inside than out, so immediately he took some firewood from the pile, tapping each piece on the splitting stump to dislodge the snow. He lit a fire in the stove, leaving the door open so he could stare into the flames as he sat on the cot taking pulls on the schnapps. He felt his way over to the table to get the kerosene lantern. He looked around in the soft, dim light, figuring out what he could take on the train and what would have to be left. He wished he would have told Mario to come out to the shack tomorrow and take some of the things left behind: his guitar, books, the notebooks. Maybe the kids would come out anyway to check it out. He finished the rest of the schnapps, lit another smoke and lay back on the cot, just for a minute, feeling warmed by the liquor if not yet by the stove.

Usually the booze or wine dulled even his dreams, but not always. Sometimes he would awaken terrified, sweating, nightmare images playing in his unconscious mind. Sometimes they came with the acrid smell of gunpowder and explosives. He didn't hear the crash, but this time when he awoke suddenly the smoke didn't go away with a vanishing dream.

At first he thought about the train. How long had he been sleeping? If he missed the train tonight, would he be able to get out of town in the morning unnoticed? He thought he heard snapping, crackling noises coming from the back wall. He still smelled smoke; in the dim light of the lantern on the table he could see a thin cloud seeping from the wall; an orange glow appeared in the window. Tom jerked up and spun his feet to the floor so suddenly his head felt like it got left behind, then caught up bringing with it a pounding ache. He grabbed his head in his hands and winced. Sweat, even in the cold shack, dampened his forehead. He doubled up, coughing as he had many times in the past couple of days and recently leaving blood-flecked sputum on his hands. The smoke and adrenaline brought just enough energy to his weakened limbs; he stood unsteadily to investigate whatever intrusion this might be.

In just seconds, flames blanketed almost the entire exterior of the back wall. Smoke seeping through to the interior wall, quickly became orange tongues of flame. Through the window Tom could see the whole area behind the shack brightening in the light like a huge bonfire. He ran outside around back and started throwing scoops of snow on the blazing wall.

Already raging, the fire hungrily consumed the pittance of snow. The futile effort seemed to make the fire rage even more and the heat forced Tom back. Turning away he glanced toward the woods, seeing what appeared to be dark figures moving away among the trees, and this time he was not dreaming. He heard the sound of a small motor and thought he saw a beam of light bouncing away through the distant trees. Investigating that mystery had to wait; he went back inside to try save some of his belongings.

He opened the door, and a searing blast came at him like a freight train of suffocating heat and smoke. He dropped to the floor and crawled toward the hiding place under the floor board for his cash box. His teeth clenched in defiance of the scorching heat singing his hands as he pried up the board and pulled out the box. Crawling backward he looked around for the box with his notebooks. He crawled on his knees over to the shelf where it sat, trying to keep below the thick smoke billowing overhead. His warm parka still hung in the storage closet at the state hospital. Carrying the box of notebooks with the cashbox perched on top, he reached for the red-and-black plaid wool jacket hanging by the door.

His head spun dizzily when he struggled to his feet; his lungs burned almost as much as the heat he felt on his face and hands. Reaching the open door, he felt relief from the cold air rushing in, but it was fueling the blaze like a blacksmith's bellows.

THE FIRST CLARETON FIRE FIGHTER to find him came directly from home on the east side of town. Dispatch had already received the alarm when he called. Instead of going to the fire station first, he left his car on the road by the trail and carried his own fire extinguisher from the trunk into the woods to the shack. Everybody knew about the shack, but not everyone knew some old man lived there. Gary Beckstrand, a fourteen-year veteran of the Clareton Fire Department, knew about Tom. After nearly seventeen years owning and operating Gary's Electric Service he knew almost everyone in town, and if not the people, he probably was familiar with the house they lived in or building they worked in. He had been out to the shack several times in years past, mostly out of curiosity about the abandoned hunting shack that had drifted into disrepair.

He happened to look out his kitchen window toward the lake and saw an orange glow in the trees on the south side by the point, and immediately guessed what had happened. They saw it so many times. Someone smoking and falling asleep, perhaps drinking too. The cigarette falls on a mattress, flames erupt and the fire quickly spreads. He knew it would be too late to save the structure if it were worth saving at all. But he had to do everything possible to try rescue anyone inside, no matter who it might be.

Tom had made it about twenty-five feet before collapsing in the snow. Gary set down the fire extinguisher and knelt down by the unconscious figure. He pressed his fingers against a jugular vein in the man's neck trying to feel a pulse; he was still alive, but the pulse was very weak. By this time a giant ball of flames engulfed the shack. Gary turned the man on his back, grasped under his armpits and dragged him farther away, turning his own head away from the ferocious heat as much as he had ever experienced before.

Almost instinctively, Gary's thoughts engaged in trying to determine cause of the fire. Had it been a cigarette on a mattress, the victim deep in unconscious, drunken sleep he likely would have been overcome by smoke, awakening too late to escape if he awakened at all. There was something different going on here. It happened so quickly, yet the victim was able to awaken, gather some belongings and get outside. It suggested arson, when someone ignites a sufficient amount of inflammable material, which in turn rapidly ignites a large area, not like a small, smoldering ignition that takes its time to develop.

A county sheriff's deputy arrived next, ahead of the other fire fighters. He had driven part way on the trail into the woods before losing tire traction on a small rise. It blocked the way for the fire department's rural grass fire rig, an Army surplus two-ton with dual rear wheels and a 250-gallon water tank. The two fire fighters could do nothing else but to abandon the truck and go in on foot.

The roof of the shack collapsed, sending a huge cloud of sparks and bright, orange embers shooting up into the black winter night sky. With no hope of saving the structure, the fire fighters and the sheriff's deputy crouched beside Tom, linked their hands beneath him and carried him to the sheriff's patrol car. He slumped over when they placed him in the back seat. Gary reached in and again felt for a pulse.

"He's not doing too good. You better get him to the hospital quick," he told the deputy.

"That's where he was. That's where he should have been," the deputy said.

"What do you mean? I knew there was somebody staying out here. I never met him. I think this fire is suspicious, too," Gary said.

"This guy escaped from the Dakota Falls State Hospital a couple hours ago. He's a dangerous psycho."

"He don't look too dangerous now. You better take him to the hospital in town here. He's sure to have smoke inhalation. I didn't see any serious burns, but it looks to me like he wasn't doing too good to begin with. He needs medical attention right now," Gary said sternly.

The deputy took the two-way radio microphone and called dispatch. He was at the fire location, an old hunting shack in the woods across the lake from town. He had found the state hospital escapee there unconscious and possibly suffering smoke inhalation. No indication of other injuries. He would be transporting the individual to the Clareton hospital as soon as he was able to get the patrol car back onto the county road. The fire fighters hooked a towing chain to the back of the patrol car and slowly backed their truck to the road.

෨ 26 ෬

HORACE SAT IN THE PATROL CAR on the west end of town about a block off the main street where he could keep an eye on traffic and also the high school a block in the opposite direction. A break-in there two weeks ago remained unsolved. While unlikely that another would occur so soon, the police had to make sure it wouldn't. A person or persons had broken a window in the back door by the gymnasium. The police and school administrators couldn't find any damage or anything missing, and the not knowing annoyed them even more.

When the weather turned cold, the frequency of these minor infractions in the community dropped off considerably, replaced by domestic disturbances often exacerbated by alcohol, motorists stranded either by a dead car battery or wheels sunk in a snow bank, or fender-bender vehicle crashes. People just never learned to slow down on the slippery snow and ice-covered streets, especially at intersections and stop signs where quickly braked wheels skidded, creating slick patches of ice, making every stop in town potentially dangerous. Even the high school hot-rodders cooled their wheels in winter, spending more time in the shop working on their beloved cars.

Now Horace began to regret the traffic stop with Larry. He could have ignored the burned out taillight, although doing so would have bothered him also. He didn't know why he handled things the way he had, trying to ignore Tom like that. Now he worried because if anyone found out there could be serious consequences. It still angered him, the way he was duped into taking Tom to the state hospital and keeping him there by force, which he thought he was doing for Tom's good, that he agreed to go voluntarily. Horace should have been told about the judge's legal commitment even though it had been contrived. Even if he wouldn't have agreed to it as a law enforcement officer, he would have done his duty irregardless.

The fire call coming over the patrol car's two-way radio startled him out of his thoughts. The Clareton Fire Department was being called out to a structure fire, located somewhere in the woods out of town on the south side of the lake. Horace instantly thought about Tom. He shifted the '57 Ford squad car into gear and sped away from the curb, wheels skidding sideways, wondering what could have happened. Being on the west side of town he decided to go counterclockwise around the lake. It was about the same distance but might be a little quicker.

Unlike the east side of the lake with its low-lying terrain around the creek inlet, the higher ground on the west side had led to development, small cabins and houses hugging the shoreline accessed by a parallel road about 200 feet in from the shore. At one time the road ended in a cul-de-sac near the southwest shore. As the number of summer cabins grew in the early 1950s, many resulting from the growing prosperity among area farmers, the call came for an extension of the lake road back out to a county road. Farther south it intersected an east-west township road along the section line. It would take Horace just a couple minutes, even with some slippery spots, to travel around to the county road on the east side and up to the trail into the woods.

Horace gunned the patrol car along the lake road. It always felt good to spring into action on an urgent call with the adrenaline overpowering lethargy and boredom, even if it happened to be an injury crash or some tragedy disrupting people's lives. Having the power to do something to help people, or make them obey the law, made it feel like it all mattered. Later he would empathize about their troubles and then let it go. He knew Tom was in trouble. Horace tried to push aside the thought that he was responsible. He knew something bad was happening at the shack, and he worried about what he would find. He would worry later about any possible repercussions from his decision to refrain from apprehending Tom. The decision was partly out of uncertainty how Tom would react if Horace had tried, if Tom resisted, and because it had been in front of the kids Horace tried to avoid that ugly scene. Now, it looked as if things might turn out even worse.

The bouncing light coming out of the trees along the south shore caught Horace's eye as he made the turn from the lake road toward the county road. What were they doing out on that thing this time of night? Absent the fire call Horace might have turned around and tried to hail the snow machine or at least turn around and try to follow it. It caught his attention like a bored dog that suddenly saw a squirrel dart across the ground nearby. Tempted to give chase, the dog knew better. It might have gotten up and trotted over to where the squirrel had been, but only to catch a scent and look around just in case it hadn't escaped up a tree.

Horace tried to remember who owned the snow machine. He remembered someone talking about it at the station, but could not recall anyone saying to whom it belonged. It looked like a bobsled. A noisy, two-stroke engine under the orange-colored cowling in the front buzzed like a giant bee, spewing bluish, oily exhaust. The engine and gears turned a long track like a conveyor belt, propelling it forward. Two metal skis in front connected to handle bars for steering. It scooted across the snow and ice over thirty miles per hour and could go just about anywhere across the snow-covered terrain. When it reached the lake road, the snow machine turned abruptly, roared between two cabins and sped out onto the lake. Horace looked for it in the rear view mirror and caught a glimpse of the machine's taillight dancing away into the distance until it blended in with the lights from town.

Away from the cabins on higher ground west and south of the lake gave Horace a better view of the woods on the south side, where he could clearly see bright, orange flames shooting above the trees right about where the shack stood. How in the world could a fire have started so quickly, engulfing the entire structure in a huge fireball? Horace turned grim at the thought of Tom being unable to escape, if he were still inside. Maybe it was a diversion. Maybe he set the fire himself before leaving for town to catch the train. Torching the shack would be one final act of leaving town for good and not leaving anything behind. The patrol car's two-way radio crackled with a Clareton fire fighter calling in a report to dispatch. They were en route in the grass rig to a structure fire on the south shore of the lake.

Horace began responding to the call in the usual quick, efficient, calm manner growing from his training and ten years of experience, until a discomforting thought intruded. He became angry with himself for the fleeting thought that maybe it would be best if Tom was in the shack and didn't escape. It would solve any future problems that might develop in getting him back to the hospital, any trouble he might cause Maria, Jim and Mario, and lessen any chance that someone other than the kids would find out about his decision to ignore Tom at the traffic stop. With Tom out of the way, the authorities and community quickly would forget about him. Horace suddenly felt ashamed. Tom would be okay. He would go back to the hospital, get treatment, and start to live a productive life once again.

Horace turned north on the county road along the east side of the lake. Looking left toward the woods he could see taillights like glowing red eyes of some large, nocturnal creature moving slowly, unsteadily from the woods toward the road. Approaching closer, he recognized the Clareton Fire Department grass rig backing out onto the county road. In the beam of its headlights he saw a heavy chain stretched out in front, hooked to a county sheriff's patrol car, a '54 Dodge Hornet.

When Horace made the traffic stop earlier, he observed the burned out taillight infraction while Larry and the kids still were in the city limit. Even following them out of town on the county road, he still had jurisdiction. At the fire and whatever else was happening, the deputy had jurisdiction along with the fire department. Horace was not optimistic that the sheriff's department would try very hard to find the cause of the fire and, if it were arson, look for suspects, just as they hadn't bothered too much about solving last week's attack on Tom's dog, Ike. It was just a dog, they said, and the old drunk probably did it himself. Horace switched on the red light just in case any vehicles happened along the road. He got out and walked up to the deputy's car just as it made the final last lurches onto the road.

"Hey, Horace, you know this guy?" Deputy Jorgenson said getting out of his vehicle and motioning to the back seat. "We found him, I don't know, about fifty feet from that shack. It was fully engulfed before we got there."

"That's Tom Nathan. Is he okay?"

"He was unconscious when we got there. Doesn't appear to be burned except maybe on his hands. He's the guy we've been on the lookout for, right?"

"Yeah, he ran away from Dakota Falls. He's really not dangerous like people say."

"Well, I wanted to take him back there, but Gary here says we got to take him to the Clareton hospital. I guess it don't look like he's going to cause any trouble, at least for now."

"He's got to get medical attention right away. I'll follow you in," Horace said. He asked if he could take a look at Tom first; the deputy shrugged and opened the back door.

Tom sat slumped to the side across the back seat, his head near the driver's side rear door. Horace shined his flashlight on Tom's face, which looked pale except for the shadows on the side pressed against the seat. Horace took off his glove and reached in to try find a pulse on the jugular vein on the right side of Tom's neck. It was there, slow and weak. Tom's forehead felt warm and clammy.

"Let's talk about this after we get him to the hospital," Horace told the deputy. "Gary, you too." Beckstrand and the other fire fighters had unhooked the chain and had been standing there waiting to go. "The way this happened so fast, I don't think it was an accident," Horace said. Gary agreed but said they would have to wait until morning and daylight to investigate.

Doc Croft waited at the Clareton hospital emergency door. Living only two blocks away he could get there quickly. He still took his turn being on call for emergencies. In most cases the nighttime calls for his patients meant the arrival of a new addition to the community. This would be different, and if not welcome, at least a change from the routine. All the dispatcher knew was that it was a middle-aged male with unknown injuries at a structure fire. On the way over, Doc Croft immediately started planning what he would do and where he would find the supplies for treating burns. Not since the war had he done much with burns. When they saw the vehicles approach, Doc Croft and the night nurse wheeled the gurney out the back door.

Deputy Jorgenson opened the car door and waited for Horace. Together they reached in, grabbed Tom under his armpits and pulled him from the backseat. They paused for the fire fighters to position themselves to grasp Tom's legs, then hoisted him onto the gurney. Even as they wheeled it in the door, Croft felt for a pulse and shined a small flashlight into Tom's pupils. The nurse pulled up his left sleeve and wrapped a blood pressure cuff around his arm. Inside, Croft pressed his stethoscope against Tom's chest and listened intently. Horace and Gary stood in the emergency room doorway watching and waiting. Deputy Jorgenson sat on a chair in the hall writing notes. The other two fire fighters asked if they could leave. Horace said he would give Gary a ride home. The deputy went to his car to call dispatch.

At Dr. Croft's order, the nurse wheeled an oxygen tank up to the bed, put the face mask over Tom's nose and mouth and slowly opened the valve.

"I think he's got pneumonia besides smoke inhalation," Dr. Croft said. He looked toward Horace and Gary standing in the doorway. "He's in a coma. We'll get him on antibiotics right away. He'll be here awhile. Is this the guy that Harold wanted committed to Dakota Falls? Does he have any family? Anybody you can call?"

Horace nodded and asked where the phone was.

Mario answered.

"Hey, Mario, what are you doing up so late? You been riding around town?" Horace teased although it was only a little after eleven o'clock. "Is your mom around?"

Maria took the phone; Mario watched her face turn serious, listening intently. A foreboding feeling flooded him, hearing her ask Horace questions: "Is he okay? Where is he now? What happened?"

She hung up the phone, giving Mario a concerned look.

"Tom's in the hospital here in Clareton. Horace said he ran away from the state hospital. They had to rescue him from a fire at his shack there in the woods."

Mario felt his face start to burn; a queasy sensation began to well up in his stomach. He fully expected her to know how Tom got there, what they had done. He had worried about the escapade all along and now the worst had happened. He just wanted to die. He was about to confess, stopping short when Maria picked up the phone again to call Jim and Thelma. Jim said he would pick them up and take them to the hospital. Horace would be waiting for them. Quiet, numb and nauseous, Mario got into his parka. It felt like a crushing weight. He sat quietly on the stuffed armchair by the front door. In a few minutes Jim arrived.

Normally at this time on a clear, cold Friday night in winter, Mario would be staying up late watching TV or reading. Sometimes they munched popcorn while playing chess or Scrabble. On December 20 of another year the living room would be cozy, glowing in the lights from the Christmas tree, Christmas music playing on the phonograph, a few wrapped packages arranged on the white, fluffy tree skirt sparkling with shiny sprinkles. Sometimes late in the evening they would turn out all the house lights and sit in the living room looking at the lighted Christmas tree, sipping hot chocolate and listening to Christmas music.

After 11:00 p.m. along the city streets en route to the hospital the holiday decorations hung dark and silent from the streetlight posts. All the Christmas shoppers were home now watching late TV, wrapping packages and getting ready for bed. Passing through downtown, all the stores had closed, and the streets were quiet. Outdoor Christmas lights still glowed on trees and shrubs around some houses, their windows casting a warm glow into the dark winter evening. Silver flickers of light from the television danced on many living room windows.

In a few minutes they picked up Thelma. No one said much on the drive back to the hospital. Horace opened the hospital emergency entrance door and ushered them in.

"Hi, Maria. You got here quick," Horace said. "They took him up to intensive care. Doc says he's in a coma. Thinks he already had pneumonia. The fire and smoke only made it worse."

"What happened? Is he going to be okay?" Maria asked.

"Sure hope so. They've got him on oxygen and IVs with fluids and antibiotics and stuff. All we can do now is pray."

"Why didn't they do something at Dakota Falls for the pneumonia?"

"Don't know. Who knows . . . maybe they did."

"How did he get out of there? How did he end up back here?" Jim asked.

Horace hesitated, casting a quick glance at Mario, who looked stone-faced but could not hide a slight quiver at the corners of his mouth.

"I don't really know how he got away from the state hospital," Horace lied. "Somebody probably could have given him a ride back here. That happens sometimes. That's why they have those 'DO NOT PICK UP HITCHHIKER' signs there on the highway by the state hospital. It's not all that uncommon to have runaways."

"I thought he agreed to go there. I thought he wanted to get help, to get better," Maria said.

"I believe that he did, at first. Maybe after he got there, he changed his mind. Who knows?"

"How did the fire start?" Jim asked.

"We don't know for sure, but we're pretty certain it was intentional," Horace said.

"What if he did it?"

"That's a possibility. We won't know until we can investigate the scene and question Tom."

Dr. Croft stood in the doorway of the hospital room writing on a clipboard. He smiled and gave everyone a firm handshake, the contact sending a current of reassurance and encouragement. He said they had done all they could; now it was a matter of time, waiting for Tom's condition to improve. He said he believed he would pull through. They could stay as long as they wanted in the lounge. Someone would make coffee. If they wanted to go home the hospital would call if anything changed.

Dr. Croft moved aside so they could enter the room. Tom looked pale even in the dim light casting shadows under his eyes, his upper body raised slightly in the hospital bed. The only sign of life appeared in the thin, moist fog inside the oxygen face mask. His shallow breathing barely showed any movement of his chest. The nurse had wiped his face with a damp cloth, removing most of the soot and grime.

Maria sat on a chair by the window looking at Tom, a slight furrow on her forehead. Jim stood at her side. Thelma stood in the doorway with Mario, who began to feel like he was in a nightmare.

Horace used the phone at the nursing station to tell dispatch that he probably would be at the hospital until his shift ended at midnight. Gary Beckstrand said it wasn't too far and he would just walk home from the hospital. He asked Horace to call him in the morning if anyone would be going out to investigate the fire scene. The nurse asked if anyone wanted coffee. Horace accepted a cup but the others declined. The nurse apologized for not having anything that Mario might like—milk or a bottle of pop. He didn't want anything; his stomach was too queasy and he felt very tired.

Pastor Carl Olson leaned over the bathroom sink, washing up before going to bed when he heard the city's fire alarm, a large steam whistle blasting from the power plant. He said a little prayer for whoever might be in danger and for the fire fighters. He stayed dressed just in case, turned on the TV and sat on the couch, waiting.

After about forty-five minutes and several queries from his wife about how long he was staying up, the phone rang. A nurse from the hospital asked if he could come down to be with Maria Reese and her son. Jim Andersen, the dentist, and Thelma Harris also were there, and also Horace Greene, one of the Clareton police officers. They were with a man named Tom Nathan in intensive care. He had smoke inhalation and some minor burns from a fire, and also had been suffering from pneumonia.

Pastor Olson told his wife he would be out for a while at the hospital. After more than twenty years as a pastor's wife, the past nine in Clareton, she was used to the calls at all hours of the day or night. She would say a prayer for him and the others and then go to sleep, accepting that her husband could return in fifteen minutes or not until morning.

According to the rotation among the pastors in Clareton, this was not Carl's turn to be on call at the hospital. The nurse knew that the Reeses attended Immanuel Lutheran so he had been called anyway. She kept to herself questions why the Reeses were there in the first place.

Passing by the nursing station, Pastor Olson greeted the nurse and Horace and continued down the hall toward the intensive-care wing. The local ministers knew their way around the hospital very well, some spending most of their time there outside their churches. They talked with patients and family members, trying to express concern and compassion. They prayed for God's help and comfort, always concluding that whatever happened, it was God's will.

Seeing Pastor Olson walking down the hall toward them, Mario felt comforted and terrified at the same time. The kids at Immanuel Lutheran liked Pastor Olson for the most part. He was kind and tried to be understanding. The Olsons had three children of their own and understood the sometimes erratic behaviors resulting from youthful minds attempting to grow into adulthood. Pastor Olson took comfort in the belief that prayer and trusting God were the only ways to deal with the indiscretions of youth, which in most cases did not result in permanent or irreparable damage.

In his fifties with reddish brown hair and slightly balding, Pastor Olson was still genuine in his manner of greeting everyone with a firm, warm handshake, friendly smile, and engaging blue eyes peering over the top of a pair of bifocal glasses part way down the bridge of his nose.

"Hi, Mario. I just came down to see how you folks are doing." He looked down smiling, reached out to shake Mario's hand and rested his left hand on Mario's shoulder. He shook hands with Thelma, then took Jim's hand, grabbed a chair and set it down next to Maria. He took her right hand, held it cupped in his and asked how Tom was doing. Maria repeated what Dr. Croft had said.

Although he was very curious, Pastor Olson did not ask why they were there or what their connection to the vagrant was. He simply said a prayer, asking for God's presence, healing, and comfort, one that he had said many times before, some in that very same room. Hearing the words, Maria threw her hands over her face and began to cry. Pastor Olson put his hand on her shoulder. Jim handed her his handkerchief. She regained her composure and began to recount the recent events, how the kids befriended Tom, how they learned about his identity, how he had agreed to go to the state hospital. She held back on detail about it all started years ago, and Pastor Olson did not ask; that would be revealed in time when the longing to have the burden lifted would be fulfilled.

The nurse returned to check on Tom. Horace went with Mario down the hall to the lounge, followed by Thelma and Pastor Olson. Horace turned on the TV even though he knew all they would see after midnight was the test pattern. He turned it off. He looked over at Mario, trying to imagine how Tom had escaped from the hospital, how he showed up riding with a car full of kids. He regretted letting them go after stopping Larry's car.

At first Horace thought he would be able to avoid any mention of the minor traffic stop in his report. Now an unsettling feeling tumbled over him that this was just the beginning of their troubles. Mario looked at Horace, the secret weighing too heavy for him to bear alone. Pastor Olson tried to make conversation, asking Mario how school was going, what were they doing for Christmas. He thanked Mario for participating in the nativity scene. Too bad about the forecast for colder weather Saturday, but it would be the last night. It would have been special to stage the nativity scene again next Wednesday, Christmas Eve, he said, but agreed with the committee that most people would prefer to be home with their families.

Maria and Jim entered the lounge, somber and tired.

"I think we should probably go home," she said. In silent consent everyone rose from their seats and filed slowly out of the lounge. The nurse said the hospital would call if anything changed. They could return in the morning.

A high pressure system of bitter cold Canadian air had slowly moved in during the day, pushing out the warmer temperatures of the low pressure system that had left about two inches of new snow. By midnight the temperature had dropped to five below zero. The winter equinox approached under a crisp, still, clear night sky teeming with countless stars and planets, pinpoints of light across the ink-dark dome of infinity. Inhaling the icy air outside the hospital burned his lungs and cleansed them at the same time. Mario looked up through the tree branches trying to find Orion and the Big Dipper, which pointed to the North Star. Seeing them gave him a brief moment of calm reassurance and stability, a respite before facing the morning and whatever might lie ahead.

‰ 27 ‰

B Y THE TIME THEY SAW THE SHORT ARTICLE in the *Clareton Chronicle* Monday afternoon the burning of Tom's shack had become old news for many readers. "Fire destroys hunting shack; man injured," read the one-column, eighteen-point, three-deck headline over four column inches of a news story on page eight. The story was a frequent topic of discussion around town Saturday at the Legion, in aisles at the grocery stores, and Sunday before and after church services. Even so, everyone looked for the story in the *Chronicle* Monday afternoon. It confirmed what they already knew and set the record straight in crisp, black letters on newsprint they could hold in their hands and even smell the ink. But questions still remained.

The story did not identify the injured man, who had been transported to the Clareton hospital, nor did it report any information on the cause of the fire. The fire chief said the cause was still under investigation but so far believed to have been accidental, very likely started by a cigarette or perhaps a kerosene lantern, or an ember from the wood stove. The story mostly gave background information about the hunting shack on the old Nielsen property, how for many years in the thirties and forties a group of local hunters had gathered there each fall. As they advanced in years and the duck populations gradually declined from the gradual loss of wetland habitat from drainage to create more cropland, the shack fell into disuse. It had been empty and unused for almost ten years.

Clareton Chronicle editor August Ditmarson leaned back from his typewriter Monday morning and reminisced about the shack, how he had enjoyed the inclusion and camaraderie of those hunting parties in the latter years. The good old boys had invited the young newspaperman along so they could get to know him, so they could decide how he would fit into the community's power structure. He was young, idealistic, and dedicated to journalistic integrity but also desired to belong to the group of business and civic leaders who ran the town, even if that loyalty sometimes meant pulling journalistic punches now and then. He agreed that it was good for the community to have an unstable drunk removed from the streets.

Only recently had he learned the name of the drifter who had been hanging around town. He was going to identify him in the story and tell readers about Tom Nathan's heroic military service, but that he had suffered from the experience, never fully recovered, and fell into drunken despair. He wanted to tell Tom's story because of the strong human-interest angle because it would edify the community about the importance of looking past outward appearances and because it was true.

The inspiration faded after he had returned from morning coffee at the café. Most of the men there, Police Chief Harold Stark and Earl Harley among them, advised August against getting too carried away with the story. "What's done is done. Keeping it before the public eye would only stir things up." They agreed it was necessary for a small story telling about the fire; a large blaze in the woods on the south shore of the lake on a dark winter evening would have been difficult to ignore.

Chief Stark expressed greater concern about how Tom showed up back at the shack in the first place. He had been in a locked ward at the Dakota Falls State Hospital. Somebody had to have helped him escape.

Stark had no ambivalence about the cause of the fire. Obviously it had been started by Tom, intentionally or accidentally. He felt no remorse at all and some relief when the county coroner called Saturday evening to report that Tom Nathan had died of complications resulting from pneumonia and smoke inhalation. He had informed Earl and several others, but August still didn't know, and Harold was not about to tell him. Harold was a little surprised that the newspaperman hadn't yet found out; he usually checked with the hospital for any news over the weekend. Perhaps he had been just too busy with Christmas or all the countless chores of publishing a newspaper.

Every weekday a few minutes after twelve noon, August waited at the end of the big press to grab one of the first copies of that day's edition, flip through the pages and, most days, feel relief that all were in order, that there were no glaring typos in any of the headlines, and most important, that the big grocery store, clothing store, and auto dealership ads looked good. He tucked the paper under his arm and, depending on his mood, went either to the café or home for lunch. Today walking home he noticed about a dozen cars parked outside the Johnson Funeral Home. He didn't recall there being any obituaries in the paper last Friday or Saturday. It irritated him, so that he almost stopped in to find out what was going on, but he didn't. He decided to call later.

MARIO SLEPT ALMOST UNTIL TEN O'CLOCK Saturday morning. They ate breakfast without saying much. Maria said Jim was coming over, and they could get their Christmas tree. After lunch they went to the hospital to visit Tom. The nurse said there was little change in his condition; he remained in a coma. They stood for a moment looking in the door of his room. Mario's legs felt weak, like they were going to buckle under the weight of his guilt about what had happened to Tom, no matter who he was.

In the afternoon, they decorated the tree, a balsam fir almost six feet tall. The activity helped to lighten their spirits, but the worrisome, private thoughts about Tom kept burrowing back in. After an early supper of sloppy joes and potato chips, they drove to the church, taking Mario to the final night of the nativity scene.

Pastor Olson staked out a spot by the door of the Immanuel Lutheran fellowship room, smiling and occasionally conversing with people in the refreshment line following their visit to the nativity scene. When Maria and Jim arrived to pick up Mario, Pastor Olson invited them into his study, just for a moment, he said. He asked how they were doing. He said he had also visited Tom later in the afternoon and had prayed for him.

Pastor Olson wheeled his chair out from behind his desk, directly facing them. A shelf of books lined the wall behind the desk. Religious pictures and symbols hung on the walls of the small office, Da Vinci's "The Last Supper," a cross, a picture of Jesus leading a flock of sheep. Maria and Mario sat on the two wood chairs in front of the desk; Jim brought in a folding chair.

Pastor Olson took a matchbook and lit a thick candle in a ceramic bowl on the corner of his desk. Flickering candlelight seemed to relax and captivate people. For him it helped keep in mind the presence of God whenever he counseled and ministered to people in his study.

Again he thanked Mario for participating in the nativity scene. It took a lot of dedication to stand out in the cold. It added a lot of meaning to the celebration of Christmas. He asked what they planned to do for Christmas. He hoped they could make to the Christmas Eve candlelight service. Maria said they were planning on it.

"I can't believe someone would deliberately burn that shack. Did they find anything out today?" Pastor Olson asked.

"I know Horace and the fire chief went out there. But I haven't heard anything," Jim said. "Horace thinks it was arson."

"That Horace . . . what a guy. He's been a real friend. I know it hasn't been easy, but he's been a real blessing for our town. And so have you," Pastor Olson said, looking at Maria. "You've been such a blessing teaching summer school for the migrant workers and their children. I'm embarrassed to say that as a church we ignored them. If it hadn't been for Mrs. Bauer being moved by the spirit to do something we'd probably still be ignoring them. People get so used to being around their own kind, then someone comes along who looks different or talks and acts different, and people become fearful. Of course, they don't show it but sometimes it comes out in other ways. But inside and in God's eyes we're all his children. I didn't really know who Tom was. I saw him around town a few times. Sometimes I would wonder if anyone had been reaching out to him and others like him.

"So, he's Mario's father?" Pastor Olson posed the question gently, quietly looking at Maria.

She stared down at the floor, unconsciously folding and unfolding her hands on her lap. Slowly, softly she began to tell about her life growing up in California, how she'd met Tom when she was eighteen. He was older, in his thirties, good-looking and fun-loving. They got back together when he returned from service in the Seabees.

He wouldn't talk about his experiences on the front lines on Iwo Jima. He had changed becoming morose, nervous and fidgety, unpredictable. He drank a lot, and it began to show on the job. When she became pregnant, Maria tried to hide it from her family. One day she couldn't hide it any longer. Her mother had to drive her to the hospital. Her father exploded in wrath. Eventually she moved out and tried to make a life for herself and the baby, but it could not include Tom as he had become. Then she saw an escape in the ad for a Spanish-speaking summer school teacher in Minnesota. It was supposed to be only temporary.

Sitting there in Pastor Olson's study on Saturday evening, December 20, 1958, was the first time Mario and Jim had heard from start to finish what Maria had already confided to Thelma.

Pastor Olson placed his hand on hers and smiled gently. Jim put his arm around her shoulders. Pastor Olson looked at them and then at Mario, smiling.

"It's good to talk things over now and then," Pastor Olson said quietly. "We don't have to carry such burdens all the time. We can talk to each other; we can talk to God. He is always listening.

"Mario, it was good of you visit Tom out at his shack and bring him sandwiches. You were doing God's work, did you know that? Feeding the hungry, visiting the lonely and the sick. That's what God wants us to do."

Mario nodded and began to understand what Pastor Olson was saying. It had never occurred to him that it might have meant more than just something to do, playing after school or on a Saturday. But Friday it had gone too far. Tom lay in a coma at the Clareton hospital because he and the others helped him escape from Dakota Falls. His shack had been burned to the ground. His stomach in a knot and lips trembling, Mario began to tell what had happened Friday and the days leading up to it.

"We weren't at the movies Friday night," he said, casting quick glance at Maria and then down at the floor. His eyes moistening and lower lip trembling slightly, he continued: "When we went to Dakota Falls, we went to the state hospital. It wasn't all my idea. Rosalyn and Aaron made up this plan to get Tom out of there. We were afraid they were going to operate on his brain or something there. It would have turned him into a zombie. That's what Rosalyn said. Then Aaron made this key so we could get in where Tom was. Rosalyn had the pattern from one of her dad's keys from work, and she knew where Tom was. Larry drove us there, and LeeAnn pretended to fall on the ice out in front of the building, and the guy who was working there went out to help her. That's when me and Jake snuck in the back and let Tom out. We drove back to town and were going to drop Tom off by the shack when Horace pulled us over because one of Larry's stoplights was burned out."

"Oh, Mario, honey, is this really true?" Maria looked stunned. "You should have talked to me."

"Horace knew about this?" Jim asked incredulously. "Why didn't he say anything?"

"I don't know. He just let us go," Mario continued. "When he stopped us, he pretended like he didn't even see Tom sitting in the back-seat. He said we weren't supposed to say anything to anybody or we'd all be in trouble." Mario struggled hold back tears being squeezed out from the weight of the betrayal of Horace on top of the confession.

345

Pastor Olson reached over and placed his hand on Mario's shoulder. "It's good to get the truth out. It would come out eventually anyway. Now we'll just have to pray for God's help and guidance to see this through."

He drew back his hand; the candle on his desk flickered and then the flame went out, sending up a thin, wavering column of smoke, quickly dissolving in the air and leaving behind a faint, pungent odor.

They looked at the candle, curious why it had extinguished. There had been no noticeable air movement. Pastor Olson looked questioningly, briefly at the candle. No one said anything, so he simply thanked them for coming in to talk things over. He closed with a short prayer, and they left for home.

Driving back to the Reeses Jim struggled with his thoughts, then tried to say something reassuring and philosophical about the situation. Maria and Mario sat in silence, looking out the car windows. Moisture from their breaths froze on the side windows of the car where the defroster didn't reach. Out of habit, Mario scraped his fingernails on the glass trying to clear an opening in the thin film of ice enough to see out, beyond the dark trees and the lighted windows of homes looking warm and cozy inside, off into some infinite space where thoughts wandered and then faded away.

Their somber mood followed them into the house. Jim stayed for a while. Maria made hot chocolate and buttered toast even though neither she nor Mario felt much like eating anything at first, but still it tasted good.

Just before ten o'clock, the phone rang. Jim answered it. His face turned serious as he listened. He asked a few questions, then handed the phone to Maria. She listened without much expression as Dr. Croft told her that Tom Nathan had died around nine o'clock. He never emerged from the coma. They had done everything they could, but his initial physical condition, the pneumonia, and smoke inhalation were too much to overcome. He had been a heavy smoker, which had already done some damage to his lungs. Maria thanked him for calling and hung up the phone.

She looked at Mario and suddenly realized that this was more about him than about her. She had shut Tom out long ago. The recent contact may have cracked open that door slightly, but that angered her more than anything. With Mario it was different. This was his father, and although Tom had been absent the first twelve years of Mario's life, their recent encounters may have led to something of a relationship. For a few brief moments he had had a father.

"That was Dr. Croft. Tom died about an hour ago," she said softly.

The words seemed to have no effect. Mario sat quietly on the couch, munching toast and looking at the TV. He began to feel numb when he began to realize the consequences of what they had done, mostly at the instigation of Rosalyn and Aaron. Although he was afraid, Mario went along because he had to. It had been a scary, exciting escapade. Like noble rescuers they had believed they were doing the right thing.

Maria suggested it was time for bed. She called Thelma and told her the news. Thelma said she should call Pastor Olson, which she did. Jim stayed awhile longer. Mario went upstairs to bed. Alone in his room, he felt as if the world were ending, and if not the world, his life as he knew it would be when they sent him to reform school. Still, it was so unfair. Tom hadn't done anything to hurt anyone and now he was dead. Exhausted, Mario fell asleep.

The routine of Sunday school and church held the demons from the night before at bay. No one knew about Tom except for those who had to. Thelma had told her parents, and they invited the Reeses, Jim, and Horace over for dinner after church. They sat in the living room watching a basketball game while Mrs. Harris peeled and cut up chunks of potato and carrots into the pot roast, which had been cooking in a low oven while they were at church.

Pastor Olson was coming over to the Reeses in the afternoon to plan Tom's funeral service Monday. Maria consented when Mario asked if he could play hockey in the afternoon. He hoped there would be enough kids to get a game going. You never really knew on Sundays. The weather had warmed up a bit since Saturday. Still, the temperature stayed in the low teens, and the rink ice was hard and only a little faster.

AUGUST DITMARSON FELT REFRESHED WALKING back to the newspaper office after lunch. Snowflakes sifted from the cloudy winter sky. December 22—it finally was winter according to the equinox, although according to the weather it usually started around the first of December in Minnesota. August had written newspaper columns about that curiosity twice, which was enough even though most readers didn't notice when he repeated a topic.

Walking past the Johnson Funeral Home, August followed his curiosity up the steps and into the large, gray, three-story former mansion. Opening the heavy, ornate, wood door he shivered when it creaked slightly. Sometimes he still had to convince himself that he could go anywhere at any time because he was a newspaperman, and it was his duty to know what was going on and, if newsworthy, report his findings to the community. Stepping softly on the carpet, he entered the back of the large parlor converted into a chapel. He sat down in the back row of seats, sturdy, oak chairs similar to those in the library except with pale green cushions.

Standing behind a small pulpit in the front, Pastor Olson saw August and gave a nod so slight that others hardly noticed. Mario turned and looked back, not sure who the guy was who just came in the back. He wondered what he had to do with Tom.

The number and identities of the audience surprised August. Maria Reese and the boy must be her son, Jim Andersen the dentist, Thelma Harris the teacher, Horace Greene, Doc Ahrends the vet. What were they doing here, and who was in the casket? A VFW honor guard in full uniform sat in the front row. An American flag draped over a plain, wood casket in front. Two flower stands one on each side held small floral arrangements. He began to think that this was connected to the fire at the old hunting shack and the hobo who had been living there, but he still didn't know for sure. This funeral had no program with an obituary on the back. Maybe there was newspaper column topic here. It would be more difficult trying to generate insight and wisdom without making it too controversial, but far more satisfying than writing about safe subjects such as humorous incidents of home life, the antics of children, ice fishing, the weather, or the lunacy of the county board.

He made mental notes while Horace Greene and Steven Ahrends stood up and said a few things about the deceased, Tom Nathan. Horace related some of the things Tom had told him about serving in the Seabees on Iwo Jima, that he was real hero. Doc Ahrends said that once you got to know him, Tom was personable and intelligent, a good worker. Pastor Olson's homily elaborated on the scripture in the Old Testament book of Micah, chapter six, verse eight: ". . . and what does the Lord require of you but to do justice, and to love kindness, and to walk humbly with your God."

From what he had learned over the past two days, Pastor Olson said he had no doubt Tom Nathan truly was a child of God, and now in a renewed body his spirit was with God. Thelma Harris sang two songs, "Amazing Grace" and "Just a Closer Walk with Thee." Pastor Olson recited an abbreviated funeral liturgy, and all joined in reciting the Lord's Prayer. Immediately at the end, August stood quietly and left; he didn't want to have to explain his presence, and he had to get back to the newspaper office and write another obituary, but not about Tom Nathan.

MAYBE IT JUST SEEMED THAT WAY, but sometimes the big stories all happened at once, sporadically between long periods when nothing much happened. The big local story on the front page of Monday's paper told about the misfortune of Darwin Bauer. The tragedy would color the Christmas holidays at the Bauer farmstead forever after.

Darwin reportedly left the bar at the VFW late Friday night, hopped on his snow machine and sped out across the ice-covered lake. The snow cover concealed a ribbon of thin ice near the inlet, and the heavy machine broke through. The Bauers missed church Sunday, a rare occurrence. All day Saturday and still on Sunday, they were trying to find the whereabouts of Darwin, not that they had much to say about it, but they usually found him the next morning sprawled across his bed, fully clothed and unconscious while his digestive system and liver churned to process a large amount of alcohol.

Finally, Sunday afternoon a search party spread out across the lake. For a moment Monday, August thought the mysterious funeral had something to do with Darwin, even knowing that was impossible because the searchers still hadn't found his body, and there was a strong possibility that they wouldn't if it was in the lake because the current might carry it out into deeper water away from where the snow machine apparently broke through.

The photo on the front page of the CHRONICLE drew several phone calls Monday afternoon from readers incensed about the insensitivity of showing searchers in a boat on the open water by the inlet dragging the lake bottom with grappling hooks. One of those calls came from Mr. Bauer himself. He shouted into the phone that his wife was overwhelmed by grief, and they would never be able to look at the paper in the same way again. The tragedy seemed to put the whole town in a somber mood over the Christmas holidays. August felt badly but tried to distance himself; he was just reporting the news, and why did people have to do such stupid things anyway?

The Bauers had planned their family Christmas get-together the following weekend, between Christmas and New Years, when their other adult children and families would have time to travel back to the farm. Daughter Emma's children were old enough to join in singing "over the river and through the woods to grandmother's house we go . . ." The little children would not fully understand the sadness coloring the trip this year, although it might occur to them when they attended a funeral Saturday instead of a warm and cheerful Christmas celebration.

The women of Immanuel Lutheran took charge during the week helping the Bauers prepare for the weekend. Mrs. Bauer had at first been inconsolable, but toward the end of the week, she began to help with the cooking and cleaning. The church women brought cookies and other holiday pastries, provided hot dishes and other meals all week.

On Wednesday, Christmas Eve, Maria Reese and her son went out to the Bauer farm with a four-quart kettle of chili. Jim's sister and her family were staying with him, and he would stop by the Reeses about nine. Thelma was home with her parents. Horace had to work as he had every holiday. His request for a few days off to visit his family in Detroit over Christmas had been denied. By Thanksgiving, it had become obvious that Chief Stark had no intention of alternating holiday duty between Horace and John, the other patrol officer. When Thelma learned that Horace would be working both Christmas Eve and Christmas Day she became furious. She would have complained to the chief but Horace persuaded her to refrain, saying he was accustomed to it and it didn't help.

Mrs. Bauer asked Maria and Mario to stay, and that's where the Reeses spent the early part of Christmas Eve. They had planned to return home immediately and open their presents. Maria said they could do that the next morning.

As they sat around the dining room table eating chili and fresh-baked bread that had been provided by Mrs. Swanson, Mr. Bauer asked what happened last weekend, about the fire at the shack and the small funeral Monday. Maria told them about Tom Nathan, who he was and what he had done in his life as far as she knew.

Mrs. Bauer listened intently, escaping for a moment the intense grip of uncertainty and sorrow over Darwin's absence. She had always liked Maria since the first time they met seven years ago. She had always wondered about what circumstances and events led up to this young, beautiful woman and her young son moving from California to Clareton, Minnesota. She was glad they had. Over the years she had grown to view Maria as a daughter and Mario as a son or grandson. Mr. Bauer seemed to respond in the same way. When they visited the farm, which they often did for Sunday dinner, Mr. Bauer took Mario along doing chores. Mario learned how to milk cows, drive a tractor, and now was getting big enough and old enough to work like a hired hand. His contribution had made a noticeable difference this past summer baling hay.

After supper they sat in the living room looking at the Christmas tree and watching TV. Most of the wrapped packages under the tree were labeled for children and grandchildren and would remain there until the weekend. Mr. and Mrs. Bauer and Darwin would have exchanged gifts with one another on Christmas Eve except this year his absence and their grief prevented them. Then Mrs. Bauer got up from the couch, found a package under the tree, removed the label and handed it to Mario.

"Please, I want you to have this."

He looked at his mother.

"Oh, Arlene, you shouldn't," Maria protested. Arlene Bauer insisted, and when she looked as if she were going to cry, Maria had to approve. She looked at Mario, "What do you say?"

"Thank you."

"Go ahead . . . open it, please," Mrs. Bauer said quietly.

Green wrapping paper with pictures of Santa Claus in his sleigh covered the long, rectangular box. Mario tried to be careful separating the taped edges of the wrapping without tearing it. For a moment the sorrowful mood of the evening lifted. Mrs. Bauer actually smiled when Mario held up the box, looking in awe at the label showing a real hunting bow and arrows, not the toy kind like those at a tourist gift shop in the Black Hills of South Dakota. Mario had seen this bow before in the sporting goods section at the hardware store, not even wishing to have it because he knew it could never be. Delight surged through him but he could not allow it to show. The gift had been intended for Darwin, and that made Mario feel undeserving, like a scavenger taking advantage of someone else's misfortune.

Maria stared at Arlene, then at Bill—he had a slight smile, wistful and warm. Maria felt embarrassed. Maybe Darwin would return. Maybe he had gone to Dakota Falls or even Minneapolis. He had done things like before. How could they give up like this when he had not yet been found? And the gift, it could be dangerous for a young boy.

"That's a nice one, eh?" Bill said. "Don't worry, Maria. I'll show him how to use it safely. Maybe we could even keep it here at the farm and he can come out whenever he wants to and use it. You can't really use it in town, even for practice. We can set up some straw bales in the grove and put a target on there. Next year I'll take him deer hunting. How about that, Mario? Would you like to go deer hunting next fall?"

He had been out in the woods several times before with Darwin, shooting at rabbits, squirrels, whatever moved, but never hunting for real, hunting big game such as deer. Perhaps just him with Mr. Bauer it would be different, not make him feel uneasy as it did with Darwin. He felt deeply threatened once this past October when Darwin pointed a Colt .45 caliber pistol at Mario. They were walking in the grove on one of those perfect fall days, sunny, cool, clear blue sky above the silver and golden leaves of giant cottonwood trees rattling softly in a breeze. Darwin's forced, ominous laugh only frightened Mario even more. Darwin said the pistol wasn't loaded and he was just kidding around. Darwin did things like that a lot, and while it may have seemed funny at the time and Mario had actually laughed or tried to, it often left him feeling uneasy.

Sometimes when they were doing chores or out in the grove hunting rabbits, Darwin told stories about his Army days serving in Korea. His unit arrived after the U.S. and allied forces already had been pushed back by the hordes of Chinese troops back to the Thirty-eighth Parallel. He told about lying on his belly among rocks on a hillside and firing his M-1 rifle at what they believed were North Korean troops. When Mario asked if he killed anybody, Darwin became coy and would only say, maybe, but that he didn't know for sure.

Whenever they returned home from visiting the farm, Maria tried to project curiosity as she gently interrogated Mario about what they did when he was with Darwin.

One Saturday evening in August, driving back to town after an afternoon of chores—Mario had mostly helped bale hay and Maria had helped Arlene bake bread and fry chicken for supper—Maria thought she smelled gasoline when Mario got into the car. They cranked open all the windows to the cool evening air carrying the sweet aroma of harvested alfalfa fields. It partly washed away the gasoline odor, but not the questions floating in Maria's mind.

"What's that gas smell? Do you smell gas?" she asked.

The twilight concealed any visible evidence of the guilty tension Mario felt spreading across his face. He fumbled around in his mind for something to say.

"I don't know."

"I smell gas." She leaned over across the seat, her eyes still on the road, and sniffed. "It's from you. Did you get gas on your clothes or something?"

"I don't know. We were putting gas in the tractor, I guess. I don't know. Maybe some got spilled."

"You should be careful. That can be dangerous. How did it get spilled? That doesn't happen too often when you fill up the gas tank. Are you sure?" Most times Maria accepted Mario's explanations. He had always been honest and truthful. The exceptions to her trusting him usually involved time spent with Darwin. Although he did not fully understand, Mario anticipated and continued to answer as best he could.

"We were at the dump hole in the grove. Darwin made this gas bomb."

"What? You mean like a Molotov cocktail?"

"Yeah, like that."

As soon as he had emptied them, Darwin broke most of the whiskey bottles in the dump hole, hoping to conceal the evidence from his parents. But today after supper he looked for entertainment in showing Mario how to make a gasoline bomb. He took the nearly empty bottle of Old Crow from its hiding place in the machine shed and chugged it down. He drained gasoline through a funnel, filling the bottle about half full. He found an old rag, tore it in half, and tied a knot in the middle. Inserting one end of the rag into the bottle, he then jammed the knot into the top. He warned Mario never to soak the exposed part of the rag in gasoline, but to use only kerosene. He let Mario carry the bottle on the way back to the dump hole. At the edge, he took the bottle, told Mario to stand back, and flicked his cigarette lighter to ignite the kerosene-soaked rag.

The old wood-burning cook stove that used to be in the kitchen still protruded from the refuse in the dump hole. Darwin aimed for it and threw the bottle. Sometimes the liquid gasoline extinguished the burning wick, but not this time. His aim was true, and the bottle smashed against the cast iron stove. Gasoline vapor ignited in a ferocious flash settling back into flames, setting bits of trash ablaze.

"Honey, that's very dangerous. You should have come back to the house," Maria scolded.

"I'm sorry," Mario said.

She wondered why Darwin did some of the things he did and at his age. Sometimes she felt sorry for him and his parents, too; sometimes she thought she could sense disappointment and dismay in a look or tone of voice when they had to acknowledge some of his behavior. It hurt Bill Bauer more the time he caught Darwin shooting at the hogs with a BB gun, watching them jump and squeal, and he struck Darwin hard across the face with the back of his hand.

EXCEPT FOR A BREAK ON THE AFTERNOON and evening of Christmas Eve authorities continued to search for Darwin. Thursday afternoon, sitting in his ice fishing shack and peering into the hole in the ice, an ice fisherman became startled when he saw a large shape suspended in the dark green, cold water. Sheriff's deputies arrived and using a chain saw quickly cut through the eight-inch-thick ice and dragged Darwin's stiff, cold body out of the open water and onto the ice. It had drifted about three hundred feet under the ice from where the snowmobile broke through. The obituary in the Friday edition of the *Chronicle* came in time to announce the funeral Saturday. It would be a big one, almost filling the sanctuary at Immanuel Lutheran church.

ஐ 28 ൬

BENEATH THE WARMING SUN OF LENGTHENING daylight in early
spring, open water soon appeared along the northeastern shore of
the lake in front of the Carlsons. Jake and Mario pushed away
from the dock in the wooden rowboat and rowed out to the edge of the ice
sheet. They imagined piloting a Coast Guard ice breaker trying to plow
its way through. Rowing mightily they crunched the prow into the rotting
ice. A few miniature glaciers broke away from the foot-thick sheet that
had covered the lake all winter long. The prow rode up on the ice, making the boat tip back and forth sideways when they shifted their weight.
They pushed off and swung the boat around parallel to the edge of the
ice.

They commenced a spring ritual of chopping at the ice with the
oars. Soon large and small chunks floated in the water surrounding the boat.
They chopped away at the edges of the ice sheet where melting and wave
action eroded the frigid strength of the frozen water until the pounding no
longer succeeded. Resting from the exertion, they surveyed their accomplishment fueled partly by their impatience with the pace that the sun and
waves took, and by their satisfaction in venting destructive energy that

brought no harmful consequences except perhaps for blunting and shred-
ding the tips of the oar blades, which Mr. Carlson might complain about but
not too seriously.

All of the fish houses except one had been hauled off the ice
weeks ago. The one left would have looked like an outhouse had the
design been more square than rectangular. It remained frozen into the
surface after a thaw followed by a cold snap in late February. It would
have been easier to remove the upper portion and leave the base still
frozen to the ice instead of trying to chip it loose. The owner made neither attempt, so there it sat out on the ice over the sunken island where
most all of the other fish houses had been. If the warm weather held, soon
it would be bobbing in open water and have to be towed ashore. Jake
derided the owner's failure to take action when he should have.

Mario looked across the lake to the southern shore. Again he
thought about what would have happened if things had turned out differ-
ently. Even after several months had passed and the warmer, brighter
days of spring stood poised to take command, he still blamed himself.
The small oak savannah jutting out into the lake showed only the charred
remains of the shack. As the leaves budded and small, delicate green
shoots emerged from the warming soil, the black earth soon would be
covered by weeds. He wondered what would have happened if all this
hadn't started with the fight between him and Frank Harley.

They thought they were doing the right thing, trying to rescue
Tom. He didn't really miss Tom. Sometimes he found himself thinking
about the times they sat by the fire and talked. How Tom studied him in
the firelight and asked a lot of questions. Sometimes he appeared in
Mario's dreams. Just last week he awoke in panic, dreaming about trying
to drag Tom away from the shack engulfed in the blaze. Maria came into
his room. She seemed weepy when he described his dream. She hugged
him and left a soft kiss on his forehead. She told him to not worry. It was
nobody's fault. Tom was in a better place now.

Mario couldn't be late for supper, so they rowed back to shore,
leaving the remainder of the task of thawing and opening the lake to the

sun and wind. Jim had made a reservation for six-thirty the Lakeside Supper Club. His parents and sisters were in town for the wedding. Maria's mother and two of her brothers were driving almost non-stop, hoping to arrive sometime Saturday afternoon. They would miss the Friday rehearsal, which was to follow the dinner at the supper club. The reservation for sixteen took up most of the small, private banquet room. The rehearsal at Immanuel Lutheran would start about eight. Mario looked around the table, savoring the warmth and intimacy of the small group; everyone seemed happy, talking and laughing.

PASTOR CARL OLSON STOOD IN FRONT OF THE ALTAR at the front of the sanctuary and smiled. He loved wedding ceremonies, most of them. Over the years, he had spent many hours trying to patch the relationships of those breaking under the strains of work, children, illness, poverty, midlife crisis, all eroding the cement of commitment and caring if it really was there in the first place. He thought he did a pretty good job of assessing the potential for a successful marital relationship. He felt very confident about this match.

Robins chirped from the high branches of the elm trees surrounding the church. The setting sun still reflected off the dry, brown grass, turning it golden beneath the pale-blue evening twilight. With a little timely rain and warming sun in a few weeks, new leaves and blades of grass suddenly would proliferate. Twilight filtered through the reds, blues, greens and yellows of the stained glass windows in the church sanctuary. Pastor Carlson gave instructions to the wedding party standing in back. On such a sweet early spring evening, Mario would yearn to be outside playing in the neighborhood with his friends except this time not as much. Rosalyn stood next to him in the aisle where they waited for Pastor Carlson to cue the ring bearers. Mario glanced at her, and when his gaze lingered on her pretty, smiling face, her long, light-brown hair flowing in soft waves over her shoulders, he felt captivated and self-conscious; he looked away but the feeling remained for a moment.

Pastor Carlson nodded to the first bridesmaid to begin the procession. Without Maria's brothers present, they had to pretend they were there. Jim's sister pantomimed taking the arm of her absent groomsman, and everyone laughed. His other sister followed, trying to outdo her sibling's acting. Then followed Horace and Thelma as best man and bridal matron.

THE TRIP TO ST. PAUL BACK IN JANUARY for Horace and Thelma's wedding brought some joy and excitement to an otherwise ordinary winter. After the investigation into the events surrounding the fate of Tom Nathan, the already-strained working relationship between Horace and Chief Stark broke down completely. Perhaps he could have fought back, but Horace had had enough. He wanted to go back to the big city, and Thelma wanted to go with him. Just before New Year's Day, he resigned after Mayor Fairbanks provided a highly favorable letter of recommendation, which he persuaded Chief Stark to co-sign.

After getting to know him, after reaching the point where they could see past the color of his skin, Thelma's parents had grown to really like Horace and welcome him as their future son-in-law. Still, that didn't quite prepare them for the wedding at the Freedom Baptist Church in St. Paul. Riding together with Maria, Jim, and Mario from Clareton to St. Paul, they filled the car with excitement and apprehension. It rubbed off on Mario, and along with his usual reserve, helped keep him off to the side in the church fellowship hall during the reception, hoping to avoid any conversation and wishing he were invisible. He had never experienced this before, being in a large room among a crowd of people, strangers and all Negroes except for his mother, Jim and the Harrises, and several others.

"Hi. My name's Edgar. What's yours?"

"Mario."

The boy looked to Mario to be about kindergarten age. He wore a light beige-colored suit and a bright green-and-gold striped tie. His white shoes looked like polished mirrors. Mario had never seen white dress shoes before.

"I'm five years old. I'm in kindergarten, and I can read already. Where are you from?"

"I'm from Clareton."

"Where's that?"

"It's about a hundred miles or so northwest of here like on the way to Fargo."

"Where's that?"

"You know, up in North Dakota. That's where Horace was before he came to Clareton."

"Who's Horace?"

"He's the man getting married." Mario pointed him out at the head table with Thelma.

"They're like chocolate and vanilla," Edgar giggled. "My momma says God made everyone the same, but some of us got a chocolate coating because all the angels liked chocolate. She says that no matter what happens, all the angels are watching over us because of that. We're all the same on the inside, but we just look different on the outside. Do you like chocolate?"

"Sure."

"What grade are you in?"

"Seventh."

"My daddy's a policeman. What's your daddy do?"

Back in Clareton the question never came up much. In school, at the park, or wherever, kids usually didn't address such matters. They knew the makeup if not always the inner circumstances of everyone's family and accepted it. Until recently the few times he faced the question, Mario easily brushed it off by answering that his dad got killed in a car crash a long time ago. Since December it had become more complicated, but now everyone in Clareton knew, so they didn't have to ask.

"I don't have a dad."

"Why not?"

"He died."

"How'd that happen?"

Edgar's persistent questions began to diminish his initial charm. Mario answered tersely and looked around for some means of escape.

"He got sick and then he was in a fire."

Edgar asked if he got burned up, and Mario said no, he hadn't.

To Mario's relief, Jim came over and sat down next to Edgar, balancing a plate of potato salad, a ham sandwich, and a piece of wedding cake. Edgar looked at the food, got up and took Mario's hand, leading him to the food line. "I'm hungry. Let's get some food." Mario would have done so earlier; he was very hungry but had refrained from getting into the line by himself. Maria, looking almost glamorous in her bridesmaid dress, mingled in the crowd, meeting people, Jim at her side until his considerable patience ended and he joined the food line. Horace, Thelma, and her parents sat at the head table, and Mario was pretty much on his own.

After the wedding, Maria would have liked to stay for the night. It would have been awkward with the Harrises along. At Christmas Jim had made it formal, presenting her with a diamond ring. They decided to hold the wedding in late March or early April after the snow season, so her family would be able to make the long trip from California with less chance of getting stranded in a blizzard.

They stayed at the reception until about eleven. It was a long ride back to Clareton, and in the middle of a bitter cold January night they worried a bit about making it without any car trouble or other mishaps. They talked almost all the way back, the Harrises mostly, which made the time seem to pass more quickly. They talked about the wedding and the people they had met there. They felt proud that Horace had finally been hired by the St. Paul Police Department. The Harrises had come a long way since they first realized that their daughter and the handsome, dark-skinned police officer had embarked on a serious relationship. They had arrived in St. Paul for the wedding and after they saw the people and their church in the friendly, close-knit community, they finally believed and understood what Thelma had found.

361

They were sorry to see Thelma go, but they finally realized that she needed to get away from home, away from Clareton. Going places and meeting new people brought growth and opportunity. By coming to Clareton, Horace not only met Thelma, he also made the contact that led to the St. Paul police job.

JUST BEFORE THE CLARETON-DAKOTA FALLS football game last fall, their eyes had locked instantly. Horace was carrying a water cooler over to the sideline area, while one of the referees was talking to the Clareton head coach. At his day job, the referee was one of a handful of Negro officers on the St. Paul police force. During the school year, he moonlighted, officiating at high-school football and basketball games in small towns around Minnesota. When he saw Horace, the referee did a double take, finished his conversation with the coach and strode over to Horace. He held out his hand and gave Horace a broad smile. He looked about Horace's age or a few years older, maybe close to forty.

He shook his head in amazement as he listened to Horace's story, how he arrived in Clareton on the bus, stopped in the hotel for a cup of coffee, met the mayor and ended up staying in town as a police officer.

Just after Christmas he was the first person Horace called following the events surrounding Tom Nathan, when the chief gave Horace an ultimatum: Resign or be dismissed for violating policy and, worse, aiding a suspect in a potential felony case. Horace resigned and left Clareton for St. Paul, taking with him Thelma Harris and the mayor's letter of recommendation.

BY THE END OF MARCH THE MEMORY of another cold, dark winter faded in the growing daylight hours. Rain showers washed away the grit left by the melting snow. Horace and Thelma had returned to Clareton several times for visits. They stayed with the Reeses, which Thelma's parents did not challenge. Once in February, they invited Maria and Mario to visit them at their new apartment in St. Paul and took them to a Lakers basketball game. Later, lying in bed waiting for sleep, Mario would reminisce about the perfect weekend riding down in the Greyhound bus, going out to dinner at a fancy restaurant, and watching the Lakers play at the Minneapolis Armory.

IN SPRING HORACE AND THELMA BROUGHT their happiness back to Clareton, which Jim and Maria hoped to emulate. Laughter and jokes rippled through the rehearsal for Maria and Jim's wedding. Happy excitement filled Maria in anticipation of seeing her family; they had hoped to arrive in time for the rehearsal.

Mario and Rosalyn stood arm in arm in the back of the sanctuary waiting for their cue. Their attention toward the front became distracted behind them by the sound of laughter and voices filtering through the church's main entrance door. The door opened slowly letting in more of the sound until a loud "Shhhh!" quickly reduced the volume.

After several nods from Pastor Carlson to cue the ring bearers, and impatient, expectant smiles among the wedding party, everyone noticed the door and heard the commotion. Mario turned and saw Grandma Ruiz' face peek through the opening door, alternately smiling and shushing those behind her. They'd made it and brought the greatest gifts, joy and a sense of completeness. Ruth Ruiz pushed the door open, motioned her family to follow and stepped into the narthex. She let go of the door and rushed toward Mario. She gave him a hug and Rosalyn, too. Maria came almost running up the aisle.

Behind her mother, Maria saw Oscar, Juan, and Reynaldo entering, waving and smiling. She reached Ruth, and they embraced. Then Ruth stepped back, and her sons continued to hold the door open. During phone calls making plans for the wedding, the matter never came up until three weeks ago. Ruth said she still didn't know if Ricardo would be coming for sure. It weighed on their hearts, seeping into and tainting the happy anticipation.

They stepped back from the door intently watching. Ricardo stepped inside the door, uncertain about what the verdict would be. Maria stood staring at him, at first looking stunned. Tears welled in her eyes. She walked slowly across the narthex, stood in front of her father and for a few seconds they searched each other's eyes. Maria stepped closer, hesitated, then Ricardo reached out and pulled her into his arms. Maria wrapped her arms around his back and buried her face in his chest.

"Hola, mi hija hermosa." "Hello, my beautiful daughter." Ricardo released his embrace and held her shoulders just looking at her. His dark moustache framed his white teeth in a big smile. "It's good to see you again."

"It's good to see you, papa," Maria said just above a whisper. "Thank you for coming."

"I had no choice. I must meet this man of yours. Mama says he's a good man."

"He is."

"And we came to play at your wedding party. We must have music and dancing. You remember how we danced when you were a *pequeño niña*? May I dance with you at your wedding party?"

"Yes, papa."

"Gracias."

Ricardo looked up at Jim and held out his hand. Jim smiled and took Ricardo's hand, making solid eye contact. "I'm honored to meet you, Mr. Ruiz."

"Ricardo, call me Ricardo. It's an honor to meet you, Jim Andersen. You are a dentist? That is good."

Jim looked at Maria and back to Ricardo. "I guess I never thought about this, but I suppose I should ask for your daughter's hand in marriage. May I marry Maria?"

Ricardo tossed back his head and laughed. "And what if I say no? Don't worry, she wouldn't listen to me anyway. She'll do what she wants to do."

"That's because she's just like her father," Ruth quipped.

"Of course you may marry my daughter," Ricardo said. He gestured toward Mario. "And you will be a good father to my grandson." Jim said he would, that they seemed to get along fine so far. Everyone looked at Mario, making him feel more self-conscious than he already was. It was the first time he remembered hearing Ricardo refer to him as his grandson.

Oscar, Juan, and Reynaldo surrounded their sister and each gave her a hug. She asked how the trip went and how they got there so soon. The trip went well, and now they did not feel how tired they had become. They traveled non-stop, taking turns driving and resting when they could. Despite Ruth's protests, they managed to switch drivers without stopping. The driver would slide over, keeping his foot on the accelerator and hand on the wheel while the new driver climbed over from the rear and into the driver's seat of the '56 Oldsmobile pulling a small trailer containing their band instruments: guitars, drum set, and amplifiers.

Pastor Carlson resumed command of the rehearsal. Maria's brothers strutted like roosters, trying to outdo one another with their gallantry, taking the arm of a bridesmaid. Horace and Thelma walked arm-in-arm down the aisle to complete the wedding party, whose smiles radiated through the soft, dim light of the sanctuary toward the back where Maria took her father's arm. Everyone laughed when Oscar mimicked the processional music: *Da dut duh da, da dut duh da.* Sitting in the second row of pews from the front, Ruth turned to watch them, happy to see Ricardo look so happy and proud.

Nearly two hundred guests attended the wedding Saturday, including most of the Clareton school teachers. When they became aware of the crowd size, Mrs. Bauer and Mrs. Harris, who were in charge of the food at the reception, made hurried phone calls from the church office to some of the regulars who provided bars and hot dishes for weddings, funerals, and other church functions. Maria had planned enough food only for about one hundred fifty.

∾ 29 ∽

MARIO STOOD ON THE STAIRWAY about half way up, watching the commotion below. He couldn't remember their house ever being so full of people, full of voices and laughter. It drowned out the sound of the 10:00 p.m. news program on TV in the living room; no one was paying any attention anyway. He could hardly walk through the kitchen. Maria's family had not eaten since leaving the café on the outskirts of Omaha.

Reynaldo and Ruth helped Maria and Jim make pizzas, the Chef Boy-Ar-Dee boxes with the little plastic bag of dough mix, can of sauce and package of parmesan cheese. Jim worked on a pound of hamburger, dropping small chunks around in the dark-red sauce. Maria insisted on baking them until the crust became golden and the bits of hamburger well-cooked, fending off her brothers who would have devoured them before they were ready. She made a face of feigned disgust when she saw that someone had left two six-packs of beer in the refrigerator.

Grandpa Ricardo sat in the living room talking with Horace, Thelma, Jim's family, Oscar, and Juan. The doorbell rang, and, before anyone in the living room made a move, Mario scooted down the stairs to open it. He had asked his mother if he could have some friends over. Everyone in the living room watched, anticipating the new guests. Jake entered first followed by Rosalyn, LeeAnn, and Larry. Mario helped them with their coats, adding them to the pile already on the bed in Maria's room. Thelma initiated the introductions. Mario hadn't expected to see Larry and LeeAnn or even Rosalyn. Jake looked at Mario and shrugged.

Larry's car was parked across the street toward the corner streetlight. Oscar had looked out the front window to see them arrive, letting out a low whistle mostly to himself.

"Hey, Larry, you got some nice wheels," Oscar nodded approvingly after the introductions had been made.

"Thanks."

"What is that? A '55 Bel Air? Okay with you if we go out and take a look?"

The direct and warm words and smiles of the visitors from southern California swept over Larry's initial native reserve. Seeing them around town on summer weekends, or distant figures in wide-brimmed hats sprinkled across vast farm fields rippling in the summer, they were just "the Mexicans," or less accommodating names, who arrived every summer and pretty much kept to themselves. Seeing them sitting in the Reeses' living room, Larry felt unsure how to respond until he settled on what might be common ground—he knew nothing about them except that they were different, but they appreciated his car, which he didn't share with just anyone. He looked at LeeAnn for a clue about what he should do. She seemed eager to join the party in the living room with or without him, which he wouldn't have minded doing himself, persuaded mostly by the aroma of pizza. But the chance to show off his car to some new admirers didn't happen every day.

The Ruiz boys finished eating their pizza. Maria handed Larry a paper plate with several slices, which he ate smoothly and swiftly in a few large bites. She handed him a bottle of RC Cola and said he could take it outside. Oscar, Juan, and Reynaldo followed him out the front door, laughing and jabbering in Spanish.

The polished black finish of the '55 Chevy Bel Air four-door hardtop parked near the streetlight made it seem powerful, ominous like a panther ready to leap in a roaring explosion of speed.

"Hey, Larry, why'd you paint it all black?" Juan asked.

Larry was already opening the hood. "I don't know. It just seemed cool."

"She's a *belleza*, a beauty."

They crowded around the engine compartment. The streetlight reflected off the chrome valve covers. Larry pointed out the fuel injection system. With dual exhaust and a four-speed transmission, he claimed to have the fastest car in town. It almost reached a hundred miles per hour in the quarter mile in just under fifteen seconds.

Larry looked at his watch. "You guys want to take a little spin?"

"*Si, muy bien!*"

They jostled their way into the car, laughing and talking, Larry being slightly mystified and uncertain. He didn't understand a word they were saying. He turned the key in the ignition. Hearing the throaty rumble of the exhaust and sensing the smooth, powerful revolutions of the engine, they giggled almost like children.

"What's there to do in this town?" Oscar asked as they drove off.

"It's really nowhere most of the time," Larry said. "We drive around, hang out at the show or the bowling alley . . . that's where I work sometimes. Sometimes we go to Dakota Falls or St. Cloud." He drove down main street and continued out of town, intending to find a quiet stretch of road in the country to open up the Chevy's 283-cubic-inch engine and let loose all 225 horses under the hood.

"You got a nice girlfriend. She must keep you busy," Reynaldo teased, and they all laughed. "Hey, you got anything to drink?" he asked. "Some beer or anything?"

Larry had made sure his car was clean before they went over to the Reeses, so he didn't lie when he said, 'No,' if it meant his car and not the cooler he kept hidden in the storeroom at the bowling alley. They were older and he did not know them well enough, so he tried to change the subject.

"So, you guys have a band? That's what Jake told me," Larry said. "He's my little brother. He's friends with Mario, so that's why we came over."

"*Si*, we are the Latin Caballeros," Oscar said. "We play mariachi. We try to—we don't have any violins. But you gringos wouldn't know the difference anyway. We're going to play at Maria's wedding party."

"You mean at the church? I'd be surprised if they let you play there," Larry said.

"I don't know. We'll find some place. We didn't haul all our stuff two thousand miles for nothing."

"Maybe we could move it over to the Legion or something. I could check with my dad."

Larry slowed the car to a stop. Thick darkness under a canopy of stars surrounded them on the country road, illuminated ahead only by the headlights. Distant farmyard lights surrounded them like starlight fallen to the earth. Larry looked at his passengers with a little grin. He revved the engine, shifted into first and dropped the clutch. The engine roared, tires squealed, and they whooped and laughed as they accelerated down the road. Larry put aside thoughts about the cost of tires; sharing his passion with admirers was worth it.

He thought they had gone far enough into the country to avoid detection. Approaching the outskirts of town on the return from the joyride, Larry saw the gumball on the roof of the vehicle closing in from the opposite direction. He did not worry. He felt sure no one had seen them in the country. He recognized the officer, John, passing by in the Clareton police car. He groaned, looking in the rear view mirror to see it make a U-turn and flashing red light go on. Innocent of any traffic violation, at least in the city, Larry felt more annoyed than concerned in pulling over and waiting for the officer to approach.

"Evening, Larry. What you boys up to?"

"Just driving around," Larry shrugged. "Just giving my friends here a ride."

"I thought you were going a little fast there."

"I was not, and you know it. Why'd you pull us over?"

"When did you get your license back? I didn't know you got it back."

"Friday."

Larry had almost made it through his senior year in high school without once losing his driver's license. And when it was taken away a month ago, he wasn't even driving.

Every winter the Clareton Jaycees hauled an old car out onto the ice. A fund-raiser for the club, people would pay a dollar to guess when it would fall through the ice sometime during the spring thaw.

This year it had been a 1938 Chevrolet. Not long after it was hauled out in late February, late one evening a bright orange fireball erupted out on the lake. The jalopy had been set ablaze. The ensuing investigation stalled until someone squealed, implicating Larry Carlson and five other guys. Chief Stark couldn't think of a punishment more fitting than revoking their driver's licenses for a month, and he convinced Judge Holmes of the same, mostly because the infraction involved a motor vehicle even if it didn't run. The kids also had to chip in to pay for the fire call, which was pointless anyway.

The officer peered into the car. "Who are you guys?"

Oscar, Juan, and Reynaldo sat quietly, impassively. They had been pulled over several times on the long trip here. In Nebraska they got a speeding ticket for going sixty-three miles per hour.

"They're Maria Reese's brothers. They're here for her wedding tomorrow. Their band's going to play at the wedding party at the Legion."

"Oh, really? Along with the polka band? That ought to be something," the officer laughed. "I think you better come up with a better story than that."

"I'm not lying. They have a band. What do you guys call it? Marchichachi or something?"

"Mariachi," Oscar said. "It's a type of Spanish music."

The officer looked at him. "You speak English?" He looked back at Larry. "I'll let you go this time. You just remember to take it easy.

Where are you heading now?" Larry said they were returning to the Reeses after a little ride. He drove off and the police car followed.

RICARDO GAZED ADORINGLY AT HIS DAUGHTER. Ruth's wedding dress fit Maria with minor alterations. His pride filled the church sanctuary more than co-workers and parishioners filled the pews, seeping into every corner and crevice. He stood straight and held his head high. Maria at his side looking radiant under the white veil, waiting for the processional music to begin.

Following the ceremony, Pastor Olson invited everyone downstairs to the fellowship hall for the reception, which ended up being part planned menu and part potluck.

At Ricardo's request and with Pastor Carlson's agreement, at the end of the ceremony Father Morgan from St. Andrew's Catholic Church bestowed a blessing on the couple and offered a prayer of thanks for the food. Ricardo did not object to his daughter being married in a Lutheran Church. In making his request to Pastor Olson, Ricardo said they're all in the same family, and like all families there are differences of opinion, but they still have the same father and mother and down deep they still love each other no matter how much they fight and argue. When Pastor Carlson relayed the request to Father Morgan, he was more than happy to comply.

Instead of a sit-down meal with servers, Maria took the advice of the kitchen ladies and agreed to buffet style. That eliminated having to decide who would receive the planned menu of turkey or ham, potatoes au gratin, and green beans, and who would get potluck. They laid out the main menu platters and baking dishes and surrounded them with a variety of hot dishes and molded gelatins, red, orange, green and some with canned fruits mixed in.

Maria felt bad when she had to tell Ricardo that their band would not be able to play for a wedding dance at the church. When Maria asked him, Pastor Olson said he didn't object personally, but he did not believe it would have had unanimous support among the parishioners, and he did not want to create another source of conflict or incident that could be used against him later. Maria understood, but did not feel she was able to make her father understand. He felt even greater disappointment having to tell his sons. They huddled in the hallway discussing what they might do. Juan said as long as they can't play they might as well drink. He went to the car and returned with a paper bag holding a bottle of tequila, several limes, and salt.

Father Morgan, returning from the men's bathroom down the hall, heard laughter and voices coming from a Sunday school classroom. He looked in at Oscar, Juan, and Reynaldo, and at the bottle on a table.

"Hello there, fellas. What are you doing here?" he asked, appearing to look more with intrigue than suspicion. "Having some refreshments, I see," he winked.

"Hola *Padre*. We are drowning our sorrows," Juan said smiling and laughing with some embarrassment. "They won't let us play here for a wedding dance. How can you have a wedding without a wedding dance?"

"That's what I heard. That's too bad. If Maria had listened to me years ago, the wedding would be happening over at St. Andrew's, and you could have your dance."

Reynaldo held up his glass. "Would you like some tequila?"

Father Morgan stepped back and looked both ways down the hall. He hesitated.

"It's okay, *Padre*. It don't really count here anyway," Juan said. "We won't tell anyone. God understands. It is fruit of the earth, for our health!"

Father Morgan stepped into the room and accepted a glass. He bit into a lime wedge, and the corners of his eyes crinkled. He sprinkled coarse salt on the back of his hand, licked it off and tossed back a shot of tequila.

"*Gracias*."

"*No hay de que*," Reynaldo said. Don't mention it.

"*Padre*, maybe you know someplace can we have a wedding dance?" Oscar asked. He refilled Father Morgan's glass, and they all had another round, and another.

Father Morgan pondered out loud about some possibilities. He mentioned the Legion, but they always had a polka band on Saturday nights. He stayed and talked for a while, asking about their work, where they lived, about events in their childhood growing up with their older sister. What was she like as a young child? He studied them for clues about the blending of their Latino and Scandinavian heritage. Reynaldo's hair was a little lighter than the others, almost with a reddish tint like his mother's. With Maria it was hard to tell; she could blend into either group, although he knew she was fluent in Spanish. A few times during the summer he called on her to help interpret when he ministered to migrant workers at the hospital. Rarely did any show up for Mass Sunday mornings.

"You should be proud of Maria. She has been a real blessing to our community," Father Morgan said. "I will ask around. Maybe we can do something about having a dance." He thanked them for sharing and excused himself to return to the fellowship hall, feeling warm and mellow, ready to engage in friendly conversation. He scanned the room looking for Mr. Carlson, who was on the board of the Legion club.

The Clareton American Legion owned a large, rectangular brick, one-story building one block off main street on the west end of town. The bar formed the centerpiece between the dining area and the dance floor ringed by tables and some booths. Even with all the lights on, it seemed dark inside. Stale tobacco smoke permeated everything. Saturday evenings the Jolly Jesters played polka music, drawing dancers from up to fifty miles away.

The bartender picked up the phone, held up his hand signaling a timeout from the banter around the bar. Listening, he looked over at the dance floor, then he looked at his watch. Going on ten thirty the polka dancing crowd had thinned, some spending more time at the tables sipping Grain Belt drafts or seven-and-sevens. He said a few words into the phone, replaced the handset and walked over to where the band was playing. While the band still played, he approached the tuba player and leaned close. Cupping his hands, the bartender talked directly into his ear. The tuba player looked around, then back at the bartender, shrugged and nodded.

"GOOD LORD. DARRELL, LOOK OVER THERE." The woman jabbed her elbow into her husband's ribs. Into his sixth Grain Belt, he was beginning to feel the effects, which had been greater this particular evening because he had twisted his ankle that morning and hadn't been doing much dancing. "Somebody's coming the back door. Looks like a bunch of Mexicans. Where'd they come from?" She sat up straight and gathered in her voluminous bright-blue skirt, which had been cascading down the side from where she sat at the edge of the booth. She looked at Darrell for some response. "There's a bunch of Mexicans coming in the back door," she repeated. She looked around at the other tables seeing that a few others had noticed, too.

Several men wearing some kind of uniform began carrying in band equipment, guitars, and amplifiers. Their dark hair and moustaches, except for one, framed their tan, smiling faces. They wore tight-fitting dark pants with gold braid down the outside of the legs, except for one who wore a robins-egg blue suit, also with the braid trim. Their short, gold-braid-trimmed jackets fit tightly over white shirts adorned with a string tie. One carried in a stack of wide-brimmed hats and set them down on an empty table near the stage. At the bar, heads turned to see people coming in the front door. They recognized mostly local folks although many not regular patrons at the Legion.

The bartender went over to the microphone.

"Evening folks. Hope you've been having a good time tonight. We always really enjoy hearing the Jesters," he said motioning toward the bar where band members were placing their orders on the house.

"Hope you don't mind but we've got a special treat for you tonight, all the way from southern California. Many of you know we had a big wedding in town tonight, Maria Reese and Jim Andersen. You know Maria; she's a school teacher. And Jim, well, some of you might wish you didn't know him." A few chuckles and knowing smiles came from around the room. "But he does a good job, keeping some of us Claretonians in big, bright smiles. Anyway, we're going to help them celebrate their wedding tonight. Turns out they didn't have a place lined up for a wedding dance. Not 'cause they didn't plan. They didn't know they were going to have a dance until these gentlemen showed up."

The bartender looked behind him. Ricardo smiled broadly, poised with his trumpet.

"Please welcome the Latin Caballeros." He leaned back and asked Ricardo, "What's that mean in English?"

"Latin gentlemen," Ricardo replied.

The bartender turned back to the mike and stepping away began to applaud, "Ladies and gentlemen, the Latin Caballeros."

The opening blast from Ricardo's trumpet shot through the dance hall like a jolt of electricity. In vibrant harmony, the guitars hanging from Oscar, Juan, and Reynaldo joined in on the loud, energetic rendition of an old Latin folk song.

Around the dance floor the empty seats remaining from the sprinkling of polka dancers were filled by the wedding party and guests. Maria had never been so happy, surrounded by her new husband, her family and friends, and watching her father and brothers standing in the spotlights playing the music she remembered hearing as a child. She had several LPs of Latin music but hadn't listened to them for years. Lately, Mario had assumed control of the hi-fi and selection of radio channels with teenage rock-and-roll.

Watching and listening, she couldn't stop smiling. Jim smiled back, and they applauded loudly after the first tune ended.

After two more songs, Ricardo invited people to dance. "This is a wedding dance, so we must dance," he said. First one, then another polka couple tentatively walked onto the dance floor. Ricardo and the boys smiled and applauded. "Bravo! Bravo!"

The band started up, and the dancers did their best to keep time with the music. The polka dance steps almost matched the rhythm of the band music. Everyone laughed and applauded, watching the polka dancers on the floor and mariachi band on the stage. The men sitting around the bar stared at the scene, giving each other incredulous glances.

"That's gotta be a first," one said. "Look at those polka dancers trying to keep up." They chortled and wagged their heads while sipping their beer.

The wife from a couple who had been sitting in the dining area approached the bar with a notepad. When the wedding crowd arrived and took their places a few began looking around for a waitress, and she volunteered.

Between songs, Ricardo urged wedding guests to dance, especially Maria and Jim. Mr. Carlson stood up and announced that he would collect the money for a dollar dance with the bride. Maria looked surprised and embarrassed but couldn't object once it had been said. Jim nodded his approval. As the wad of dollar bills clutched in Mr. Carlson's hand thickened Maria's energy seemed to increase. She stopped once to take a sip of soda. Ricardo and his sons played song after song, mixing in some popular tunes.

Between songs Ricardo motioned to Jim. He approached the stage, and Ricardo whispered something. Maria sat at the table watching them, curious. Others saw, too. They watched him return to the table and whisper to Maria. She feigned a look of surprise. Her hand covered her mouth. She looked at Ricardo, shaking her head as if to plead against whatever had been said. Ricardo tilted his head to the side with a pleading smile, begging her to agree. Ricardo looked back at his sons and nodded. He lifted the trumpet to his lips and began to play the song, the one that accompanied Maria in her teen years learning to dance flamenco style. She looked at Jim with a worried smile. She looked around at the tables; everyone was looking at her. She took a deep breath and leaned down to remove her shoes. Oscar stepped off the stage and brought over a pair of castanets and thick-heeled dancing shoes. He plucked a red carnation from the bouquet that had been part of the head table centerpiece at the reception, pinched off most of the stem, and gently inserted it into the side of Maria's hair, which had been done up in a bun instead of worn long like she usually did.

"*Bravé, bravé hermana.*" He squeezed her shoulder and returned to the stage. Ricardo stopped playing and waved his hand sharply like a director's cut to stop the music.

Maria took the castanets in her hands, slightly trembling. She stood and slowly, gracefully stepped to the center of the dance floor. A spotlight shone on her white wedding dress, its slim waistline above a full skirt. She lowered her face demurely, casting a shadow over her tan skin above the low yet modest neckline. Her hair shone in the spotlight. She gripped the castanets, turned her head sharply toward the stage and signaled with a crisp nod.

Ricardo's trumpet flared with the explosive opening bars. Maria threw her head up face forward, her focus intense on some time and place long ago. The castanets burst into sound like a string of firecrackers flying with her arms above her head at the same time she spun into the passionate, wild dance, looking more like a gypsy than a bride.

The guests and bar patrons stared in awe. Mario's surprise and some embarrassment settled down into pride and wonderment. From their visits to California, he had learned some things about Spanish culture, especially the language, but he had no idea his mother could do this, nor did Jim, Thelma, or any of her other friends and co-workers.

Father Morgan, smiling widely, began tapping his foot and clapping his hands trying to keep in time with the music. A few others joined in and kept going until the dance ended, when everyone stood and applauded, some whooping and whistling.

Jim stepped out on the dance floor, embraced her and took her by the hand back to the table. Her chest rose and fell trying to catch her breath. Perspiration coated her face and shoulders. She smiled and looked around her, nodding to acknowledge their applause. From the stage Ricardo and the boys paid homage with deep bows.

The party and dancing continued after last call at 1:00 a.m. at the bar. Ricardo and the boys each had a dance with their daughter and sister. After much cajoling Mario danced with Rosalyn a couple times when the band played popular rock-and-roll tunes. Someone had brought some of the leftover food from the church and spread it out on several tables. Two bottles of tequila and a cooler of beer mysteriously appeared on a table over in a dark corner. The band would have played all night.

Some of the guests glanced at their watches, noting that it was already several hours into Sunday. Some contemplated staying home from church, but knew they couldn't. Pastor Olson had stopped by the Legion briefly, leaving well before midnight. Even Father Morgan went home before midnight, torn between staying to enjoy the warm fellowship, but not wanting to feel too tired or hung over at 8:00 a.m. Mass, particularly this one.

Looking around at the thinning crowd and the mess on the tables, Thelma began to organize the clean-up. Mr. Carlson had graciously offered use of the Legion at no charge. He began straightening tables and chairs. Mrs. Carlson went into the kitchen and brought out two big trash cans. She ordered Jake to begin collecting trash and by default the command passed along to Mario and Rosalyn. They had been reveling in staying up so late with the adults at a party. Suddenly they felt tired but could not leave; there was work to do.

When one garbage can became full, Mario grabbed the handles, hoisted it up against his right thigh and carried it bumping along as he walked out the back door to the alley. It felt good to be away from the crowd and commotion. He didn't notice how stuffy the air had become inside until going outside and breathing and smelling fresh air.

Except for a few scattered remnants of drifts lingering in the daytime shadows all the winter's snow had melted, trickling off into storm sewers, ditches, streams, and lakes. The cool night air in early April carried a faint fragrance of the gradually warming soil, strangely sweet from last season's decaying vegetation and the new growth poised to emerge in the lengthening sunlight, occasionally washed and sustained by rainfall.

Mario let go and the trash can landed on the pavement with a scraping clunk. He turned to go back inside when something, a movement, caught his eye. He looked back down the alley over the row of garbage cans and saw a figure standing about fifteen feet away. The man's face hid in the shadow of the street light at the end of the alley. Mario hesitated, startled yet not afraid.

"Isn't it kind of late for a young fella like you to be out?" the man said in a gently teasing tone of voice. "Must be some kind of party going on in there."

Mario remained transfixed. He wanted to retreat quickly back inside, yet he felt something that made him hesitate longer.

"Don't worry about me. I was just looking for whatever I could find here," the man said. His kind voice blended in tones that seemed both wise and melancholy. "It's amazing what folks toss out. If something doesn't look just right or is just a little bit broken they toss it out. Sometimes all it takes is a little fixing."

Mario squinted trying to make out the face.

"Must have been a big party," the man said. "I saw a lot of cars. Must have been something special."

"It was a wedding party. For my mom," Mario heard himself say, almost like in a dream.

"Your mom? How old are you?"

"Twelve."

"So now you got a step dad?"

"I guess."

"Well, that's good. I hope you all get along. I'm sure you will. I bet the party was fun. Weddings, births, birthdays, that's what life's all about. Someday it comes to an end, but then it starts all over again. I used to be afraid of that, what happens at the end. I don't suppose you think about things like that yet. I should shut up. Talking about things like that. Sorry. I don't want to spoil the party. There's a lot more I could say, but it wouldn't do any good anyway. We all have to live our lives. I will say one thing, though. We are all accountable for what we do. We can make mistakes, but God forgives if we let him and we try to do better. I know I made a lot of mistakes. Then sometimes you think you're doing the right thing and it turns out to be a mistake, or you think you make a mistake and it turns out to be the right thing. I guess when that happens you just have to leave it behind. You just have to look ahead and hope you're a little bit wiser. But I don't think you're like I was. I don't think you'll make the same mistakes I did. Sorry, I'm blabbering again. You better get back inside or folks will worry."

Mario stood completely still, almost mesmerized by the voice from the shadowy figure. The man said a few more things, some of which Mario didn't fully comprehend. A sense of peace enveloped him, allowing him to feel calm and relaxed, helping to dissipate memories and thoughts that had haunted him for months. He had never told anyone about the burden of guilt that followed the incidents of last December. He was reminded almost every time he saw Frank at school or around town, although Frank never bothered him anymore, which was a relief. He was reminded when he looked across the lake to where the shack once stood, or when they drove to Dakota Falls, passing by the state hospital, or when Ike lay curled up by his feet in the living room. Sitting on the couch watching television, gently stroking the big dog's black-and-brown coat sometimes it brought back memories of sitting by the fire outside the shack and talking.

"Hey, Mario!" Grandpa Ricardo stood in the doorway. "What are you doing? We have to go. You know what time it is?"

Mario turned toward his grandfather, looking as if he had been startled from a trance.

"Come on, *hijo*. Come on, son," Ricardo urged. He stepped out the doorway and walked toward Mario. "I thought I heard voices. Were you talking to someone?"

Mario turned and looked back toward the row of garbage cans. The man was gone.

"There was a man there. He was just talking." Mario looked back to Ricardo, embarrassed. "There really was."

Ricardo believed in the boy's sincerity, yet could not entirely believe what he had just said. "What did this man say? Were you afraid? Did he bother you? You should have come inside right away and told someone."

"He wasn't mean or anything. He was just talking. I don't know who it was. I don't know. He asked about the party. He was talking about life stuff."

"Life stuff. What do mean by life stuff?"

"You know, like what people do in their lives, good things and bad things. I don't know."

"Okay, I believe you. A mysterious philosopher in an alley at 2:00 a.m. I suppose if he's saying good things, what's wrong with that?" Ricardo put his arm across Mario's shoulders to escort him back inside. "We have to get up early you know. We can't miss church. I know this was not a good weekend for the wedding but it was the only time we could make it. We should be thankful that Pastor Olson and Father Morgan agreed to do this wedding now. You got to get to bed so the Easter Bunny can drop by before you get up."

Back inside, the building was almost all cleared out. The tables had been cleared and put back in order. Almost all the guests had left. Maria and Jim were putting on their coats. Her brothers lugged the last of the band equipment out to the trailer behind the station wagon. Horace and Thelma were saying good-bye. They had to head right back to St. Paul. Horace had tried to get Sunday off, hoping that an out-of-town wedding of a close friend the day before would be sufficient reason, but it wasn't. He had to be on duty at 7:00 a.m.

Maria and Jim planned to leave Sunday afternoon for a few days in Duluth, taking an early springtime drive up the North Shore of Lake Superior. Mario would be staying at the Carlsons with Jake. Right now everyone just hoped to get a few hours' sleep before the sun rose on Easter Sunday morning.

1969

April 19, 1969
Flores, Guatemala

Dear Roz,

Sorry it's been so long since I last wrote. Maybe you didn't even get some of the letters. The postal service in Guatemala is like everything else around here these days—chaotic. Maybe with your studies you wouldn't have time to read them anyway. I hope things are going well for you. I miss you a lot. Things are really crazy around here. You probably don't see much in the papers, and it's probably just as well. One bad war is enough. Down here we're fighting, too. Supposedly against Communist rebels, mostly among the native population in the countryside. It's really ironic—we're here with the Peace Corps trying to help the poor natives improve their lives and at the same time helping the government try to suppress them. Awhile back I saw some U.S. Special Forces guys with a Guatemalan Army unit drive through our village. I guess a couple years ago they went on a major campaign against the rebels, and thousands were killed. Now, I can't leave our village without some natives along with. They say if I was out on my own I wouldn't last too long. The papers here are controlled by the government, so you don't see any of the bad stuff, but we hear a lot of stories about killings and torture. I wish someone had told me this before. Anyway, the work is going well. Mostly I'm helping the villagers improve their crop production. It's incredible . . . just about anything grows here, but they're so backward about farming. We're trying to figure out ways to reduce damage from insects without using so much chemicals. We're trying to use soil conservation practices. What they really need is a bunch of old farmers like Bill Bauer, but I'm trying my best. But enough of that. If and when I ever get out of here I hope to see you again. I know you're swamped the next bunch of years in medical school, but what about after that? I've never told you this before, but I've always thought about us being together. There were times when

382

I wanted to say something, but I guess I was just chicken. I think about you all the time. Sometimes it gets really lonesome here, and thinking about you keeps me going. If you think I'm nuts to say this, that's okay. I'll get over it. I know it seems a little weird to be talking like this when growing up we've been such good friends, almost like brother and sister. But that was then, and this is now. We're not kids anymore. I know there are a lot of other fish in the sea, and I don't blame you if you don't want to get stuck with some small-town kid you grew up with. I've always cared about you, thought about being with you. At least we wouldn't have to spend a lot of time getting to know each other. We can focus on the future. Well, now it's all out. Maybe you suspected it. As smart as you are, you probably did. If you didn't say anything because you don't feel the same way, I'll understand. But if there's any chance you do, I would do everything in my power to make it work and make you happy. We could really do some great things together, building a life together and helping others. God knows the world needs all the help it can get. Not sure yet if I'll be here through the summer or not. I should be back by September at the latest. I can hardly wait to see you.

    Love,

    Mario